❧ EXCERPT ❧

"Do you fancy a swim?" Christian asked, pointing to a declivity nearly hidden in the trees.

Samantha peered downward and drew in a gasp. A waterfall sparkled like liquid silver as it cascaded over a cliff face, creating a mist rising as thickly as a London fog. Whiteness foamed where the water tumbled into a turquoise pool edged by green bushes and trees heavy with orchids. She turned to him with a wishful smile. "May we?"

"If you like. First allow me to establish that no grasshoppers are lurking in the water or bushes."

She found it impossible to contain her enthusiasm and darted away to slide down a few feet of the steep slope.

He clasped a hand around her arm. "Wait. I'll go first."

They clambered down the rocky hillside, Christian keeping a careful eye on the way ahead, checking his footing before moving forward. When they encountered a particularly steep area, he helped Samantha with a steadying hand.

At length they stood beside the pool. After dropping the packs, Christian beat the bushes for unfriendly wildlife, then began to unbutton his shirt. "Wait until I tell you to come in."

Samantha paid no attention. She squatted on the ground, dipped her hands in the cool water, and rubbed it on her parched face.

He cupped her chin in his hand and tipped it up until their eyes met. "Did you hear me? Don't enter the water until I tell you it's safe."

"Quite clearly. Do hurry, Chris. I want to swim."

He sat down to remove his boots and stockings. When he rose, he pulled his shirt out of his trousers.

Samantha's eyes grew large and round. She caught her lower lip between her teeth. Why did it not occur to her until now that they would be required to disrobe? When he stripped his shirt over his head, she stuck a finger in her mouth and nibbled on the nail.

"I'll have to do something about that, Sam," he muttered.

Her gaze jumped up from the muscular chest covered with dark, curly hair, which held her undivided interest, to his face.

"Chewing your fingernails." He gestured at the finger in her mouth and cast her a chiding look. "Do I make you nervous?"

She dropped her hand and spun around, twining her fingers together behind her back. "Of course not. 'Tis merely a habit that has naught to do with you or my nerves. I have no notion I'm even doing it."

He unbuttoned his trousers, the buttons sliding from the holes sounding as loud as gunshots.

"Perchance we can break that habit," he went on. "Dr. Freud would say your mother denied you oral gratification as an infant. I'll have to devise a substitute to occupy your hands and mouth."

Her face burned hot. Though she had noa notion what he meant, she suspected his thoughts were less than gentlemanly. "You will do no such thing," she said.

He laughed, and the splash of his body hitting the pool came from behind her.

When she collected the courage to turn about, Christian was swimming underwater. He surfaced and bent at the waist. His bare legs shot straight up out of the water, and he disappeared again.

She must look a ninny, cowering on the bank, gawking at him. Though she possessed the courage to face down a deadly snake with the grace of Queen Victoria, she was incapable of viewing a nude man without her knees turning to marmalade.

When he dove again, it became clear that he was not completely unclothed. He still wore his linen smallclothes. Being wet, they clung to every ripple. Were she to concentrate, she could see through them to the powerful flesh beneath. So he only *appeared* to be bare. Her bones threatened to liquefy.

He popped up close to her, shaking his head, sending glittering droplets scattering across the pond and over her clothing. "It's safe," he said, scrubbing his hair away from his face. "You may swim now."

STARLIGHT & PROMISES

CAT LINDLER

MEDALLION
P R E S S

Printed in USA

STARLIGHT & PROMISES

CAT LINDLER

DEDICATION:

To Jeffrey Geoffroy's cat, my own saber-toothed tiger and an endangered species in his own right, who so enriched my life. Run easy, sweet boy, in a vast pampas full of game, where spotted coats don't mean fur coats.

Published 2010 by Medallion Press, Inc.

The MEDALLION PRESS LOGO
is a registered trademark of Medallion Press, Inc.

Names, characters, places, and incidents are the products of the author's imagination or are used fictionally. Any resemblance to actual events, locales, or persons, living or dead, is entirely coincidental.

Typeset in Adobe Garamond Pro
Printed in the United States of America

ISBN: 978-160542093-6

10 9 8 7 6 5 4 3 2 1
First Edition

ACKNOWLEDGMENTS:

My thanks to everyone at Medallion Press, especially Helen Rosburg, who first recognized the promise in my books and graciously shared her knowledge of Samoan culture. Thanks also to my critique partner, Chalene Fleming, who always speaks her mind and, although we tussle over changes, is usually right in the end, and to Tammy Seymour, who read the original manuscript.

Chapter One

An uncharted island in the
Furneaux Islands off Tasmania
1892

"*Smilodon*," he whispered, barely uttering the word.

"What?" Richard Colchester, sixth Earl of Stanbury, sharply turned his head. "Let me have the glass."

James Truett grinned and slapped the spyglass in Richard's outstretched hand. Richard cut him an annoyed look and examined the distant figure on the rock cairn. Heat coming off the sandy ground distorted the vision. Richard focused the glass again.

He gasped, and as a breeze stirred the heat waves, his eyes watered. He blinked away the moisture. A cat sat on the rocks—a cat as large as a lion. Richard laid the glass on the ground beside him and wiped his face and eyes with his handkerchief. Hesitating a moment to slow his heart, he picked up the glass again and studied the cat.

Sleek yet heavily muscled. An abundant dark mane ran along the ridge of a thick, arched neck. Bunched

1

muscles moved under a tawny coat spotted with irregular white blotches. It moved, stretching out short front legs, warming its belly on the rock surface. Massive paws with long toes ending in sharp, nonretractable claws; a lean abdomen, plainly outlined by the ribs underneath; and powerful, densely packed rear haunches. Small, rounded ears set well back on a broad head. A wide, square muzzle, and dark green eyes, large and tilted at the outer corners. The cat washed its legs, taking leisurely swipes with its tongue, and the unmistakable gleam of eight-inch curved canines extended outside the mouth to below the jawline.

"*My God.*" Richard sucked in a breath through parted lips. His hands shook, jiggling the glass, wavering the image. "'Tis a bloody Smilodon." He turned to his companion and grinned. "James, we've found a bloody Smilodon."

For two hours, Richard recorded his observations, and James sketched the cat in detail. Though Richard's primary interest centered on the island's flora, something of this magnitude was impossible to ignore. He made notes as precisely as he would have done had the cat been a new bromeliad.

Comfortable in each other's company, the two men—Richard a noted botanist; James a nature artist and disciple of Audubon—worked in silence. At thirty-five, James was ten years Richard's junior. For twelve years they had traveled together through the world's unknown corners, observing, recording, collecting samples, and sketching the plant life, producing detailed monographs with illustrations accurately depicting the vegetation of exotic locales. The scientific community eagerly awaited each new contribution.

When the cat moved on, Richard and James backed away from the sandy plain in the island's interior and worked their way through the dense brush of the jungle toward the temporary camp they had established on the beach. A sultry breeze rippled through the thick foliage, carrying the meaty scents of decaying vegetation and the whistling calls of parakeets and cockatiels. A six-inch-long, rust red lizard scurried across their path, twirling its tail like a propeller. The trail it left on the sandy ground resembled a corkscrew. It halted at the edge of the trees, expanding its red throat sac in a display of miniature bravado. A long-tailed shrewlike animal shrieked overhead and swung off through the treetops. Still dazed by their discovery, Richard and James tramped along, their tongues stilled, each engrossed in his thoughts.

James suddenly stopped—as he was often wont to do when he sighted a strange plant—causing Richard to nearly tread upon his heels. He gestured expansively with one hand. "Just think, Richard, if that storm hadn't caught us and blown the ship off course to this island, we never would have had this opportunity. We should give thanks to the Lord for His intervention."

"Fate moves in mysterious ways, as do the vagaries of the ocean in these waters," Richard replied with a wry smile. "In this case, perhaps we should extend our thanks to Neptune."

James chuckled. "Ah, Richard, always the heretic."

Hobart, Tasmania

In the boisterous, smoky Blue Boar Inn, the air hung close and thick with odors of boiled mutton, a blazing pinewood fire, and unwashed bodies. As they dodged pinching fingers and wandering hands, serving maids with platters balanced on their palms and mugs of ale dangling from their fingers swung through tightly packed patrons. Outbursts of ribald laughter followed their swishing skirts.

Richard and James sat at a scarred table in one corner, ignoring the tumult around them and the mutton chops cooling and congealing in their own fat. Their heads close together, the two men conversed in lowered voices.

Richard pulled a pen, a bottle of ink, and a sheet of stationery from his pack and laid them on the table. "I plan to write to Samantha, explaining the situation and the importance of maintaining secrecy. Knowing her, she will pull together an expedition in record time."

James frowned and took a swig of ale. "Samantha? Our Samantha? I cannot help but worry. I fear your expectations exceed her talents and her ability to be discreet. This discovery is far too important to remain a secret for long. My God, a Smilodon! 'Tis beyond the wildest imaginings of even the most optimistic scientist. Done properly, it will ensure the career of the first person to record it."

"That's why I'm depending on Samantha. I feel certain she can be cautious and still get the job done. I have no doubt she'll manage without creating a stir. Samantha's not one to take no for an answer; though now that I think about it, she may muddy the waters a bit, in a manner of speaking. Her tenacity could be our undoing."

James raised an eyebrow. "How?"

"I'd place a wager of a hundred pounds that when the expedition shows up Samantha will be heading it."

"Surely not!" James looked shocked. "This is not an expedition for a lady."

Richard leaned back in his chair and laughed. "And what does that have to do with Samantha?"

"Samantha may have, um, spirit, but she *is* a lady. If she *does* arrive with the expedition, you shall simply have to send her back. You cannot possibly take responsibility for her under the conditions of a jungle expedition."

Richard grimaced. "I'll certainly try. But Samantha,

as you are well aware, does not take orders in good cheer. That *spirit* with which you so generously gift her is more akin to obstinacy. At best, I might convince her to remain behind in Hobart."

"You are her guardian." James bent a stern eye on his friend. "I realize Samantha can be difficult at times, but you must be firm. Rein her in, or she will never be manageable and suitable for marriage."

"Believe me, I've tried," Richard replied with a cynical smile. "Nonetheless, Samantha considers herself a *modern* woman. Nothing I say or do seems to have effect."

James cocked a brow. "A modern woman? I cannot say I have familiarity with that term, nor have I heard her express such sentiments. What does it mean?"

"Cannot say I truly understand it myself. To Samantha, I gather it means she does not take orders from men, any men, myself included. I finally stopped fighting it. Her arguments wore me to a nub."

James waved with his mug of ale. "Then marry her off. She's certainly old enough. A husband will curb her rebellious nature."

Richard snorted, nearly choking on his ale. "I would, but I know of no one I dislike enough to inflict so vile a torture. Perhaps you would offer yourself as sacrifice?"

James gulped his ale with haste, unlike his normally moderate self. "Not me," he mumbled. "I'm a con-firmed bachelor."

Richard pushed the paper aside, stuck a fork in a chop, and transferred it onto his plate. "Enough about my recalcitrant niece," he said through a mouthful of stringy mutton while gesturing with the fork. "She is the best qualified to handle this situation. When she arrives, we'll deal with her. My primary concern is planning a successful expedition from our end. We must be ready."

At a prickling on the back of his neck, Richard half-turned in the chair to examine the tavern's patrons. 'Twas as if someone, or some malevolent presence, was watching them, listening in on their words. His survey revealed only heads bent over platters and eyes focused on tankards of ale. The mixture of sailors, merchants, and settlers seemed to pay them no heed. He dismissed his edginess as due to the secretive nature of his conversation with James.

While dividing his attention between the mutton and the list of supplies and personnel he jotted on the paper, he discussed with James their needs for a fully equipped expedition. Confident he had recorded all his requirements, Richard extracted a new sheet of paper. Taking up the pen and dipping the nib into the ink bottle, he began . . .

My dearest Samantha . . .

Two tables away, a man sat with his back to Richard and James. While eavesdropping on them, the man clenched and unclenched his hands beneath the table.

A serving maid edged up to him, her bovine bosom threatening to spring loose from the tight confines of a low-cut bodice. She regarded him with a lascivious gaze and ran her tongue across her lips. Bracing her hands on the table, she leaned over, nipples visible in their insecure nest. "What can I get fer ye, luv?" She wet her rouged lips again with the tip of her tongue.

When he turned and sent her a malicious stare, she jerked back with a sharply inhaled breath and hurried away, the heels of her shoes clacking in a rapid pattern on the plank floor.

Chapter Two

"Blast it!" Samantha tripped over a tangle of sedge grass and landed on her hands and knees in the muck of the bog. A marsh hawk, skimming the vegetation, released a piercing cry and wheeled over her head, as though to mock her clumsiness. She canted her face to the bird, saying, "You needn't be so ungallant." Sitting back on her heels, she examined her muddy hands and ruined walking outfit. No help for it now. Wiping her hands on her skirt, she looked down and, from her vantage point, spied her quarry. Movement in the grass. The wriggling of a common lizard, also known as the viviparous lizard, *Lacerta vivipara*. It hid beneath a clump of shiny, dark green leaves, its gray green color merging into the stonewort, round-leaved sundew, and marsh orchids.

"Aha. There you are, and you would choose stinging

9

nettles for your refuge. For the longest time, I thought I should have to go home empty-handed. I shall call you Albert."

Pulling down her sleeves to cover her arms, she poked beneath the nettles. The elusive lizard burrowed farther into the muck. She dug a bit under it, tipping it into a hollow in the ground, and scooped it up, tucking it into her pocket.

More of the tarlike bog mud now smeared her gown, and burrs clung to the skirt. A tear along the length of one sleeve added to the outfit's disreputable look. *Oh, bother!* Given that her clothing was beyond repair, she crawled about, in the event she should come across some other interesting creature. When shrill young voices rose nearby, above the trilling of frogs and whistling of sparrows, she lifted her head and peered over the spears of grass to view three schoolboys wielding sticks and beating at the reeds.

Samantha lumbered to her feet and approached the boys. They halted their activity and turned sullen faces her way. She now recognized the trio, the unruly offspring of her aunt's hay man.

"What have you there?" she asked with a tight smile, letting her sharp gaze touch on each boy.

The one she knew as Bradley spoke up. "Nut'n, m'lady."

She crouched down and searched the vegetation they had beaten flat. "Well, it must be something, or you would not have taken such care to punish the reeds." She sucked in a breath at the sight of the battered grass snake, its long, heavy body twitching in obvious pain. She gathered it into her hands and gently lifted it from the ground. It still had life in it and wriggled in her palms. Cradling it in the crook of her arm, she stood and faced the boys.

They hung their heads and shuffled their feet, making a rustling in the grass. The youngest, Madden, she recalled, snuffled and wiped his nose with a dirty sleeve.

"You shall receive a switching for this," she said, barely able to contain her ire.

"'Tis only a snake," Bradley said, raising his head and sending a mutinous look into her eyes.

"'Tis the snake's home, Master Bradley. It has the right to be here. You do not. It caused you no harm. Indeed, it could not, as it is a harmless species. I shall speak with your father tonight." Wrapping the snake in her shawl, she strode off through the marsh, eager to get the injured reptile home and nurse it back to health.

A mile from the house, the lowering sky sagged farther, the ragged scraps of clouds knitting together into dirty gray sheets. A misty drizzle evolved into rain, and by the time she reached the steps of the country manor, her hair hung in a wet, matted mess. She pushed it away from her face with a grimy hand. Her rain-soaked wool jacket weighted down her shoulders, and her dragging skirt wrapped about her legs.

She circled the house to enter by the servants' door. Muddy footprints following her across the wide oak-plank floors of the kitchen, she sloshed into the hallway in relative silence, considering her condition.

"Samantha!"

Aunt Delia's voice issued with authority from the drawing room. Before Samantha could squish her way to the staircase, Delia appeared ahead of her, bursting through the opening framed by double pocket doors, and confronted her like a mongoose challenging a king cobra. Delia came to a halt, her bow-shaped mouth puckered into an expression of censure.

"I do declare," Delia said, "I have looked everywhere for you. I should have known you were tramping about the bog, communing with those slimy creatures. I only hope you did not bring another reptile into this house."

Albert stirred in Samantha's pocket, and the grass snake flexed in her arms. She hugged the shawl closer to her chest.

Delia waved a hand. "No matter. The postman brought a letter from Richard. It has come all the way from Tasmania."

"Tasmania? How wonderful." Samantha stretched out a hand. "Let me see it."

"Not until you change. From the looks of the hall, I believe you have brought the entire bog into the foyer."

Samantha fled up the stairs, deposited Albert and the grass snake—who had yet to inspire her with a name—with the rest of her reptile collection, threw off her muddy clothing, and pulled on a day dress. Tugging on the waist of her dress to center the seam over her hips, she stepped over to the cheval mirror.

With her butterscotch hair straggling down her back and about her shoulders and the hectic flush in her cheeks, she looked younger than a twenty-year-old spinster. She laughed at the turn of her thoughts, her golden eyes sparkling back at her in the mirror. Tripping out of the room and back down the stairs, excitement bubbling up inside her, she sped into the drawing room.

Richard in Tasmania. How delicious!

"*Smilodon*," Samantha breathed and hugged the letter to her chest. She read it again and broke into laughter, spinning around the room, her skirts flinging papers from the desk to the floor.

"*Lady Samantha Eugenia Colchester*! That is no way for a proper lady to behave in the drawing room." Delia's booming voice seemed out of proportion to the round, diminutive figure from which it issued.

Samantha stopped, swaying dizzily for a moment, and faced her critic. She beamed and waved the letter in the air. "Something wonderful has happened. Uncle Richard has found a Smilodon!"

"That's nice," Lady Delia said with a distracted air. "Have you seen my sewing box?" She hustled from corner to corner, peering behind Empire divans and wingback chairs.

Samantha's brows dipped downward. "Auntie, this is a monumental discovery. Perhaps the most important in hundreds of years. Simply think of it. *A living Smilodon.*"

Delia straightened up from where she had bent over a Tudor chest in the corner. "For heaven's sake, girl, what is a Smilodon?" she asked, as if Samantha spoke in Swahili.

"'Tis a large cat about the size of a lion." She raised her arm to waist level.

Delia sniffed, tiny hands resting on her plump hips. "Then I am sure I saw one at the zoo. The London Zoo is world famous. It has every animal imaginable."

"No. You don't understand." Samantha laughed again. "The Smilodon is a saber-toothed tiger. It has been extinct for over ten thousand years."

Delia tapped a finger on her chin. "You make no sense. If this animal is extinct, how could Richard have found one?"

"That's exactly what I plan to find out."

A week. Such a long week, full of frustration and disappointments. Lost in thought, Samantha stared out the parlor window at the pouring rain. She sat in the overstuffed chair, shoes off, feet curled beneath her, and chewed her fingernails. Her pet iguana, Narcissus, stared at his image in a polished brass flower pot beside the chair. He hissed at the mirrored intruder, and the serrated crest on his neck raised and lowered.

Aunt Delia, established in a comfortable wingback chair by the fireplace, stitched turquoise flowers onto the pillow slips she was embroidering. Chloe, Delia's eighteen-year-old daughter, played chess with the butler, Pettibone, at a corner table. When Chloe made a particularly clever move, squeals of laughter bubbled from her pouty lips, causing Pettibone to scowl, reposition his spectacles, and squint harder.

"Samantha, dear," Delia said, peering myopically over at her niece. "Whatever could be on your mind? Ladies do not put their fingers in their mouths."

Samantha pulled her fingers, topped with the familiar sight of ragged fingernails, from her lips and blew out a breath. "'Tis this expedition Uncle Richard has asked me to organize. I'm to hire a competent mammalogist to pursue the Smilodon. I'm afraid my dear uncle has overestimated my qualifications. I've never even *been* on an expedition, unless you count the time Richard took me to Scotland to look for a rare sea grass when I was twelve or my reptile-collecting trips into the countryside. Perhaps he misinterpreted my slight exaggerations in the letters I wrote him."

"A mammalogist?" Delia asked, her brow wrinkling.

"You know, a scientist who studies mammals, those with fur and teeth and, um, nipples."

"Nipples?" Delia squeaked. She extracted a lacy handkerchief from the bosom of her gown and fanned her fiery face. "You shouldn't even know such a word. You are an unmarried lady."

Samantha sighed. "'Tis a perfectly legitimate scientific word. Never mind. You must help me out here. I have no idea even how to begin to find the proper man or put together this expedition."

"My dear," Delia replied, still visibly shaken by Samantha's shocking language, "you must understand that I am utterly opposed to your taking on such a dangerous quest." She inhaled and released a deep breath, her lumpy bosom rising and falling. "Nonetheless, I know you well. I suspect I will not hear the end of this until it is done. Therefore, I shall impart some advice. I have found that it is always best to start at the beginning."

Samantha sent her aunt a perplexed gaze.

"What I mean to say is, if you *must* do something and have *no* expertise in that endeavor, simply find the person who does."

Samantha dismissed the statement with a wave of her hand. "I've already approached all Richard's friends at the academy. They are either currently immersed in their own research or simply uninterested. I think they did not believe me on account of my gender." Rising quickly from the chair, she clasped her hands behind her back and strode across the room, tossing the next words at her aunt. "They laughed, as though I were playing a jest on them. Ha! A jest. Merely Richard's silly goose of a niece playing a jest."

Delia lowered the sewing to her lap and settled her gaze on Samantha. "They are only men, my dear, and British men at that. Surely you can expect no less. If you cannot gain their cooperation, then you must ask yourself who has the most to gain, the expertise and daring to carry it out, and the interest necessary to travel halfway across the world on a possible wild-goose chase."

"I do know of one person," Samantha said softly, halting in the midst of the room and tapping her lower lip with a fingertip. "However, he's an American and almost impossible to contact. You see, he no longer carries out expeditions and has become a recluse."

"There now." Delia sent her a satisfied smile. "Woman prevails. You have already thought of someone suitable. And being retired, he is not likely to be engaged in other research. Nevertheless, I am concerned that he is an American. They are such ruffians, you know. I'm averse to the idea of you and Richard tramping through the jungle with a ruffian. Then again, if he is retired, he must be an older gentleman and will be of a more settled nature." The corners of Delia's mouth made a sudden turn downward. "I say, your scientist isn't another of those reptile people, is he?"

Samantha chuckled at her aunt's turn of phrase. "No, he studies cats."

Her aunt's brows went up. "Like Horatio? Very strange, I must say, to be one who studies cats."

From his warm bed by the hearth, Horatio lifted his head with a plaintive meow.

"No," Samantha said, "not like Horatio. Wild cats."

"Humph," Delia said with a sniff. "My dear, as you well know, Horatio can be quite wild when he wishes to be."

On a fine, sunny day the following month, Samantha came through the drawing room at a run. "Aunt Delia," she yelled, searching the parlor and the dining room before finding her aunt in the breakfast room with Chloe. Pettibone was forking kippers off a serving tray onto Delia's plate and frowning at Narcissus, who preened over his image in his water bowl in one corner of the room and pawed at the water, wetting the Oriental carpet. When Samantha entered so hurriedly, the iguana lifted his head with a jerk and scurried under the table to tangle himself in Delia's skirts.

"Decorum, Samantha. Young ladies of breeding do not run."

Samantha grinned and waggled a letter. "I received a reply to my inquiry. I have an appointment in Boston in four weeks."

"Goodness me!" Delia exclaimed, tossing her napkin onto the table. "We must rally the troops immediately. We have no time to waste. We must pack and book passage to America." She rose from the chair and shook the clinging reptile off her skirt hem.

Some of Samantha's elation drained away. "We? I planned to go alone."

"Alone?" Delia planted her fists on her hips. Narcissus seemed to echo her question by cocking his head at Samantha. "It just isn't done, my dear." She shook her head. "Of course you cannot go alone. An unmarried woman must have a chaperone. I will fulfill that function, and we will require your maid, Gilly." She tilted her head to one side, as though mentally counting. "We really should have a male escort, especially when we get to Tasmania." She smiled. "Pettibone will do nicely."

Pettibone, having moved to the doorway, rolled his eyes up to the ceiling. Exceedingly tall, built like a stork, blind as a badger without his spectacles, and older than Methuselah, Pettibone had served the Colchester family for longer than anyone could remember. Worry lines permanently crinkled his bald head, and he attributed every white hair in the tufts above his ears to dealing, on a daily basis, with a most eccentric female household. "As though I do not suffer enough," he muttered, "now they are contemplating dragging me off to the wilds of Tasmania, where my noble head will most likely become a shrunken decoration in some heathen's hut."

Samantha's shoulders sagged at the growing retinue.

"And this would be the perfect educational opportunity for Chloe," Delia continued. "Travel is such a broadening experience. Yes, Chloe must come along, too."

Chloe? Pampered Chloe? Samantha's hopes for a quick, efficient passage to America died. Delia's daughter was as spoiled as a three-day-old leg of mutton left languishing on the kitchen counter in summer's heat. She cried for weeks if she broke a fingernail or scuffed her favorite shoes.

"Leave the London social scene for the hinterlands?" Chloe said with a whine. She curled a blond ringlet about her finger and scowled. As though remembering scowling produced wrinkles, she smoothed out her face with her fingertips. "Tasmania is primitive and dirty and teeming with transported criminals," she declared.

Delia smiled at her daughter. "We shall visit Boston first. Boston has become a modern, lively city. We have relatives there, and with your beauty and aristocratic grace, you will become the cream of Boston society. Perhaps you will even meet a handsome, wealthy American and fall in love."

"And perhaps I can talk you into leaving me in Boston while you shuffle off to Tasmania," Chloe whispered beneath her breath while beaming her sweetest smile. Her voice returned to its normal volume. "It sounds like a marvelous idea. When do we leave?"

Samantha groaned and argued and pleaded but to no avail. Delia remained firm. Samantha's mind whirled, grasping for a solution. Perhaps in Boston, she could foist off her crew on their relatives while she slipped out of the country with her elusive scientist.

CHAPTER THREE

In the countryside outside Cambridge, Massachusetts

"Professor Badia, the hem of my gown is positively mud soaked. I wish to return to the college. You must fetch me back immediately."

Recognizing the shrill quality of the voice, Christian Badia swore beneath his breath and turned his gaze on Miss Simpson. "I specifically informed you," he said, swinging about to include the entire class of young ladies in his look, "that you were to don appropriate clothing for this outdoor excursion."

Miss Simpson pouted. "I did. This is my smartest country outfit. However, I imagined us to be riding in a carriage. I had no notion you would expect us to tramp through a swamp."

Christian struggled to contain his temper. "This is a class on marsh ecology, Miss Simpson. I could scarcely escort you to the Boston shops to study spring marsh birds."

"But the ground is so . . . so muddy."

"That's why it's called a marsh," he mumbled, squelching the derogatory response that sprang to mind.

Beside him, Garrett Jakes chuckled. "You'll not win, Chris. I only bless the Lord for allowing me to witness this spectacle."

Christian rounded on Garrett. "Exactly why are you here?" he asked, his words sharp. When Garrett's gaze wandered over to the curvaceous Miss Simpson, Christian sighed. "I suppose I need not have asked. Nonetheless, you shall hold your tongue and refrain from seducing my students, or you will find the hike back to Harvard long and lonely. These women are under my protection"—pulling out his pocket watch, he consulted the time—"for another hour and forty-three minutes."

"If this is so painful for you, why did you agree to take on Professor Bradshaw's lecture?"

"I can only assume that, as I grow older, my brain cells die at a more rapid rate, and my thinking has become muddled. At any rate, we need the additional income."

"That or your brain is fixed on courting the favors of the most luscious Mrs. Anderson."

Christian scooped up a plug of muddy grass and flung it at Garrett's head, and the young man ducked with a laugh.

Christian wiped his hands on his breeches. "Let us

simply say I could not refuse the dean's imploring me to help her out of a most difficult spot."

Garrett shook his head. "Notwithstanding the charms of Mrs. Anderson, in my estimation, you miss the expeditions. I must admit, however, this seems a poor substitute, at best, though I do thoroughly enjoy accompanying you and your harem."

"Mister Jakes!" The cry came from a willowy redhead who had stumbled to one knee in the mud.

Garrett grinned at Christian. "Pardon me, but my assistance is required elsewhere." He loped off through the marsh. "Coming, Miss Carter!"

Christian rested his hands on his hips and examined the group of floundering females. No bird in its right mind would alight within a mile of them. He rued his caving in to Margaret's pressure and accepting this commission after Professor Bradshaw fell from his horse and broke his leg. A lecture course for females on marsh ecology. What an absurd idea. These women were as at home in the out-of-doors as he was at a Buckingham court function.

Harvard had admitted women in 1879, giving them their own annex, apart from the men. In 1894, the annex became Radcliff College, a wholly feminine institution. Since Radcliff offered no science courses, Harvard allowed the women to attend segregated classes on the hallowed campus. Christian scoffed at the notion.

Few women had the fortitude to pursue science, though a small minority showed promise. He glanced at Miss Browne, a sturdy brunette in a heavy tweed skirt, scuffed boots, and a workingman's cap. But then, Miss Browne came from working-class stock and attended Radcliff on scholarship. She had the incentive to make a better life for herself, unlike the more privileged young women who sought only a husband among the professors.

"Professor Badia!"

Miss Simpson again.

"Yes?"

"We must leave straightaway. A rather large creature is attacking me." When the grasshopper crawled farther up her skirt, she squealed loudly enough to flush the red-wing blackbirds from the cattails ringing the distant pond.

"No. Please wait in the carriage until the others finish with their sketches."

"But—"

"Garrett! Kindly come rescue Miss Simpson from the depredations of a giant grasshopper!"

Christian wiped his brow with his sleeve. By the time he fetched the young ladies back to the college, he would have lost another thousand brain cells.

"*Smilodon*?" Christian snorted. "What tripe is this?" He crumpled the letter in his fist and heaved it at the wastebasket in the corner. It banked off the wall and landed dead center. He swiveled around in the desk chair and shouted, "Garrett, get in here!"

Garrett popped his head around the corner and peeked into the room. At the lack of flying missiles, he sauntered in and perched on the edge of the desk. Brushing back a hank of wavy blond hair, he turned his innocent blue eyes to Christian. "Have we a problem?"

Christian shoved the rolling chair away from the desk and stood so abruptly the chair wheeled away, crashing against the back wall. Combing a hand through his thick hair, he glared at Garrett, paced to the middle of the room, and whirled around. "*We* don't have a problem. *You* have a problem. I thought you screened my mail. That's what I pay you for. You *are* my secretary, are you not?"

Garrett's mouth turned up in a charming smile no woman within three counties could resist. He picked up an ornate gold fountain pen from the desktop and twirled it in his fingers. "Of course I'm your secretary, among other duties." His smile grew broader, the innocent expression positively cloying. "Did I miss something? Is that why you feel compelled to yell?" His heavy sigh echoed about the study. "I do my best, but do you show appreciation? No. You belittle my attempts—"

"Stow it!" Christian stalked to the wastebasket. He plucked out the delicate vellum stationery and held it up. "*This*, Garrett. *This* is the problem. I pay you well to keep crackpots" —he smoothed out the letter and reexamined the signature—"like Lady Samantha Eugenia Colchester off my back. Especially women crackpots, and *most particularly*, women crackpots of the British aristocracy."

Garrett looked up from the appointment book he pretended to inspect. "You know, someday you will have to come to terms with this unreasonable loathing for aristocratic ladies. Not all of them are she-wolves in ewe's clothing. Some are quite nice. What happened to you happened long ago. The time has come for you to let it go."

Something broke inside Christian, and he fought to take a breath. "I have no earthly desire to discuss my past with you or anyone else," he said, his words blasting Garrett.

Garrett lowered his gaze, staring down at the desk. Hurt suffused his face. "I only thought I could help."

Christian regretted taking his anger out on Garrett. But, damn it, he didn't want to think about the past, much less banter about it with Garrett. "I need no help," he said gruffly. "Particularly the help of some young pup."

An affronted expression still plastered to his face, Garrett looked up. "As to the letter, I was mistaken in thinking I tossed it into the rubbish. Somehow it became mixed in amongst the bills, and you are quite aware of our financial situation and how monstrous that pile has become."

"What?" Christian said, preferring not to dwell on his finances. "Been too busy bedding the entire local female population that you can't find a few minutes to carry out your duties with a bit of diligence?"

Garrett's face crumpled. "A low blow, Chris."

"Obviously not low enough, if what I hear is true." Christian shook his head. "Sometimes I rue the day I plucked your disreputable, criminal carcass off that dock in San Francisco. I should have left you with the rest of the wharf rats."

"What if she's not a crackpot?" Garrett asked quietly, shifting the subject back to the point.

Christian made his way to the hearth and poured a whiskey from a cut-crystal decanter sitting on the mantel. He turned back around. "Not a crackpot? You mean what if her uncle really *found* a Smilodon?"

Garrett nodded.

One side of Christian's mouth edged up. "You know damn well the Smilodon has been extinct for ten thousand years." With a jerk of his hand, he downed the whiskey. "Even if it wasn't, you wouldn't find one in the South Seas. Impossible. Smilodon never existed in Oceania." He dropped the letter on the floor and fell silent for a moment. *Suppose Garrett is right?* His hand cupped his chin, lashes lowering to half-mast, and racked his brain for possibilities. His chest tightened, and his heart picked up its pace. Striding over to the bookcases, he yanked out several volumes, rifling through the pages.

"Inspiration strike?" Garrett ventured.

Christian raised a hand, throwing Garrett a quelling look over his shoulder.

Garrett clamped his lips together.

Christian stopped flipping pages, his gaze skimming a passage. "It could be a *mesonychid*," he mumbled. "No. Impossible." He slammed the book closed and shoved it back onto the shelf.

Garrett retrieved the letter from the floor, holding it to his nose and sniffing. "But, Chris," he moaned, "she wears a most intriguing scent."

Christian snorted a laugh. "Sometimes I forget how devious you are. Your mind permanently resides between some wench's thighs." He returned to the mantel, reached for the decanter, and downed another slug of whiskey, this time straight from the bottle. "Okay," he said with a sigh. "Give her an appointment. I'll relent this once and let you check out her assets while I listen to her crackpot claim."

At the smug smile on Garrett's face, Christian's eyes narrowed.

"I already have."

"Already have what?"

"Given her an appointment. She'll be here next week."

"How?" Christian sputtered. "She's in England, for God's sake. Did you exchange missives by carrier pigeon? Is she flying over on a pterodactyl?"

Garrett held out the letter. "Check the date."

Christian snatched it from Garrett's hand and examined it. It was dated two months ago. "More devious than even *I* imagined." He laughed softly and reached, once more, for the whiskey.

CHAPTER FOUR

Hobart, Tasmania

Richard and James prepared for Samantha's arrival as best they could with the meager resources in Hobart. Each day at high tide, Richard met the docking ships, anxiously awaiting a return letter from his niece, and his impatience grew out of proportion to the distance between England and Tasmania.

He didn't truly expect a reply so soon, and James admonished him to be patient. Nevertheless, images of the Smilodon raced through his head. For it to have escaped extinction for so long, it wouldn't be a lone animal but rather one of a population. Evolution and the rules of mortality decreed that no animal existed in isolation.

His need to return to the island grew stronger each day, but he held it inside, fearing expressing too much interest in the Furneaux Islands, too many questions relating to tides and reefs and ocean depths, might alert others to the location's importance.

On their way to the tavern one misty evening, Richard and James passed through a street darkened by extinguished gaslights. A chill worked its way down Richard's back, and he shivered. Wary of the darkness and unusual silence, he urged James to gravitate toward the center of the street, away from the ebony pools of shadow hugging the storefronts.

They traversed half the street's length before encountering a malodorous puddle of water stretching across their path. As they circled around it, four men stepped out of a black alleyway in front of them. Glare from a lone streetlight flashed off knives in the fists of two of the men; the others displayed pistols. All were taller than average height, wider than the broad side of a ship. Their faces were lumpy and hard, framed with bristly beards. Their eyes glittered like chips of marble and held cold stares.

Richard tensed and reached for the pistol inside his coat.

"If I were ye, mate, I wouldn't de it," said a harsh voice.

The man who spoke stepped forward. Richard had never laid eyes upon a more fearsome creature. Tall, beefy, red-haired, scarred, and one-eyed, with a whitened, puckered hole where the missing eye had been, he wore a ragged, dirty frock coat over a bare, furry chest.

"I'll just take that," the man said, leaning forward

and plucking the pistol from Richard's inside coat pocket. He inclined his head toward James. "Now ye."

"I'm not armed," James said stiffly. "Take what coin we have and leave. We have little of value."

The man squinted from his one good eye, and his gaze ran over Richard's and James's clothing, which was obviously well-cut and made of fine fabric. "A couple o' swells like ye two should be good fer a fair amount o' coin. Ye dinna look like no charity cases ta me." He turned to his men and grinned. "De they, lads?"

The others remained silent, faces devoid of expression. Slowly they moved, as soundless as wraiths, and surrounded the two men.

James threw a well-aimed fist at the man in front of him, knocking him back on his heels, but he was no match for four men bigger than he. Richard knotted his fists and gathered himself to fight when a cudgel came down on the back of his head. His vision receded to black, and he soon joined his friend, lying unconscious in the street.

James opened his eyes to near darkness. Odors of rotting fish and harbor sewage permeated the air, gagging him. Damp planking lay beneath his body, and timbers creaked about him. The floor swayed and dipped gently, a jarring bump arresting the motion at intervals. His mouth was dry, his eyes gritty. He tried to rise, but scratchy rope bound his hands in front of him and also trussed his feet.

Richard!

James struggled to speak. His voice came out in a raspy whisper. "Richard?"

No answer, and James shuddered. He dug his fingernails into the wood floor, squirmed and inched and pulled himself across the rough planks. After a few feet, he bumped up against a body. He ran his hands over the body's shape and clothing: Richard, lying motionless on his side.

A sudden bright light seared the darkness, making his eyes sting and water. The light came from a lantern, a looming black shape discernible behind it.

"So ye're awake. 'Tis about time."

James recognized the voice of the one-eyed man and tried to wet his cracked lips. "What have you done to Richard? Have you killed him?"

A booted foot swung out and kicked Richard in the ribs. The unconscious man moaned.

"Nah, 'e's still alive. Ye must 'ave a 'arder 'ead." He let loose with a guttural laugh.

Rage at the man's actions flickered through James. "Where are we?"

"'Board the *Manta Ray*, bound fer New Zealand.

We be sailin' t'night. Behave yerselves, answer our questions like nice gen'lemen, an' ye'll be a'right."

"Why are we here? What do you want with us?"

The man fell silent, and the light receded into the distance. Once again, the smells and darkness enfolded James.

When Richard recovered consciousness, the pain began. He lay on the planks in a pool of wetness he suspected was his own lifeblood. Richard wiped the gore streaming into his eyes with the back of his arm and looked up at James, whose back was striped by a whip, wrists tied by rope to the rafters above, body hanging limp and swaying with the ship's motion. Blood dripped from his flesh, coating his legs and forming a puddle on the deck beneath.

The man with the cat-o'-nine-tails, a fine specimen of scurvy manhood, had ceased the flogging and now turned his gruesome face toward Richard. "See what ye an' yer mate made me de?" he snarled through broken teeth. "I've gone an' killed 'im. Make it easy on yerself. Can't save yer friend now. Tell ol' Smythe where ye saw that animal, an' the cap'n will put ye ashore at t'next landfall."

A cold fury welled up in Richard. "I'll tell you nothing. You'll kill me either way."

Smythe grinned, a bone-chilling sight, particularly

in the hold's shifting shadows tossed about by the dim lantern. "Well now, ain't ye t'smart one?" He pulled a knife from his belt and sliced through the ropes holding James. The body fell in a boneless heap to the planks. "I guess ye need more persuadin' from me cattail." Stepping toward Richard, he stroked the whip as though it were a woman's breast.

When shouts broke out, coming from overhead, replacing the sound of sighing timbers and slapping waves, Smythe cocked his head toward the sounds. "Bloody 'ell!" he swore and bolted for the ladder, leaving Richard and James alone.

Richard crawled over to James and cradled his friend's battered head in his hands. "Are you alive?" he whispered.

No answer came.

Richard pressed his ear against the bloody chest and listened. Nothing.

But then a faint heartbeat. Richard feared he only imagined it, but it came again, ominously slow and faint. His own heart lifted. James was still alive.

The shouts above grew louder, followed by stampeding feet and cannon fire. An explosion burst on deck. Timbers crashed, sending a shudder through the planks, as though from a fallen mast. Acrid smoke seeped through the hatch to the ship's bowels.

They were under attack, and for the first time, Richard

tasted the hope of freedom.

After endless minutes of cannon barrages, the impact of a large object rammed against the hull, transmitting a quake through the ship. Now the metallic clash of steel against steel and pistol fire mingled with shouts and curses, as attacking sailors boarded the *Manta Ray*.

Richard fought his way to his feet, faltering from pain and loss of blood, and staggered up the ladder. He threw back the hatch cover leading to the deck, gaze sweeping over the battle in progress.

The crew of the *Manta Ray*, which Richard suspected to be a pirate ship, fought fiercely to beat back the invaders. Richard hoped to see uniforms, British uniforms, and possible rescue, but that wasn't the case. The other ship's crew appeared as evil and ill-featured as his captors, and his faint hope turned to despair. From all accounts, they had fallen into the midst of two pirate ships battling for supremacy.

They had to leave the *Manta Ray* before the battle was decided. Even if the invaders won, he and James would be no better off than they were at the moment. Perhaps even worse. The two crews appeared evenly matched, and the fight would probably rage on for some time.

In the confusion, they might be able to slip away. But where? He peered through the railing. Ocean lay in every direction, with no sight of land. His jaw clenched tight. Land or no land, they had to seize their chance.

The possibility of drowning or becoming a meal for sharks daunted him a bit, but 'twould be an easier death than the pirates on the *Manta Ray* planned for them.

Adrenaline and resolve moved Richard's body and masked his pain as he struggled back down the ladder, slipping on his blood, which squelched beneath his feet. He tied a rope around James's chest below his arms and dragged him topside. The trail of gore they left behind might telegraph the route of their escape, but he hoped the pirates found themselves occupied with more pressing matters.

The engaged pirates, battling for their lives in tight groups over the splintered deck, spared them hardly a glance. Clasping James to his chest with one arm, Richard used his other arm to pull himself along, half-crawling, half-sliding to the ship's gunwales. He lashed two nearby empty water casks together with rope and heaved them over the side. Squeezing under the railing, he said a prayer and rolled overboard into the ocean.

CHAPTER FIVE

Massachusetts

"*Trespassers will be shot. Survivors will be hanged.*"

"Humph," Lady Samantha Colchester said after reading the painted wooden sign to the crow perched on the fence post. "Professor Badia cannot discourage me that easily. In any event, I have an appointment."

The bird cocked its head, examining her with a shiny black eye.

Wan sunlight bled through a gray November sky to scatter light on neat, square fields, meadow swells, and midnight green spruce copses. Frost coated brittle autumn grass, and an ice film skimmed atop water in roadside ditches. She turned toward a noisy flock of crows settling on an adjacent field to glean corn stubble for kernels the harvesters had missed.

"You had best join your friends," she said, coming

back to the sociable crow on the post, "or you shall miss your dinner."

When a wind caught the edges of her cloak, she shivered, pulled it tighter around her shoulders, and consulted the watch on a gold chain about her neck. "Blast it!" she said to the crow. "I'm damnably late. Though why you should care, I wouldn't know."

With a squawk, the crow took to wing.

Squeezing between the fence slats, she forced her bustle through behind her. When she limped up to the house and climbed the front steps, her reflection in the door's glass panels provoked a frown. Hair trickled out from the pins beneath her hat. Her bustle sat askew at a most unbecoming angle, and dirt smudged her face. Perspiration dribbled down her sides and gathered between her shoulder blades, causing her damp dress and underpinnings to cling to her beneath the dusty cloak. If that weren't enough, a rock in her boot cut into her foot.

She tugged at the bustle, plopped down on the top step, and unlaced her boot. While she wrenched it off and dumped out the rock, the door opened behind her.

"My, my, what have we here?" a melodic male voice said. "Surely not a damsel in distress."

Over her shoulder, she peered at the speaker. No older than his early twenties, tall and slender, with a chest and shoulders beginning to broaden with maturity, he was the most stunning young man. Blond hair fell in soft waves, touching his shoulders and framing his face. Lush lashes edged blue eyes. The paintings of the angel Gabriel in the London National Gallery surely depicted this man.

She found herself unable to form a suitable answer with her normally glib tongue.

The angel circled around her, went down on one knee. "Allow me." He held out his hand for her boot.

She blinked and drew a breath. "No, no, I shouldn't. 'Twould be improper. I need no assistance, truly. I shall do it." With heat surging into her cheeks, she shoved the boot back onto her foot.

"Then allow me to lace it up for you." When he tilted his head, his flaxen hair picked up the scant sunlight as though drawing it from the sky. "Please?"

With a flustered smile, she allowed him to retie the laces. Afterward, as he rose gracefully and offered his hand, she released a groan and swayed to her feet.

The angel escorted her through the door and accepted the cloak she doffed, hanging it on a coat tree. Dropping into a chair behind a wooden desk at the foot of the hallway stairs, he leaned back, propped his feet on the desktop, and crossed his boots at the ankles.

"Garrett Jakes at your service," he said, his tone now crisp and professional, his slender hands folded across his flat abdomen. "How may I help you?"

She reached into her reticule, drew out her calling card, and passed it across the desk. "Lady Samantha

Eugenia Colchester." As his dreamy gaze wandered over her figure, she cleared her throat. "I have an appointment with Professor Christian Badia."

She prayed Mister Jakes would be gracious enough to overlook the tiny detail of her late arrival and her disheveled appearance. She attempted an unsuccessful swipe at tucking her straggling tresses beneath her hat, but an errant curl persisted in dangling in front of her eye. She blew at it, trying to will it into obedience.

Garrett's smile nearly blinded her. "You've no reason to fret, Lady Samantha. You look ravishing." Then he sighed, waving toward a door to the right of the hallway. "You're expected." When she remained stationary, he gave her a questioning look from beneath those incredible lashes.

"Were you planning to announce me?" To her dismay, her voice emerged high and squeaky.

He smiled again and batted his lashes.

Her stomach jumped in counterpoint.

"Completely unnecessary. You may enter, and don't bother to knock. Professor Badia eschews ceremony."

Samantha tugged down the jacket of her traveling dress, struggled once more to tame her hair, walked over to the wooden pocket doors, and entered. The empty room suggested that Professor Badia must have stepped out for a moment, and she took the opportunity to look around the study. Bookshelves crammed with hundreds of tomes lined the paneled walls, and a wrought-iron stairway spiraled upward to a second-story library loft ringed with a wooden catwalk.

She had never met the professor but felt as if she knew him. Christian Badia was a zoologist with a specialty in wild cats and, more importantly, an animal tracker, the best in the world. She had managed to uncover little information about the reclusive man's personal life. Supposedly affiliated with Harvard University, he rarely appeared in public. He had discovered dozens of new species but declined the honor of naming them. Only one species tempted him to a touch of egotism: a small, reddish gold wild cat he found on the island of Borneo and dubbed *Felis badia*.

Drawn to a blaze in a marble-fronted fireplace, she rubbed her hands together, baking her chilled fingers. Two cut-glass decanters sat on the pink-veined mantel. She removed the stoppers, one at a time, and sniffed the vapors: brandy and whiskey. A little medicinal brandy could perhaps alleviate the cold that had settled into her bones from the forced walk. She choked down a quick sip, gasping when the strong liquor burned her throat, and replaced the decanter.

She strolled over to a wooden desk sitting in front of a sweep of royal blue velvet drapes. Floor-to-ceiling windows, crafted from octagon-shaped panes, looked out on terraced gardens. She moved closer for a better view, but in late autumn, naught was in bloom.

The study lacked the normal animal heads and other stuffed hunting trophies prevalent in the spaces men called their own. From what she recalled, Professor Badia held great contempt for trophy hunters and rebuffed their efforts to hire his tracking skills, sometimes gracefully, and, on occasion, forcefully. London was all atwitter when he broke the Duke of Pembroke's nose with his fist for badgering him to lead a big-game hunt into Africa. Being acquainted with the stuffy duke, Samantha smiled at the mental image.

However, Professor Badia had a greater charm than simply humiliating the insufferable duke. He wrote brilliant, exciting papers and books about the wildlife he encountered and his experiences on expedition. And through devouring those writings, she came to know him.

Her mind's eye held the picture of a white-haired gentleman in his sixties, distinguished, cloaked in an aura of loneliness. He would have a thin, dark face, seamed from long exposure to tropical climes, a figure spare and wiry from exhausting treks into the jungles. Thick spectacles would cover eyes watery and weak from squinting into the African sun. His thin, callused fingers would be stiff and permanently ink-stained from his prolific writing.

Samantha released a long sigh and sank into a chair before the desk, speculating on when Professor Badia would return, had he not already departed for the day. Surely the angel Jakes would have informed her should that be the case. He said the scientist was expecting her. Professor Badia simply had to see her.

While she waited, a faint thudding hummed through the air, coming at regular intervals from outside. She rose to her feet and strolled to a door beside the desk, opened it, and walked out into the sunlit cold. The noise emanated from a weathered barn behind the house. After looking around and noting no prying eyes, she made her way across the narrow yard and cracked open the barn door. A tall, dark-haired man at the other end of the rambling space was bouncing what appeared to be a leather ball. Standing in the doorway, she watched him.

"Shut the bloody door!"

Samantha hopped inside. The door slammed shut behind her. When she moved into the space, her boots' hard soles clattered on the floor.

He spun around to face her with the ball held in his hands. "And either take off your boots or get off the damn court!"

Court? Looking down to the highly polished wood planks gleaming beneath her feet, she tiptoed toward the wall.

The man glared, standing with his legs apart, one hand splayed on his hip, the other balancing and spinning the ball on his fingertips.

"You have no need to curse," Samantha whispered. Moving up against the wall, she studied him as he glided across the floor, bounced the ball, and tossed it at what looked like a peach basket with no bottom mounted high at one end of the barn. An identical basket was at the opposite end, and lines, circles, and curves were painted on the floorboards.

From the agile way he ran about and jumped up to the basket, Samantha could see the man was young. A student from the nearby university? He wore shockingly short cutoff trousers that exposed a long expanse of muscular calf and thigh covered with dark hair. A tight, sleeveless pullover shirt hugged his chest. His athletic attire was most immodest, but his supple movements and the sleek length of his frame extending to the basket mesmerized her. His body brought to mind an otter leaping through the marsh and diving deep beneath the reedy pools.

He stopped at the arc of a painted curve far from the wall, jumped into the air, and released the ball in a smooth motion with both arms extended over his head. The ball arched toward the basket and swished through its middle. When he turned, walking in her direction, she sidled toward the exit.

"Don't move," he snapped.

Samantha flattened her back to the wall, examining him through her lashes. He was taller than she surmised at first glance, more than a foot taller than she. 'Twas not unexpected. She stood only three inches over five feet, and most of her male acquaintances towered over her. His flesh exposed not an ounce of fat and looked to be carved from stone. Golden stone. Wide shoulders tapered to a trim waist and hips and a flat belly; muscles rippled along his chest and abdomen under the shirt and flexed down his bare arms and legs. Sunlight filtering through a high window lit his face, revealing brown hair streaked with golden highlights that fell thick about his cheeks and to his shoulders in the back. Harsh planes and angles chiseled his arresting features. Heavy, dark brows, nearly black, slashed across his forehead above brilliant green eyes as sharp as cut emeralds. Their intensity pinned her shoulders to the wall.

He moved closer, striding seamlessly, like a predator stalking prey through the tall grasses of the veldt. Despite the softness of his step, irritability dripped from his expression. An odd little shiver went through her. She threw a desperate glance at the door. It seemed unimaginably distant, so she settled for closing her eyes.

His footsteps neared, a whisper on the polished floor. They stopped. When she looked up, he stood directly in front of her. Her nose nearly touched his chest; his heat surrounded her. She craned her face upward. He was older than his agility indicated. Small lines radiated from the corners of his eyes, a few silver hairs touched his sideburns and temples, and dark stubble shadowed his cheeks and deeply cleft chin. Her shoulders drew inward a bit as something strange and hot twisted in her belly, fanning out through her toes and fingertips. Fear, no doubt.

"Who are you? What the hell are you doing here?" he asked, his voice as sharp as the angles of his cheekbones. "Do you make a habit of intruding on private property?"

She straightened her spine. "Who are *you*?" she countered. "An employee, I would assume. I am unaccustomed to being addressed in a surly manner by servants." Moreover, he had cursed at her. Three times, no less.

His lips curved in what could be considered a smile on any other man. On him, it more resembled a sneer. "I asked you first."

She nibbled at her lower lip. On second reflection, could he be someone of importance, such as Professor Badia's son? If that were the case, she had made an inauspicious first impression.

"Lady Samantha Eugenia Colchester," she said, her voice underlain with an annoying tremble. Men didn't ordinarily unnerve her. She thought of them, for the most part, as silly creatures concerned only with the cut of their coat or the fall of their cravat. This man managed to disorder her senses, and she swallowed with difficulty before gaining her composure. "I have an appointment with Professor Badia. Please tell me where I can find him."

"Well, *Lady* Samantha Eugenia Colchester, you

missed your appointment."

"I realize I arrived a bit late—"

He snorted a laugh. "No, not a *bit* late; a *good deal* late. In fact, you're an hour and a half late."

Samantha stiffened. "How could you possibly be aware of my situation?" He had no right to speak to her in such a tone of voice and treat her with disrespect, regardless of his position. "I demand to speak directly with Professor Badia. 'Tis exceedingly urgent. If you were simply to fetch him for me, he will thank you for your service."

A dark eyebrow winged upward. "You *demand*? And you command me to fetch him?" He grinned, grasped the bottom edge of his shirt, pulled it off over his head, and used it to wipe the sweat from his face. "I beg your pardon, Lady Samantha. I'm Professor Badia's secretary, and believe me, you missed your appointment. His office is closed for the day."

Facing an endless expanse of bare masculine chest liberally covered in fine, dark hair, she blinked, his words flying past her ears all but unheard. She caught her breath, what breath remained after shock drove the main portion of it from her lungs. "Y-y-you are indecent. Cover yourself this instant!"

He chuckled. "You overstep your bounds. I seem to recall that you barged in here uninvited."

She processed what he had said before she lost her concentration, and wet her lips. *Professor Badia's secretary?* She lowered her eyelashes. "You see, 'tis dreadfully important I meet with Professor Badia. I came all the way from England with a proposal I know he'll wish to hear. 'Tis a matter of life and death," she finished on an inspired whim.

He propped a hand on the wall beside her head. Two long, tanned fingers settled under her chin and tilted up her face. Closing his eyes, he took a deep sniff. His brows hunkered together in a scowl. "Have you been drinking?"

"N-no, indeed not." She held her breath, her face growing hot.

His eyes gleamed. "You said a matter of life and death? I must say, that changes things. Are you in need of another appointment?"

"I am." She pulled away from his hand, looked down.

He leaned closer, and his voice turned soft. "How badly?"

"Qu-quite badly," she said, voice shaking from the proximity of his hard, hot, sweaty body.

"*How* badly?" Slowly, drawn out this time. His fingers lifted her chin again, and his mouth descended.

Her gut twisted. "How dare you!" She jerked her head sideways, bringing up her hands between them to shove on his chest. Never before had she touched a man's bare chest. Slick with perspiration, hot and disturbing, as if it were on fire. Springy hair tickled her palms. Taut muscles moved beneath his skin, and he was as hard as he looked. "I shall have you dismissed, you malodorous masher," she said, pushing against him and fighting the *frisson* of heat speeding through her veins.

He eased back and laughed, a bone-deep rumbling across the small space between them.

A melting in the private area between her legs, a sudden moisture, sent a hot rush of blood into her face again.

"Whatever is the matter, your ladyship? Am I not up to your aristocratic standards?"

She panted from the exertion of pushing on him and the strange feelings upsetting her equanimity. "Please. Let me go. I beg you."

He stepped back, rested his hands on his hips, and eyed her with an inscrutable expression. "Very well. I apologize if my actions were untoward. You may have another appointment."

A glimmer of hope trickled through her.

"Next month." He spun on a heel, walking away.

Samantha ran after him, grabbing at his arm. "No, wait. Please. I must see him sooner. I have already waited more than six months. I would not have been late, but my hired carriage lost a wheel. I walked for miles in the cold. I had rocks in my boots. The gate was locked. I was obliged to climb through the fence. My bustle nearly fell off—"

He stopped midway across the floor, held up a hand,

and cast an ominous glower at her boots, which were making a racket on the wood surface. "You are *now* on the court."

She looked down; her lips pursed. "Oh." She plunked her bottom on the floor and tugged on the laces of the half boots, her fingers fumbling as though they were made of iron sticks, and she muttered, "What a bloody nuisance! How ungentlemanly! Remove my footwear! What well-bred lady traipses around in her stocking feet? In point of fact, what lady plops herself on the floor to remove said footwear? Not even a chair for my comfort. Only an uncivilized half-wit would expect a lady—"

She suddenly recalled the man's presence and glanced up. Was he listening? It appeared not. His profile was revealed in the dusky light. His eyes were turned away, and his expression showed total unconcern for her ignoble position.

Pulling off the boots at last, she flung them against the wall, climbed back to her feet, and tugged at his arm. "I have discarded them. See?" She hitched up her dress hem and wiggled a tiny, stocking-covered foot.

His lips twitched at the corners, and he beckoned with a finger. "Come with me." When they stood beneath a peach basket, he looked up, as though measuring the distance between the top of her head and the height of the basket.

"Not a chance," he mumbled.

"Beg pardon?" She hadn't quite caught the meaning of his words.

He looked down at her. "I said, 'You don't have a chance.' You're such a little one." His eyes sharpened, and his gaze swept up and down her body, making her flush with warmth. Then again, perhaps he was measuring her for a coffin. The errant thought gave her a chill, but she brushed it off as mere fancy. Truly, the man's dour mood was transferring itself to her.

"You know," he said at last after his leisurely perusal, "you remind me of a tigrina."

She tilted her head to one side and narrowed her eyes, the better to project her disapproval. "A what?"

"Tigrina," he repeated.

Her mouth firmed. "I'm certain, even on our short acquaintance, that you mean insult with that remark, do you not?"

"Not at all. A tigrina is a rather small cat with spotted fur. All fluff, pointy teeth, and sharp claws. It has a contrary nature, spitting and hissing and then running away at the first sign of confrontation."

The blood in her veins turned to rock, as did the marrow in her backbone. "Sir, why you should presume to speak to me in such a familiar way and deign to make personal remarks on my appearance and character, when we have not even been properly introduced, is beyond my comprehension." Her hands fluttered in concert with her words. "My size, lack of size, or nature, contrary or otherwise, can be of no concern to you. When I have left your presence, which will be soon, I pray, we need never meet again. My business is with your master, not with you." Beneath her breath, she added, "Thank the saints."

An amused twinkle settled in his eyes. "I beg your pardon, m'lady. It was merely an observation and not meant to be taken personally."

"Humph." She settled herself with a shake of her shoulders. "For your information, sir, though why I should tell you, I do not know, I am of average height for a woman."

He blew out a breath, picked up the ball, and placed it in her hands. "If you say so, *tigrina*, then I must agree."

She failed in her attempt to burn him to cinders with her stare. "Do not presume to call me by that odious appellation. To you, I am Lady Samantha."

"As you wish," he replied with a slight nod. "Let us, then, conclude this business as quickly and painlessly as possible so you can deal with my . . . master."

She turned her attention to the ball that she held in two hands as carefully as if it were a prickly horned toad. "And I am to do what with this?"

He pointed up. "Throw the ball through the basket, and I'll give you an appointment for tomorrow. One try."

Samantha tilted back her head, studied the distant basket. "Three tries."

"Two. My final offer."

She nodded, took off her hat and gloves, set them on the floor, and brushed the hair from her face. Closing her eyes, she said a silent prayer. *Please, Lord, guide my hand!* Then she threw the ball into the air. She peered through her lashes as it soared aloft and descended toward the man's head.

He reached out with one hand, caught it, and passed it back to her, pointing to the basket again. "Concentrate. Open your eyes and watch what you're doing. Though I realize your inclination may well be otherwise, the objective is to hit that, not me. Feel the ball go through the basket. Be the ball."

"Concentrate. Be the ball," she whispered and paused to inquire, "What sort of ball is it?"

"Does it matter?"

"It does if I'm obliged to be the ball."

"A basketball," he said with his first genuine smile. It transformed his face into something close to human.

"A basketball," she whispered again. "Concentrate. Be the basketball."

With her eyes open this time, she moved under the basket and threw the ball upward. It shot through the bottom and flew out the other end.

She clapped. "I did it!"

"It's supposed to go through the other way."

"You were not specific."

He chuckled. "Right you are, Lady Samantha. I suppose I wasn't. I'll have to be more precise in the future. Tomorrow morning at eight. Arrive on time. Professor Badia demands the courtesy of punctuality." He retrieved the ball, bounced it several times on the shiny boards, and threw it at the basket.

"Mister," Samantha called out. "Um, I failed to catch your name. How should I address you?"

"Save your breath. Don't," he said without looking around, having recovered his previous surly manner.

"You see," she persisted, "I require a ride back to town. Do you not recall? I informed you that my carriage broke down."

"See Garrett." He gave her his back, darting across the floor to the basket at the far end.

"See Garrett," she mocked softly lest he hear her and she lose the concession she had so recently gained. She retrieved her hat and gloves and walked over to her boots. *What a rude, obnoxious man. Somewhat compelling, perhaps, but obnoxious nonetheless.* Recalling Garrett, the dreamy blond angel, she snatched up her boots and hurried out the door. Garrett had manners. He was a gentleman, unlike this hairy American ruffian.

That night, after an uneventful ride in a hired carriage

back to her lodgings, Samantha drifted halfway between sleep and wakefulness, her nerves thrumming, and she dreamt.

He stalked her through a meadow carpeted in grass as golden as ripened wheat. Bright sun penetrated to her bones, and she parted the high stalks, moving quickly and silently. She stopped and crouched down to listen. How close was he? He panted through parted teeth and sniffed the ground, following her spoor. Large paws padded softly, drifted toward her. She rose, lifted her head above the tallest vegetation, saw the rounded top of his tawny head. His thick mane, a fusion of dark and light strands, arched upward from the nape of his neck.

He raised his head, clear green eyes catching her gaze, holding her in thrall. While she stood utterly still, unable to move, he wove a flowing path, drawing in on her by sight instead of scent. The world fell still. All sound and motion ceased beyond this one spot in this golden meadow. Yellow sunlight poured down, the world beyond its sphere turning as black as the ocean depths. A curtain of life drew around them, as if nothing else existed outside its enveloping folds. They were the only living creatures on Earth.

As the cat drew nearer, a quiver shook her. 'Twas inevitable he would track her down. His canines, long and curved, gleamed in the sun, and his pink tongue lolled outside the wide mouth, which lifted into a knowing grin. A grin meant only for her.

She had nowhere to go. No escape from his piercing teeth

and lethal claws. Fear tore through her, hot and screaming in a high keening. Or was it her voice?

He crouched, his thigh muscles bunched into steel coils. His tawny tail whipped back and forth, flattening the grass and sending a wave of seeds into the crystalline air. Resigned to her fate, she lay back and bared her throat. When he sprang, he arched across the sky, a streak of golden fire and overwhelming strength. She closed her eyes, waiting for his weight to bear her into the earth.

Samantha awoke with a jerk, tossing Narcissus off the bed and onto the floor. Her breath came in short, hot gasps. Her heart slammed against her ribs. She pressed a hand on her chest and released a small, whispery laugh. "My goodness," she uttered into the darkness. When she turned over and closed her eyes again, the iguana climbed back onto the counterpane and curled up beside her.

CHAPTER SIX

On the dot of eight the following morning, Samantha stood at attention in front of Garrett's desk. He melted her with a smile, gesturing toward the door. "He's expecting you," the dreamy man said, then gave her a warning look. "You'd better knock this time."

Considering her scruffy appearance the preceding day, Samantha had taken especial care with her wardrobe. She had brushed her hair into submission and coiled it into a becoming style under a jaunty blue hat and dotted veil. Her navy blue suit fit snugly, but modestly, with long, tight sleeves and a high collar edged with white lace. The skirt swept back to a bustle draped with a velvet train. Smart black leather half boots with a medium heel peeked out from beneath her hem. White gloves completed the ensemble. Aunt Delia had inspected her earlier with a critical eye and pronounced her quite acceptable.

For most of the previous night, Samantha had tossed and turned, plagued not only by her disturbing dream but also by visions of a broad, hairy chest and hard, green eyes. In addition to addressing the business bringing her to Professor Badia's door today, she had every intention of mentioning the rude employee's behavior.

The man had tried to kiss her. And, good Lord, she'd almost let him! She even recalled his scent: salty and earthy, distressingly . . . male. Each time she called to mind his disrespect and reprehensible behavior, an unpleasant cauldron of heat seethed low in her belly. She attributed the reaction to disgust. A man of his ilk should be locked up, kept away from decent women.

She dared not inform Delia of the man's inappropriate attentions. She had enough difficulty convincing her aunt to allow her to visit Professor Badia without a chaperone.

Samantha knocked on the pocket doors. She interpreted the grunt coming from beyond the wooden barrier as permission to enter. She went inside and quietly closed the doors. The drapes were drawn, the sole light coming from a fire on the hearth and a small table against the far wall.

Professor Badia, she presumed, bent over the table, his eye pressed to a microscope. Candlelight, reflected in a tilted mirror, illuminated the specimen on the stage. His outline revealed a large body, and she smiled. So much for spare and wiry. Standing in silence with hands laced at her waist and tadpoles wriggling in her stomach, she waited for him to acknowledge her.

He readjusted the mirror and fiddled with the lens, ignoring her for endless minutes. At last he straightened, walked over to the windows. Tall and sturdily built, he wore formfitting trousers and a dark frock coat. He pulled back the drapes and turned around.

Her hands tightened into fists, and the breath stuck in her throat. She released it in an explosion of sound. "You!"

Professor Badia waved toward a chair. "So it seems," he said dryly.

Samantha remained at the door, as though her boots were nailed to the floor.

He gestured again. "Please have a seat, Lady Samantha, unless you wish to leave now. My time is valuable. I'm here at your request, and I'm not a patient man."

She forced herself to move, slid into the chair, and clamped her lips together, fearing only nonsense would spew forth, or worse yet, vile oaths. She fought the urge to leave at once, but he represented her last hope, so she swallowed her pride.

He sank into the desk chair, rotating it to face her, crossing his legs, and bracing his elbows on the armrests. Listing his head to one side, he stroked his chin with the fingertips of his right hand while his eyes held hers in a penetrating gaze. After a long silence, he sighed. "I suppose I'll have to initiate this conversation, since you appear to be tongue-tied. Exactly what do you require from me?"

"Your expertise," she said without thinking.

His mouth turned up in a slow smile. "Your request could be interpreted in many ways, my lady."

The heat of a blush ran down to her toes. "Y-y-you know perfectly well I meant your animal tracking and expedition expertise." She hadn't truly noticed his lips before, though she did now. Full and sensual, they appeared soft in contrast to the sharp points of his cheekbones, the firmness of his jaw, and the ruggedness of his body. When she realized she was staring at his mouth like a smitten schoolgirl, she glanced away to focus on a point beyond his left shoulder.

"What do you want to do with them?" he asked softly.

Her eyes widened, her gaze bouncing back to him. Of course, he meant his scientific talents. She inhaled a calming breath to prevent her mind from wandering again. "As I told you in my letter, my uncle Richard discovered a living Smilodon."

He shifted, as though bored, and looked out over the room.

"I realize how ridiculous that must sound," she quickly went on, "seeing as the saber-toothed tiger has been thought to be extinct for at least ten thousand years, but Richard is a serious, respected scientist, an

Oxford-educated botanist. He says he has found a Smilodon, and you may trust his word. He is not prone to delusions, pranks, or exaggerations."

Professor Badia sat straighter. "Your uncle is Lord Richard Colchester, the Earl of Stanbury?"

"Yes. You have heard of him?"

He inclined his head. "I have several of his monographs. They're quite excellent."

A smidgen of optimism settled in her chest.

"Well, get on with your story," he said. "How did Lord Stanbury manage to find this Smilodon?"

His apparent interest, lukewarm though it was, encouraged her to continue. "Uncle Richard was in Tasmania, arranging a botanical expedition to explore an isolated region of the interior, when a native approached him with a dried flower Richard had never seen before. The native said he found it on an island in the Furneaux Group. Uncle Richard became quite excited because the plant fit no recorded family of flora. He chartered a small boat with his friend James Truett, the botanical illustrator, intending to make a cursory survey of the island preparatory to a full expedition. A storm at sea caught them and sent them off course. You see, it was the typhoon season. When they reached the nearest landfall, an uncharted island with no landing harbor for boats, Uncle Richard and James swam ashore and camped out on the beach, while the crippled boat limped back to Tasmania with the crew."

He gestured for her to halt. "Why did they not return with the boat?"

She chuckled. "You would have to know Uncle Richard. For the opportunity to explore completely unknown territory, he would swim across the English Channel. And the boat's crew promised to send back rescue."

He leaned back in the chair and tapped his full bottom lip with his steepled fingers. "I understand."

"Do you?" She attempted a small smile. "I suppose all scientists feel they are compelled to seek out new adventures. Even you."

"Indeed." His eyes twinkled beneath half-closed lids. "I also enjoy exploring unknown territory . . . and seeking new adventures."

Something in his tone struck her as less than respectful. Samantha blushed again, losing her smile and her train of thought. The man was insufferable! Were all American men this ill-mannered?

He filled her speechless silence. "And on this uncharted island they found a Smilodon."

"Yes," she said, unable to meet his eyes. She pulled a paper from her reticule, leaned forward, and laid it on the desk. "James drew this illustration of the cat."

Christian picked up the drawing and perused it, his brows lowered in concentration. "Again," he said, handing it back, "why do you need me? This seems like a task

Lord Stanbury and his colleague would prefer to handle on their own."

Samantha bit her quivering lower lip. Her stomach plummeted, and tears gathered in her eyes. He would refuse to help her; she just knew it. "Richard is a botanist, not a zoologist. He requested that I engage a competent scientist with the right qualifications. But I . . . I fear something terrible has happened. Once I read his letter, I immediately wrote him back and received no reply. I'm the only other person who knows the island's exact location. So you see, I must ask you not only to lead the Smilodon expedition but also to find my uncle."

His face took on a pensive expression. "A *true* living Smilodon would be an incredible find. Your uncle is widely known for his scientific integrity. However, I'm obliged to ask myself whether I wish to become involved, to throw my bucolic life into turmoil. As I'm sure you're aware, I no longer pursue wild animals."

"Please, Professor Badia. I cannot do this without your assistance."

He sighed. "Tell me about the two vessels, the one your uncle arrived on and the rescue ship."

"I checked with the Naval Ministry. Both sank with all hands aboard a month later."

"And James Truett?"

"Also missing."

Christian left the chair and walked to the mantel,

pouring himself a brandy. "Would you care for something? A sherry, perhaps?" He turned, sending her a look of inquiry. "Brandy?"

Her blush escaped before she could suppress it. Honestly, the man must believe her red face to be a permanent affliction! "No, thank you. I dislike strong spirits. Will you head my expedition? I have the funds, but I require your expertise."

He stood at the hearth with one boot resting on the fender, gazed into the fire, and said nothing for a long time. At last he lifted his head. "I must admit it's intriguing, my lady, but I'll have to give your proposition some thought. I can fit you in again . . ." He strode over to the appointment book on his desk and flipped through the pages.

Samantha sprang to her feet and slapped a palm down on the book.

He raised his eyes to hers.

"Tomorrow," she stated.

A vein throbbed blue against the skin of his temple, surely an ominous sign.

A steel band clamped around her chest, restricted her breathing. "This could easily be the most important discovery of the century," she said before she could lose her nerve, "and you have played with me long enough. Should you decline, I have other interested parties. I repeat, I shall give you until tomorrow." He could not possibly know she was bluffing, but he had humiliated her and was now tugging her about like a toddler on a leading string.

He chuckled. "Very well, Lady Samantha Eugenia Colchester, tomorrow it is. Be here at seven o'clock sharp."

"On the contrary. This time *you* are obliged to make an appointment with *me*." She handed him her card. "You may call on me at *precisely* nine o'clock at this address. Should you arrive even five minutes late, I shall assume you have no interest in the expedition and will contact my other sources." She tilted up her nose and walked away, prepared to make a haughty exit. Though she was taking a risk, a colossal risk, she assured herself that the possibility of such a monumental discovery would sway him to reason. Besides, men such as Professor Badia must be dealt with firmly, lest they gain the false impression that they were in charge.

His voice stopped her before she reached the door. "What do your friends call you, Lady Samantha? I would wager something insufferably charming, such as Mandy or Sam."

She whirled back around. "My friends call me Samantha. You, Professor Badia, may address me as . . . *my lady*."

He threw back his head and laughed.

As she left, she managed to pull the door to without slamming it.

Samantha's scent had barely cleared the air when

Garrett opened the door and popped his head inside. "Spicy, isn't she?"

Christian scowled. "Were you listening at the door again?"

"Wouldn't have to if you would invite me in."

"Indeed," Christian muttered. "She's spicy all right, like sour pickles."

"Come, Chris, are you not being a bit judgmental?"

"Judgmental? Damned right. She's a bloody aristocrat!"

Garrett frowned. "She's not Lady Jane, you know. Don't even look like her."

Christian swung the door closed with emphasis, nearly bouncing it off Garrett's head.

"Cork-brained clodpate! Lack-witted lobcock! Reprehensible reprobate! Moronic muttonhead! Vituperative villain! Boorish bacon brain! Thick-witted troglodyte! Addlepated, addlepated . . ." Samantha ran out of additional appropriate alliterations for Professor Christian Badia. She paced past the clock yet again and glared at the hands: a quarter of ten. Snatching a picture off the mantel, she smashed it against the wall. What was she to do now? Should he fail to come, and that appeared to be his intention, she had no options left. She scowled at the clock and slumped into a chair. The minutes ticked by.

Tension twisted the muscles of her neck into knots and accelerated the pulse banging against her temples. Why, oh why, was Christian Badia the only person qualified for this expedition? She racked her brain for other possibilities. None came to mind.

The clock struck ten, and a knock resounded on the door.

Samantha rose, running her hands over her hair and green damask dress. "Enter," she said.

Pettibone opened the door. "Professor Christian Badia," he announced in his bored, nasal tone.

Samantha composed her expression. "Please see him in, Pettibone." She would be damned if she would allow Professor Badia to see how his tardiness upset her.

Christian strolled up to the door, handing his hat and cloak to Pettibone. He wore fawn-hued riding breeches and black boots. His white lawn shirt was cravatless, open at the throat, exposing the dark hair Samantha was painfully aware also covered his chest. A brown hunting coat molded to his shoulders. His blond-streaked brown hair swept back into a queue tied with a rawhide strip. Odors of leather, horses, and brisk autumn air accompanied his entrance.

"You are late," she said, the words simply springing from her mouth of their own volition. She nearly bit her tongue for giving him such an obvious opening.

He grinned as wickedly as Satan at a feast for the newly damned. "I fear so. But only a *little* bit late."

She flinched and walked over to a fireside table. "Tea, Professor Badia?"

"No thanks, Sam. I would rather have coffee if it's available."

Her hackles rose at the diminutive of her name. Did the man have no manners at all? The tea she was pouring overran the cup rim, spilling into the saucer. She clenched her fists to stop her hands from shaking and rang for the butler. "Professor Badia would prefer coffee."

Pettibone bowed stiffly and sniffed. "Yes, m'lady."

"Please be seated, *Professor Badia*." She indicated a seat by the fire.

He inclined his head, settled into the chair, and stretched his legs, so muscular in the skintight breeches, out in front of him. When he crossed one ankle over the other knee, she looked up, her gaze colliding with his. His eyes glimmered with amusement and something else: something dark and knowing, barely detectable behind the mirth.

She nearly dropped the cup of tea. Heat crept up her cheeks and down her neck.

"Perhaps I should go first," he said as she managed to find her chair. "Once again, you seem to be at a loss for words."

She started to open her mouth, thought better of it, and stirred her tea instead.

"I'll agree to head this expedition only if you consent

to my conditions."

She arched her brows. "Conditions?"

"Conditions."

Samantha looked away. What mischief dwelled in his mind now? Perhaps he would require her to row the ship to Tasmania or catch sharks with a hatpin. She caught herself nibbling on her fingernails and halted the nervous gesture. Had he noticed? She glanced at him. *Oh, bother*, he had. She dropped her hand and pressed her spine against the wooden spindles of the chair. In spite of her reservations of there being "conditions" to which she must agree, she gave a jerky bob of her head.

As Christian relaxed into his chair, Pettibone appeared with the coffee. "Cream or sugar, Professor Badia?"

"Black will be fine. Thank you." He accepted the cup and sipped the brew. "Great coffee," he said to Pettibone. "You aren't looking for new employment, are you? I could use a majordomo."

"I hardly think so." Pettibone snorted under his breath, shuffling out and closing the parlor door with a rather loud bang.

"I suppose not." Christian smiled wryly and directed his gaze to Samantha once again. "We were speaking about conditions."

"You were speaking. I was listening. I continue to do so."

He saluted her. "*Touché*. Conditions, then. First,

you'll pay all the expenses incurred."

"That was my intention."

"Next, Lord Stanbury and I will share authorship on any publications resulting from the expedition."

"I agree," she said, surprised his conditions were so reasonable. "Uncle Richard should have no difficulty with coauthorship." The tension lifted from her shoulders.

He grinned like the hare confronting the tortoise prior to the race, his teeth flashing in his tanned face. "Fine. Now for the difficult one. This is to be my expedition. I'll take sole charge, make all the plans, and give all the orders." When she started to speak, he cut her off. "I'll brook no opposition on this. I'm familiar with that part of the world. It's primitive and dangerous, infested with sea pirates, criminals, headhunters, and cannibals. In assuming responsibility for the expedition's safety, I'll tolerate no interference or challenges to my authority."

She controlled her voice with difficulty. "I understand. I realize you have the superior experience. I shall follow your orders." Surely that could not be *too* difficult. Step here; do not step there; hide behind this tree . . .

"You had better. You can travel with us to Tasmania. I have friends there who run a respectable boarding-house. I'll send reports to you when I can."

"No!" She jumped up, and her cup of tea went flying. It splashed across his breeches. "You go too far. I must go to the island with you."

He stood just as abruptly, cursed, pulled himself up to his full height. His cup dropped on the side table with a clatter. The liquid remaining in the cup sloshed out and spilled onto the table. With a handkerchief drawn from his coat, he brushed at the scalding tea on his leg. "You will not!"

"I will!"

His eyes narrowed, darkened. "Not!"

"How will you find the island without me?"

"You will inform me of its location before we reach Tasmania."

Her mouth quirked into a wide smile. Slowly and distinctly, she said, "No . . . I . . . will . . . not."

"Damn it, Sam," he said on an explosive breath. He threw the soaked handkerchief to the floor. "Have you any notion of what you're saying?" Raking a hand through his hair, disheveling it, he stalked away, pacing across the room, his large form seeming to dwarf the space. "The South Seas are treacherous enough for armed men, much less pampered society ladies. I've already mentioned the unsavory human elements we will meet: not *might*, but *will*. In all likelihood, we'll encounter spiders the size of dinner plates and centipedes over a foot long, whose bite can cause your arm or leg to swell to four times its normal size." He paused, skewering her with his gaze. "Snakes, too. Have you ever heard of the two-step viper?"

"No, but it sounds interesting. What color is it?"

"What color is it?" he sputtered, rumpling his hair again. "This is no joking matter. Its venom is lethal, killing before the victim can take two steps. Even the plants, deceptively beautiful, harbor poisonous spines or sap that strips skin from flesh. And were that not enough, the men I hire will be no gentlemen. You would have no privacy. I cannot afford to make a mistake and risk lives because I'm distracted by playing nurse to you."

Samantha returned his stare. "I have no need of a nurse. I'm far from being a child. I have no fear of your flesh-stripping plants nor two-stepping snakes and headhunting cannibals. I'm not a helpless, pampered female, but a modern woman. I am perfectly capable of taking care of myself in any situation. In fact, I have a reputation as a well-respected amateur herpetologist. I accompanied Uncle Richard on many such expeditions." Her conscience thumped her a bit at the lies. Small lies, but lies nonetheless. "I will not give you the island's location. I shall obey you in all else, but I must go with you. This is *my* expedition. I have to find Uncle Richard."

Christian blew out an oath she'd not heard before, then said, "So be it. It's your funeral, Miss *Modern* Woman, whatever the hell that means. I wash my hands of all responsibility regarding you." He leaned forward, pointing a finger at her, his eyes hard, voice low. "But I warn you, should you disobey my orders *just once*, I vow I'll turn you over to the nearest cannibal tribe and join them for dinner. If I cannot find any cannibals, I'll shoot and cook you myself."

He bent over, picked up his cup, drained his coffee, and started toward the door. With his fingers on the handle, he turned to meet her gaze once more. "We leave a week from tomorrow. Be prepared and pack light. I want this agreement in a contract. Write it up, sign it, and send Pettibone over to the house with it before we leave. You'll not board ship without it."

"Even the part about the cannibals and shooting me?" she asked with a tilt of her chin and a tight smile.

The smile flickering across his mouth would have given a bull elephant pause, and he departed, throwing the answer over his shoulder. "Especially that clause."

After he left, Samantha allowed her nerves free rein. Goose bumps spurted across her skin when she finally realized what she had talked him, and herself, into. And, good Lord, she'd forgotten to tell him about Aunt Delia, Chloe, Gilly, and Pettibone, who had insisted on accompanying her from England and expected to come along for the journey. He would be annoyed at that disclosure.

Mayhap that was an understatement. He would be furious!

Chapter Seven

Boston Harbor

Christian stood on the deck of the *Maiden Anne* under a leaden sky brushed with wispy, mare's-tail clouds. Hundreds of ships clogged the busy harbor, jockeying for space at the docks. Older clippers, schooners, and barques competed with more modern wooden or metal paddlewheel steamers of the Cunard Line, sporting masts and barque rigs, and the most recent propeller-driven steamships.

The *Maiden Anne* possessed the qualities Christian required: speed, seaworthiness, alternate power, and defense. He knew well the dangers of South Pacific sea travel. The waters along their planned passage could range from balmy to full-blown typhoons.

With the *Maiden Anne*, flexibility was key. The ship was a hybrid design, a steamship masquerading as a clipper. Two screw propellers driven by a double-expansion engine and fueled by a steam boiler provided her main power. She could make nine knots under propellers alone in calm seas, though she looked and responded more like a clipper designed for long-distance commerce, combining speed and seaworthiness. Elongated, slender, and sharp-bowed, she carried a full complement of four masts in addition to the steam engine and made better time under sail with favorable winds and currents, leaving the screw propellers for the doldrums and stormy weather. Designed to sail in the U.S.-China trade, the ship carried thirty-six small cannons for defense against sea pirates. When confronted with calamity, they would have the options of running, maneuvering, or fighting.

Below decks space was at a premium, but Christian cared not the least for passenger comfort. Lady Samantha would have had her fill of bare-bones ocean cruising by the time they reached Hobart. He planned on it, neither wanting nor needing a woman on his hands. In the case of Lady Samantha, the thought occurred to him, he was more likely to have his hands on *her*. He grinned. In spite of that delightful image, he could not afford the distraction and danger she posed to the expedition and to his sanity.

He looked over the railing, regarding the twisting movements of dozens of jellyfish species teeming in the water between the docked ships. While ticking off their scientific names in his mind, he waited for Garrett and Samantha and again wondered why he had agreed to head this improbable expedition. Was he persuaded a Smilodon still existed? He supposed it was possible, considering the thousands of unexplored islands in the world's oceans. He gave a short, bitter laugh. *About as possible as humans walking on the moon,* as Jules Verne described in his fanciful tale.

Straightening, he pulled a cigar from his coat pocket, struck a lucifer on the wooden rail, and touched the flame to the tobacco. He leaned back against the rail, smoke wreathing his head. Flicking ashes into the harbor waters, he tilted his head up at the squawking call of a circling seagull and narrowed his eyes to a spear of sunlight that pierced the cloud cover. Tangy salt-sea air and lapping waves bathed his soul, propelled his thoughts. Though he had left this all behind years ago, the surroundings still lifted his spirits.

Considering the obstacles, why was he here? What possessed him to accept her ladyship's commission? He could say that he felt a slight obligation to Richard Colchester, a fellow scientist, but the search for a missing person was best left in the hands of the authorities.

He contemplated the alternative. Was his motivation Samantha herself? Had he convinced himself there existed an attraction, other than lust, a pedestrian emotion easily managed? Certainly, the feisty lady fetched his attention, piqued his curiosity. Was it enough? He shook his head, drew deeply on his cigar, and rejected the thought. The lady was haughty, outspoken to a ludicrous degree for a woman, impossibly stubborn, and too high in the instep. Aristocratic ladies were not his preferred cup of tea. In fact, he despised nothing so much as a highborn lady. Memories surfaced of Lady Jane, and a bitter taste coated his throat. He shoved the painful past aside.

Were he any judge of women, Samantha would defy him at every opportunity and make his life hell. Only one reason for his acquiescence remained—boredom. For six years he had moldered on the farm, writing books and breeding horses. He missed the field expeditions, the excitement, and the danger. Scientific curiosity still burned in his blood, although he had tamed it somewhat in recent years. As a result, he led a stale, passionless life. The opportunity presented by Lady Samantha Eugenia Colchester and the Smilodon, as improbable as it sounded, stirred that part of him still longing for the chase. The expectation of discovery engulfed him, stimulated him, and ignited a fire he'd not felt for many years.

One last expedition, successful or not, would pacify his wanderlust. He could retire to the farm in contentment. On this final trip, perhaps he would regain some of the satisfaction in his scientific skills he once enjoyed, and it was damned good to have a ship's rocking deck beneath his feet again. It had been too long.

Jonas Lindstrom, a dignified, no-nonsense ship's captain, motioned to him from the helm. Christian pushed away from the railing. Soon he and Jonas became engrossed in a discussion of charts and passages, and Christian immersed himself in the familiar details of a well-planned expedition.

When the carriage arrived in the drive to transport them to the ship, Samantha was as jumpy as a mouse caught in a pit of death adders. Bedlam reigned in the hallway behind her. Aunt Delia directed servants and family alike in a thundering voice, sending them scattering about the house to retrieve and pack treasures she could not possibly bear to leave behind. With her round figure and unfashionably large bustle, she resembled a mushroom cap floating across the hall on tiny feet too small to support her bulk. Chloe, her blond ringlets flying, whined, tugging at her mother's arm and begging to remain in Boston with their relatives. Pettibone countermanded Delia's orders, sending luggage back upstairs and trying to explain that ships had severely limited space. Gilly, Samantha's Irish maid, cried and cast mournful glances at the attractive American footman who hauled luggage downstairs at Delia's command and lugged it back up when ordered to do so by Pettibone. The iguana basked on a foyer tabletop, bathing in a stray sunbeam pouring in from the window above the door, while he supervised the chaos with unblinking eyes and admired his image in the polished mahogany surface.

All Samantha needed now was another argument with the abrasive and intimidating Professor Badia. No, they would more than argue. While she watched her noisy brood in perpetual motion, fingers of panic clutched her throat. 'Twould be a proper row, perhaps even with fists swinging. No, not fists; surely he would not dare. However, 'twould be a scene she would just as soon forego.

At a knock on the door, she swallowed around the boulder in her throat. Her stomach churned with queasiness, and her inability to take a proper breath made her limbs light and tingly. A headache threatened to crack open the top of her head.

When the footman made for the door, she waved him aside and opened it wide enough to slip outside, then closed it behind her. Garrett—beautiful, wonderful, gentlemanly Angel Garrett—stood on the porch, a wide-brimmed hat in his hands. She peered over his shoulder for any suggestion of a tall, dark body with piercing eyes.

"Chris sent me to collect you, my lady," Garrett said, wrinkling his brow, she supposed, at her furtive movements and transparent unease. "Are your bags ready?"

"You may as well call me Sam," she said while continuing her search for the mad scientist. "Professor Badia does. He seems to forget I'm a lady and we are barely acquainted." She leaned to one side to see around the back of the carriage, but Professor Badia could not possibly be lying in wait there.

A frown marred his perfect mouth. "I beg your pardon, but are you feeling quite well?"

She jerked up her head, hand instinctively going to her mouth, and she nibbled on a fingernail. "Is he lurking in the carriage?" she whispered.

His lips lifted in a puzzled smile. "No, Sam, he's at the ship. Perhaps you should spill the beans to me before we meet him. You obviously have some concerns on your mind."

Cracking open the door without saying a word, she allowed him to look inside. The babble of shouting, crying, whining, and commanding assaulted their eyes and ears. Samantha slammed the door closed again.

"My God!" Garrett gasped as though in pain. "Surely not *all* of them are coming with us?"

She nodded.

"And you didn't tell him?"

She shook her head. "I never found the perfect moment."

He shuddered. "Chris will murder you."

"Murder?" she squeaked, fingers clutching her

throat like she imagined Christian might do.

"Perhaps not actual murder, but it's bound to be ugly."

His thin smile was thinner than she might have wished, and the sincerity in his voice made her quake.

Opening the door with the caution of a man entering a feeding frenzy of starving crocodiles, he stepped into the fray, raised a hand over his head. "Quiet!"

A hush fell over the hallway. All heads turned his way. Delia sniffed and looked affronted. Pettibone sighed and looked relieved. Chloe's mouth fell open; she looked lovestruck. Gilly paid no attention and still sniffled away. The iguana climbed down from the table, wiggled over to Garrett, and wound around his legs.

He looked down at the three-foot-long green reptile and sucked in a breath. "Good Lord! What the hell is that?"

Samantha darted over, picked up the animal, and cradled him in her arms. He opened his mouth and closed his eyes in an expression of pure pleasure. "A South American iguana and quite tame, as you can plainly see. I named him Narcissus because he enjoys looking at his reflection. He is a good traveler and will be no trouble at all."

Garrett grimaced, pointing a shaky finger at the iguana. "He's coming, too?"

She nodded again, feeling as if she were transforming into one of those bobble-headed dolls sold at Harrods department store in London.

Garrett closed his eyes, lips moving, mumbling

something inaudible. Opening his eyes, he faced the others. "Listen up. Each of you, excluding the iguana, may bring only one small chest. You will leave the remainder behind."

They grumbled in competing voices.

"You have exactly ten minutes to load your baggage and be in the carriage, or I'll leave without you."

They flew into action with only ten minutes to accomplish the impossible, managing to cage up Narcissus and sort out their belongings within the allotted time. In a cacophony of noise, they climbed into the carriage.

As Garrett passed by Samantha, he muttered, "When he sees this . . . I wouldn't wish to be in your shoes."

Had she a choice, neither would she. She tried to force a smile and failed.

When the carriage pulled up to the quay in front of the ship, Samantha inched back the curtain to peek out the window. Christian stood on the aft deck with his back to the dock, conversing with a man who looked like the captain. The situation appeared hopeful. If only she could keep everyone quiet, she could sneak her family aboard without attracting his attention.

The carriage brakes squeaked loudly enough to raise the moldering bodies from the graveyard. The coachman yelled at top volume to the dockhands for assistance. The horses whinnied more shrilly than Samantha ever heard a horse whinny. And as soon as Garrett opened the carriage door, Delia, Chloe, Pettibone, and Gilly spilled out onto the quay like chickens leaving a hen-house—squawking stridently, flapping their arms, and milling about aimlessly. Narcissus nudged open his cage door and plopped out onto the roadway. He looked around, spied Samantha, and made a beeline for her. She scooped him up before the wide-eyed dockhands could make a grab for him.

Clearly audible over the riot of noise came the voice Samantha had dreaded hearing all morning.

"Sam! Fetch your backside over here!"

Her stomach twisted with a sickening lurch.

"They are my family," she said after she boarded the ship. Hugging Narcissus tighter to her chest, she caused him to squirm. "And gentlemen refrain from referring to ladies' body parts in such a crude manner in loud voices in public places. I shall expect you to restrain your impulse to do so in the future." She trusted a preemptory strike would throw him off balance, distract him from her entourage.

He resembled the Colossus of Rhodes, legs spread wide apart, arms folded over his chest. His face was a thundercloud, his eyes so razor sharp they could have pierced a caiman's hide.

"For your sake," he replied in a tightly controlled voice, "I hope they're here to see you off."

"No?" she whispered, losing a bit of her backbone.

He eyed Narcissus. The iguana returned the stare measure for measure. "Well, you can send them and that armful of reptile, whom I presume to be another of your relations, back to whichever insane asylum you sprung them from. They'll not set foot on this ship."

Samantha pulled herself up to her full height, stuck out her chin. She tried to look down her nose at him but found it impossible. He was too tall. She settled for a haughty sniff. "If they go, so do I."

"Very well. I find that an acceptable solution. You have no business on an expedition of this sort." He turned away, striding off across the deck.

"Have you not forgotten something?" she called out.

He halted, swung around to face her. "Indeed. My wits when I agreed to this."

She tucked her mouth into a smile. "Only *I* know where to find the Smilodon."

"On an uncharted island in the Furneaux Group. Now that I know it exists, I'll find it without you. It might take me longer, but I'll find it." He walked away.

Samantha deposited Narcissus on the deck and ran after Christian. Cutting in front of him, she blocked his path. "But we have a contract!"

He scowled. "If you will recall, that contract specifically stipulates obedience to my orders."

"You never told me I could not bring my family. So I did not disobey your orders. Did you really think an unmarried woman would travel alone?"

He rolled his eyes. "I'm beginning to believe I didn't think at all. I certainly didn't imagine, even in my wildest nightmares, that a woman would be traveling with a damned iguana. Have we finished now?"

Anger surged up, choking her. She doubled her hand into a fist, drew back her arm, and punched him in the stomach.

He flinched, but clearly only from surprise.

She winced and shook her smarting hand. When she looked up to the expression on his face, she wished she could take it back—almost. She could hardly believe she had hit him. "I intend to hold you to the contract!" she shouted before he could lay hands on her. "I have a cousin who is a Boston barrister. Should you dare to touch me, I shall sue you for assault as well as breach of contract! You cannot treat a modern woman in such a manner."

"America has lawyers, not barristers," he said dryly, rubbing his stomach.

When he failed to retaliate, she drew on her reserves. "If you refuse to cooperate, I shall head up my own expedition," she said with a toss of her head. "Though I would find you useful, much as one finds a shoehorn a useful tool, I do not need you. I will find the cat on my own and return with it to England while you are still wallowing in the doldrums."

"*You*, Lady Samantha, are a lunatic," he said, his

eyes narrowing. "You will do no such thing. As you so succinctly stated, we have a contract."

"And *you*, Professor Badia, are an unmannered lout whose presence I can very well do without."

An odd look stole into his eyes, and he smiled. 'Twas not a smile that comforted her. If a gila monster could smile, it would smile like Christian at that moment. "I believe I have reconsidered," Christian said, "but not on account of your threats."

"Then why?" she asked, though her mouth was as dry as the gila monster's shed skin. At the smirk on his face, a hard knot formed in the pit of her stomach.

He draped his arm across her shoulders, yanked her up close to his side, and all but pulled her off her feet.

While his heat seeped into her, her heart pounded as loudly as a herd of stampeding Galápagos tortoises and jumped into her throat.

"I'll make your family comfortable and will enjoy ensuring you pay for their ease. When I finish with you, you'll beg me to send you home. But mark my words. I'll keep you by my side until I'm quite prepared to relinquish you." He lowered his head until his face came within inches of hers. His hot breath scorched her skin. "Are you familiar with the crow's nest?" He pointed.

She looked up, way up, to a small bucket at the top of a tall mast. Her eyes widened.

"Hand me one more unanticipated problem, and

you'll find yourself spending your days and nights up there, standing watch. By the time we reach Tasmania, you'll believe you've sprouted wings."

He laughed softly, leaving her standing there, trembling, her emotions so jumbled she was incapable of even remembering why she was on a ship.

His shouting shook her out of her daze. He gestured at Narcissus, who was chewing on a line securing a sail. "And cage that animal before I make him into soup!"

CHAPTER EIGHT

The cabin door burst open and banged against the bulkhead.

"On deck, Sam!"

Samantha's eyes popped open. When she sat up abruptly, her hammock flipped over, dumping her onto the deck. Narcissus hit the boards beside her and scrambled for cover. She brushed away the snarled hair obscuring her vision and blinked at Christian. The black outline of his body filled the doorway. He grinned, teeth gleaming in the semidarkness. She began a slow burn.

"Fifteen minutes," he said. "Then I return for you."

The door slammed shut.

Heavy with sleep, she pushed herself to her feet, rubbed her sore bottom, stumbled over to the washbasin, and splashed water on her face. The cabin was darker than it should be, illuminated by a lone lantern swaying from an overhead beam. She glanced at the porthole in the left bulkhead. The pink blush of predawn faintly tinted the sky. The sun still languished beyond the horizon! Her slow burn worked itself into a simmering boil.

She lit another lantern and searched for her clothing among the jumble. Bodies and baggage filled the suffocatingly small cabin to bursting. The ship offered only three cabins, and the women had appropriated the larger one, normally taken by the captain. Aunt Delia and Chloe slept in the double bunk. Hammocks hung from the rafters for Samantha and Gilly. Narcissus now curled up on the narrow window seat along a bank of windows set in the bow, the only flat surface not piled with clothing. Christian and Garrett shared a tiny cabin next door. The captain made do with an even smaller cabin, more like a wardrobe, across the companionway running below deck. Poor stuffy Pettibone, much to his indignation, was obliged to bunk with the ship's crew. She failed to comprehend why Christian had not engaged a more comfortable ship.

She cast a look at her family, and her lips pursed. They slept the sleep of the dead. She would never understand how they slumbered through Christian's bellowing.

She hurried with her dressing, knowing Christian's threat to return was not an idle one. What new torture had he devised for her today? The first morning after sailing, he pulled her from her hammock when she refused to rise at dawn and hauled her topside, dressed only in her night rail. Once there, he presented her with a mountain of clothing that required mending.

"Since you took it upon yourself to drag a gaggle of extra bodies aboard without requesting permission, you've burdened the crew with additional work. While we're at sea, you'll make yourself useful." He pointed at the clothing. When she opened her lips to protest, he cut her off, saying, "You may consider that an order." He parted with a venomous smile.

The second morning proceeded much the same as the first. Only this time, he assigned her to laundry duty for the entire crew. By the third morning, Samantha learned 'twas in her best interest to rise, dress, and rapidly present herself topside when he awakened her. Now if she could only master that damnable hammock!

Dressed and scrubbed but still not fully awake, she shuffled down the companionway and up the ladder to the deck.

Christian waited by the railing, consulting the watch in his hand. "Not bad. And with two minutes to spare. You learn quickly, nearly as quickly as a dog. I once read that a dog can learn any trick in three days."

Samantha growled.

"Tame that temper, or I'll tame it for you and have you climbing the rigging."

"So, what is your pleasure today, *Master*?" she said,

her good sense having taken flight. "Emptying the bloody slops? Scraping the bloody barnacles off the bloody hull? Keelhauling the bloody damned malingerers?"

He made a clucking sound with his tongue. "Watch your mouth. Your aunt raised you to be a lady."

"As though you would know a lady from a stinkpot turtle," she muttered.

He wagged a finger. "Temper, temper. You'll only make it harder on yourself. Until now, I've taken it easy on you."

She snarled, gathered her nerve to punch him again, and sighed instead. 'Twould be a futile gesture. He was too big, and she could not truly hurt him. Why expend the energy and damage her hand only to have him laugh at her? Besides, he would then chop her up for shark bait and toss her overboard. Failing that, he would surely set them ashore, bag and baggage, at the first landfall.

"Can you cook?" he asked.

She looked up, eyeing him with suspicion. "Of course."

Christian crossed his arms over his chest. "*What* can you cook?"

She tapped a forefinger against her chin and rolled her eyes skyward. "Well, let me think. I can make canapés and French finger pastries, radish roses, which are difficult in the extreme because the little edges tend to break off, pâté swans—I sculpt those especially well—and cucumber sandwiches. You know, those little triangles without the crust? My specialty would be strawberries dipped in chocolate silvered with sugar." She flashed him a triumphant smile.

"In other words, you cannot cook."

Samantha poked a finger in his chest and stamped a foot on the deck. "Of course I cannot cook, you bloody halfwit! I'm a *lady*. I *employ* a cook."

One dark eyebrow arched sharply. "Beg pardon, what did you call me?"

"Nothing you would wish to hear again," she mumbled, dropping her gaze. Her finger ended up in her mouth, where she trimmed the edges of a tattered nail.

"Hitch up that skirt, your ladyship. You're going up the rigging. You can stand watch in the crow's nest."

Halting her unconscious manicure, she gave him a startled look. Her bottom lip trembled. "I will not!"

The eyebrow rose higher. "You what?"

"I cannot." Her voice wavered, and her lashes swept downward to shield her emotions from his relentless stare. "I suffer from a fear of heights," she whispered.

He exhaled a long breath. "Then report to the galley." He gestured at a small building sitting on deck. "You'll learn to prepare meals. This ship is feeding more mouths than one cook can handle."

When Christian turned and walked away, Samantha mocked him with an insolent parody of a salute. "Aye, aye, Captain *Bluebeard*."

Chapter Nine

The *Maiden Anne* docked at Charleston, South Carolina, the first landfall since sailing from Boston. Samantha propped her elbows on the rail, rested her face in her palms, and gazed at the gleaming city. Morning light glittered on graceful brick homes adorned with wrought-iron balconies and towering white columns. Late-blooming magnolias overpowered the odors of salt and fish with heady perfume, and lacy shawls of Spanish moss draped stately cypress and live oaks.

They would load supplies for only one day and leave on the dawn tide. The crew and Samantha's family readied themselves to go ashore and chattered in excited voices behind her. Captain *Bluebeard* had ordered her confined to the ship for some slight and completely justifiable insubordination. Christian was making her life miserable, which 'twas his obvious intent. She sighed. Arguing only merited more punishment.

Aunt Delia came up beside her and patted her on the cheek. "No long face, Samantha," she said with the carefree air of one whose head didn't permanently rest on the block beneath the headsman's axe. "You can weather whatever he dishes out. Never forget you are a modern woman, and modern women do not pine."

"Then why do I feel like a prisoner?" Samantha grumbled. "He is exceedingly unfair. He gains a perverse pleasure in torturing me. The way this journey is developing, the first land I shall set foot upon will be Tasmania."

A sympathetic look spread over Delia's plump face and deepened the creases of age in her neck and jowls. "I'm sorry, my dear. Perhaps you should agree to stay in Hobart with us. Then the professor will have no reason to be so beastly to you. He acts in this manner only to convince you to give up this dangerous quest."

"Most certainly not," Samantha said with a toss of her head. "I refuse to grant him what he attempts to force upon me. I shall not reinforce his despicable behavior. Surely he cannot continue in this fashion for the entire expedition. It must terribly strain his small mind to devise new punishments for me daily."

Delia's expression was soft and thoughtful. "You are quite correct. I do not expect he can."

"I shall simply have to outlast him," Samantha said.

"He expects to coerce me into submission, into giving up. I am determined he'll not succeed."

"Of course not."

Pettibone waited by the gangplank and waved at Delia. When she ignored him, he shook his head and started toward her.

"I regret leaving you alone while we troop off into town," Delia said, "but I must find a floor that does not sway. I know you will persevere." She patted Samantha's cheek once more, took Pettibone's arm, and accompanied him off the ship.

"I'm not alone," Samantha murmured. "I have Narcissus to keep me company."

Narcissus raised his head from his bed on a coil of rope beside her and yawned.

Garrett disembarked next with Chloe clinging to his arm. Chloe, dressed in her best gown, basked under the attention of the handsome young man. She had mooned over Garrett since the first day at sea, and he appeared to return her regard. Another unfair development. Samantha had met Garrett first. He was *her* angel, not Chloe's. Gilly followed closely behind them with the ship's purser, Alan Smith, whom she seemed to find at least as fascinating as the footman she left in Boston.

Christian was the last to leave the ship. He paused behind her before departing.

She refused to acknowledge him.

"I shan't be gone long," he said, his words coming from over her shoulder.

"You have no need to cut short your lark on my account," she said, fighting to conceal the tears in her voice.

"Stay in your cabin and catch up on your sleep. The docks are dangerous for a woman, but you'll remain safe on board."

When he left, she softly said, "As if you cared."

After a long, lonely afternoon and a dinner she could barely swallow, Samantha sat cross-legged on the deck under the evening sky and stared out at the city lights, softened into downy halos by the haze of a misty night.

What was she doing here alone? Why had she been so stubborn? From their first meeting, when Christian began to order her around, she should have strived harder to curb her explosive temper. Little good that did her now. She had carried their frequent clashes too far. She normally was not this easily driven to ire, but he had the oddest ability to burrow under her skin and prick her independent nature, causing her to lose her customary restraint. And when that restraint fell by the wayside, he scooped it up and employed it to club her over the head.

Samantha looked up to laughter and the murmur of conversation carried on the air from nearby houses and taverns and sighed. A light breeze ruffled her hair, bringing with it the pungent smell of raw shellfish from an open-air market and occasional hints of delicious cuisine from an outdoor café. Her mouth watered, and her eyes swam with tears.

She had met her fair share of arrogant males, who considered it their divine right to dominate a woman's every thought and action, but she always managed to steal the reins of control before they realized what she was about. She'd never encountered a man quite like Christian. He seemed to read her thoughts even before they sprang fully formed in her mind.

Most of the time, Christian treated her like a schoolgirl who required his guidance and discipline. How would it feel if he were to treat her like a woman? Sometimes when she watched him on deck, his sun-tinted hair blowing in the wind, the strange sensations he stirred in her when they first met surfaced again. She still dreamt of his hairy chest and muscular body. How he felt and the heady smell of his bare skin. *No!* If she was incapable of managing him now, how would she handle his manly regard? She would have better luck swimming back to Boston and towing the ship behind her by a rope clenched between her teeth.

Was she expecting too much for Christian to treat her as an equal partner in the expedition, to feel free to contribute her own ideas and suggestions? He likened a woman with sound opinions to a child who required silencing. If she intruded, he shooed her back to the schoolroom and locked the door behind her. If she insisted, she found herself on the receiving end of one of his vile punishments.

Boots tapped on the gangplank, and Samantha wiped away her tears with the back of her hand. When she turned her head, Christian, still dressed in evening clothes, stood beside her.

"Have you been crying?" he asked.

"Absolutely not." She averted her watery eyes. "Nothing you do or say could make me cry."

He squatted on his heels. "Stalwart, aren't you?" His warm breath feathered her hair.

"Indeed," she whispered.

Christian straightened his legs to stand. "Go to your cabin and change your clothing. I'll take you into town."

She lifted her gaze to him. "Why? Because you pity me?" As soon as the words flew from her mouth, she wished she could take them back. No doubt she had angered him. He would depart and leave her here alone again.

A frown firmed his lips. "It was not pity that brought me back to the ship when I should be enjoying myself ashore—where I would be now had I half a brain in my skull. I'll give you fifteen minutes. If you're not ready by then, I'm leaving without you."

When she jumped to her feet and dashed to her cabin, he called after her, "And wash your face."

Christian stared at her retreating figure. Despite Samantha's noble birth, she had an allure he was helpless to define. From the moment she had clattered onto his basketball court, he found himself intrigued, fascinated, challenged, and *damn it*, as hard and horny as a stallion stabled next to a mare in season. She had a mind as sharp as a blade, wit like the crack of a whip. He admired her spirit as much as he lusted after her body.

Her small, curvy figure, that butterscotch hair and those golden eyes, eyes like a wild cat's, tormented him. He despaired of catching a whiff of her scent, a hint of lavender entangled with her own uniquely arousing odor. Her image filled his dreams. Samantha gloriously nude and moving in wild abandon beneath him.

Hard already, he cursed and shifted his erection. The night was shaping up to be longer than he would have wished. He should have remained in town.

Samantha bounced back on deck and stopped in front of Christian. She nearly stopped his heart. She wore a jade green satin gown that shimmered in the moonlight. It tightly hugged her small waist, pulled into graceful folds across her flat belly, and swept back into a bustle and train. The bodice dipped low, too low in his opinion. Creamy breasts swelled above the material. It wouldn't take much for that bodice to slip and expose her bosoms.

Now that evoked an image he would recall in paradise! Short, puffed sleeves capped her slender shoulders and left her upper arms bare. White gloves stretched up to her elbows. Her long hair flowed back and up into a waterfall of curls tumbling down to her shoulders. Topaz earrings twinkled in her ears, and a gold chain with a topaz pendant encircled her neck. The pendant dropped dangerously close to her cleavage, calling his attention to it. Not that his attention wasn't already fixed on that enticing valley. He resisted the temptation to adjust his trousers in front of her.

"Well?" she said, spinning slowly in front of him.

His cock swelled to monumental proportions, and Christian swallowed hard against the ache. "Will you not be cold in that?" he asked in a strangled voice.

She laughed, a gleeful, tinkling sound. "No, silly." She flung out a hand clutching a gold cashmere shawl. "I have a wrap. See?" She pulled it around her shoulders and rested her gloved hand on his arm. "May we go now?"

His gut told him to say no and send her back to her cabin. Despite the intuitive message, the excitement sparkling in her eyes caught and bewitched him. He very much feared the night was going to be *exceedingly* long.

Christian drank more wine at dinner than he should have, but the liquor was not what intoxicated him. Samantha sparkled like champagne, and he reveled in her bubbly light. Amusing and full of joy, she proved to be a quick and witty conversationalist. He could scarcely drink her in fast enough. When they waltzed, he held her a little too closely, and the heat of her soft body in his arms threatened to unravel him. His brain wandered uncensored into dangerous waters. He cinched her slim, uncorseted waist, and his devious mind rejoiced that he wouldn't be required to fight that bloody boned contraption to undress her. Of course he would not, but the thought bedeviled him nonetheless. At that moment he wanted her more than he ever wanted anything—more even than the Smilodon.

When his hands roamed and brushed her tempting breasts, clearly, he had reached the edge and was losing his footing. Withdrawing into himself, he tried to barricade his mind and body against her allure. When his attempt failed, he aborted their dance, grabbed her hand, and snatched up her shawl, dragging her out of the restaurant.

"Where are we going?" she asked, breathless and running to keep up with his longer strides.

He remained silent.

She dug in her heels, pulling him to a halt.

He faced her straight on, the muscles of his jaw tight and stiff.

Her face fell. "What is wrong? What have I done now?"

He consciously relaxed the tension in his face. "Nothing. It's simply time I took you back to the ship."

"May we stroll along the boardwalk first?" She peered up into his eyes, her emotions plainly visible in their depths. "I have always dreamt of visiting Charleston and strolling on the boardwalk in the moonlight."

I'll bet you have! He doubted she'd even heard of Charleston before this trip.

"Please, Chris?"

She looked so pitiful and . . . hopeful. He would be a cad to spoil her evening. "Very well, but don that wrap."

They sauntered along the boardwalk, passing couples who ambled by or embraced in enclaves shadowed by overhanging buildings. The boardwalk was known for assignations, and Christian felt like a voyeur witnessing the intimacies of others.

Samantha stopped by the railing and gazed out on the ocean. Moonlight silvered whitecaps on the lapping waves and turned the beach into a sea of sparkling diamonds. She lifted her face to the salty air coming in off the ocean, breathed deeply, and closed her eyes, her curls lifting in the wind. Her shawl slipped down around her waist. Every time she inhaled, her breasts swelled and strained against the satin dress.

Christian reached the end of his tether. Lust ran through him like a runaway locomotive. Steam would rise from his ears at any moment. He was so hard, his cock was likely to shatter into pieces if he accidentally bumped against the rails of the track. Hot blood beat thickly in his ears until he no longer heard the sound of the waves hitting the beach.

Turning Samantha into him, he twisted one hand

through her curls and tilted back her head; his other arm encircled her waist. Brushing his lips over hers, he slanted his mouth to find the perfect fit. She tasted like wine, strawberries, lavender, and innocence.

He pulled her closer, pressing her against his body while he ran his tongue across the seam of her lips. They parted, and he swept inside, delving for her essence. Deepening the kiss, harder and more demanding, commanding her response, her surrender. His tongue flickered and stroked, seeking and finding her tongue and dueling with it.

His free hand slid in a slow caress down her back, cupped her buttocks, and lifted her off her feet, molding her groin to his aching erection. He rocked her against him, wanting more, and groaned low in his throat.

Her arms swept around his neck. The moan that came from her brought Christian to his senses. What was he doing out here in plain view, bare minutes from laying Samantha down on the boards and taking her like some dockside whore? She was a virgin, an innocent under his protection, and he was taking advantage of her inexperience.

He slid her down his body, until her feet found the boardwalk, and released her, stepping away and retaining only her hand. "I do believe it's past time for you to be getting back," he said in a husky voice, "before something happens we'll both regret."

She nodded, lowered her eyes, and tugged her shawl around her shoulders. Ruddy color spread across her face and neck.

They walked back to the ship without speaking.

After leaving her at the top of the gangplank, her small, whispery "Thank you" followed him into the darkness. He stopped at the first tavern to cross his path. Faced with liquor or the attentions of a talented, well-endowed strumpet to dampen his passion, Christian chose a head-banging drunk.

CHAPTER TEN

Samantha awoke at dawn to light sifting through the porthole. While she snuggled farther under the blankets and waited for Christian to rouse her in his usual manner, she retreated to their evening together. Christian had looked so devilishly handsome in his black evening clothes. Instead of the brash American she knew—and despised—he showed her a different side of his personality: gentlemanly and cultured, witty and charming. Her senses reeled under his smoldering eyes.

He had kissed her. Ever since she noted the softness of his lips in contrast to the hardness of his face, she longed to touch them, run her fingers across their surface. But she dared not be so bold. Besides, Christian afforded her no opportunity.

When his lips touched hers, she became drunk with

pleasure. They *were* soft and firm at the same time, like silk over steel. They roused feelings she never experienced in the fumbling, dry kisses of her past suitors. A flame kindled in her belly, and when his tongue plunged into her mouth, the flame flared into life, its fire licking her with heat, soaring higher as he stroked deeper. Her legs turned to butter, and an ache plagued her woman's place between her legs, wanting *something*, anything to ease its distress.

She found what she wanted when Christian picked her up and pressed that spot to his manhood. She felt his hardness and length—his heat—through her clothes. He rocked her against himself, and she believed she would die from pleasure. Dizziness overwhelmed her.

Her pounding heart beat against his. His masculine odors of leather and musk and something darker and utterly male. The heady flavors of wine and salt and mystical desire brought into her mouth by his tongue. Moonlight limned the blond highlights in his dark hair, and her image reflected in his half-lidded eyes, stormy with passion. The fire from him mingling and merging with her heat.

When he set her away, her limbs grew cold, her heart utterly alone.

Overly warm from her reverie, she threw off the blanket and flipped out of the hammock, landing on her feet. Having learned his lesson, Narcissus now slept on the window seat instead of in the hammock. She patted water on her face, and the heat abated. Glancing at the clock, she saw that an hour had flown by.

Where was Chris?

After dressing, she went topside to look for him. Not only was he nowhere in sight, very little was. Fog embraced the ship, shrouding the masts and sails in thick, gray sheets. Weak morning light bleeding through imparted a ghostly glow to objects and sailors about their duties. The fog lay so densely about her, she had difficulty distinguishing the dock at the end of the gangplank. Gulls cried from the quay. Even they were walking instead of flying to find their fish breakfast. She suspected the ship would remain in port this morning.

Samantha made her way to the galley and helped Jasper Poirier with breakfast. She now enjoyed her time with the ship's cook. Though hard on her at first, Jasper warmed up as she learned her way around the cramped space and put genuine effort into unraveling the mysteries of cooking. He was Jamaican and British to the core, with an upper-crust, drawing-room accent that would put the stuffiest peer of the realm to shame. A sheen of sweat from the galley fires continually gleamed on his coal black face. Glistening black hair, braided into multitudes of tight, slim plaits, hung about his face, even with his chin. In one ear he wore a gold earring with a shark's tooth dangling from it. One day he pulled up the leg of his trousers and showed her the scar on his calf he received while fighting off the shark. "Of course," Jasper said in his cultured tones, "I daresay I had the last laugh." He tapped the hanging shark's tooth, set it swinging, and laughed heartily.

Samantha prepared a breakfast tray for Christian. First she asked around, but no one had seen him on deck. She carried the tray to his cabin and knocked. "Chris, I brought your breakfast."

A string of shocking curses followed a loud groan, then, "Begone!"

She knocked louder. "Have you taken ill? Can I do something to relieve your discomfort?"

"Cease that infernal racket! And stay the hell away from me!" Heavy feet stumbled across the floor, and retching came from the depths of the cabin.

When she tried the door, it was locked, so she sought out Garrett and cornered him.

"Good morning," he said with his usual captivating smile. "It appears as if we'll not set sail until the next tide, if the fog lifts by then."

"I took breakfast to Chris," she said, skipping the pleasantries. "He yelled at me and has locked his cabin door. I'm concerned for his health."

His gaze flicked to a distant point beyond her head. "I believe your best course would be to leave him alone today. I don't imagine we'll see him on deck for several hours."

She placed a hand on his arm. "I thought I heard

him vomiting. Is he ill?"

"You could certainly say he feels poorly. Don't worry. I suspect his condition is minor and will pass quickly. Simply leave him be."

She frowned. "Very well, if you are certain he is not seriously ill." She left, returned to the galley, and spent the remainder of the morning peeling potatoes for luncheon.

By the time the noon meal rolled around, Christian had still failed to make an appearance, and Samantha searched for Garrett again. She had completed all her work and was in need of a task to occupy her.

"Will you teach me how to shoot a gun?" she asked him.

"Why?"

"If I was capable of defending myself, became competent with a rifle and a pistol, I would be more useful on the expedition. Chris would worry less about my coming along. Since we'll not sail until the midnight tide, we have time to ride out of town where you can teach me the fundamentals."

A touch of uncertainty appeared on his face. "I don't know if that's such a good idea. Chris might not like it."

She clasped her hands together in front of her. "Please? I want to surprise Chris with my marksmanship."

"I suppose it would do no harm," he said with a shrug.

While Samantha changed into a riding habit, Garrett gathered up the rifles, revolvers, ammunition, and other supplies. They hired horses from a nearby stable and rode into the countryside, farther inland and away from the fog.

Christian gained full mobility in the early afternoon. He had missed two meals, and his stomach cleaved to his backbone. It certainly had reason to complain. His innumerable trips to the chamber pot ensured its current empty misery. Along with the food he expelled, he finally purged the liquor from his system. Now only a splitting headache and bloodshot eyes attested to the night's excesses.

He grimaced at the notion of food and had a bleary recollection of yelling at Samantha again. Shame pricked him, not a feeling with which he had a close acquaintance. The poor girl. He was either blistering her ears or climbing over her like an octopus. He owed her an apology and fully intended to pursue one as soon as he felt human again.

Before washing and shaving, he opened the porthole to let in fresh air and empty the chamber pot. The dense fog explained why the ship had not gotten under way. He dressed, climbed up on deck, and prepared to face the day, or what remained of it.

A knot formed in his chest when he failed to find Samantha. He questioned Delia, Chloe, Pettibone, and Gilly as well as the captain and crew. No one seemed to know where she had gone. His gut clenching, he recalled the previous night with startling clarity and not a small amount of guilt. Had he so frightened her with his lecherous advances that she fled the ship to escape him? She could be alone in town now—lost or hurt or *being* hurt by a gang of sailors bent on forcing their attentions on any unescorted woman to wander across their path.

With precious time flying by, he burst into the galley. "Jasper, have you seen Sam?"

"Good afternoon, Professor," Jasper said. "I see you remain among the living."

Christian glowered and combed a shaky hand through his hair. "Samantha?"

Jasper grinned, showing a wide expanse of perfect white teeth. "Why, indeed, I saw her earlier. She departed with Garrett. Didn't say when they would return, but I would not expect them back before supper."

With a growl, Christian whirled on his heel and stomped out of the galley. Nasty claws dug into his temper. While he was worrying himself to a nub, Samantha was gallivanting around the city with Garrett. She had disembarked without permission and hadn't bothered to inform him or anyone else, other than Jasper, of her intentions.

A sudden thought struck him with the force of a broadside. She was with Garrett, the stud of the Western Hemisphere! The lad had no control when confronted by anything in skirts, and he would find Samantha an irresistible temptation. She had little experience with men, especially men like Garrett. Her naïveté could mire her knee-deep in trouble before she realized her predicament. Garrett wouldn't restrain himself simply because Samantha was untouched. Garrett never considered the consequences before plowing ahead in pursuit of his own pleasure.

Christian fumed and swore vile curses, making the crew edgy. He stalked around the ship like one of the wild cats he studied. When they returned . . . Well, Garrett would be well advised to find a hole to climb into and Lady Samantha best hold on to the seat of her pantalets.

Samantha and Garrett found an isolated meadow surrounded by forest where the sun had burned off the fog. Garrett got right to work, setting out the weapons, showing Samantha how to load the rifle and sight the target. She had a good eye, but at first try, the rifle's kick knocked her off her feet, onto her bottom, and bruised her shoulder.

"Brace yourself with your legs apart, knees slightly bent," he said, going through the procedure more thoroughly this time. If he returned her with a dislocated shoulder, Christian would break his neck. "Position your left leg in front and shift your weight onto it. When you fire, keep the stock snug to your shoulder.

The impact will rock your body back onto your right leg instead of slamming against you. You'll remain on your feet with less damage." He demonstrated. "The recoil will still smart. With your small frame, you have little upper body strength for serious shooting. But if you were forced to shoot something, or someone, you could."

She tried a few more times until she complained that her arms ached and she could no longer hold the heavy rifle upright. He then taught her to shoot from a sitting position and while prone, lying on her belly on the ground. In this position, where she could brace her elbows on solid earth, she hit the target almost every time. When she could do no more, he disassembled the rifle and cleaned it.

They moved on to the Colt .45 revolvers. After explaining how to load the gun, Garrett said, "Stand the same way you would as if you were shooting a rifle. Hold the gun in your right hand with your arm out level with your shoulder, but relaxed, elbow slightly bent. Sight along your shoulder and hand in a direct line to the target. Squeeze the trigger, and when it fires, allow your elbow to bend as the gun kicks back. Your arm will fly up into the air over your head and absorb the impact."

Samantha showed real talent, quickly mastering the handgun. When she wanted to practice the quick draws and shooting from the hip featured in penny dreadfuls, Garrett laughed. "You'll hit naught that way, Sam, except perhaps your foot. For that sort of shooting you must be *exceptionally* good, and you're far from that category yet. Give it a few years, and then you'll be ready to rob trains."

When they expended their ammunition, they flopped down on their backs in the dry winter grass to look up at the sky. Garrett chewed on a long grass stalk while Samantha described the shapes she saw in the clouds. "That one looks like Chris," she said, pointing to an anvil-shaped cloud.

"That's a thundercloud," he said in a chiding tone.

"I'm well aware of that. 'Tis big and stormy, black and seething inside." She laughed. "And with a big head on top."

"You know, Chris truly has your best interest at heart."

She rolled onto her stomach, fastening her gaze on him. "How did you and Chris meet?"

"I robbed him." He gave a short laugh. "At knifepoint, no less."

"No, you did not!"

"Oh, indeed, I did. I was thirteen and had lived on the San Francisco docks for six years. I existed hand to mouth for a long time, scrounging what food and shelter I could find. Then I fell in with a gang of thieves. I suppose you could say they adopted me. At ten, I was rather appealing."

She grinned. "You still are."

He rolled his eyes and sent her a melting smile. "So

I've heard and must agree."

She punched him on the arm.

"Ouch! You pack a mean right cross. We could have used you in our gang."

"Go on with your story."

"They taught me everything I know. How to shoot a gun and fight with a knife, slitting a man's throat before he knows what's happening. Pickpocketing finesse and diversion tactics. The more gentle arts of brawling, drinking, and wenching. Eventually I became a second-story expert, gaining entry to houses thought impregnable. I can scale a wall like a spider. My exploits became legendary."

"I would wager they did. What happened when you robbed Chris?"

"He broke my arm."

She abruptly sat up. "He did not!"

He smiled wryly. "He did and most effectively. He grabbed my wrist and broke my arm over his knee. Never have I seen a man move so fast. I never saw it coming."

She gasped. "My goodness."

"Then he flung me against a wall as though I were no heavier than a sack of feathers. I managed to get my feet beneath me and took off running. I suppose the impact addled my brains, because I cannot remember any pain after the initial jolt. But I ran like the wind. I was known to have the fastest feet in the gang. Chris caught me as easily as if I were running through swamp mud. I later found out he was a sprinter in university."

"Where did Chris go to school?" she asked, changing the subject.

"Harvard and then Oxford."

"Is he English?"

Garrett let a beat of silence pass, and his gaze slid away. "Chris prefers I not talk about his past."

"Then tell me what happened after he caught you."

He sighed, giving her a lopsided smile. "He slung me over his shoulder and took me to his hotel chamber, brought in a doctor to set my arm, fed me, cleaned me up, and clothed me. There I was, filthy, ignorant and uneducated, disreputable and corrupt, even at thirteen, and spewing curses like a drunken sailor. And then he took me home to Boston. As you can see, I've yet to take my leave."

Samantha turned away to look out over the meadow. "I find it hard to believe he could be so compassionate."

He brought her back to him with a tug on her chin. "You know very little about Chris. You see only the hard exterior, but he's soft underneath."

She snorted in an unladylike manner.

His look was censorious. "He *does* have a heart, and it's less unassailable than you believe. I know. He saved my life. He saved my soul and gave me a home and a future. He educated me and taught me right from wrong. I would give my life for him. He's a good man, Sam."

"Then why does he treat me so horribly? Does he hate all women, or am I the lone exception? And why does he not want me on this expedition?"

He got to his feet and laughed down at her. "You truly have no notion, do you?" Garrett had noticed the way Christian's gaze followed Samantha when she was unaware of his scrutiny. Neither anger nor dislike glinted in Christian's eyes, but something else, something Garrett had never seen before. He suspected Christian donned his façade of brusqueness to keep Samantha at arm's length. Perhaps it was for the best. The good professor wasn't the settling-down sort.

"About what?" she asked as he helped her stand. She brushed the grass off her skirt.

He raised his hands in front of him. "Far be it from me to be the one to enlighten you. Chris would kill me."

She gave him a puzzled frown.

"Listen to him, and do what he tells you to do. I know he's been difficult, but he considers you his responsibility. He has no wish to see you get hurt."

When she tried to pursue the topic further, he shook his head. "It's late. Chris should be up and about by now. We better return before he becomes worried."

She mounted her horse with his assistance. "Exactly why *did* he sleep so late today?"

"I'm not saying another word," he said with a grin. "Why don't you ask Chris?"

They arrived at the ship, and leaving Garrett to unload the horses, Samantha ran up the gangplank. Christian occupied the top of the long boards. His expression stopped her in midgallop. His brows were drawn to a dark slash above his eyes; his lips formed an inflexible, thin line. His body stood as rigid as the main mast, and his eyes filled with fiery anger. A muscle jumped wildly in his tight jaw.

She went still, the blood draining from her brain, managing only to utter, "Oh no."

"Where the hell have you been?" He caught her arm in a hard grip and hauled her onto the deck.

When Garrett started to speak from a few yards away, Christian threw him a fulminating glare. "I'll take care of you next. I asked Sam a question."

Garrett closed his mouth and walked away with the horses.

Never having seen Christian quite so angry, Samantha mislaid her voice. Quivering seized her limbs. She grabbed hold of the railing to steady herself.

"Where were you?" he demanded again, shaking her sharply.

"With Garrett," she gasped and tried to wrench her arm from his grasp. "He gave me a shooting lesson."

"What other sorts of lessons did he give you?"

"None. What is your problem?" She twisted like an eel. "You are hurting me!"

"Stop squawking. Who gave you permission to leave the ship?"

"No one. I finished my work and wished to learn how to fire a gun. Garrett was gracious enough to teach me."

"How gracious?" he grated out between clenched teeth.

Samantha finally freed her arm and shook it to relieve the numbness. Recovering from the first rush of panic, she allowed her temper to leap to the forefront. "Gracious enough."

He towered over her, glowered down at her. "Should you ever even *think* about taking off again without my permission and without letting me know where you are and what you're doing, I'll turn you over my knee so quickly you won't know what hit you. And when I get through with you, you'll be standing for the rest of this trip!"

Propping her hands on her hips, she returned his glower. "You and how many grenadiers?"

"I'm warning you. Don't dare to try my patience any further," he spat.

"What patience?" she spat right back, prudence not being her best quality.

Bending down, he butted one shoulder into her stomach and flung her up and over. Her head and half her body hung over his shoulder and down his back. When she beat on him with her fists, screamed obscenities, and stiffened her spine, he smacked her buttocks hard enough that the blow and her outraged cry resounded across the ship and turned heads. A tight arm across her legs held her in place while he stalked across the deck to the ladder, climbed down, and dumped her on his cabin deck. Leaving her in a heap of skirts and jumbled hair, he slammed and bolted the door.

CHAPTER ELEVEN

Samantha pounded on the cabin door until she was certain she had bruised her fists. Christian was a rat! And her family was not far removed from that. By the time Aunt Delia came to the door, several hours had sped by, and Samantha's voice was hoarse from yelling.

Delia sided with the rat. "Samantha, I understand you are distraught, but Professor Badia explained everything. You really should not have disappeared. Never have I seen anyone so distressed as was the good professor. You may say your prayers he had not the inclination to chain you in the hold on naught but bread and water. Should you only cease sparring long enough to get to know him, you would find him to be quite a likeable gentleman."

Likeable gentleman? *Hah!* Her sweet, sensible, bumbling aunt had defected to the enemy. Normally

Aunt Delia showed good judgment of character. How could she have gone blind so quickly and thoroughly?

"Embrace this confinement as a relaxing holiday from your chores," Delia said, "a soothing break that will allow you to reflect and garner your strength for the trip ahead."

Her aunt's attempt at logic only made Samantha's chest heave. "Release me, Aunt Delia!"

"Oh, I could not possibly do that, dear. Professor Badia will release you later."

Samantha slumped against the door. "How much later?"

"I do not recall his mentioning, but you will be fine."

Gilly paid her a visit later. She had turned coat, too. "Ye're lucky he didn't beat ye, m'lady. He was ever so worried and angry."

"Fetch me some dinner," Samantha pleaded, seeing no use in arguing with Gilly. Christian had obviously mesmerized her and Aunt Delia or drugged them or done something equally vile.

"Beggin' yer pardon, m'lady, but I canna do that. He says ye're ta go without yer dinner."

"Whom do you work for, Gilly? Him or me?"

"Why ye, o' course, but I couldn't defy him. He's such a nice man, an' it's fer yer own good."

Her own good? Now he was truly stretching it!

Pettibone and Chloe also stopped by to share her misery. Christian had influenced them as well. Samantha gave up and sank down on Christian's bunk, where she drifted in and out of slumber. His scent on the sheets and blankets assaulted her senses and brought her dreams she could very well have lived without.

She sped through the meadow, her feet tangling in grass as golden as ripened wheat. A sweet smell surged upward and merged with the scent of perspiration seeping from her pores. Bright sun baked the day, causing her head to swim. Fear pushed her faster, farther, toward the edge of darkness surrounding the sphere of light trapping her in its yellow web. If she could only reach it!

A rustling came from her right. Her heartbeat roared in her ears. She stopped, knelt down. How close was he? Vibrations from his heavy footfalls made the ground tremble beneath her knees. The snapping of stalks grew nearer, and she rose up, lifting her head above the tallest vegetation. Not more than a dozen yards away, he raised his head, tawny with a thick mane, a fusion of dark and light strands arching upward from the nape of his neck. Clear green eyes caught her gaze, holding her in thrall, reflecting a menace that pricked her skin with ice. His canines gleamed in the sun.

The world fell still. All sound and motion ceased beyond this one spot in this golden meadow. A curtain of life drew around the two of them, as if nothing else existed outside its enveloping folds. She feared they were the only living creatures left on Earth.

She glanced around for a frantic moment—whirled

and ran. Grass blades sliced at her legs. She neared the shadowy world, and a great weight slammed into her from behind. She fell forward, flattened the grass, borne to the ground by his strength. She lay on her stomach, tears pouring from her eyes. His paws pressed her shoulders into the rich soil. Would he truly hurt her? Hot breath and the slide of ivory teeth on the back of her neck penetrated her senses. She arched back her head and screamed to the sky.

Samantha tossed on the cot, whimpers escaping her lips. When she finally pulled herself from the nightmare, damp clothing clung to her body.

Samantha remained locked in the cabin for five long, boring days. She had no notion where Christian and Garrett slept during that time. The ship had sailed out of Charleston harbor on the night of her incarceration, and a never-ending expanse of ocean greeted her whenever she gazed out the porthole.

The first morning of her confinement, Christian unbolted her door at dawn and, without a word, shoved a tray of food across the deck. Pulling the door to, he secured it. From her perch on the bunk she looked down at the tray—bread and water. Her stomach uttered a protesting gurgle. Was that all she would have for breakfast? Wrong, she soon discovered. For the entire day.

She doubted Aunt Delia was aware of the *good* professor's plan to starve her.

Each successive day began in the same manner, and Samantha, like a fawning puppy, began to look forward to her only contact with a human, brief as it was, and her daily meal. When his footsteps came from the companionway, her mouth watered. She recalled correspondence in her uncle's papers about a Russian scientist who thought dogs might salivate simply from the stimulus of ringing a bell. *Hell's teeth!* She was becoming Christian's dog. On the third day, fruit and meat supplemented her bread and water.

On the fourth morning, she ventured to address her jailer. "May I kindly have something to read? I'm becoming weary of counting the planks on the ceiling."

Christian cut her an impassive look and closed the door more gently this time. The door opened an hour later, and a book flew through, bouncing off the deck. "Thank you," she started to say, but he pulled the door shut.

Samantha plucked up the book and read the title: *The Flora and Fauna of the South Pacific Islands.* "An interesting choice. Not what I would have chosen had I a library at my disposal, but under the circumstances, better than naught." Turning onto her stomach, she devoured the author's journal.

Christian threw open the door on the fifth morning and stood in the doorway. "You're free to go," he said and, walking away, left the door ajar.

The days wore on, and Christian treated Samantha as if their confrontation and her subsequent incarceration never occurred. She knew better than to refer to the incident and was more than willing to let it go. They engaged in no more arguments, and no further romantic encounters ensued. They maintained a polite but distinct distance, like opposite poles of a magnet.

Samantha fell into a routine, and life aboard ship gained a sameness. She spent the majority of her time with Jasper in the galley, learning to prepare such delicacies as jambalaya, crawfish stew, and a spicy concoction he called "jerked chicken." She enjoyed his lessons and company and fast became quite the journeyman cook. They put into port often for fresh meat, produce, and water while traveling down the eastern shore of South America, though at most stops, the passengers and crew remained on board. And thus far, good weather and steady winds sped them along on calm seas.

Samantha soon developed a friendship with the young cockney cabin boy, Cullen O'Dare, and spent hours tutoring him in reading, writing, and arithmetic. An intelligent, engaging boy, he had a quick, gap-toothed smile in a gamin's face topped with an unruly mop of black hair.

One sunny day she tried to talk Cullen into allowing her to cut his hair. He backed away while she stood on deck with a pair of scissors in her hand. "No ye don't!" he said with a scowl and plowed a hand through the thick strands, his unconscious action reminiscent of an exasperated Christian. The boy's blue eyes snapped. He jutted out his jaw. "I ain't stupid like Samson. No Delilah's goin' ta cut *my* 'air!"

He found Samantha later and apologized with a lopsided grin. The remainder of the day he spent with Christian, whom he worshipped and imitated with uncanny accuracy. Cullen told Samantha, "Someday, if'n I study 'ard an' learn 'nough, I'm goin' ta be a scientist, just like Chris."

Samantha's balmy family surprised her by how well they adjusted to the voyage. Each found his or her own niche among the crew and contributed useful labor.

Gilly assumed Samantha's mending chores and became an expert at patching up sail. The afternoons she reserved for Alan Smith, learning about inventory and accounting. She improved her skill with numbers, and Alan praised her efforts at every turn. A romance seemed to be developing. They often appeared on deck in the evening, Gilly standing at the railing with Alan's arm around her waist, their heads close together.

Their obvious attraction tugged at Samantha's heart

and reminded her of Christian's kiss. Her gaze sought him out wherever he was on deck. Every once in a while, she found him watching her, but often far away, she was unable to discern the expression in his eyes.

Chloe—delicate, spoiled, demanding Chloe—washed laundry. 'Twas a freak of nature to see her with her arms in hot, soapy seawater up to the elbows. Nonetheless, Samantha suspected her cousin found the work worth the effort when Garrett massaged fragrant lotion he had purchased in Charleston into her hands each evening. During the nightly ritual, Chloe sighed and fluttered her blond lashes while Garrett enthralled her with seductive smiles. Christian kept a close eye on the two.

One evening when Garrett finished applying lotion to Chloe's hands, he moved on to her neck. Soon afterward, Christian called Garrett aside for a private talk. Samantha happened to be close by and eavesdropped on the ensuing argument, audible only to her and the two men. From her hidden position, she had a good view of them.

"You cannot be planning what I know you're planning," Christian said.

Garrett placed his hand over his heart. "Chris, you wound me! *She* has been flirting with *me*."

"She's eighteen and a maid of gentle breeding. In English society, females learn to flirt while still in their cradles. They have no idea of where it leads. Regardless, that's no excuse. Every female between the ages of ten and eighty, even the blind ones, flirts with you. Do you have to fuck them all?"

Fuck? Samantha pursed her lips. She was unfamiliar with the word, though she had no need of a crystal ball to divine its meaning.

Garrett's features settled into an affronted expression. "I resent that implication. Though I appreciate the flattering allusion to my manhood, it would be physically impossible, not to mention morally reprehensible, for me to do so."

Christian snorted. "Since when have you and morality had more than a nodding acquaintance? I'm cautioning you, Garrett, if you compromise Chloe, you'll marry her."

"M-m-marry?" The word bubbled up from Garrett's throat the same way *manure* would have had he stepped into an odorous pile whilst in his best boots.

"Marry." Christian's voice was firm, his eyes steely. "And I'll walk behind you with a pistol in your kidneys to ensure you carry out your obligation. Do we understand each other?"

Garrett swallowed hard and nodded. Then he smiled. "Since you mentioned the 'M' word, old man, isn't it time you considered settling down? How about Sam? You two seem to suit quite nicely."

Samantha clapped her hands over her mouth to muffle the squeak. Her marry Christian? What an appalling notion!

"Bite your tongue," Christian growled and marched away from Garrett.

After the men's discussion, Chloe, much to her apparent dismay, received only hand massages.

When the ship rocked at anchor, Aunt Delia held decorum classes on deck after supper. Before long, the sailors were dancing like drawing-room dandies to hornpipe music and drinking tea out of battered pewter cups with their pinkies sticking out to the side. Samantha asked Delia why she deemed it important for sailors to learn the fundamentals of society protocol.

"A generous dose of civility and manners never hurt anyone," Delia answered with an aggrieved sniff.

Samantha saw the most astonishing transformation in Pettibone. He worked a sailor's day, dressed in clothes borrowed from some accommodating soul, coiling rope, hauling on lines, winching up anchor, standing watches, and taking a turn at the wheel. She marveled at the old man's strength and stamina. His stuffiness and haughty manner fled and left a jovial, hardworking man in its place. He looked and acted years younger, tanning in the sun and hardening from the work. Samantha caught a glimpse of the powerful young man he must have been centuries ago.

Christian and Garrett also worked as common sailors, carrying out whatever tasks the captain required and always at hand when the crew needed a strong arm or back. Christian spent much of his time spelling the captain at the wheel, where the scientist showed a surprising expertise and familiarity with sailing ships.

Christian had brought along a trunk filled with basketballs. He nailed empty bushel baskets to two facing masts, and when the ship sat at anchor or sped smoothly along by steam power, he shot baskets, often accompanied by Garrett and Cullen.

On a still, muggy evening while anchored off the coast of South America, Christian dug out a basketball and taught the game to the crew.

Rowdiness ensued with a plentitude of what Christian called "flagrant or intentional fouls." Everyone not actively engaged in the game stood along the sidelines to keep the ball from disappearing overboard. Narcissus, who now had the run of the ship and the affection of the sailors, chased the ball whenever it wandered out of bounds. Though unable to pick up and retrieve the large object, he kicked it like a football, which it was, and batted it with his tail, out of his pursuers' hands, until he tired of playing and allowed them to rescue it.

Samantha even joined the game after a while, but when she pulled her old trick, Christian, acting as referee, pointed at the basket. "No goal," he yelled. "Sam, you know it's supposed to go through the top of the basket, not the bottom."

She argued, citing as defense her relatively shorter

height. He slapped her with a foul and confined her to a barrel of nails until she regained her temper and apologized.

They naturally gravitated into two teams, the Redcoats and the Yanks, and played whenever they had the opportunity. Samantha developed into a valuable player on the Redcoat team once she mastered the fundamentals. With her small size and quickness, she dribbled circles around the bigger, clumsier men. Only Christian or Garrett could steal the ball from her, and even they had difficulty doing so. However, her main threat soon came from young Cullen, who began to outshine them all.

To Samantha's frustration, the Redcoat coach, Aunt Delia, told her niece that she would permanently bench her should she try to shoot baskets. But whenever a Yank committed a foul against Samantha, even Aunt Delia was unable to prevent her from taking her foul shots. She never made them. A few times in the middle of a game, Christian clearly took pity on her and lifted her up by her waist to the basket, allowing her to dunk the ball. His team always booed and hissed and contested the points.

The first time the unfortunate Garrett ran full tilt into Samantha and knocked her flat onto her back, Christian dashed over and picked her up. She blinked at him with crossed eyes.

"You're too small to take charges," he said tightly. "If you ever do that again, I'm banning you from the game."

She marked it as one of the few occasions they

agreed on an issue. Despite her shaky condition, she demanded her foul shots.

He shook his head. "Most certainly not. I believe we can all agree to grant you the two points."

She remained as adamant as he, and eventually, after much shouting and a few tears, she got her way. This time she tried a different strategy. She tossed the ball underhanded by bringing it up from between her knees . . . and came close. The next one went in the basket, and both teams patted her on the back. Samantha later learned that, while she was recovering from her collision with Garrett, he took a brutal charge from Christian, and the ball had not even been in play. He complained about the lump on the back of his head for a week.

Owing to his age and superior wisdom, Pettibone normally assumed the role of referee and called fouls with much whistling on a hornpipe. Affecting a composed, disdainful manner when the players questioned his calls in a less than polite manner, he tilted his long, sharp nose up in the air and pointed stiffly to the sidelines, tossing recalcitrant players out of the game with abandon at the slightest infraction. Once he even ejected Aunt Delia. He demanded she retire to her cabin when she stomped onto the court, shook her fists at him over a decision she saw as unfair, and called him a "blind, old fool."

The Yanks were the better team, with both Christian and Garrett, who had more experience with the game, and Cullen, who played as if he had emerged from his mother's womb with a basketball in his hands. At times, Christian took Pettibone's place as referee, especially when the Yanks grumbled about the British referee showing bias toward the Redcoats. But Christian could not remain on the sidelines for long; his love of the game called to him, and he soon returned to the court.

One afternoon when azure sky seamlessly met the sea and gulls from the coast described lazy spirals about the ship, Samantha leaned over the bow railing to watch dolphins leap across the ship's path. Having learned to separate his firm strides from the others' long ago, she heard Christian approaching. When he stopped behind her, his masculine odor enveloped her.

"Why do they do that?" She pointed to the dolphins and turned her head to look at him. Tied back with a ribbon and tossed by the wind, her long hair streamed behind her like a banner and flowed across his chest and face. He brushed it aside, draped it over her shoulder, and rested his hand there to keep the tresses in place. His eyes were bright today and crinkled at the corners in the sunlight. They held soft interest instead of the angry or indifferent light she had seen too much of lately.

He looked out at the dolphins, and his expression

grew thoughtful. "No one really knows. Sailors believe dolphins steer them to safe waters. They've saved drowning sailors by using their bodies as floating buoys or by towing unconscious men close to shore. For some unfathomable reason, dolphins seem to have an affinity with humans. Lord knows why. They're hunted for meat in most parts of the world."

Her lips slanted upward. "Why do *you* believe they leap like that in front of the ship? You must have some theory."

He returned the smile. "I daresay they're playing, enjoying the thrill of the close encounter. I also believe they're waiting for us to throw the galley waste overboard so they can obtain a free meal. They have an especial fondness for fish heads." He winked, and a hint of devilry flickered in his eyes. "But I've noticed they have little liking for your jerked chicken."

When she turned back to the rail, his lips whispered across the back of her bare neck, though she could have imagined it. Dare she find out?

Two nights later while Christian stood watch, footsteps tapped on the boards. Turning, he leaned back against the railing, folded his arms over his chest, and crossed his ankles. In the radiance of the lanterns and stars, Samantha came into sight, pausing by the ladder and nibbling at her fingernails—a familiar habit, one in which she indulged when nervous or fearful.

His heart gave a leap, as did his cock. He dismissed both unruly organs.

She moved toward him, seeming to push her feet forward.

He smiled warily, suspecting their meeting privately in the night boded ill for his peace of mind. "Dare I ask what mischief you're about at this late hour?"

"Nothing." She lowered her head and paid particular attention to worrying a nail head in the planks with the toe of her half boot.

"I beg to differ with you. What do you want?"

She looked up with luminous eyes glowing in the starlight. "I wish to request a favor."

Warning bells clanged in his brain. "What?" he asked with caution.

"You see, I have developed this theory. You are a scientist, and scientists are fond of theories, are they not?"

"What makes me suspect I'll regret my answer if I say yes?"

She pouted prettily. "Set aside your reservations for once and simply answer the question. I assure you the ship will not sink if you do."

"Right, I'll bite. I cannot wait to discover where this is leading. Indeed, I'm fond of theories. Now I suppose you plan to tell me yours?"

"Of course."

Her infectious grin coaxed a smile from him.

"I have contemplated our kiss in Charleston and formed a theory," she said.

"I die with anticipation." He recollected that kiss, and a jolt of searing heat danced along his nerves like Saint Elmo's fire.

"I imbibed a great quantity of wine that night," she said after taking a deep breath, "and when you kissed me, I felt dizzy and . . . and strange. I can only conclude that my condition resulted from becoming foxed on the wine. You see, I seldom imbibe strong drink."

His lips twitched. She consumed two small glasses of wine. She really *was* an innocent if she had no inkling of the emotions that flared between them. Though he suspected her ultimate destination, he allowed her to plow ahead into rough seas.

"The only true way to test my theory is to try it again when I've had naught to drink. Do you not agree?"

"I most emphatically do not." He moved to turn away. Her small hand on his arm stopped him. Her eyes revealed a vulnerability that grabbed his soul and less saintly parts of his body. Blood pumped slow and heavy into his loins, and he groaned.

"Will you kiss me again, Chris?" Color rose into her face. "As a scientific experiment to test my theory?"

His resistance wavered, and he cursed his weakness. If he were to kiss her, could he trust himself not to become overwhelmed by this blasted obsession with her?

"For science?" she asked, her voice becoming very small.

"Very well, in the interest of scientific inquiry . . ." He bent over and bussed her on the cheek.

Her face fell, and tears welled up in those marvelous eyes. "You are mocking me, pretending to misunderstand. I should have known you would not take me seriously."

He released his breath in a slow stream of air. "Why yes, Sam, I suppose I was, though I had no intention of giving offence. We'll carry out this experiment properly. Pucker up."

Holding her wrists in his hands, he pulled her arms behind her back and gently drew her up against him. A tingling shiver swept all the way to his toes. He dipped his head and moved his mouth as lightly as a breath over hers, kissing the corners and running the tip of his tongue over the curves. When she parted her lips, he moved on, kissed her nose and her eyelids, placed fleeting kisses across her forehead and temple and down her cheeks.

At last he settled his lips over hers and slanted his head, fitting and molding to the shape and softness of her mouth. He flicked his tongue barely inside, out again, ran his tongue over her teeth and tantalized himself with quick thrusts. When her tentative tongue found his and caressed it, heat fired his groin, and he eased back, leaving her lips, and pulled her up tighter against him, allowing his erection to pulse against her belly.

"So sweet," he murmured. "You have the most luscious mouth, Sam, soft as a jaguar's fur, sugary as a mango, and smooth as butter. Hot, melted butter."

When she opened her mouth, he delved back inside, deepened the kiss, filling her sweet cavity with his tongue and stealing her breath. He thrust rapidly in and out in imitation of what he ached to do, and she moaned and trembled, her head falling back. His tongue went deeper, his lips growing harder, greedier. She kissed him back with her lips, her tongue, and her body undulated against him. Heat rose swiftly and unbearably. His testes ached, and he rubbed his swollen shaft against her softness to dispel some of the discomfort.

Samantha broke the kiss. "Release my hands," she said in a quavering voice.

"Not on your life." He continued to trace a moist trail across her throat and under her chin, his tongue traveling across skin like hot silk.

"Why?"

"It keeps both our hands occupied," he murmured against the hollow at the base of her throat, gliding his mouth downward, as low as her modest dress would allow. He brushed kisses back to her mouth again, tonguing the corners and the enchanting dip in her upper lip.

"Chris," she said, her face heated and flushed,

"please release me. I want to touch you."

Had she thrown a bucket of cold water on him, he could not have pulled away faster. His back stiffened, and though he still held her hands, he stepped back until their bodies no longer touched. "Bloody hell," he said, "you have no notion of what you're saying."

"I do. Please release my hands." Her eyes darkened into turbulent golden pools. "I merely want to touch you, and I would like for you to . . . to touch me."

Her words sliced the air like a pirate's cutlass. He dropped her hands and backed up another step. "You know nothing," he said harshly. "Your innocent touching wouldn't stop there. Return to bed. I give you fair warning that next time you attempt a stunt like this, you'll find yourself on your back with your skirt up around your ears, and I'll be inside you faster than you can say . . . theory."

Visibly stung by his words, she lowered her eyes, spun around, and ran away.

With a deep scowl, Christian watched her leave. Though he was relieved at her withdrawal, shame and disgust at his behavior pricked him. How could he set an example for Garrett when he couldn't even keep his hands off Samantha? It made no difference that she had instigated the encounter. He had the experience, was older, supposedly wiser.

What attraction did the little imp have that drew

him in so tightly? His mind and body had tangled into knotted threads, and he was helpless to find the ends to straighten them out. He had only to look at her, and his cock mutinied. He had to resolve this unseemly state of affairs in some fashion, but damned if he knew how. One wed a girl like Samantha; one didn't simply fuck her. *Marriage!* He was disinclined to pursue that path, particularly with an aristocrat. From his perspective, the situation was more satisfactory when she hated him.

What was happening to him? Lust, love, insanity, middle-aged senility? He supposed he could take his pick.

CHAPTER TWELVE

They approached Cape Horn on the southern-most tip of South America, and good weather paced them. Other than occasional rolling swells, the ocean remained glassy. Clear blue skies stretched from horizon to horizon. When the wind freshened and filled the sails, Captain Lindstrom cocked a weather eye skyward and pointed out the subtle signs of changing conditions. Gannets, gulls, and cormorants no longer accompanied the ship. Their desertion predicted heavier weather ahead.

Well known for its stormy, unpredictable seas, this stretch of water was the most dangerous they planned to cross. They would swing around the Cape through the Drake Passage, a narrow strip of ocean between South America and Antarctica. An alternative passage existed through the Straits of Magellan, but it would have added several weeks to the journey, and both Christian and Samantha expressed their impatience to reach their destination.

When they neared the Cape, sailing between the Falkland Islands and Tierra del Fuego, the ocean swells rose higher, lifting like the exposed backs of marine leviathans. They progressed beyond the islands dotting the coast, and deep troughs and foaming whitecaps began to mar the waters. Cold ocean currents streaming off Antarctic glaciers met warm tides flowing down the South American coast, creating a volatile mix. The waters clashed, and the sea grew turbulent, tossing the ship about.

The clement sky held until they reached the western edge of Tierra del Fuego and moved northward into deeper ocean. There the East and West Furies came together, and so many breakers disturbed the ocean's surface, early explorers had named it the Milky Way.

Storm clouds crouched on the horizon, hanging low and dark. The sea churned, buffeted the ship, and made passage along the deck perilous. The captain ordered lines strung as handholds and commanded the women to retire below deck.

Samantha languished in the cabin beneath the wind's roar—screaming around the ship, growing in strength—as hard rain pellets struck the deck. The cabin floor pitched and bucked. Sailors' shouts, words shredded by the rising wind, came from overhead. Gilly and Chloe huddled on the bunk and clutched each other, moaning and whining nearly as loudly as the wind. Samantha snapped at them and savaged her fingernails. Delia took the storm in stride, sitting in a captain's chair bolted to the deck while she sewed and timbers groaned around her. Meanwhile, the ship shivered and screeched, plunged into and out of deep swells.

When Samantha had gnawed her fingernails to the quick, she threw herself out of the hammock onto the sloping deck. "I cannot remain here any longer! I must go up to see if I can help."

"I'm sure you mean well," Aunt Delia said, looking up from her sewing, "but the captain said we would be safer in our cabin."

"Not if this ship should plunge to the ocean bottom." Her reply elicited another loud wail from Chloe and Gilly. "Forgive me, but I must get out of here."

She careened to the door and clambered up the ladder. Cold wind and rain blasted her in the face before she reached the top. By the time she crawled out on deck, the rain had turned to sleet. Biting wind whipped her skirt around her legs and threw her hair into her face. Sitting on the slippery boards, she tied her hair into a knot at her neck before climbing to her feet again. As the ship plummeted, she staggered, her legs braced far apart, buffeted by icy rain and sleet, tossed about by howling wind and a pitching deck.

Men ran in all directions, yelled into the wind, pulled in sail, and lashed down cargo. Samantha struggled against the gale and heaving planks to make her way forward, hugging a mast when a frigid wave smashed against her back. It soaked her clothes and almost swept her overboard. Clinging to the timber, she lifted her tearing eyes to the rigging, where sailors scrambled and climbed the ropes like spiders on a gigantic web. They swayed to the ship's violent movements, furling sails and untangling lines.

She gasped. Over her head, Cullen hung upside down, halfway up the rigging, from a line wrapped around one leg. She screamed for help, but the wind stole her words, casting them overboard. The closest men, intent on their own missions, failed to note Cullen's predicament. When the mast holding the rigging cracked and leaned, she released a sharp cry, then pressed her lips together to keep them from trembling.

Ripping off her skirt and petticoats, she flung them into the wind. In her blouse, short chemise, and pantalets, she scaled the rigging. Ice coating the ropes froze and deadened her hands, but she clung to the netting. When her boots' leather soles slipped, she kicked them off and let them fall to the deck. She continued upward, keeping her gaze fixed on Cullen far above.

Samantha had almost reached the boy when a faint shout came from below. She dared not look down, terrified her courage would abandon her. She was so very close. When she came alongside Cullen, she grasped his freezing arm in her icy hand and pulled him forward, allowing him to grab the rigging above and untangle his leg.

"Can you climb down?" she shouted.

His eyes round with fear and his lashes coated with frozen tears, he nodded and began his descent.

She glanced down. 'Twas a dreadful mistake. The world spun before her eyes, and a vise gripped her vitals. Clutching her arms about the rigging, she closed her eyes. She could not possibly climb down! Her chest cramped with vertigo and constricted her breathing. She would die up here, an icicle frozen to the ropes. The sailors would have to cut off her stiffened limbs to fetch her down.

Out of nowhere, a strong arm curled around her waist. A warm body moved up behind her and leaned against her back. Large hands gripped the rigging above hers.

"I have you!" Christian shouted, unbuttoning his heavy coat with one hand. "Turn about and put your arms around my neck."

She could not do it, could not let go.

"I gave you an order, Sam!" When she remained frozen in place, he pried her arms off the ropes and turned her upper body into his chest. "You're safe now. Wrap your arms around my neck like you did when I kissed you." Her arms crept up, then clasped him with all her strength. "Good girl. Now put your legs around my waist." He had to help her, but soon her thighs gripped his waist as tightly as her arms squeezed his neck. With some difficulty, he fastened one button on his coat behind her back. "Keep your eyes closed. I'm taking you down."

Christian descended the rigging with her clinging to him like a leech, snug under his coat. Tears ran down her face to mix with the rain and sleet soaking his shirt. She could breathe again but shivered from a bone-chilling cold.

When he reached the deck, he carried her to her cabin. In front of the astonished looks on the faces of the women, he unbuttoned his coat, peeled Samantha off his chest, and wrapped her in a blanket.

"Dry her off, get her warm, and don't allow her to leave this cabin again!" he barked and stalked back out into the storm.

The tempest blew itself out hours later, and Christian, having changed into dry clothes, returned to Samantha's cabin. Without saying a word, he hooked a muscular arm around her waist and picked her up. Tucking her against his hip, he carted her into his cabin, tossed her onto the bunk, and bolted the door on his way out.

That night, Samantha lay on Christian's bunk and tried to close her ears to the thud of a basketball on deck overhead. The sound had become a familiar one when she was in Christian's bad graces.

Samantha endured a full week on bread and water for disobeying orders. Why did she not see this coming? If she'd only planned ahead, she could have stowed clean clothes and extra food in Christian's cabin before he returned for her. She cursed her dirty, hungry state. Taking a deep breath, she let it out slowly. Oh well, now she could finish her book.

By the time Christian released her from his cabin, which Samantha now openly referred to as "the brig," the ship sat at anchor in a cove off the western coast of Chile. When she arrived on deck, the men were scuttling about and replacing the cracked mast. She avoided Christian and found Jasper in the galley. He piled a plate high with food and shook a finger in her face.

"Though your actions were heroic, you took a witless risk. Thank the good Lord Chris saw you, or you would still be hanging from that rigging. The ice would have stiffened your body so completely, we could have used you for a figurehead on the prow." He chuckled.

Samantha pulled a face. "I know. Refrain from feeding me a lecture. Simply feed me! I served my time in the brig. If he should lock me up again, I'll become so skinny he'll be unable to find me. I shall merely turn sideways and disappear at will."

"Now watch your cheeky mouth, especially around Chris," he warned. "That man has a temper."

"I am well acquainted with his temper, thank you very much. His wrath puts to shame the wrath of God," she replied while stuffing her face.

Jasper *tsked* and shook his finger again. "You should learn some manners, young lady."

She talked around a mouthful of the drumstick of some mainland game bird. "Not before Chris does. 'Tis he who lacks manners. Perhaps you should suggest he attend Aunt Delia's decorum classes."

A few days after Samantha's release, Christian strolled into the galley. When he crooked a finger at Samantha, she looked at him with suspicion. "Do you intend to yell at me or toss me in the brig again?"

"My plans didn't include it. Have you a guilty conscience?"

"I do not," she mumbled.

"Glad to hear it. I wished only to speak with you."

"About what? Can we not speak here?"

He shook his head and walked away. "When your curiosity gets the best of you, you can find me outside."

She felt safer in the galley with Jasper close at hand, but the cook gave her a pointed look and nodded. "Go to him. He would not hurt you."

"Indeed." She blew out a breath. "He would not lay a

finger on me but contents himself with starving me to death."

"Is fear the reason you avoid him? Are you truly so timid?"

Samantha untied her apron and slapped it on the weathered wooden table. "Most certainly not."

She found Christian aft, hunkered on his heels, coiling rope. Samantha sat on the deck in front of him, drew up her knees to her chest, and hugged them. While she waited for him to complete his task, she quietly admired his strong body and rugged face. How could a man who looked so delicious be so sour? When he finished with the rope, he lay on his side facing her, propped on an elbow with one leg stretched out and the other bent at the knee. He perused her for a long minute, his eyes giving away nothing. She chafed under his thorough inspection.

"Would you enjoy leaving the ship on an animal expedition?" he finally said. "We're approaching a small island I visited once before. I asked the captain to lay up for a few days now that we're through the Drake Passage and entering calmer waters. The men deserve a bit of sun and relaxation on the beach after freezing in Tierra del Fuego and repairing the mast."

His words poked her brain with a sharp stick. "I believe we agreed to make all haste to Tasmania. Have you some nefarious plot to deposit me on an isolated speck of land where I shall be required to survive on lizards and coconuts?"

He chuckled. "I hardly think ridding myself of you would be to my advantage, as tempting as the notion may be."

Despite his smile, she detected a nuance of affront lurking about his eyes. "Then why pause our journey now?"

"We also require new water stores. We lost many casks in the storm, and the island will be our last landfall for weeks."

"How long would we be gone?"

"Three days."

She tilted her head toward Garrett and Chloe, who chatted by the railing. "Are the others coming along?"

"No. Only you and I." His gaze ran over her gown. "Of course, you'll have to shed those clothes."

Her spine snapped rigid. "I beg your pardon?"

His eyes twinkled, and he laughed. "I only meant you'll have to wear trousers. The terrain is rough and no place for skirts. I would think you could fit into a pair of Cullen's old trousers."

"You've been planning this trip all along, have you not? It explains the book you gave me to read."

"I trust you had sufficient time to finish it. Bring it along. You might have need of it." When she remained silent, he asked, "Did you enjoy it?"

"The plot was dreadfully slow, but I found the characters intriguing."

He chuckled and got to his feet. "I'm pleased to see

you've managed to retain your sense of humor. However, you've sorely tested mine on this voyage. See Cullen for some suitable clothing, and I'll take care of the rest. We anchor in a cove off the island tonight. I'll meet you on deck, prepared to go, at dawn."

Samantha climbed topside, clad in Cullen's old clothing. Christian eyed her from a distance. The outfit strained at the seams, but it would be more appropriate than one of her gowns. When she strolled up to him, he inhaled sharply at the curve of her hips in the tight-fitting trousers, her small, firm breasts jutting against the shirt's thin material. He handed her a wide-brimmed straw hat. "Wear this to keep the sun off your face." She turned and walked away. "And for God's sake, don't . . ."

When she bent down to collect her pack, his hand itched, and he stepped up behind her to pat her tempting bottom so nicely displayed beneath the tight wool. She straightened with a gasp. He grinned and winked. "Nice fit, Sam."

She sputtered, struggled into the pack's straps, and settled them over her shoulders, a blush covering her face.

He picked up his pack, went to the ladder leading over the side, and climbed down into the dinghy.

As Christian pulled on the oars, he granted Samantha a smile. She returned it, all innocent and unsuspecting. Were she able to interpret his thoughts, her sunny mood would flee in an instant. Wait until she encountered *live* wildlife, the kind existing outside the London Zoo. Suffered from exposure to extremes of heat and cold, constant dirt, prickly plants, and biting insects. Experienced firsthand a lack of privacy. Limped along on sore feet and nursed an aching back. Then she would be content to remain safely ensconced in Hobart. His smile inched into a grin.

Samantha trudged behind Christian across the island's arid landscape and entered a fantasy world. They traversed bizarre terrain so extraordinarily alien, as though the ship had landed them on another planet, perhaps Mars, instead of an island in the Pacific. She always believed the tropical oceanic islands consisted solely of green, moist jungle, huge ferns, and overhanging vines. The area through which they traveled was as far from jungle as was her London drawing room.

Few trees graced the sandy plain, and those were twisted into grotesque shapes, as though tortured by a sadistic gardener. When she rubbed her palms against the trunks, gray, hairy bark flaked off. The wood beneath was ironlike, dry and dense. Sparse, grayish green leaves drooped from the branch tips, and when she touched one, it felt fat, waxy, and smooth.

They encountered little wildlife. A few circling hawks and the occasional lizard or beetle scurrying across the hot sand. A brown fox darted across her path in pursuit of a strange mouse hopping ahead of it on impossibly long back legs. Misshapen cacti, scattered amongst the trees, arose in the near distance, and a small, curious, wrenlike bird flitted around one tall cactus, sticking a sharp probe into holes on the plant's surface. Samantha looked for Christian to ask him what the bird was doing, but he ranged far ahead, and she lacked the strength to catch up with him.

Her pack grew heavier with every step, and the straps cut painfully into her shoulders. Christian had set a brisk pace, and with her shorter legs, she found it difficult to keep up. The hot—no, searing air dried her throat and sucked the moisture from her skin, like walking through a furnace. Was it truly December? Snow would have fallen in Boston by now, but here at the bottom of the world, high summer reigned.

Despite her discomfort, she reveled in the open space and the freedom, especially the freedom of wearing trousers. She questioned why society had condemned women to drafty, unwieldy skirts for so many centuries. If every woman should have the opportunity to wear trousers, just once, they would soon be all the rage. Skirts, petticoats, and corsets could be naught but a male plot designed to keep women in bondage, and she resolved to acquire several sets of male trousers when she returned to England.

Several hours went by, and her ache evolved into acute physical pain. She cast a glance at Chris's back, far in the distance. "Chris?" she gasped as loudly as her parched throat would allow.

In the still, dry air, her plea carried to his ears, for he halted and turned around.

She commanded her aching legs to trot forward until she drew alongside him. "May we take a short break? Your legs are longer than mine, and you are walking too fast. I'm not accustomed to carrying a pack. It hurts my shoulders."

"An animal expedition has several rules," he said with a patronizing expression and in a similar tone. "First, to actually *find* animals, you must refrain from talking. Second, this is not a stroll through Regent's Park. If you cannot keep up the pace because you have shorter legs, walk faster. And third, my pack is heavier than yours. If you wished to carry a lighter load, you should have packed fewer items."

Her face fell. "But you are larger than me. Your pack *should* be heavier."

"Do you wish to trade?"

She closed her mouth, though she had a notion to remind him that he had filled the packs, not she.

Turning away, he focused on the horizon. "No? Then allow us to move on—quietly. I want to cover more territory before we stop. We'll take a break about an hour from now." He nodded toward a steep ridge in the distance.

She groaned and shifted the pack, moving it a scant inch off the grooves in her shoulders.

When he finally called a halt in a depression shaded by a line of stunted trees straggling along a creek, Samantha dropped her pack with a grimace. She stumbled past him and knelt beside the creek, cupping her hands and splashing water over her face and neck.

He allowed her to rest for an hour before he stood and came to her side. "Ready?"

She mumbled to herself and struggled to her feet.

Christian walked to the creek and dipped his canteen into the water before taking off at a more modest speed. Samantha missed his detour as she fought with her pack and tried to find the least painful position. Three hours out into the hot sun, she ran out of water. "Chris, may I have a drink of your water? My canteen is empty."

"Rule number four, always fill your canteen when you have access to fresh water. You never know how far you might have to walk to the next water hole. Next time, use your head." In spite of his chastising words, he passed her his canteen and allowed her to drink.

Chapter Thirteen

By the time they made camp, light was fleeing rapidly on the short-lived heels of a tropical dusk. The lowering sun hit the cacti, throwing Brobdingnagian shadows—like the giant characters in *Gulliver's Travels*—stretching across the barren plain. Samantha staggered, and sweat drenched her clothes. She could not even remove the pack. When she raised her arms, cramping pain seized her shoulders and back.

Christian came over and lifted the pack. "Why did you not tell me the straps were cutting into your shoulders?" he asked, his voice thick with concern.

Tears of pain stung her eyes. She turned to look at the bloodstains on her shirt. "I thought you knew."

His eyes darkened. "Devil take it! Had I known, I would have called a halt before now. Slip down your shirt. Those cuts need treating."

Too tired and in too much pain to argue, she unbuttoned the shirt, eased it off her shoulders, and grimaced at the wide, raw patches on her skin. When he wet a handkerchief and cleaned the bloody stripes, she whimpered and flinched away.

"I know it hurts, but I have to clean the injury, or infection will set in." He reached into his pack and withdrew a brown bottle. "Now clench your teeth, because this may burn."

When he poured the weak solution of carbolic acid on the open wounds, she bit back a scream, and wetness streamed down her cheeks. She dragged in a shuddering breath. "It hurts terribly now."

"Wait a minute, and the pain will ease." He left her to tramp through the area beyond the campsite.

She could not believe her eyes. What was he doing now? Chasing after some animal while she was suffering? She failed to keep the angry edge from her question. "What are you looking for?"

"Aloe. Ah, here's one." He returned with a fat leaf in his hand that had a waxy skin, silver green with spiked edges. He squeezed it until a clear, jellylike sap oozed from its cut edge and rubbed the substance over her wounds. An immediate cooling seeped into her skin. After a short while, the pain ebbed to a dull ache.

"How does it feel now?"

She allowed a smile to creep over her mouth. "Better."

"Capital. You can collect wood for the fire. However, don't stray from my sight. Have a care where you step and what you grab. Snakes can resemble branches."

Her good humor fled, and she sent him a goggle-eyed look. Was that a hint of mercy in his features? If so, it swiftly disappeared.

"I hardly expect you to carry the wood on your shoulders," he continued. "A minor injury should not excuse you from your fair share of work."

After she had collected enough firewood for a dozen campfires, he demonstrated the technique for starting a fire using twigs and dry grass. "Why go to all that trouble?" she asked. "Why not simply use lucifers?"

He shook his head and clucked his tongue. "Matches become wet, and you might not have any. A fire could mean the difference between life and death. You must become competent with alternative methods and using the materials at hand." As soon as small flames appeared, he smothered them and handed her the twigs. "Now you do it," he said, rising. "I'll hunt for dinner. I expect to find a fire when I return."

"Chris—" He vanished before she could finish her objection. The infuriating man moved as quickly as a chameleon. She stared at the twigs, thinking perhaps she should have paid closer attention to Christian's rambling. Images of sleep, a bath, and a ten-course meal had caused her mind to drift while he droned on about twigs and fire. Never did she believe he would expect *her* to do it.

When Christian returned, Samantha still sat in front of the fire pit, her right thumb in her mouth, biting on the nail. The twigs lay undisturbed on the ground. He halted and silently studied her, aware of what she was going through. He recalled his maiden voyage into the field. Her pain and frustration were genuine. Why could he not simply carry her pack and start the fire? Remembering his ultimate motive, he shook his head as though to suppress the urge to give in to the sight of her misery. She would learn naught if he were to make her wilderness jaunt a pleasurable stroll. Capitulation now would ruin his intentions. He supposed he could slow down the pace . . . a bit. She *was* considerably smaller than he. Perhaps he would remove a few items from her pack. He could still make his point by the time they returned to the ship. His goal was to discourage her, not kill her.

"Aren't you a bit old to be sucking your thumb?" he said from directly behind her. *I have something else you can put in your mouth,* the devil on his shoulder suggested.

She jerked out her thumb. When she looked over her shoulder, he arched a brow. "I cannot help but notice we don't yet have a roaring fire."

"The twigs declined to cooperate," she said in a sullen voice. "I have no option but to believe you gave me defective wood."

He suppressed the smile tugging at his mouth and sat on the ground beside her. "Then I suppose we'll have to eat our dinner raw." He pulled out a wriggling grasshopper from a pouch hanging at his belt. "But I must admit they taste better roasted."

Her eyes opened as wide as saucers. She scrambled away, her knees churning up the sandy ground. "That is a bug!" she screeched. "I will not eat bugs. I care not what you do to me, but you'll not force me to eat a bug!"

He couldn't control his grin. "Sam, Sam, calm down. What did you expect? My returning to camp with lamb stew and meat pasties slung over my shoulder? Bugs are less disgusting than you might imagine. They're full of energy. You enjoy lobster, do you not? And shrimp and crayfish? All are arthropods, exactly like this grasshopper. Sometimes insects may be the only meal you can capture."

"No!" she yelled, her eyes filled with fire. "You cannot trick me. I will not eat bugs!"

He popped the insect into his mouth and made a production of crunching and swallowing it.

She shuddered, her face turning green, leapt to her feet, and ran into the bushes. He heard her vomiting and shook his head. After extracting a box of lucifers from his pack, he started a fire. He caught her voice at intervals, still defiant, coming from the camp perimeter. "I will not eat bugs! You cannot make me! I shall starve first!"

Having checked the surrounding area for snakes and other hazards, Christian allowed her to crash about beyond the fire's circle for an hour. Meanwhile, he cleaned the fish he had caught, spitted them, and grilled them over the flames.

"Sam, dinner is ready. Return to camp before you hurt yourself in the dark."

"You cannot force me to eat!" she shouted from wherever she was hiding.

"If you say so, but this fish looks tasty."

"Fish?" Within a heartbeat, she stormed up behind him with a leafy branch clutched in both hands. It smacked him across the shoulders, over the head, and on his back. By the time he made it to his feet and wrestled the weapon away from her, she managed to smite him with more than a few hard licks.

Her hair escaped the braid she had fashioned this morning and whirled in a chaotic storm about her head. She pushed the strands out of her face, features contorted with rage. Her eyes snapped, and she pointed a shaky finger at him. "You did this on purpose! You had no intention of having me eat bugs. You are trying to frighten me and convince me to quit this expedition. The same with your walking too fast and giving me a pack too heavy for me to carry. But I will not! I will not quit! No matter what evil schemes you have in your twisted mind, I refuse to buckle under to your attempts at intimidation!"

She tossed her head, and her butterscotch hair went flying. Her face glowed as red as the campfire, eyes wild and dark. Christian had never seen her looking so beautiful. A disturbing ache settled inside his chest, right around the region of his heart.

"I should have known"—she sucked in a ragged breath—"you would not take me on an excursion because you believed I might enjoy it, or because you wished to be nice to me, or wanted to spend time with me. You are the cruelest, most devious, most obnoxious, insufferable man I have ever had the misfortune to meet." Tears painted muddy tracks down her dusty cheeks. "And I hate you, Christian Badia!" she sobbed. "I hate you!"

He caught her shoulders and gathered her shaking body into his arms. While he stroked her back, her sobs subsided to hiccups. All this brouhaha over a grasshopper? He had expected revulsion, perhaps anger, but not hysteria. Perhaps he had pushed her too far. The situation wasn't working out quite as he had planned. He wiped her face with his handkerchief. "You're quite right. I *did* want you to give up. I now realize you desire this too greatly to crumble at the slightest obstacle. I promise, no more games. Instead, I'll teach you what you need to know to survive and help out on the expedition."

When she looked up, hopefulness combined with wariness lined her features. "You truly mean what you say? This promise of yours is not another trick?"

He put genuine warmth into his smile. "Honestly. No more tricks. We'll see how well you get along. If I'm satisfied you'll be safe in the field without constant supervision, you may accompany us. I vow to keep an open mind and grant you every chance to succeed. When we reach Hobart, we'll discuss it."

She pulled back from him and grinned. "Wonderful. Let us eat. I'm starved!"

He suffered a pang of loss when her warm body left his arms. "Help yourself." He gestured at the fish. "You'll find tin plates and utensils in my pack." While she retrieved the eating implements, he brought out a bag of native fruit he had picked earlier.

He handed her a wrinkled green fruit. She gave him a cautious smile, and her eyes narrowed. "Is it edible?"

"You'll like it. It's sweet."

She bit into the fruit, and juice ran down her chin. "Delicious," she said, a mouthful of fruit and tender fish garbling her words.

Christian had the sudden, inexplicable urge to lick the stickiness from her skin. He barely prevented himself from acting on his desires.

While they finished their meal, the sky became ebony and the stars sharp and bright, true darkness falling over the desert. Samantha looked up with wonder written across her face. "I never imagined such an absolute night could exist. The stars are so incredibly brilliant and close. I do believe I can catch one." She stretched out an arm and pretended to grab a star and put it in her pocket. Throwing him a triumphant glance, she laughed.

She skipped through the camp, catching stars as though they were fireflies, and his throat tightened at her pixielike play. She was too alluring tonight. He tried to tell himself she was merely a girl, not yet fully grown, but he knew better. A woman's fire ran through the veins of her small body and ignited him whenever he drew close. Part girl, part woman; he wanted it all. Carnal thoughts bedeviled him, and he consigned them to the recesses of his mind.

"I love the desert," he said, dragging his gaze away from her intoxicating play and turning to make up the bedrolls. "Only when you leave civilization can you experience true night . . . and quiet." When his pointed words failed to quell her capering, he called to her.

She gave him an impish look. "I have yet to catch them all," she said, pointing up at the sparkling stars.

A smile came unbidden. "Leave some to guide the sailors, Sam, and come here."

When she approached him, he examined her wounds, coated them with another layer of aloe, and pointed to a bedroll. "Now lie down. You're exhausted, and we have a long day tomorrow."

Though Christian snuggled into his bedroll and seemed to have no trouble finding sleep, Samantha's mind declined to shut down. Despite her anger at Christian and her body's exhaustion and pain, her imagination spun unfettered. She speculated about Christian. He was such a contradiction, strong with a masculinity that sent her heart thumping. Conversely, he could make her want to commit murder—his. He could be tender and sensual and utterly arrogant and infuriating. She wondered what made him the way he was.

"I know nothing about you, Chris." She spoke more to the darkling sky than to him.

"Of course you do," he replied in a sleepy voice.

She smiled at the opportunity to quiz him. "I mean, I know you are a scientist, a respectable one, and you study wild cats. I've read everything you have written."

He rolled over and folded an arm beneath his head. The dying embers of the fire outlined his long body. "Everything?"

She sat up and bobbed her head. "Every word."

"Good God, Sam. You must lead a boring life and have a great deal of idle time on your hands."

"Not at all. I find your writing brilliant. You have such passion for what you do. Your essays reveal a deep love of wildlife. You see nature in a way few people can.

What I meant to say is, I know nothing of the man behind the scientist. No one seems to. Who are you, Chris? I don't even know how old you are."

He settled onto his back and slipped his hands beneath his head. "Does it matter? I have no grisly skeletons rattling around my family closet. I am what you see. My life is no more complicated than that."

She leaned forward. "But it is. Our roots, our upbringing, families, friends, and mentors determine who we are. Tell me something personal about yourself. I wish to know what made you who you are."

"I'm a private man." A note of reserve etched his voice. "I take no enjoyment in discussing the past, because it's simply that, over and done with. It has no relevance now. I do what I do because I take pleasure in it, and when it ceases to satisfy me, I'll do something else."

She scooted her bedroll closer so she could rise above him. "Please?"

He looked up into her eyes and groaned. "Very well, if my surrender should convince you to go to sleep, I'll answer *one* personal question."

"Three," she said automatically.

He laughed and looked away. "You're still a tough negotiator." He brought his gaze back to her and said in a firm tone, "Two questions. My final offer."

She smiled. "Shall we start with your age?"

He snorted a laugh. "Is my age truly so important

that you would waste one of only two questions? Your prospects appear bleak if you were ever to discover a magic lamp with a grateful genie."

"I'm simply curious. You have the, ah, the strength and stamina of a man in the prime of life, but sometimes your mind seems older than Pettibone's. And at times, your behavior is closer to that of a young man, someone of Garrett's age."

He grimaced. "Very well, Sam. I have no desire for you to compare me with either Pettibone or Garrett. I turned thirty-eight this year."

She placed her forefinger to her lips and blinked. "That old."

A grin flickered across his mouth. "Practically one foot in the grave."

"I would hesitate to put it that way. You are quite well-preserved for such an advanced age."

"I thank you for the somewhat dubious compliment, madam," he said dryly. "Now ask your second question so I can get some sleep and some of that peace and quiet for which I visit the desert."

"Are you a British lord?"

Christian remained silent, his expression guarded.

"You promised to answer two questions," she ran on quickly, "and I recall no restrictions on particular subjects."

"My mistake again. When I'm in your presence, I seem to find myself in that predicament more often than not. No, I'm not a British lord. I claim ownership to no peerage. The only title I've earned the right to use is Doctor of Philosophy, one I gained through hard work and perseverance. You see before you merely Christian Badia, American citizen."

"But are you an aristocrat?" she persisted.

His brows came together. "You intend to beat this subject to death, do you not?"

"I find myself compelled to do so when you allow me only two questions."

He took a deep breath. "My father was a British earl. I was born on our estate in England, but I came to my majority in Massachusetts."

She wrinkled her nose. "What do you mean he *was* an earl? A peerage is normally inherited. If your father no longer lives, the title would go to his eldest son, whom I presume from your prickly answer to be you."

"My father discarded his title, relinquished all claim to it, renounced it, denounced it, and became an American citizen. He petitioned the Crown to award the earldom to some other inbred drain on society."

"It sounds as if you admired him for what he did," she said more softly. "Tell me about him."

Christian cast her a stern glance. "Is that not question number three?"

"I do believe it to be a statement and still part of question two."

Staring up at the stars, he said, "My father was a remarkable man but too idealistic for the times in which he
lived. He was a reformer, one of the earliest. He felt true
spiritual and emotional empathy for the misery he saw
every day—the poverty, disease, starvation, injustice, and
prejudice. Not because one man was inherently superior
to another but because of the circumstances into which he
was born. An accident of birth determined a man's place
in life. My father saw the established hierarchy, based on
inherited privilege, conspiring to maintain the inequity.

"He did what he could to aid those less fortunate,
lobbied in the House of Lords for reform, lent his support to labor unions, and used his wealth to effect good
in an attempt to change the system. He established and
supported hospitals for the poor, schools, homes for
unwed mothers and orphans, and employee-owned fac-
tories. And when the money was gone, he sold and gave
away the contents of the estate.

"Society mocked and shunned him. We even received
death threats. The newspapers, controlled by the aristocracy, lampooned him in political cartoons, dubbing
him 'The Battersea Earl,' referring, as you know, to the
meanest section of London."

Her heart twisted. "That must have been distressing
for you."

"No, Sam," he said with a quick look at her. "It was
most gratifying and quite wonderful. I championed my

father's ideals and still do. He believed inherited wealth to be unearned money tainted by the sweat of slaves and serfs and penniless croftholders for hundreds of years.

"When we had naught left to sell, when he had given it all away, we sailed to America and homesteaded in Massachusetts, where we built the farm through our own sweat and labor. Everything I have, I worked for, and therefore, it means much more to me."

A frown plucked at her lips. "Do you, then, hate British lords so dreadfully?"

"I have no hate for individuals." He gave a short laugh. "Perhaps I should qualify that by saying, not all of them. Many are as much poor dupes as everyone else—victims of their birth. What I hate is the system that perpetuates the nobility, one that stubbornly allows an archaic institution to continue while the world changes around them."

His gaze darted to her face. "Forgive me if I should hurt your feelings, but can there be any more useless creature than an aristocrat? They neither work nor do they contribute anything useful to society. Their sole legacy is noble offspring, who in turn become an additional burden on the working class. The aristocracy bemoans a welfare system yet refuses to acknowledge that their own class structure perpetuates the most heinous form of welfare—living off the sweat and backs of the poor."

She contemplated his words, and her mouth pursed.

"Have you the same animosity toward British ladies?"

He laughed, reached out, and tweaked the tip of her nose. "With the proper guidance and incentive, women, even British ladies, can be whipped into shape, taught to work and carry their own weight."

"Humph. I do believe I have no liking for that 'whipped into shape' part of your answer. Be that as it may, with your reformist leanings, you must favor women's suffrage."

"Well, I wouldn't go that far—" When she slapped him on the shoulder, he grinned. "Most assuredly. I support the notion in principle. Men and women should have the same rights but only the rights they earn. Unfortunately, society has prevented women from learning what they need to know to compete with men on an equal footing. In that way, men protect their own interests and maintain domination of the home and the workplace. Women can learn as capably as men, but they've not had the opportunity on account of men controlling the institutions and governments."

"Then why do you insist on being in charge?" she challenged.

Christian rose up on an elbow to face her. His voice became serious. "Because on this expedition, I have the most experience. I assume that fact to be the reason you hired me. A party with more than one leader foments rebellion, and confusion sets in, resulting in preventable harm." His tone softened. "Were we planning a shopping expedition to Harrods, I would gladly allow you to take the lead."

She affected a small pout and changed the subject. "Do you ever regret your father's decision? His abandoning an earl's lifestyle, the wealth and prestige?"

"What is there to regret? I have everything I could wish for—my work, my home, my basketball court. I have as much wealth as I deserve. How much does one man need? And as for prestige, I have the respect of my professional colleagues and friends not because of who I was born but because of who I am and what I've accomplished."

"Is there nothing else you want? A wife? A family?"

His eyes glinted with emotion, but she had difficulty deciphering what she saw in them. "Garrett is like a son to me and quite the handful, thank you very much. I suppose someday I might consider marriage and children."

"I daresay you had best consider quickly, as you are not getting any younger," she replied.

"I thank you for reminding me." He stretched out and rolled away from her on his side. "Now, go to sleep, or you'll regret your lack of it tomorrow. Some way, I'm not certain how, you managed to slip more than two questions by me."

CHAPTER FOURTEEN

Dawn blazed forth in a fiery yellow ball, a wave of scorching heat, and a loud buzzing on Samantha's bedroll. She lay on her back, her stiff body aching, her brain slowly rousing. Lifting her head, she peered down the length of her legs. A snake with a tail of rattles coiled on the blankets between her spread knees. It watched her with flat, elliptical eyes, a red tongue flicking in and out of its mouth.

She turned her head a fraction to find Christian's bedroll empty. She had encountered a few venomous snakes in her reptile-hunting career, all of them adders. She now eyed the snake with fascination and remained motionless, examining it and trusting it would decide to leave on its own. Yellow spots marched down its length above a red stripe painted on a background color of tropical sand. It shook its tail again, and the noise that had awakened her buzzed like a hive of bees. *A rattlesnake. How delightful!* She recalled the ones the London Zoo imported from America. A thrill rippled through her. The longer she studied the animal, the more beautiful it seemed, in a cool, sinister way.

Perhaps she could charm it, like she had read about in books on India. She'd had no success with English crowned snakes, but a rattlesnake could prove more susceptible. She began a rhythmic humming and stared into its eyes. The snake calmed down and rested its head on its coils.

A wiggling movement came from the ground beyond her feet, and Christian's low voice reached out to her. "Don't move, Sam. Lie still."

She had no intention of moving.

The wiggling came again, and a brown mouse with a pointy nose scurried into view. The string tied around its tiny waist led to a long, spindly branch that waved back and forth.

Christian was fishing for the snake! At the idea of fishing for snakes, she stifled her laugh for fear of startling the reptile.

The mouse ran back and forth on its tether, and the snake lifted and turned its head, its oval gaze intent on the small creature. Its forked tongue flickering in and out, the snake uncoiled in an unhurried motion to slither off from between Samantha's legs and move past her feet.

Christian swung the branch in a wide circle, backing up into the brush, drawing the snake farther away. A loud squeak came from the mouse when the snake caught its breakfast.

Christian trotted into sight, ran to her, and bent down on one knee. "Are you unharmed?" Muscles across his cheeks tightened and etched deep lines in his forehead.

She threw back the blankets, came to her feet, and stretched. "Of course I am."

He rose beside her, grasping her upper arms. "Did it bite you?" His words came out in a tremble. When she shook her head, he inhaled a straggly breath. "I assumed you would be terrified and do something foolish, like try to kick it off the bedroll. You took at least ten years off my life."

She lifted and firmed her chin. "Calm yourself. At your age, I doubt you can afford to lose ten years. I already informed you of my herpetological background. I have no fear of snakes, nor am I foolish."

He regarded her with new respect, his mouth relaxing into a smile. "Perhaps you'll prove to be less troublesome than I originally believed."

Samantha responded with a grin.

He winked. "However, I'll not wager money on it. Next time our intruder could be a grasshopper."

She snorted and scooped her blankets into her arms to ball them up. "You used quite the unique method for luring it away. A result of your eons of experience, I presume?"

He took the bedroll from her hands, shook it out, and rolled it into a neat, tight cylindrical bundle.

"I thought rattlesnakes hunted only at night," she said.

"Normally they do, but when it's chilly at night, like it is now, they hunt when the sun comes up, then digest their meal in the heat of the day. Anyway, that fellow was a bit thin. It hadn't eaten in a while, and I had a suspicion it would not turn up its nose at a mouse." A lazy smile tugged at one corner of his mouth. "And surely by now you've discovered I'm a unique fellow."

"To be sure, you are," she murmured, lowering her eyes and walking away to load her pack.

Christian carried Samantha's pack, along with his own, to allow her shoulders time to heal. However, he warned her she would bear that responsibility the next day. Samantha gave him a careless shrug. Without the heavy pack, she skipped along as light as the clouds floating above, keeping pace with him more easily. She even forged ahead on occasion, returning only when he shouted at her to remain in sight and watch where she walked.

All the while, her buttocks flexed beneath the tight trousers, and Christian's rebellious mind prattled, *I should have been between her legs instead of that snake.*

Toward late morning, they scaled the steep rock spanning the island's length like a spiny backbone. The golden orb of the sun raised heat waves that danced like seductive Egyptian women over the plain at the foot of the ridge. Hawks floated overhead and dipped in sultry updrafts created by the abrupt change in landscape. Christian reached the crest and halted on a ledge. He called Samantha over and gestured to the land below. "This is the western side of the island. It receives most of the rain."

"Remarkable," she said. Her gaze swung back and forth from the brown half of the island to the lush green valley. A jungle of palms and ferns covered the western slope. Lianas twisted among the trees to create aboveground highways for a host of exotic birds and small mammals.

"Do you fancy a swim?" he asked, pointing to a declivity nearly hidden in the trees.

She peered downward and drew in a gasp. A waterfall sparkled like liquid silver as it cascaded over a cliff face, creating a mist rising as thickly as a London fog. Whiteness foamed where the water tumbled into a turquoise pool edged by green bushes and trees heavy with orchids. She turned to him with a wishful smile. "May we?"

"If you like. First allow me to establish that no grasshoppers are lurking in the water or bushes."

She found it impossible to contain her enthusiasm and darted away to slide down a few feet of the steep slope.

He clasped a hand around her arm. "Wait. I'll go first."

They clambered down the rocky hillside, Christian keeping a careful eye on the way ahead, checking his footing before moving forward. When they encountered a particularly steep area, he helped Samantha with a steadying hand.

At length they stood beside the pool. After dropping the packs, Christian beat the bushes for unfriendly wildlife, then began to unbutton his shirt. "Wait until I tell you to come in."

Samantha paid no attention. She squatted on the ground, dipped her hands in the cool water, and rubbed it on her parched face.

He cupped her chin in his hand and tipped it up until their eyes met. "Did you hear me? Don't enter the water until I tell you it's safe."

"Quite clearly. Do hurry, Chris. I want to swim."

He sat down to remove his boots and stockings. When he rose, he pulled his shirt out of his trousers.

Samantha's eyes grew large and round. She caught her lower lip between her teeth. Why did it not occur to her until now that they would be required to disrobe? When he stripped his shirt over his head, she stuck a finger in her mouth and nibbled on the nail.

"I'll have to do something about that, Sam," he muttered.

Her gaze jumped up from the muscular chest covered with dark, curly hair, which held her undivided interest, to his face.

"Chewing your fingernails." He gestured at the finger in her mouth and cast her a chiding look. "Do I make you nervous?"

She dropped her hand and spun around, twining

her fingers together behind her back. "Of course not. 'Tis merely a habit that has naught to do with you or my nerves. I have no notion I'm even doing it."

He unbuttoned his trousers, the buttons sliding from the holes sounding as loud as gunshots.

"Perchance we can break that habit," he went on. "Dr. Freud would say your mother denied you oral gratification as an infant. I'll have to devise a substitute to occupy your hands and mouth."

Her face burned hot. Though she had no notion what he meant, she suspected his thoughts were less than gentlemanly. "You will do no such thing," she said.

He laughed, and the splash of his body hitting the pool came from behind her.

When she collected the courage to turn about, Christian was swimming underwater. He surfaced and bent at the waist. His bare legs shot straight up out of the water, and he disappeared again.

She must look a ninny, cowering on the bank, gawking at him. Though she possessed the courage to face down a deadly snake with the grace of Queen Victoria, she was incapable of viewing a nude man without her knees turning to marmalade.

When he dove again, it became clear that he was not completely unclothed. He still wore his linen smallclothes. Being wet, they clung to every ripple. Were she to concentrate, she could see through them to the powerful flesh beneath. So he only *appeared* to be bare. Her bones threatened to liquefy.

He popped up close to her, shaking his head, sending glittering droplets scattering across the pond and over her clothing. "It's safe," he said, scrubbing his hair away from his face. "You may swim now."

Her fingers automatically moved to her mouth. She realized in time what she was doing and jerked her hand back down to her side. Despite his promise to teach her what she needed to know about the expedition, was this another attempt at intimidation? If so, it would not work. He could take his intimidating tactics and put them right in . . .

What are you waiting for, Samantha? Be brave. Show him he cannot frighten you.

That was not her problem. Her hesitation stemmed not from fear of Christian but of the fire inundating her body. She had already allowed him to kiss her. No, were she being truthful, she begged him to kiss her and found it pleasant.

Pleasant? No, 'twas ecstasy!

Samantha harbored no illusions she would ever wed. After four disastrous London seasons, she admitted her dubious assets and love of scientific achievements were unlikely to attract a serious suitor. Between her appalling temper and reptile collection, she made an abysmal choice for some peer's wife. That fact became clear when a grass snake crawled out of her reticule while she and Jeremy Coulten strolled along the Serpentine at Hyde Park. After screaming like a fishwife, he fell into the water. His natty suit covered in duckweed, he climbed up the bank and escorted her home without uttering a word. Gossip of the incident spread through the Ton, and her suitors dwindled to naught. She was destined to remain on the shelf forever. Whether or not she sullied her reputation now seemed a moot point. In any event, she was a modern woman with no need of a husband or a reputation.

Christian swam away with strong pulls of his arms, slicing through the water like a fish. When he reached the other side, she ducked into the bushes, ripped off her boots and stockings, and stripped off her shirt and trousers. She shimmied into the water still wearing her camisole and pantalets. The pond was cool and wonderfully refreshing on her heated flesh, and she treaded water, sun warming her shoulders. Swimming out into the middle, she flipped onto her back, closed her eyes, and floated like a fallen leaf. With cool water laving her body and sun penetrating to her bones, she felt as if she could float forever.

Samantha opened her eyes at a splash. Christian was cleaving through the water toward her. She glanced down the length of her body to her lawn camisole and pantalets, and they were as transparent as a spiderweb. Rose nipples, plainly visible through the thin cloth, puckered tightly from the water's chill. And, my God, the water even put the triangle of hair in her private area on display!

She dropped her legs, sank in the water. He drew nearer, swimming in circles around her. She spun with him, giving him a puzzled smile. What was he about? While treading water, she kept an eye on him.

He grinned slyly. "Were I a shark, I would see you as a tempting meal." He continued to circle. "I would take a big bite out of that delectable little bottom."

She wrinkled her nose and splashed water on his chest. "Cease, Chris."

His circles tightened, and he gnashed his teeth.

"I mean it. Stop it!"

Dropping beneath the surface, he caught her legs and pulled her under. Teeth glided across her ankle and closed lightly around her calf. When he emerged again, he came up on the other side of the pond. Swimming toward her, he circled again. This time when he drew close, she splashed him in the face. Christian ducked and shot away underwater. He came back, precisely like a shark. Circling. Circling. Closer and closer.

His features harder and more menacing this time, he said, "Suppose our ship sinks, and we have to swim for shore through an ocean of sharks? How would you deal with your dire situation? Tell the sharks to cease?" He dove again, and his teeth grazed her thigh. She kicked out, connecting with his shoulder.

He surfaced with a grin. "Better. But duck beneath the water to face me. With those luscious legs waving about and that wiggling rear end, you make an enticing target." He slapped a hand on the water's surface. "With you up here and me below you, you cannot see what I'm doing."

While he circled, Samantha plotted. As soon as he disappeared, she slipped under the water, pushing him away with a foot planted in his belly. He released an explosive stream of bubbles.

Entering into the spirit of the game, she analyzed his strategy, planning her countermoves, giving as good as she got. Christian praised her initiative when she eluded him and scolded her when he snuck in close enough to bite. At last he flipped belly up and floated away on his back.

Nerves jangling and limbs weary, Samantha exhaled a breath when his mock attacks came to an end. Closing her eyes, she floated and daydreamed about the Smilodon. It had Christian's green eyes and stalked her from the high grass.

Christian shot up from the pond bottom and hooked an arm about her waist. She squealed. He drew her back against his chest and bit her on the neck. "I won," he growled. "You dropped your guard too soon. Never assume the shark has given up until you know it's dead."

His bite gradually changed character, becoming a caress, moving down her neck to her shoulder. While he swam backward, he towed her toward the shoreline. Her back lay against his chest, and his hard manhood pulsed against her buttocks.

The water boiled where it touched her skin. She should push away. Fatigue made her limbs weak and limp. Her energy drained away. *And she was so damnably hot!* Though a mouse of apprehension gnawed at her mind, she knew Christian would not truly harm her. She relaxed and told herself she could trust him.

CHAPTER FIFTEEN

Christian's mouth grazed her ear, and Samantha floated, unresisting, through the silky water. Circling the shell of her ear with his tongue, he dipped inside and traced the inner whorls. She shivered and steamed at the drag of his teeth along her skin and soft biting at the lobe. His lips traversed the back of her neck in small kisses and ended up at her other ear, nibbling and tonguing. If he did not stop, she would surely burst into flames.

She concentrated on the sensations of his mouth, and his hand moved upward to her breast, his palm traveling in lazy circles, brushing the nipple. Her breasts ached; her nipples hardened. The fleshy globes swelled, pressing into his hand. Taking the nipple between his thumb and forefinger, he rolled it and gave a gentle tug. A low moan strained against her throat. Sharp pulling streaked from her breast through her belly, straight to the tender flesh between her thighs, as though an invisible thread connected her chest and groin. She yearned to rub her thighs together or press her womanly flesh against something firm to alleviate the disturbing twinge.

When he slid his hand to her other breast, Christian stopped moving, having halted in waist-high water with his back against a tree growing out of the pond. Samantha tried to turn in his arms, to face him, insist he stop caressing her. Surely he took improper liberties, and even a modern woman would not allow a gentleman to go so far. But his arm around her waist held her firmly in place, and she did not really want him to stop. Both his hands settled on her breasts, kneading and pulling, stroking and teasing, and she whimpered. She had truly lost the game. Or had she won? Sagging against the hard wall of his chest, she gave up to the pulsing streaks of fire.

At her capitulation, Christian spun Samantha around. Holding her up, his hands under her arms, he bent one knee and braced his foot against the tree trunk. He seized her lips in a deep, scorching kiss, sweeping his tongue through her mouth with abandon, and lowered her astride his upraised thigh.

Her woman's center made contact with his rigid leg. She released an explosive breath, squirming to press herself closer.

"Gently, Sam," he whispered. "Allow me to lead, or you could hurt yourself."

She puzzled over his words, but when he kissed her again, she forgot to ask their meaning.

Clasping her about the waist, he raised and lowered his thigh, slowly and smoothly. She slid along his slick skin as though gliding on a greased board. While he kept her from settling against him too deeply, she clutched his shoulders.

The hair on his thigh created friction against the opening of her sex through the slit in her pantalets. It soothed the ache at first. He took her nipple between his lips, nipping it and licking it through the camisole. His mouth closed over her breast, taking it into the moist warmth and gently sucking. Flames shot from her nipple to her groin. Her ache evolved into an acute, twisting pang, originating deep inside and working its way outward.

Her need grew, and Samantha wriggled to settle deeper on his leg. She *needed* firmer contact. He kept her where *he* wanted her, and the rocking sped up. The drag against her sensitive flesh turned torturous, no longer easing her ache but driving it more profoundly into the walls of her woman's passage. Swollen and hot inside, a taut heaviness gathered in her belly until she could no longer tell pleasure from pain.

She was so hot!

Her breasts and belly flushed with heat searing to her core, spreading upward over her throat and face, and that place inside her became the hottest of all.

She was burning up!

Tension coiled in her lower abdomen, tight and hard and distinct from the tugging ache or the heat. It slid down and inward, like a shark, circling tighter and tighter, moving closer to the discomfort in her sheath. Her legs trembled. She braced her hands against his chest, pushing.

"No! Stop, Chris," she gasped, her voice cracking, a hot, wild wanting sweeping over her. "You are frightening me."

"Shhh." His breath whispered across her nipple, and he rocked her even faster. "I'll not hurt you. Relax. Let it come."

Let what come?

He sucked hard on her breast, her nipple, matching the rhythm of her hips, and with a groan, she gave in. Her confusion fled on the wings of an explosion, a crescendo of glorious pleasure that overwhelmed her discomfort. Stars burst behind her closed eyelids. She bucked hard, and Christian finally stilled her, lowering her as deeply as she wished to go. Undulating spasms moved down her sheath, spread outward and through her limbs, leaving searing heat in their wake and melting her bones. She collapsed against his chest, burying her face in its crisp hair. Christian lowered his leg, shifting her off his thigh and holding her closely until her tremors subsided.

"Welcome to the wonder of passion, tigrina," he breathed against her hair.

Samantha opened her eyes, blinking rapidly when her lashes brushed up against a hairy chest. She was as limp and boneless as a rag doll but warm and contented, floating in velvety water . . .

Hairy chest? Oh, Lord, a hairy chest!

What had she done? She was not exactly certain. She remembered water and a leg and heat, oh, so much heat, and someone lit fireworks . . . and . . . Christian! Vivid memories crashed over her. Even her toenails blushed.

What would he think of her now? She'd not imagined their game would go to such extremes. Swimming together in near nudity was scandalous enough, b-b-but what? But what they had done? Exactly what *had* they done? Perhaps if she were to close her eyes again, he would go away, or she would wake up from this embarrassing situation, safe in her London bedchamber. She squeezed her eyes shut.

"You cannot hide your face all day."

Oh, Lord! Her cheeks flamed.

Christian cupped her chin. She peeked up through her lashes and met the sparkle of amusement in his eyes.

He was laughing at her!

The flush heating her face nearly ignited her. A notion struck her like a fist to the chest. Tears filled her eyes, and her heart pounded. She dropped her lashes again, shielding her emotions.

Christian's smile dissolved into a frown. He didn't plan this encounter—truly he didn't—and now he had mortified her. He turned Samantha around until her back fetched up against his chest and buried his nose in her hair, inhaled her essence. "There. Now you cannot see me. Do you feel more comfortable?"

She gulped and nodded.

Christian took a breath to slow his heartbeat. "Talk to me. Tell me what so upsets you. I assure you that what happened between us will remain our secret. I'll not ruin your reputation."

Samantha sniffled and made a small movement with one hand. "'Tis not that."

His frown deepened. "Then what?" He sensed her struggle in trying to form the words.

"I do not know what happened to me, but I feel certain it should not have." She hid her face in her hands. "I do not, do not wish to—" Her voice choked.

"What?" His heart rate kicked up again. What so frightened her? Samantha was not one to be easily cowed. She must have some genuine concern about which he was unaware.

". . . have a baby." She forced the words out in a whisper.

Christian's heart twisted, and he released a quick breath. "Christ, Sam. We've done nothing that would make a baby. Has no one ever spoken to you about relations between men and women?" He supposed her to be inexperienced and a maid, but according to Delia, the girl was twenty years old, older than he had presumed at their first meeting. And from her ardent response to his touch, he assumed *some* experience. What he'd not expected was complete ignorance. Did women still lead such insular lives? It was nearly the twentieth century. Surely she had gleaned some information from her women friends, had boyfriends, entertained suitors. However, she appeared to have as much acquaintance with her own body as she did with starting a fire. Even less. That a young woman could reach the age of twenty with no knowledge of men was dangerous and inexcusable. He wished he had known beforehand. He wouldn't have touched her.

Yes, you would have!

Samantha said nothing for a moment; then her chest hitched with a deeply inhaled breath. "Really, Chris, 'tis not as if I know *nothing*. In theory I know about men and what they do. I simply lack the specifics of the mechanics. Aunt Delia considered men and their . . . their appetites an improper topic for a lady. She said that when the time came, I would learn all I needed to know from my husband." Her voice grew smaller. "I do not believe she was very fond of men, you know, in that way."

The pang in his heart took him by surprise. "Sweet Jesus! So much for the modern woman. And your mother?"

"She died when I was small."

Christian remained silent, groping for an acceptable explanation, knowing he could not, in all good conscience, allow her to feed her fears. How much could he say without overwhelming or alarming her again? He drew in a breath and plunged ahead. "I wouldn't want to confuse you with a lengthy, scientific explanation. How much *do* you know?"

He had no need to see it; he felt her blush.

"You needn't be embarrassed," he said, keeping his tone quiet, reassuring, or so he hoped. "What men and women experience together should be wonderful and special, and hopefully, fulfilling. It isn't shameful. We did nothing you should regret."

She should have no regrets, but I should.

"Close your eyes," he said.

When he looked down at her face, her eyes were wide open. She still trembled. He ran his hand down her face and closed her eyelids. "Now take a few deep breaths."

She drew in and expelled air, her chest rising and falling.

"Pretend I'm your . . . your mother," Christian said, keeping his voice low. "Feel free to ask me anything. Knowledge banishes fear. Trust me. What do you want to know?"

She took a breath before speaking, and her words came out in fits and starts. "What did you do to me?"

Once again, her question rocked his senses. "Have you never touched yourself intimately?"

She tensed and shook her head. "I was tempted once, but it seemed dreadfully, dreadfully . . ." Even from behind her, he could see her cheeks color. "Something a lady would not consider."

"Disabuse yourself of that notion. Though you may have been taught otherwise, touching yourself is merely a way of taking pleasure without the complications of babies. I simply showed you what you could do for yourself."

"But what happened to me?"

"When you feel desire," he said, "passion builds up inside you and seeks release, what men, and some women, call an orgasm. When the release comes, it brings you pleasure. You did feel pleasure, did you not?"

The tightness of her muscles relaxed. Her breathing slowed. "Indeed, but the sensation was also strange and unnerving, as if I were on a runaway horse. I had no liking of being unable to stop."

"It's natural to feel frightened at first because you have no knowledge of what to expect. Your trepidation will pass with experience."

"But more than simply what we did comes later, does it not?"

He chuckled. "Indeed, a great deal more, but nothing you'll learn from me."

Samantha twisted her head to look up at him. "Was it pleasurable for you?"

He cleared his throat. "Of course I enjoyed it, too."

"I once heard a man must, must—"

"Spill his seed?" Christian gave her an amused smile. "A rather quaint euphemism. Apt but not necessarily true, though some men believe it to be so. Making love involves not only taking pleasure but giving it. I received my pleasure from watching yours."

She gasped, and her face reddened. "You watched me?"

His smile widened into a grin. "You're beautiful in your passion."

Her head moved from side to side, as though denying his words. "We are not wed. I should not enjoy such intimacies. Does that not make me a wanton? Nice ladies, proper ladies, do not act as I did."

The muscles in Christian's jaw flexed. "You're not wanton," he said harshly, "merely naturally passionate. And you're a fine, *proper* lady, even when you lose control." He exhaled, wondering why he had initiated this conversation. It was going far beyond what he'd envisioned. "Have I answered all your questions?" He should have known from experience that Samantha never ran out of questions.

"When you held me, I felt your . . . your male part against me."

"It's a penis or a phallus," he said flatly. "Call it what it is. It has a few cruder names, but you have no need to know them."

"Your p-penis against me, it felt larger than I expected

it to be, larger than those in the pictures of Greek and Roman statues, and somehow, I do suspect it would not fit under a fig leaf."

A laugh exploded from his chest. Samantha was such a delightful mixture of innocence and audacity. "No, I don't expect it would. When a man becomes passionate, his penis becomes larger and harder."

"I do not believe I understand." Confusion ran through her words.

"It's similar to blowing up a balloon."

"Oh!" Her forefinger headed for her mouth. He caught it and bit her fingertip, throwing an exasperated look at the ragged nail. *Great, now I've given her the notion an erect cock looks like an inflated balloon!*

"How much larger?" she asked after she retrieved her finger from his grasp.

At her words, blood filled his groin, and he had no wish to frighten her. Christian paused before saying, "I believe that question is one I have no business answering." The first time a virgin saw an erection, the sight was shocking enough. At this moment, size, his or any man's, was an issue about which Samantha had no reason to concern herself. "Have I answered all your questions now?" he asked again.

"One more." When he nodded, she said, "May we do it again?"

He lifted his eyebrows, and she threw a mischievous grin over her shoulder.

Not on your life!

"No. Don't be greedy. Were I obliged to go through that again, you would learn a great deal more than you have a need to know."

She shifted away from him. A stillness came over her, a steeliness in her posture. "Learn? A need to know? Do you feel I am in need of a tutor? If that was your intention, I assure you that I require no lessons. Simply because I have questions . . ."

He shook his head. "No, Sam. I'm no tutor, not yours at any rate. That wasn't my intention."

"If you are not saying that merely to placate me, then only one question remains, and I will bother you no longer. Why *did* you do it?"

Christian expelled a breath. "Bloody hell, I have no idea. The water is warm and silky, the sun hot, the sky blue. I knew you would like it, and it pleased me to give you pleasure." *I did it because I'm hornier than a rooster in a henhouse, and I have no self-control!*

He took a step closer, gaining his composure if not completely suppressing his ever-present arousal, and slapped her on the bottom. "Sojourn over."

Hurt supplanted indignation on her face. "First a lesson, then a sojourn? Is that all this was to you, a sojourn?"

No, do not say what you want to say! "Please do not let us quarrel now. Climb out of the pool and pull on your clothes. We have a lengthy trip back to the ship."

They crossed the desert again, and this time Samantha's pack rode lighter on her back. She assumed Christian had transferred most of her gear to his pack. He also padded her straps so they no longer bit into her shoulders, and she silently thanked him for his consideration. He kept pace with her shorter strides, pointing out and naming the plants and animals they encountered, entertaining her with their habits and behaviors, and teaching her which plants, such as aloe, were edible or useful in other ways. With his kind acts on their return trip, she soon forgave him his comments at the pond.

They camped at sunset, and finally, after innumerable tries, she started a fire with twigs. He kept his promise to teach her survival skills and demonstrated setting snares for rabbits and ground birds and how to extract water from cactus. That night around the campfire, he regaled her with stories of the animals he had pursued and discovered throughout his long career and thrilled her with accounts of narrow escapes from warlike natives and sea pirates.

At the end of the long day, Samantha tossed on her bedroll and mused on Christian, the pool, and her . . . what did he call it? Her *orgasm*. No wonder London's morality mavens made such a big ado over intimacy. And if the act was as pleasurable for men as for women, 'twas no surprise they sought it with such abandon and so many young girls compromised themselves. She now had no reason to wonder why the details were guarded so secretively—to save women such as her from falling into wanton ways. Clearly the knowledge had come too late for her redemption.

Her musings brought her body to life, and her breasts tingled. Moisture gathered between her legs. Oh, she was incorrigible and surely beyond all hope!

She peered at Christian, who slept on his side with his back to her. With great hesitation, she touched her breast. When she rubbed her hand over it, the nipple tightened. Her flesh swelled and ached.

Oh, Lord!

Was he truly asleep? It suddenly seemed important she know.

"Chris," she whispered, "are you asleep?"

"No." His voice came back so suddenly, she jumped.

"May I sleep next to you? I'm cold."

Strained silence descended like a shroud. Face heating, she chewed on her lower lip.

"Very well," he finally said. "Come here." He rolled over and lifted the edge of his blanket.

She climbed out of her bedroll and rushed over to him, crawling in and cuddling up to his warmth. When he turned onto his back with her curled into his side, she rested one of her hands on his chest.

Lifting his head, he touched his lips to her forehead and skimmed a hand down her arm. "You lied, Sam. Your skin is as hot as the center of a volcano."

"Though I've never been in the center of a volcano, you could possibly be correct," she replied.

"Have you ever read Mary Shelley's novel *Frankenstein*?" She shook her head.

"In the story, a scientist, Dr. Frankenstein, attempts to create the perfect human and bring it to life. Purely for scientific achievement, you understand. He assembles his creature and gives it life, but it turns into a monster he cannot control. Eventually it murders him, and the frightened townspeople kill it. Since the book's publication, the name 'Frankenstein' gained a new meaning, referring not to the misguided scientist but to any uncontrollable creation that destroys its creator."

"You are making a point, I presume?"

Turning sideways, he propped himself on his free elbow and traced her mouth with his thumb. His lips curved into a rueful smile. "Indeed. I fear I've created my own Frankenstein bent on destroying me."

She pursed her mouth into a pout. "Are you suggesting I've become a monster?"

"Of course not. However, I've unleashed the fiery monster trapped inside you, and I'm very much afraid its flames will burn me to ashes." He moved his hand across her shoulder and down to her hip. "Lie back," he said, his voice descending into a rumble.

Samantha shifted onto her back, and he swept his palm over her shoulders and arms. Feathering his fingers over her face and outlining its contours, he skimmed them down her neck and around her ears. She closed her eyes. As his touch fanned the embers inside her, her limbs grew languid.

Throwing the blankets aside, he smoothed his hand down and around her breasts, neglecting their thrusting peaks, sliding to her waist and belly, sweeping circles and lines with his fingertips. When he reached the vee between her thighs, he bypassed it, causing her to groan and peer up at him. A little smile crimped his mouth, and he brushed his hand up and down her legs, massaging her calves and thighs. He worked his way back up in the same manner, bent over, stroked her lips in a light, lingering kiss. Lying back, he closed his eyes.

She wriggled about to lie on her side. "Is that all?"

He opened his eyes. "You wanted more?"

"Perhaps." Through her blush, she sent him a devilish look. Coming up on her knees, she cupped her hands into a bowl. "Please, sir, I want some more."

Christian laughed and rose back up on his elbow. "Very well, Master Twist," he said, his voice husky. "I would not want you spreading tales I'm a stingy man."

CHAPTER SIXTEEN

Christian unbuttoned Samantha's shirt, peeled it off her shoulders, and laid it aside. Grasping the edge of her camisole, he stripped it over her head.

Her stomach knotted, and she crossed her arms over her bare breasts.

Seeming to have no interest in her sudden mortification, he removed her boots and stockings, undid her trousers, and tugged them down her hips. Once he bared her to her pantalets, he looked at her, eyes crinkling at the corners.

"Stop hiding yourself. I want to see you."

His gentle smile shored up her nerve, and she slowly lowered her arms to her sides, though they remained tense, her hands knotted into fists.

Christian pulled off his boots and stockings and came

to his feet to remove his shirt and trousers, gaze roaming freely over her form. Leaving on his underdrawers, which had short legs like his basketball pants, he stretched out on his side next to her.

She ventured to glance at his covered midsection.

"Once you release the tiger from its cage, it becomes difficult to control and impossible to lure back inside until tamed," he responded to her silent question.

His words bounced around in her head, making as much sense as Egyptian hieroglyphics. "I beg your pardon?"

"I was using a metaphor," he said with a chuckle. "Trust me. I'll not take what rightfully belongs to the man you marry. We can still experiment with pleasure without the ultimate act."

The ultimate act? She was dying to know more about *that,* but her tongue tangled up too much for her to ask.

Christian reached for her, fingers trailing over her skin, following the same route he explored before. This time, while his sultry gaze followed the path of his fingers, he circled one taut breast and spiraled inward.

Like a shark.

"You're a beautiful woman, Sam, with a body so exquisitely small." Though spilling softly from his mouth, the gruff undercurrent of his words made her flesh quiver. "But beneath your clothing, your womanhood is obvious. You have lovely breasts. Only a handful, but firm and tilted up, shaped like the bowl of a champagne glass, breasts that could besot a man. Your nipples are pink rosebuds, firm and silky, tightly furled and always slightly erect, as though your passion overflows into them even when you've not been aroused. They're so responsive. Merely the touch of my gaze causes them to swell and lengthen, begging to be fondled and suckled. I feel your need—in your dusky golden eyes, the rosy hue of your skin, your quickened breathing, the pout of your nipples, and that sensual little thrust of your hips."

His hands caressed her, and his voice poured over her like warm summer rain. Samantha's eyes grew wider. Never had anyone spoken to her this way. No one other than Gilly had seen her undressed. Other men, boys in comparison to Christian, who fancied themselves in love with her, had plied her with sweet words and poetry. Their insipid prose had failed to stir her. The silky sound of Christian's voice—never mind his words—dark with passion, threw her brain into disarray, accelerated her heartbeat, and boiled her blood, hastening the aching want inside her. His eyes smoldered, dark and smoky, and scorched a path of burning need on her skin.

Before touching her distended nipple, he paused and cupped his palm beneath her breast, weighing and massaging the curve.

It swelled and heated in his hand. When he flicked his thumb over the nipple, tongues of fire licked through her. He flicked faster and more firmly, strumming the tight bud, and she strained toward him, pressing harder.

Holding the nipple gently between his thumb and forefinger, he rolled it, tugged, and rolled it again.

A pulling ache raced to her groin. This time she knew what to expect and relaxed into the feeling. Instead of disconcerting her as it did the first time, the tugging produced sharp twinges of pleasure. The inner folds of her sex wept tears, dampening the crotch of her pantalets.

He slid his hand to her other breast, giving it the same attention.

By the time he paused, she panted, her heart beating frantically. Heat built up in her lower abdomen, and deep throbbing besieged the walls of her body's cleft. She wiggled her hips against the ground, buttocks clenched, and arched her mons in minute upward thrusts, wanting . . .

Christian moved over her onto his knees and straddled her hips. Enclosing a nipple in his lips, he sucked gently and rolled it between his tongue and teeth. After tending to her other breast, he laved her chest and throat with his tongue, pressing heated kisses against her skin.

The fire in her core scorched her flesh, the pulsation in its walls coming deeper and faster.

He wedged a knee between her legs. "Open for me, Sam."

She parted her thighs, and he knelt between them, resting back on his heels. His manhood—no, *penis*— strained against the thin linen covering. It looked huge!

Her jaw slackened at the tumescent shaft stretching from his crotch to his waist. It had seemed so much smaller in the pond. She pressed her eyes closed, and her breath shortened, partly from a heightened excitement but mostly from a welling need.

Spreading her legs wider with his palms, he laid his hand flat on her heated furrow. Through the slit in her pantalets, he stroked the sensitive lips.

She gasped, keeping her eyes firmly shut.

Parting her with his fingers, he glided along the intimate folds but fell short of penetrating her passage. His finger moved up and circled a tender spot encompassing the heart of her passion, and he fondled it with a fingertip.

With a cry, she lifted her hips off the ground. He strummed rhythmically, and she gasped in great breaths. When he ceased and took his hand away, she whimpered.

"Open your eyes," he said, "and give me your hand."

Her breath suspended, Samantha inched up her eyelids and stretched out a shaky hand.

Christian positioned her fingertips over that mysterious spot, covering them with his own. A hard nub of flesh tingled when she touched it, and he guided her fingers in a gentle rhythm.

"This is your pleasure center, your clitoris," he said. "The flesh is sensitive and easily hurt. Keep your touch light. If you feel pain, back away."

Uncomfortable at first that he should witness her

perform such an intimate act, she soon forgot everything other than the storm buffeting her body and becoming more intense than anything in her experience. She lifted her hips in sync with her fingers' stroking, and the quivering center of her womanhood coiled and coiled, tighter and tighter, and culminated in a glorious burst of light. Convulsions tore through her. She slammed her hips against the ground, arched high in the air, pushed against the hands. A torrent of heat poured to the tips of her toes and fingers. In the deepest recesses of her mind, she was aware of Christian pulling her hand away.

While she was coming down from her orgasm, he kissed his way up her belly and chest, taking her lips in a long, wet, hot possession. Slipping back to her breasts, he gently nibbled until her trembling subsided.

He lifted his head from the valley between her breasts. "Put your legs around my waist, tigrina," he whispered.

More?

She could do naught but obey.

Samantha raised her weak legs, wrapping them about his waist and locking her ankles together behind him. He wedged one hand beneath her, cradling her buttocks in his palm, and thrust his erection against her core. Each thrust ground against her bud, and her hips soon picked up the rhythm, rising to meet him and bumping against his penis.

She could scarcely believe it; 'twas happening again!

The heat, pulsing, throbbing, and coiling took control. She arched and rose higher and higher on the edge of a cliff, straining to reach into the sky, to soar off the precipice and drift to Earth on wings of delight. The rapture became so intense her passage began small contractions almost immediately and took her by surprise.

"Chris," she gasped. "Can you . . . ? Could you . . . ?"

Christian moved firmer and faster against her, adjusting his angle. His muscles and tendons tensed and flexed. He clenched his teeth, groaning with the effort of holding back. When she screamed and slammed hard against him, his head flew back, his neck muscles taut and stretching. He erupted, ramming her back, once, twice. His semen spurted out in a gushing stream, soaking through his smallclothes and wetting them both in a pulsing ejaculation.

He eased down on shaky arms, wary of crushing her with his weight but too shattered to move aside yet. His heart thudded against his ribs, and he dragged in ragged gasps of air.

Rolling off after a few minutes and onto his back, he threw a trembling arm across his forehead. He was soaked in sweat and semen and as wrung out as he'd ever been after a three-day drinking bout. He'd never felt so good. His orgasm had been incredible, stupefying. He had no conception of what it would feel like once he was inside her.

Once he was inside her? What was he thinking? The errant notion surely resulted from his cock's wishful thinking. He had no designs on the willful innocent's virginity. Once they found the Smilodon and her uncle, they would part ways. He would leave her wiser but none the worse for wear. Most likely, they would never cross paths again. Why did that thought bring a tightening to his chest? He had no inclination to pursue the source.

He peered over at her. "Are you all right?"

"I believe so," she said in a wobbly voice, "but why am I so wet?"

His chest shook with laughter. "Ah, Sam, that necessitates a long story better saved for another time."

He got wearily to his feet and pulled her up beside him. "Come with me. I know of a stream nearby. We both need a bath."

During the following weeks on shipboard, Samantha and Christian sought out opportunities to be alone and continue their love play but with a restraint Christian enforced. He had aroused new, compelling feelings in Samantha, and now he paid the price. She tested his resolve at every turn, pushing him to the limits of his endurance and patience. Each day it became more difficult to adhere to the constraints he placed on himself.

Nights generally found them at the aft railing, watching the ship's wake in the starlight or embracing in some shadowy corner of the ship. She tried to entice him into taking her to his cabin. Determined to leave her virtue intact, however, he declined, and arguments flared. Strained relations resulted for a few days following their disagreements, but the siren song of passion soon pulled them back together.

On a crystalline night during the dark of the moon, Christian came up behind Samantha while she rested her forearms on the railing and gazed out over phosphorescent ripples on the ocean's surface.

Samantha pointed to the green and pink sparkles. "What causes it?"

"Tiny animals so small they can be seen only with a microscope. Some scientists believe the animals absorb sunlight during the day, store it inside, and release it at night."

"'Tis beautiful," she said with a sigh.

His mouth teased the sensitive spot behind her ear. "Beautiful," he mumbled against her skin.

She began to straighten, and he placed a hand on the small of her back. "Stay where you are." He moved closer behind her, the hard length of his manhood pressing through her dress to rest along the cleft of her buttocks. His tongue tasted her neck and ears. His hands circled her breasts, fondling her nipples through the cotton barrier. He stepped back and lifted her skirt.

Samantha stiffened at cool air wafting across the backs of her legs. "Chris, someone will see us."

Running the tips of his fingers up her calves and thighs, he caressed the bare skin below her pantalets. "No, they won't. It's dark here, and my body will shield you from view."

His hands kneaded her legs and buttocks, and sparks sped through her veins. Reckless and wanton, she leaned over the railing with her skirt up around her waist. She'd not seen his face yet. 'Twas as if a mystery lover accosted her in the darkness.

Moving his feet between hers, he spread her legs apart. The split in her pantalets opened to the night, and a breeze teased the lips of her sex. The muscles in her thighs tensed. When he rubbed his cloth-covered erection against her cleft, she moaned, hollowed her back, and lifted her hips.

He wrapped his arm about her, fingers finding the nub of her desire and stroking it until her sheath wept, and she moved rhythmically against his hand. With his other hand, Christian stroked her from behind. As Samantha moved closer to orgasm, a finger slid inside her, and she tensed at the unfamiliar sensation.

Christian whispered, telling her how good she felt, how hot and slippery, and her walls clutched his finger. He moved the digit, stroking her, dipping deeply and withdrawing, and when she relaxed, her body accepted the incursion with delight.

His finger moved faster, the rubbing on her clitoris more insistent, and she floated upward toward ecstasy and shifted her legs wider. Now two fingers moved inside her. Rivers of fire and ice flowed outward through her limbs, draining her of strength and will, and Samantha exploded inside, a cry breaking from her. She flew over the edge, splintering into shards of light, and collapsed across the railing.

Christian withdrew his hands and turned her quickly into his arms, holding her close. Aftershocks claimed her, body and breath, and her legs gave way.

While she regained her senses, his lips descended and pulled from her the last dark dregs of her passion. He still pressed heavily against her belly, and she looked up into his eyes.

"I want to touch you, Chris."

He grew still, nodded. She tried to unbutton his trousers, but her shaky fingers were unable to manage the feat. Christian brushed aside her hands and released the buttons, leaving his underdrawers as a last barrier between them.

Eager fingers explored the turgid flesh beneath the cloth, and Christian moaned and arched his neck, the tendons stretched tight at Samantha's light touch. She rubbed her palms across him and marveled at the heat, and his penis grew larger and harder, while her touch grew bolder.

Finally, with a grimace of pain, Christian pulled her hands away.

"Did I hurt you?" Samantha asked.

He uttered a short laugh. "No, tigrina, but if you continue, I'll have to change my trousers."

When she opened her mouth, he stopped her. "Leave me alone now. Go back to your cabin."

Soon she left his sight, departing with a pout on her face. He opened his drawers and, with swift, hard strokes, finished what Samantha's naïve touch had begun, all the while imagining he was inside her.

After catching his breath and straightening his clothes, he debated the wisdom of continuing with this dalliance. He feared Samantha was falling in love with him, confusing passion with more permanent feelings, although the fault lay with him. He had toyed with her heart and body and was beginning to despise himself for his selfishness.

Christian avoided examining his own heart too closely, however. He had two options: stay away from her or marry her. Perhaps he would be well advised to pull back for a while, grant them some time to cool off. But he had tried that course before, and his good intentions fell all to hell and back whenever she drew near. His need for her took over, and he wanted only to bury himself in her heat and wetness. Even thinking of how she would feel brought his penis to attention again, and he cursed into the wind.

He never should have touched her. From the moment he saw her floating in that blue pond, all her charms and secrets revealed by her transparent camisole and pantalets, he became lost. Their game of "shark" merely had inflamed him. And he *was* a shark, Sam his unsuspecting bait. In the innocence of her awakening passion, he had caught her in his sharp teeth before she understood what was happening. Her virtuous beauty and fiery nature drew him like a moth to a candle flame. And like the moth, he would rather die than forego his own fascination.

He could not recall burning this hot for one woman, wanting her constantly and walking around in a permanent state of arousal. She possessed such natural seductive enthusiasm and a great deal too much misplaced trust. Little did she know that tonight he'd been only seconds away from releasing his cock and plunging into her virgin flesh. He dared not come that close again. He had to break it off.

Christian avoided Samantha as much as possible for the remainder of the voyage. Her face reflected her hurt feelings, her inability to understand why their relationship had changed. He alone understood.

The distance he enforced was for her own good . . . and his. He declined explaining his withdrawal, suspecting that even a short, intimate conversation could lead to disaster. Each night he tossed in his bunk, unable to sleep, pounding the pillows and bemoaning his own weakness. Finally Garrett moved into the crew's quarters to get his rest.

Samantha also slept poorly, though her cabinmates slumbered like hibernating frogs and noticed naught amiss. She agonized over what offense she had committed to deserve Christian's indifference. When she posed the question, he brushed off her inquiry, saying he was too busy to take the time for conversation. Too busy? He'd not been too busy to initiate her to passion. Why then did he withdraw it? Was he already through with her?

She resorted to questioning Garrett, nigh pinning him against the railing with no means of escape, and grilled him.

"What is Christian's problem?" she asked in a shouted whisper, waving her hands in her agitated state. "Why does he blow hot and cold, being tender and loving at one moment, arrogant and bullying the next? I vow I cannot fathom what tangled thoughts run through his mind. 'Tis maddening, and I am on the threshold of taking out his heart on the point of a sword!"

Garrett raised his hands, palms outward. "Don't fly into a dither, Sam. You have no skill with a sword."

She huffed. "Well, I would if I did. And that is hardly the point, is it?" Though she pleaded with him to help her understand what demons rode Christian and made him act in such an incomprehensible way, Garrett held his counsel, and Samantha stormed away.

As Christian retreated more, avoiding any discussion regarding his sudden coolness, Samantha's temper unraveled further. She went out of her way to cross his path, defy his orders, and attract his attention, even if, more often than not, she drew his wrath and not his loving touch. 'Twas better than cold indifference, although she secretly held in her heart every sharp word and angry gesture directed her way.

A chasm of monumental proportions opened between them, and the closer the ship drew to their destination, the wider it became. Samantha was reaching her wit's end and sought to end the estrangement, return to their sharing of intimacies. Not only his tender touches and the thrilling love play, the loss of those she could bear, but also their laughter and sharing of confidences. His arm about her, his body bracing her against the ship's rocking, his voice in her ear, and the smile lighting up his eyes and face.

Her anger grew apace, and by the time they sighted Tasmania, she became as remote and unapproachable as he, ignoring his commands and flaunting her disrespect in front of the crewmen. A seething cloud seemed to hover over them, crackling like a thunderstorm with animosity and repressed sexual hunger. The undercurrents of their frustration threatened to sweep up those closest to them, who learned to keep their distance for fear of being dragged into the fray and forced to take sides. Samantha and Christian were two islands of misery, separated by stormy waters, in the midst of a vast ocean.

CHAPTER SEVENTEEN

Tasmania arose on the horizon at dawn in a dark green vision of mountainous terrain.

The *Maiden Anne* sailed into the sheltered harbor of Sullivan Cove, and Samantha inspected the town spread out along the mouth of the Derwent River. Richard had described much of it in his letters, and now Samantha reconciled his written words with the sights before her.

Docks delineated the shoreline in a half circle, with Hunter's Island, containing the guardhouse, store tents, and commissariat storehouse, on the eastern curve. The town plan formed a simple grid, with four main east-west thoroughfares and six smaller north-south streets that crossed the Derwent at their northern end.

Garrett appeared beside her, braced his hands on the railing, and leaned into the breeze coming off the water.

"See," she said, pointing, "beyond the docks are the houses of the surgeon, surveyor, and chaplain, which sit between Delvey and Macquarie Streets and next to George's Square, that large green common."

"Have you been to Tasmania before?" he asked.

"No, but I have read and reread Richard's letters. Many times he described the town in detail."

"What's that large white house?" he asked, indicating a whitewashed stone mansion.

"Government House. It has lovely gardens, and behind them sits the officers' quarters. Those rather orderly looking set of buildings across Macquarie Street are the Royal Marine Barracks flanked by convict quarters on the east and the houses of the mineralogist and Lt. Lord R.M. on the west."

"And there?" he said, gesturing to the far western end of Macquarie Street.

"Another government garden. That scattering of trees and thick brush line the Derwent River. On the other side of the river are quartered the hospital and surgeon's office, the harbormaster's house, and the carpenter and smith's shops." When she turned to look at him, he had wandered away to join in conversation with Christian at a distance, and she returned to her survey.

Small, residential houses, built and occupied by free settlers, dotted the cross streets to the west, and the inevitable concentration of taverns and inns lined Delvey

Street close to the piers. A tiny church sat in an isolated area north of town, as though distancing itself from the bustle and licentious activities of the heavily used port.

Richard had also indicated that Hobart was an important stop along the England-India trade route, and ships of all sizes plied the harbor. Beyond the harbor and town, Tasmania remained a wild, unsettled, mostly unexplored land filled with strange animals and certain death for the unwary. Steep mountains and impenetrable jungle blanketed its interior and challenged only the boldest explorers. The British had no real incentive to explore and settle the remainder of the treacherous land. They chose Tasmania for colonization solely for its deep, sheltered harbors and welcoming coastline, so important to Britain's trading community and convenient to the riches of the East. Therefore, Tasmania remained an untamed nation with only a small band of settlers along the southern coast who barely kept the inhospitable wilderness at bay.

With a frown, Samantha swept her gaze over the town. Where amidst the bustling streets or hostile wilderness could her uncle Richard have gone?

When Christian entered her cabin, Samantha was adjusting a feathered hat atop her curls. A deep burgundy suit trimmed with black velvet molded the curves of her figure. The snug jacket displayed a double row of brass buttons down the front and repeated on shoulder epaulets. The skirt draped back into a low bustle. She had inspected herself in a mirror earlier and thought she looked like a military commander ready to face battle. She turned at Christian's step and gave him a wary smile.

"Shall we go?" she asked, a militant set to her shoulders.

He also appeared prepared for battle with legs braced apart, squared shoulders, and hands linked behind his back. A stern expression rode his features, eyes hooded, and those soft lips she knew so well set in a thin, hard cast. One look at his merciless features, and the starch seeped from her. She knew what was coming. He was so damnably unfair.

"I've already informed you," he said in a tightly controlled voice, "that neither you nor your family can disembark until Garrett and I make arrangements for housing. Once you foisted yourself on me, I planned for you to stay in a boardinghouse. Of course, since you saw fit to drag along half of London on your skirt hem, that plan is no longer feasible. I'll have to lease a house, which may take a few days. You will stay on board and behave. Hobart is a rough town. Ladies have no business gadding about unescorted."

"I could remain with you and Garrett," she said, unrepentant for conveniently forgetting their previous conversation.

"We'll be engaged. I cannot escort you about. Am I to locate a house, seek information regarding your uncle's whereabouts, and get this expedition under way as soon as possible, I'll have no time to act as your guide. If my business proceeds satisfactorily, I'll take you into town tomorrow."

"Then I shall go ashore with Pettibone."

He sighed. "You will not. Pettibone is about as intimidating and as much protection as a mosquito."

"How about Pettibone and Jasper? I must find out what happened to Uncle Richard. So much time has passed already, and—"

"No, Sam!" he said, voice rising nearly to a shout. "You heard me clearly. You'll wait until I can take you ashore. That's my final word."

She gave him a sullen look, and he scowled, jaw firming into granite. "Give me your promise you'll not leave the ship without my permission."

She pressed her lips together.

"Promise. Or I'll lock you in my cabin until I return."

"I promise," she said in a small, unconvincing voice.

"Heed me well. You'd better obey me."

When she offered no comment and longingly gazed out the porthole at Hobart, Christian grasped her chin and turned up her face. Eyes as cool as a lizard's hide bored into hers. "Promise?"

"Promise," she said with a sigh.

He let loose a curse under his breath and strode to the door. "I'll return tomorrow around noon." He pointed at the cabin floor. "Be right here when I come aboard."

When the door closed, she slung her black velvet reticule across the cabin, ripped off her hat, threw it to the floor, and stomped on it with a black-booted foot. She flounced to her bunk to flop onto her belly and brace her chin in her hands.

'Twas not fair! Christian had become a tyrant! *Become?* She snorted. When had he *not* been a tyrant? Was he oblivious to how desperately she wished to find her uncle? She lived in constant fear that Uncle Richard and James had met with foul play or some horrific accident. Tomorrow Christian would decide he had a more important agenda than to escort her into town. Why could she not go ashore and conduct her own investigation? Because she was a woman? Ridiculous! Was this not *her* expedition and he merely her paid employee? Did he even realize how contradictory he was? For all his egalitarian talk about women's rights, he excluded *her* from the group deserving any consideration.

Samantha changed into a day dress and fumed until supper, all the while searching for a legitimate reason that would allow her to break her promise in good conscience. As he had extracted the vow through duress, surely she was not bound by it. With a sudden smile, she recalled some of his words in between all the blustering.

225

Only unescorted *women* courted danger in Hobart. If she were to go as a boy . . . Christian would not return until noon tomorrow. She had sufficient time. He would never suspect she had left, and *she* certainly would not enlighten him.

Samantha rummaged through her chest for her trousers and shirt and contemplated taking Cullen with her. No. Cullen worshipped Christian and would not keep her secret. She had to slip off without anyone seeing her. The ship had anchored in the harbor rather than docking at the quay, so she would have to borrow a dinghy.

Samantha approached Delia after dinner. "Auntie, I have a raging headache. The smoke from the chimneys in Hobart is beastly strong. I forgot how foul the air could be near a town."

Delia placed the back of her hand against Samantha's forehead. "You are not running a fever, dear, are you? I do hope you have no inclination to come down with some dread ailment." She grasped Samantha's elbow, trundled her down to the cabin, and helped her undress. When Samantha lay in bed under the covers, Delia stroked her cheek. "An early night will do wonders for you. You have had entirely too much excitement on this trip."

Samantha held back a smile. *If you only knew the whole of it, Aunt Delia!*

Delia paused at the door. "We shall be as quiet as mice when we retire so as not to wake you. Now try to sleep." She exited in a swirl of bombazine skirts and muslin petticoats.

As soon as Delia left, Samantha leapt out of bed and pulled on her disguise. She had borrowed one of Cullen's knit caps but could pin up her hair only after the other women fell asleep. Climbing back into her hammock, she jerked the covers up to her neck. Her thoughts whirled. Uncle Richard had mentioned the Blue Boar Inn in his last letter. That establishment would be the most obvious place to start.

By the time the watch called out ten o'clock, Delia and Chloe softly snored in the large bunk, and Gilly sighed in her sleep. Samantha slipped out of her hammock, retrieved her boots and cap, and crept out the door. She pinned up her hair in the passageway and tugged the knit cap down to the tops of her ears.

In the silent companionway, faint light came from two lanterns, one between the passenger cabins and one by the ladder. The ship rocked gently at anchor, and the lanterns cast leaping shadows in the narrow passage. A faint glow from the dock and town lights came from topside. Samantha snuck up on deck in her stockings, carrying her boots. She took a quick look about at the top of the ladder, checking the position of the night watch. After so many nights at sea, she had learned the sailors' habits.

As she expected, the watch stood on the fo'c'sle, smoking his pipe. She made her way aft to the dinghies and cranked the winch to lower the boat into the water. When the crank squeaked, she froze, but the sighing of the ship's timbers as it swayed on the incoming tide covered the noise. Slowly releasing her held breath, she clambered down the rope ladder and rowed away from the ship toward Hobart.

Samantha shifted from foot to foot in the street fronting the Blue Boar Inn, her fingers and toes tingling. Bedlam assaulted her ears from the crowd inside, and she nibbled on her thumbnail. Mayhap this was not her best inspiration. As she paced in front of the tavern, dredging up the courage to go forward, three sailors careened out the door and collided with her.

"Watch it, mate!" the one missing most of his teeth slurred. An odor of stale beer and onions blasted her in the face before the man cuffed her on the ear, knocking her askew and down on one knee. The three roared in drunken laughter and staggered off.

While pushing herself to her feet, she caught sight of two familiar figures striding down the walk toward the tavern. *Christian and Garrett!*

Her pulse raced, and her breath jammed in her throat. Sucking in a lungful of air, she burst through the tavern door. 'Twas an ill-conceived move. She crashed into a serving wench, who screeched and dropped her armload of tankards. Ale splashed up, soaking Samantha from waist to toes and covering the rowdy patrons at the three surrounding tables.

"See 'ere, ye little bugger!" the woman shouted, her overstuffed bosom heaving in Samantha's direction. A callused hand came out, grabbed her ear, and twisted hard.

Samantha spewed out a string of curses she had heard aboard ship and wriggled her way free. She clapped a hand to her smarting ear and dashed for the crouching shadows in the room's far corner.

The indignant barmaid became swept up in the ensuing commotion. A scruffy man with a scraggly beard, sitting at a table near the altercation, accused the miscreant at the next table of cursing at him. He threw a roundhouse punch, knocking the innocent man backward and toppling his chair to the floor. When the sailor's mangy friends sprang from their chairs and took revenge, Samantha crawled under a table.

The ale-soaked patrons blamed their nearest neighbors for their condition and took appropriate action, too. Fists flew, chairs flew, ale flew, and shouted curses turned the air blue. Serving maids swung trays with abandon, smiting the heads of guilty and innocent alike. The Irish proprietor leapt over his counter, shillelagh in hand, and cleaved a path through the combatants. Those he felled with his blows staggered and slumped against the walls, crawled out the door on their bellies, or lay in a stupor on the floor, sporting huge knots on their heads.

From her spot beneath the table, Samantha held her breath when the tavern door opened halfway. Christian stuck his head inside, withdrew with an expression of disgust, and closed the door. She exhaled and settled back on the floor to await the fight's conclusion.

When the melee surged closer to her hiding place, she scooted farther beneath the table, and her back hit a pair of knees. She stiffened and looked behind her. A head dipped down and peered under the table, looking straight into her eyes.

"Hallo, lad," the man said softly and chuckled. "You must be the one responsible for this fracas." He crooked a finger. "Come out from under there and sit in a chair. They've already forgotten about you."

She looked out at the room, at the fight raging on. She had no hope of making her way to the door yet. 'Twas foolish to hide beneath the table now that she'd been discovered. She slid out and dropped into a chair at the man's right side, assessing him while contemplating her next move.

The stranger's appearance was heads above the other tavern patrons. A slender, graceful frame, well dressed, clean, and neat. Sandy hair and a close-trimmed beard framed his face. Attractive middle-aged features, not dark and sensual like Christian's or bright and spectacular like Garrett's, but pleasant. She sensed no menace in his demeanor.

He offered her a smile, eyes twinkling. "Do you have a name, lad?"

"Sam Colchester," she replied without thinking. She shrugged. No one here knew her anyway. If this man was acquainted with Richard Colchester, so much the better. How many gentlemen of Richard's station could go unnoticed in a town as small as Hobart? This man might be aware of her uncle's whereabouts. After all, Richard's plight was the reason she had found herself in this muddle.

He gave her the opening she sought. "What are you doing in a tavern this late at night, Sam? You should be home in bed."

She strived for a sorrowful expression and sniffled. "I'm lookin' fer me da'. 'E didn't come 'ome last night."

"Why do you not tell me his name? Perhaps I know him."

"Richard." She knuckled a fist in her eye so it would tear.

"Richard Colchester?"

"Aye, that's 'im." She threw him a trembling smile. "De ye know 'im then?"

The girl's words hit Steven Burnett right between the eyes. While she was evaluating him, he'd been looking her over with considerable interest, knowing at first glance she was no boy. Those curves and her creamy skin gave her away. He'd also seen something familiar in her face.

At her clear, golden eyes, the Colchester eyes, his stomach lurched. A few wisps of butterscotch hair escaped her cap, strands of the same unusual hair color he had seen before on only one other person.

He could barely suppress an eruption of laughter. *The chit was Samantha Eugenia Colchester, Lady Samantha, Richard's niece!*

In the twenty years following his father's unfortunate demise, Steven had avoided England but had maintained his contacts in London. Richard's niece was born shortly after the murder and Steven's own hasty escape.

What a coup! Richard must have written to her of the Smilodon. In fact, her uncle *was* missing; she *would* be looking for him. He'd taken care of Richard Colchester and James Truett over a year ago after authorizing the use of persuasive but ultimately unsuccessful methods to force Richard to reveal the cat's location. 'Twas a shame James also met his end, but innocents often suffered. Did *he* not suffer the destruction of his career, nay, his life, when Richard was the true culprit? Perhaps Samantha knew where to find the Smilodon. He'd heard the girl and Richard were close. Richard was her guardian. Of course she would know. Richard would have confided in her. That was the reason she was in Hobart.

"I know a Richard Colchester, but he is unlikely to be your father," Steven said, modulating his voice to a sympathetic tone. "The man of my acquaintance has not been seen in some time. I recall that he departed Tasmania around a year ago."

Her shoulders drooped.

He came to his feet and extended his hand. "Allow me to take you home. You should not be alone on the streets this late. Hobart can be hazardous."

She pulled back and shot out of the chair, knocking it over in her haste, then glanced about, head swinging from side to side. Steven followed her gaze.

The fight had ended, and its participants lay in battered heaps on the floor. The proprietor cleaned his shillelagh with a bloody rag behind the counter, and serving maids . weaved among the wounded, retrieving dented tankards and bent serving trays. A few of the walking wounded staggered out the door.

"Nay, thank ye, sir," she sputtered. "I live just around t'corner, an' I 'ave ta go now." She took off, sprinting past the bloodied bodies.

"Damn Colchester wench!" Steven swore and banged his fist on the table. It would be too risky to follow her immediately. He had no wish to frighten her. A few inquiries placed with the usual sources would reveal her lodgings. If she was going after the Smilodon, he would discover that fact soon enough. In the end he would acquire everything he desired and deserved: the cat and ultimate revenge on the Colchester family.

Samantha slammed out the tavern door, sprinted

down the street, head down, arms pumping, and ran headlong into a hard body, knocking it to the ground. She fell on top of him, and her legs tangled in his.

"Damn it!" a harsh voice bit out. "Watch where you're going, lad. Have you been drinkin'? You're soaked in ale."

She looked down with horror, recognized the uniform of the military watch. When she scrambled up, her legs churned.

He caught her jacket by the collar and hauled her up on her toes to shine his lantern in her face. "What are you up to, lad? No good is my guess. You'd best come along to the sergeant an' let him decide what to do with you."

She struggled and kicked but made no progress against the firm hand of the officer. When she aimed a foot at his groin, he dodged it, cursed, and shook her like a rag doll.

"If you don't settle down an' come peaceable like, you'll find yourself spendin' the night in gaol an' likely get a beatin' as well," he growled.

His words and the realization that with all her twisting and turning she was in danger of losing her cap curtailed her fighting spirit. What would become of her if he was to discover she was actually a woman? She would be taken for a doxy and thrown into prison. If she cooperated, played the role of a poor, abused waif, perhaps she could walk away from the situation with little delay and no harm to herself. Christian could not learn of her activities this night. He would fillet her like a fish.

The man marched her down the street, his fingers biting into her shoulder, and she kept constant watch on the light pedestrian traffic. Christian and Garrett were nearby. If she could avoid them until she talked the sergeant into releasing her, she would be able to slip back aboard ship before Christian returned.

They halted in front of an ugly gray edifice with no redeeming features. The heavy iron window bars, rusted by salt air, sent a chill up her spine. Her captor hauled her through the door and into an untidy room dominated by a desk and soured by the reek of ale and male sweat. A corpulent man, with so many chins she could barely see his mouth, sprawled behind the desk. He wore a stained, wrinkled uniform unbuttoned down the front to allow room for his massive belly, and a tankard of ale sat beside his left elbow. He glowered when the duo passed into the room, and piggish eyes regarded her contemptuously.

"Well, Corporal Brent?" The sergeant sent the corporal a knowing wink. "Have you taken to lads now?" He laughed, his rolls of fat jiggling like a bowl of aspic.

At the sight and odor of him, Samantha's stomach turned over. To avoid disgracing herself and worsening the situation, she kept silent and bowed her head, casting her eyes down at the filthy floor.

"Nay, Sergeant Dobbins," the corporal said, "you know me better than that. I received word of a riot at the Blue Boar Inn. I found him outside, runnin' like the devil an' stinkin' of ale. Ran into me an' knocked me down, the little bugger did. He's probably a thief. 'Tis past curfew, an' he fought me. Want me to throw him in gaol till we check the tavern an' find out what mischief he's caused?"

"Look at me, lad," the porcine Dobbins said. When Samantha lifted her head, he pinned her with a cold, pitiless stare. "What were you about on the streets this late?"

She prayed she looked penitent. "I was lookin' fer me da'. 'E didn't come home, an' me brother sent me after 'im. Please don't lock me up. I didn't de nuthin'. 'Onest! I'm nae thief."

Sergeant Dobbins's gaze crawled over her like spider legs. "Who's your father?"

She twisted her hands in her jacket to control their shaking. "Richard Colchester. But I dinna know where 'e is."

"Where's your brother?"

"Board the *Maiden Anne*. 'E just shipped in."

The sergeant wheezed a sigh. "And he has a name, I presume?"

"Garrett Jakes." *Better Garrett than Christian!* "An' before ye ask, me name's Sam."

His eyes narrowed. "Your brother is not Garrett Colchester?"

She realized her slip and mentally cursed. "Me mum, she married again."

Sergeant Dobbins swiveled his gaze to Corporal Brent. "Throw him in the holding cell and collect this Jakes fellow off the *Maiden Anne*. We shall soon get to the bottom of this. Should the lad be lying, he'll rot for a long time in gaol. Tell Jakes to bring along the fine for violating curfew, or his brother will be our guest for a while."

Samantha's stomach throbbed sickly.

The corporal clutched her arm and dragged her through an odiferous corridor. After opening a barred door, he tossed her inside, where she landed heavily on a bug-infested straw bed. A bucket in use as a privy sat in one corner, issuing malignant odors, and three other wretched creatures hugged the floor. One, pissed to the gills, spewed the contents of his stomach into the bucket and added to the malodorous air. The second one ignored her and picked lice from his filth-encrusted body. The third occupant regarded her with licentious eyes, as though penetrating her disguise. Then again, perhaps he preferred boys. At school she had heard whispers about such goings-on, though she never fully understood them. She shuddered, rolled up into a ball, and hunched against the wall to make herself as small as possible.

Please, Garrett, come soon and rescue me from this miserable place.

Christian fought to bring his trembling under control. Their business completed earlier than expected, he and Garrett had returned to the ship over two hours ago to find Samantha gone, and no one had seen her leave.

"But she retired early," Delia insisted.

Christian sent out men to search the ship from bow to stern. When one sailor discovered a missing dinghy, the men came ashore, canvassing the docks and finally scouring the town building by building, alley by alley, but they uncovered no clues to her whereabouts. Christian ordered dinghies into the water, instructing the sailors to look for her body. Soft splashing from oars, shouted exchanges, and the gleaming bobbing of lanterns floated out of the darkness over the harbor. He swore if he should find her alive, he would kill her for shaving another decade off his life. At this rate, he would be meeting Saint Peter within weeks.

"Come morning, I'm mounting an expedition into the interior," Christian said and plowed a shaky hand through his hair. "I fear she has gone after her uncle on her own." *Damned female!* And after she gave him her promise. Her duplicity only served to confirm his opinion that a woman's promise was no more than words thrown to the wind. Concern for her safety warred with rage at her audacity and stupidity.

"Hello!" a voice called out, intruding on their dock-side conference and drawing their attention away from the flickering lights in the floating dinghies.

A lantern bobbed in the distance and moved toward them. When the man drew closer, his corporal's uniform emerged from the darkness.

"Be that the *Maiden Anne*?" The corporal waved his lantern toward the ship anchored in the harbor.

"It is," Christian said. "The *Maiden Anne* is our ship. What interest would the military garrison have with us?"

"Are you Garrett Jakes?" He lifted the lantern to examine Christian's face.

"I'm Jakes," Garrett answered from beside Christian. "Who wants to know?"

The lantern and the man's gaze swung to Garrett. "We picked up your little brother tonight outside the Blue Boar Inn. Least he says he's your brother. He's probably lyin'. Tryin' to squirm out of a thievery charge."

"What's his name?" Christian asked quietly.

"Says 'tis Sam. Scruffy little urchin he is. I can see you're gentlemen, an' he couldn't be related to you."

Christian's jaw hardened to flint. "Perhaps we should take a look. He could be my cabin boy who lost his family at sea and thinks of Garrett as his brother."

"Very well." The corporal sighed. "You're likely wastin' your time. But 'tis your time. I just do my duty." The man swung around and walked away.

When Christian strode forward, Garrett stepped around him and barred his way. "Allow me to handle this situation," Garrett said at the evidence of Christian's tense fists, rigid body, and the fury reflected in his features.

Christian's eyes glittered like splintered ice. "Move," he ordered, the word spurting from his lips like venom from a viper.

Garrett braced a palm on Christian's chest. "I will not. You're too angry to deal with Sam at this time. I've no wish to have to spring you from prison on account of your committing murder. Not that I'm saying you truly would, but I'll not have you frightening the life out of her. In any case, I rather like the chit. I'll fetch her."

Christian stepped back, closed his eyes, and scrubbed a hand across his mouth. When his eyes opened, he appeared more lucid. "Perhaps you're right. I would be more likely to wring her neck than bail her out of her scrape." He turned and walked toward town, looking back over his shoulder. "Take care of her. And make certain I don't see her for a week or two."

When Christian disappeared into the night, Garrett released the breath stuck in his throat. Now for Samantha, the little fool. His quick strides ate up the dock, following the direction the corporal had taken.

At the garrison gaol, the swinish sergeant stood, buttoned his uniform jacket, and smoothed his thinning hair when Garrett entered. He gestured to a wooden chair. Garrett settled gingerly on the shaky, sticky seat, and the sergeant offered him a tankard of ale.

"No thanks," Garrett said. "I have no wish to waste your valuable time. Please bring out the lad so I can identify him. Should he be my cabin boy, I'm prepared to pay the fine"—he plopped a hefty purse on the desk, raising a dust cloud—"though I'm tempted to leave him with you for a few days to teach him a lesson."

The sergeant's eyes bulged at the size of the purse. He waved curtly to the corporal. "Get the lad."

Corporal Brent escorted Samantha out of her cell and into the sergeant's office. The sight of Garrett sent her pulse into a headlong gallop. Though relieved at her rescue, she dreaded the scene bound to ensue when she came into Christian's clutches. Satan's own bullocks had surely scattered their droppings over her path tonight.

As Garrett circled her with his hands clenched behind his back, she examined his impassive face through the screen of her lashes. Stopping in front of her, he lifted her chin on the edge of his hand. She cringed at his flinty glare, though his angel-like features remained as expressionless as rock.

"Well?" the sergeant asked, his bloated fingers toying with the pouch.

Garrett cupped his chin with one hand, resting the elbow in his other palm, and rubbed the hand over his mouth. "It's he." He exhaled heavily. "My apologies for the inconvenience."

Sergeant Dobbins belched, his stinking breath sending out a cloud tinged with ale and poor dental care. He snatched up the pouch and dropped it into a desk drawer. "Were I you," he said with a cruel smile, "I'd give the lad a taste of the cat. Take out the fine on his hide and teach him who's master."

Garrett caught Samantha's gaze with a look that knocked the air out of her. "Perhaps someone will." He turned to the two policemen. "I owe you my thanks for finding the lad. No telling what could have happened to him alone in a place such as Hobart." His fingers sank into her elbow, and he pushed her out the door.

As soon as they hit the street, Garrett's face grew taut with anger. Samantha suspected Christian was waiting for her not far away, and Garrett was taking her to him. If she was able to beat them to the dock, find the dinghy, and board the ship first, she could barricade herself in her cabin until Christian . . . Until Christian what? Forgot about the incident? That seemed unlikely, but she had no wish to face him at this moment when his anger was bound to be at its most virulent. She twisted her elbow out of Garrett's hand and starting running as fast as she could. She was panting hard and fairly flying when a hand clamped on her collar, jerking her backward and up off her feet.

She closed her eyes, legs dangling in the air. The shirt collar cut into her throat, threatening to strangle her. But then choking to death might be her best choice at this point, before Christian had the chance to lay hands on her. Garrett held her high off the ground with one hand, like he would hold an incontinent puppy by the scruff of its neck, and shook her until her teeth rattled. She'd not realized the slim young man was so strong.

"Enough!" she croaked.

Garrett dropped her, and she fell forward onto her knees. She peered up at his censorious look and tight frown.

He reached down and brought her to her feet. "Why did you run from me?"

"From the look on your face, I feared you would do me an injury or that Christian was lurking in a dark alley where he could chop me into fish food with no witnesses."

"Stop that, Sam. Your exaggerations become tedious. No one will do you physical harm, as you well know, unless Christian gives you the sound paddling you deserve. At any rate, you're fortunate Christian has taken himself off to town. I vow you have naught but pudding between your ears. Where did you go tonight?" He shook his head. "Never mind. It doesn't matter." He took her by the wrist and towed her to a bench by the waterside. His fingers clamped on her shoulder like a crocodile's teeth, pushing downward and compelling her to sit. He settled beside her, turned sideways, and looked into her eyes. "For your own safety, it's time you learned something about Christian's past."

CHAPTER EIGHTEEN

At last! Now, when it was too late, when she had tossed herself into a fine pit of snakes, Garrett would finally disclose what she had badgered him for so long to spill.

"First, I must tell you that I came tonight not because I sympathize with your irresponsible actions, but because Chris was so incensed," he said. "I feared he would suffer an attack of apoplexy unless he was given some time to cool his head. My rescue was not for your sake. It was for his."

She hung her head. "I'm sorry," she said softly.

"As you well should be. However, your apology is unlikely to pull much weight with Chris." He paused and took a breath. "Has he divulged his background to you?"

She glanced up at the abrupt change of subject. "He

told me his father was a reformer and gave up the earldom after losing everything in an effort to ease the plight of the poor. They then came to America."

Garrett cocked his head. "That's all he said?"

She slowly nodded. "Is there more I should know?"

He gave a little laugh. "I expect there is, if you truly wish to understand why Chris has been so harsh with you."

She grabbed his hands. "Truly, I do. Please tell me."

Garrett extracted his hands from her grip and combed one through his hair. "What he said about his father is true, though only a small part of the story. The formation of Chris's character properly begins with his mother."

"His mother? Chris never mentioned his mother. I assumed she died when he was young."

He lifted a hand. "Allow me to continue without interruption, Sam. The tale is sordid enough without having to backtrack." When she nodded, he went on. "Lady Jane came from the bluest of the blue-blooded aristocrats. She was beautiful, the toast of the Ton, and the most notorious strumpet in London."

Samantha gasped.

Garrett gave her a warning look. "I daresay the path to Jane's boudoir was deeper than a carriage rut in April. After giving birth to Chris, she suffered through numerous pregnancies, none of which she allowed to come to term. As she had left the earl's bed after Chris's birth, all were the progeny of her various lovers. She spent money like it was water and flaunted her affairs as though they were badges of honor. Through it all, her husband worshipped her, denying her infidelities and defending her reputation, such as it was. Then the day came when her philandering came to an abrupt end. A jealous lover whom she spurned murdered her before killing himself."

"How awful!" Samantha said. "How old was Chris when this happened?"

"Fourteen. Old enough to understand his mother's nature but too young to take up the mantle of the earldom from his father."

She wrinkled her nose. "What do you mean? Why should Chris have to—?"

"Quiet," he said, laying a finger across her lips. "The shock of Lady Jane's death drove the earl to madness. He retreated into a childlike state and became unable even to care for himself. Circumstances forced Chris into the role of father and head of the family, his sire having become the child. Between the earl's generosity and Jane's profligate spending, the estate was soon destitute. Chris sold what they had left, which amounted to a pittance, and took his father to America, where he built a cabin in Massachusetts with his own hands and cared for his father until the earl's death three years later." Garrett gazed earnestly into Samantha's eyes. "Since the day his father ceased to be the man he once was, Chris has struggled to maintain strict control over his own life and circumstances. He fears that should he ever let go, allow himself to weaken to another's will, particularly a woman's, he will share his father's fate, his madness."

Samantha pressed her hands to her mouth, mind spinning with the implications of Garrett's revelations. "Oh, my. I can now see why he has such an aversion to aristocratic ladies and why he insists on having his own way. Had I been privy to this information earlier, I might have done things differently."

Garrett stood and, with a dubious smile, offered his hand to Samantha. "I very much doubt that, Sam. You and Chris are much alike. You both have strong characters and obdurate personalities. I consider it a blessing you haven't thrown each other overboard yet."

Steven Burnett strolled to the tavern door and walked outside. From the doorway of the Blue Boar Inn, he watched Samantha's retreat. Leaning against the rough wall, he lit a cheroot, and chuckled at her encounter with the military watch. He would not go to her aid as he could ill afford to bring attention to his interest in the girl, especially to the military authorities. She would extricate herself from her predicament, and he would find her again. Hobart was still a small town, for all its worldly pretensions.

After the watch departed with Samantha and headed

toward the garrison, two men passed by the tavern on the opposite side of the street. In the oily glow from a streetlight, Steven recognized one. Professor Christian Badia. Steven had seen him only once before in Hong Kong, but the tall figure with light-streaked dark hair and chiseled features made an unmistakable impression. Steven knew Badia's credentials and his reputation, his success in tracking down species impossible to find, and the events of the night dropped into place.

He chuckled at judging the situation correctly. They were pursuing the Smilodon. Christian Badia's presence, along with that of Samantha Colchester, confirmed it. Now, if he could only be certain of the fate of Richard Colchester and James Truett.

As Christian walked down the street, and Steven's gaze followed him, Steven recalled the meeting nearly a year ago.

The *Manta Ray* returned to Tasmania battered but still afloat, and Steven received a message from Miggs to meet him at the Blue Boar Inn. He assumed the pirates had extracted the cat's location, disposed of the two Englishmen, and now expected final payment.

Steven had entered the silent tavern on that long-ago morning in a swirl of fog to find a scarcely populated room. The proprietor, Ian Mickles, was setting up the bar and wiping down the counter in preparation for the day's trade. Sleepy barmaids wandered among the tables, sweeping trash-strewn floors and swabbing sticky tabletops.

They blinked at Steven through red-rimmed eyes, their worn features caked with runny face paint from the previous night's revels.

Mickles nodded to Steven and inclined his head toward a door behind the counter. "Yer party's waitin' fer ye in the back room. Keep it short. I ain't runnin' no boardin'house."

"We shall take ale, if it is available this early," Steven said.

"Always got ale." Mickles wiped his hands on his dirty apron and drew two tankards of ale, thrusting them into Steven's hands as he passed by.

The captain of the *Manta Ray* slouched in a chair behind a battered table. Three burly, unshaven men dressed in sailor's togs lolled against one wall. Eyes as dead as those on a week-old mullet in a fish market peered out from grim, hard faces.

Even compared to his minions, the pirate captain was a fright, and Steven suppressed a shudder of revulsion. A scar ran from the man's hairline to a puckered hole at the site of his missing right eye. His filthy frock coat gapped open over a barrel chest furred with coarse red hair. One arm rested in a sling, and a host of new scars crisscrossed his chest and face, adding to the fearsome countenance.

Anxious to be away quickly, Steven slammed the tankards on the table, ale sloshing over their sides, and · straddled a wobbly chair. He reached into his pocket, withdrew a bag of coins, and tossed it onto the table. "You have favorable news for me, I presume?"

Miggs flashed a greedy look from his one good eye. His hand snaked toward the pouch, but Steven was faster. He pinned Miggs's splayed hand to the table with a fist and narrowed his eyes into slits. "Have you favorable news for me?" he asked again, his voice dropping to a soft, lethal level.

A ripple went through the pirate's frame, and he pulled his hand away. "Nay. They wouldn't give it up. Smythe near whipped one o' 'em ta death, but t'other still wouldn't talk. Course by then, 'e was 'alf dead, too. We coulda got t'location eventually, but we was attacked by Jack Fallon on the *Rapier*. Barely got free wi' our lives an' ship. Lost 'alf me crew, I did. Least we sent the *Rapier* ta a watery grave."

With thumb and fingertips, Steven smoothed down his beard. "Where are you keeping Colchester and Truett now?"

"Ye see, that's the strangest thing. When the fightin' was over, we checked the 'old, an' they was gone."

"Gone?" Every muscle in his body stiffened.

Miggs rocked back in the chair and crossed his arms over his chest. "Yeah. 'Tis right eerie. Truett was dead. Smythe swears ta it, an' Colchester was nae much better. A cannonball punched through the 'old. They musta washed out through the 'ull. Only way I see they coulda left t'ship. They're dead now. We was in the Tasman

Sea, days from any landfall. Even if Colchester made it off t'ship alive, 'e couldn'ta made it ta land. 'E's shark bait fer sure."

Steven picked up the pouch and returned it to his pocket.

"'Ey now!" Miggs shouted. The chair legs slammed against the floor. "We earned them guineas."

Steven pushed back his chair, surged to his feet, and looked down coldly on the pirate. "I still don't have that location. Your job is finished when I do. Let me know where you're anchored, and I shall contact you when I sort out this mess. I may allow you another chance to redeem yourself. Then again, considering your incompetence, I may not."

Steven returned to the present, and a faint smile pressed the corners of his mouth. He ground out the cheroot beneath his boot heel. Perhaps he would offer Miggs that second chance. And this time, he had better succeed. The fragile girl should be easier to deal with and persuade than her uncle.

When Garrett and Samantha boarded the ship, Samantha saw no evidence of Christian. Though Garrett had told her Christian went into town, Samantha trembled nonetheless. He could have returned without Garrett knowing, and she glanced about while Garrett propelled her across the deck. Her heart beat so rapidly she was certain to expire and save Christian the effort of taking her life.

Instead of escorting her to her cabin, Garrett pushed her into the brig and closed the door.

"*Et tu, Brute?*" she called out when the bolt shot to.

"It's for your own safety," he replied.

Yes, she supposed it was. She engaged the inside bolt.

Later, the door rattling signaled that Christian had come for her. She struggled to shove his weighty chest of belongings in front of the portal. 'Twould at least slow him down. She was in no mood for another dreadful confrontation.

The boards sighed, as though he had leaned up against them. "Have you any concept of a promise, Sam?" he said calmly.

At first, the words stuck in her throat. When he didn't attempt to break down the door, she called herself a coward and rested her forehead on the wood. "I do," she muttered.

"*The devil you do!*" The blast rocked her back on her heels. "You're a *dishonest bitch*!"

Stung to the core, she tightened her hands into fists. "I am not dishonest," she managed to force out.

"Very well, I take that back. Not dishonest then. A conniving, manipulative bitch."

"I am not!" Tears swam in her eyes. After her talk with Garrett, she now understood the basis for Christian's assessment of her character, yet she still could not believe he would be so hateful.

"I have no earthly wish to listen to your defense this time," he went on. "No excuse short of the ship catching fire could possibly explain your actions to my satisfaction. You're manipulative. You give your word with no intention of keeping it. You connive and scheme, looking for a crack in the wall, any way to wiggle out of your responsibilities and have your own way. And in the process, you put your life and the lives of those around you in danger. If you were a man, I would have lashed you at the mast."

If I were a man, I would not be in this predicament!

His fist struck the door.

She jumped away and hugged her arms around her waist. Goose bumps sprinted across her skin.

"You could have been killed!" he shouted. "You're fortunate I haven't taken my belt to you. The next time you cross me, I will. That's a *promise,* and be aware *I* keep my promises. Furthermore, I shan't be responsible for someone who refuses to follow orders. You won't travel to the island with us."

She rushed to the door and slammed her hands against it. "You cannot do that! You told me I could! This is *my* expedition! You cannot bar me from it!"

Silence came from the other side.

"You are a beast," she whispered through her tears.

"A bloody, vicious beast!"

Samantha lay on her stomach on the bunk, chafing at her confinement, and counted the days slogging by. Though she suffered from Christian's reneging on his promise to allow her to accompany the expedition, even that bleak development hurt less than his deliberate dismissal of her. How could he forget the intimacies they shared? She never could.

Throwing herself from the bed, she stormed about the cabin, making circuit after circuit, working the kinks from her stiff muscles. She cursed and screamed at the bulkheads. After tearing through Christian's possessions, she tossed them around the room. Standing amid the destruction, fury vented at long last, she achieved some satisfaction and serenity.

A week passed, during which she examined and reexamined her feelings and began to see Christian's actions in a more rational light. In hindsight, the only sight she seemed to have lately, she came to a reluctant deduction: she should have waited for him to take her ashore. True to her stubborn nature, she had forged ahead without thinking and deserved the consequences. Taking off alone had been a boneheaded, perilous act, not to mention unproductive. Where did that leave her?

She smiled ironically, spinning in place and opening her arms. "Here," she said to the walls. "Stuffed away in a cabin barely wide enough to twirl a skirt." Sinking onto the cot, she dropped her chin on her steepled hands and dwelled on an infinitely more important subject. Did Christian have feelings, other than exasperation, of course, for her? If he was only using her, would he not have taken her virginity at the first opportunity? She had offered him every occasion to do so. Did his pursuit have a purpose? Had it changed now that she had broken her trust with him and probably lost his respect forever?

That he might hate her brought a crushing weight to her chest and tears to her eyes. He was everything she believed she always wanted in a man: strong, intelligent, maddeningly handsome, tender, and sensual. Someone she could . . . love.

Love?

The notion struck her like a castle wall hit by a cannonball and drove the breath from her lungs. She had fallen in love with him, in love with that impossible, infuriating, intoxicating man. She sank to the deck, pulse racing like a steam engine. Her fingers went to her mouth, and she nibbled at her fingernails until only nubs remained, struggling to divine what the future held for her now and whether that future also held Christian Badia.

By the time Samantha gained her freedom, Christian had already amassed and organized the majority of the stores he required for the expedition. He had taken on local men to help with the equipment and a pilot familiar with the ocean through which they would sail. Aunt Delia, Chloe, and Gilly were settled in Talmadge House, a two-story Georgian brick dwelling Christian leased in a respectable area of Hobart, and Pettibone would remain in Hobart with the women.

When Samantha contemplated being escorted to Talmadge House and the ship departing before she could speak with Christian, her heart ached unbearably. During her confinement, a silent sailor showed up at her door daily with her meals. Christian's absence, even in that small task, spoke volumes about his opinion of her.

Samantha emerged on deck to find Christian standing at the railing, his gaze rapt on the gulls diving for fish in the harbor water. She approached him with her feet dragging along the wooden boards. At the sound of her footsteps, he turned his head. A stone mask came down over his face, and he returned to the gulls in blatant dismissal.

Her heart plummeted to her knees. Now that she had finally accepted her heart's message, she had lost him. Falling in love with Christian happened gradually, sneaking past her defenses with no warning during their months at sea. She loved the way his comingled blond and brown hair swept back from his face, a few shorter strands always escaping his queue and tossing in the wind. She loved how his eyes lit up at the sight of her, darkened during their love play, and crinkled at the corners when he laughed. She loved his mouth, soft and firm at the same time, tasting of pleasure and . . . Christian. She loved his voice, deep and sensual—when not shouting at her—and rough with passion. She could watch him forever, tall and hard, lithe and moving with inimitable masculine grace. Mostly, she loved his mind, his deep convictions, his sharp intellect, and his willingness to patiently answer her endless questions, to teach her about love, banish her ignorance, and take away her fears.

She wanted him more than anything. She wanted to be at his side . . . *forever.* But in taking one risky step too many in her normally heedless way, she feared she had thrown away whatever they might have had together.

Desperate to reach him, she came up behind him to slip her arms around his waist and press her cheek to his back. She soaked in his scent and heat and the feel of his body. She loved him with all her heart. Now she doubted he could ever love her.

"Please do not hate me," she whispered against his shirt. "I'm genuinely sorry for the problems I caused."

The muscles in his back grew rigid.

"I don't hate you," he replied, seeming to force out the words, his chest expanding with a deep breath. "I don't hate you, but I cannot trust you, and I cannot spend all my time worrying about where you are and what trouble you've gotten yourself into."

Her heart shattered.

He released a short laugh devoid of humor. "I would have you know that for the first time in my life, I actually considered a long-term relationship. Perhaps even marriage. But how can I expect you to honor a contract as sacred as a marriage vow when you're incapable of even delivering on a simple promise?"

Her world dissolved into dust carried away by the offshore breeze. Tears rained from her eyes, wetting his shirt. "I can," she said in a tearful whisper.

"No, you cannot. And you know it as well as I. It's too late, Sam, and best we keep our distance. I'm unwilling to take any more chances. Someone will get hurt or even killed, and I cannot be responsible for that happening."

"Can you not forgive me just once more?"

He shook his head. "Not this time. When I think of what could have happened to you . . ." A shudder went through his frame. "I trust you'll forgive my past transgressions, but I cannot forgive your deliberate lying and continued disobedience. The orders I issue are meant to keep you safe. You seem to have no conception that this trip is not a pleasure cruise."

She drew away, shoulders hunching. "I'll give you the Smilodon's location in the morning. First I must find Richard's letters."

He turned around at last, bracing his hands behind him on the railing, and smiled cynically. "With what strings attached?"

"No strings," she whispered, bowed her head, and shuffled away.

The tavern atmosphere was subdued, the voices muted near Christian's table. He sprawled in a corner booth with his back against the wall, one leg stretched out along the bench. Despondency with an edge of danger radiated from him, spiked the air like a noxious vapor, and suspended the gaiety. Other patrons gave him a wide berth, darting surreptitious glances his way, and whispered among themselves. One waitress, younger and bolder than the others, with waist-length red hair and freckles dotting the bridge of her nose, brushed a firm breast against his arm when she leaned over the table to set the tankard of ale in front of him.

He looked up and licked his bottom lip, gaze skimming over the girl's opulent figure. Perhaps she was the balm he required. To bury himself in a woman's heat. Lord knew he required something, and ale was failing to soften his mood. He'd not had a woman since . . . since the night Garrett fetched Samantha from the gaol. He held only a vague recollection of his trip into town and his encounter with the tavern wench. He recalled his terror and the need to expend it. He was harsh that night, and rough, thrusting mercilessly into the girl, not his usual style. She certainly earned her coin. And afterward he got as pissed as a badger and initiated a brawl that ended with his sleeping off his hangover in a rubbish-strewn alley.

Samantha haunted him. When did she not? He still felt her softness against his back, her small arms around his waist, the moisture from her tears against his shirt. What in God's name was he going to do with her? She was tearing him apart. She had turned his world upside down, and he liked it not one damn bit. At this moment he wanted only to erase her imprint from his memory.

The red-haired wench smiled coyly. His cock twitched, and he winked, nodding toward the stairs. Picking up his tankard, he followed her swaying hips up the stairway to her room. After pulling the door to, he leaned against it and sipped his ale while she discarded her clothes. The removal of her bodice and skirt revealed a firm young body, plump and ripe, but the haste, expertise, and oft-practiced moves with which she stripped left him cold. No fumbling fingers like Samantha, no lingering, no naïve nervousness.

When she lay on the bed and spread her legs, his desire

waned. He wasn't foxed enough. He cursed under his breath and threw some coins on the dressing table.

"Come on, luv," she crooned, beckoning with her fingers. "Somethin' wrong? Want me ta give ye a hand?"

He offered an apologetic smile. "Not tonight, sweetheart. Another time, perhaps. I have too much on my mind." He turned and walked out of the room.

When he left the tavern, he wandered from tap-room to dance hall. No matter the quantity of ale he consumed, he remained sober, his thoughts dwelling on one small, lithe, curious woman, an image of butter-scotch hair and golden eyes. She possessed him, following him throughout the night. He couldn't get sotted. *God*, he couldn't even get laid! What ailed him, and what did he plan to do about it? How could he purge her from his system? Was that what he honestly desired? Questions continued to badger him until dawn's faint light crept over the horizon and washed the sky with pink.

Christian burst into Samantha's cabin at daybreak, startling her out of her hammock and onto the deck. She yelped when she landed on her bottom, pushed the hair out of her eyes, and stared up at him, swallowing her irritation when viewing his lunatic expression. He re-peatedly ran his fingers through his rumpled hair and over his bristly jaw. His wrinkled clothing looked as if he had slept in them. His shirt had three missing buttons and hung out of his breeches.

"Get dressed," he said brusquely, muttered, "Bloody hell," then continued in a softer tone. "Wear something decent . . . something"—he waved a hand in the air—"becoming. And do something"—the wave again—"with your hair."

"Chris—"

"Just get dressed."

She sat there with her mouth agape.

"Damn it," he blustered. "Get on your feet and dressed *now* before I change my mind or carry you out clothed in naught but a night rail."

"Carry me where?" she sputtered, but he let the door swing to with a slam. His boot strides thudded down the companionway.

A thrill bubbled up inside her. They must be sailing today, and Christian had changed his mind. He was allowing her to join the expedition. If that was so, why should she wear something becoming? Perhaps she was misinterpreting his words, and he had something else in mind. From his manner, though bizarre, she grasped she was no longer in his bad graces. Mayhap not completely in the clear, but he was speaking to her again.

Wide awake now, she levered herself off the deck and raced to the basin to wash. Rummaging through her chest, she pulled out a white muslin dress trimmed with lace and green ribbon around the low neckline and short, puffed sleeves. She brushed out her hair and fought the heavy mass to pull it up into curls. Her fingers trembled too much, and she settled for tying it back with a green ribbon and leaving two long curls in front of her ears. She slapped on a dainty straw hat with trailing green velvet ribbons. Jewelry? No, she had no time to look.

Time! Her pulse escalated into a mad rhythm.

Christian had neglected to tell her how much time she had. He always timed her.

She prayed she was not too late, though for what she still had no notion, and darted out of the cabin. In her haste, she stumbled up the ladder to the deck, all but falling on her face when she snagged her toe in her dress hem. Christian caught her before she banged her chin on the boards. With a freshly shaved face and slicked-back hair, dressed in snug fawn breeches, black boots, a white shirt open at the collar, and a black frock coat, he looked exceptionally striking, but his eyes still had that wild look, like a snapping turtle caught in a trap.

He spun her around, looking over her white dress.

"Is my gown appropriate?" she asked.

He nodded curtly. "It will do." Then he murmured, "The color is certainly appropriate."

She raised her eyebrows and smiled hopefully. "Will you now tell me where we are going?"

"No, and don't ask questions. Let's be off before I forget why I'm doing this." He took her elbow and helped her into the dinghy. He rowed to the dock, silence wrapping about them like a woolen blanket, where he lifted her in his arms and set her on the pier. After climbing out of the dinghy, he took off at a rapid pace, pulling her along by the elbow.

Sweat poured off Christian's forehead by the time they reached their destination, and the ocean breeze whipping around Samantha had blown her into disarray while he hurried her along. Then he stopped and turned to her, seizing and holding both her hands in a tight, clammy grip. "Samantha Eugenia Colchester, you will marry me," he said in a voice sounding as if it rumbled up from his gut with excruciating effort.

Like an unwound clock, her heart stopped in her chest.

CHAPTER NINETEEN

Samantha was a dead woman, her heartbeat only an illusion, or, at the least, she was a madwoman suffering from delirium. She turned her head slowly, as though sudden movement might cause it to unhinge, and took in every aspect of the building beside them. Built of whitewashed wood with a stubby steeple topped by a bell tower, Hobart's small church screamed of propriety in an immoral town. The sight persuaded her. She was dead, lying somewhere inside the church, her stiff body reposing in a pinewood coffin. Why then did Christian's grasp send prickles through her hands? She stared blankly at the church, unable to make a neural connection between it and his words.

Did he ask me to marry him? She mentally shook her head. He did not pose a question, did he? She did not believe so. The wind must have whistled through her ears, carrying the cries of gulls from the pier, and she mistook the sounds for what she desired most in the world to hear, the world she so recently departed. Would Christian attend her funeral? Would he mourn her?

Christian slid his hands to her upper arms, holding her tightly, and uttered a strangled plea. "I require an answer, Sam." He shook her gently.

She looked up at his face and processed his tortured look. The skin stretched so tightly across his cheekbones, she could have carved mutton on their sharp angles.

He shook her again. "Yes or no. I must know."

She voiced the sole word she could push past her lips. "Yes."

His face paled, his mouth crimped a bit, and small creases lined his forehead. "I feared you would answer that way." He straightened his shoulders, tucked her arm in the crook of his elbow, and led her into the church.

Garrett met them in the entryway. He shoved a bouquet of golden roses into Samantha's hands and whispered aside to Christian, "Are you certain you want to do this?" When Christian snarled, Garrett scurried away and took his seat, his face as pale as Christian's.

Aunt Delia, Chloe, Gilly, and Pettibone sat on the left side of the aisle with Captain Lindstrom, Cullen, and Jasper on the right. The remainder of the ship's crew lounged on pews in the rear of the chapel. Roses bedecked the altar in hastily thrown-together arrangements. Their heavy scent barely masked the odor of unwashed bodies emanating from the back rows.

A mist cloaked Samantha from that moment on, clouding the events in a ghostly haze. Sounds emerged only as echoes, faint and far away, words barely comprehensible, and voices vaguely familiar. Though she was aware of Christian standing beside her and the pastor in front of them, their images blurred, fuzzy at the edges, as indistinct as spirits. Candle flames flickered on the altar, halos of soft light, spreading a gentle glow over the assemblage. The perfume of the roses teased her nostrils, sweet and cloying at times, then drifting away, becoming elusive, as though she only dreamt it.

Christian's hand held hers. Warmth and strength flowed from his body to hers as her only link to reality, her only solid ground. She clung to him to keep from falling.

The pastor's anxious eyes monitored Christian during the ceremony, as though he expected the groom to swoon. Christian's face remained as white as paste, and moisture beaded his forehead. Nonetheless, he managed the proper responses, speaking his vows in a deep, resonant timbre that rumbled through his hand and into her bones. When Samantha opened her mouth to speak, the sound of her own voice startled her.

Christian slipped a wedding band on her finger. It held two stones, an emerald and a topaz, shaped like stars and embedded side by side in gold. His stunned expression altered only once, when he looked down on her stubby fingernails and frowned.

Aunt Delia and Chloe wept uncontrollably into their handkerchiefs. Gilly wore a wide smile. Throughout the ceremony, the men in the church, with the exception of Pettibone, sat glumly and grimaced as though in sympathy with a fellow companion falling into the trap of the leg shackle.

"Way to go, m'lady!" Pettibone yelled out after Samantha said her vows. "Now you *have* to obey him. You just made a promise to God." Aunt Delia elbowed him in the ribs, eliciting a loud grunt.

Christian claimed her lips in a possessive kiss that Samantha felt to her toes, but she still wondered whether it all was not a dream. When he pulled back, his eyes focused on her upturned face. "I trust you were listening to Pettibone. Now I have the law and God on my side. You're mine to do with as I wish."

His words shook her from her dreamlike state. She leaned back into the circle of his arms. "Is that why you married me?" she asked with an arch look.

His mouth quirked in a rueful grin. "Not at all, ti-grina, though the notion deserves merit and should have occurred to me earlier. One might speculate that the only way to ensure your safety and obedience is to keep you beneath me in bed, so I'll always know where to find you." Then he lowered his voice so only she could hear him. "In truth, I want to be inside you so desperately I can taste it."

Heat crept up her neck and into her cheeks. She wanted him, too, felt as if she had wanted him forever, though she would never be so bold as to tell him inside a church, no less!

He pressed his fingertips to her cheek, and his breath warmed her ear. "Did I ever tell you how much I adore the way you blush?"

Samantha blushed even more furiously, and Christian laughed.

Married!

Shock still rippled through her veins, though the full weight of the vows only now impacted her brain. Was it all a dream? *Perhaps I'm still locked away in Christian's cabin, delirious from hunger.* She pinched herself and winced with very real pain.

Married! The word descended like a crushing weight. *Love . . . Honor . . . Obey . . . Obey?* What had she done?

Husband and wife. Till death do you part. It seemed so . . . so frightfully final. What would happen to Samantha Colchester, modern woman? Was she now but an appendage, an extension of Christian Badia?

She whispered, "Mistress Christian Badia." The words were strange, impersonal. The name took away her individuality and reduced her to a subordinate role in one fell swoop, one moment in time.

She brought to mind an image of Christian. Tall, dark, utterly masculine, and desirable. Tender and intelligent, gentle and sensual. Short-tempered and overbearing, arrogant, infuriating, maddeningly passionate. She sighed, aware it was a tad late to cry off. They were well and truly wedded.

Samantha sat on the padded stool before the dressing table mirror to remove her hat and studied her reflection while pulling the ribbon from her hair and releasing it from its confinement. The heavy butterscotch mass slipped from its bond and rippled around her shoulders, falling to her waist in glowing waves.

Why did she waver now? She had wanted this, asked for it, pined for it. Perhaps not the wedding but certainly the bedding. She flushed at her thoughts, at the times in the past when she all but begged Christian to bed her. He would now answer her pleas and satisfy her curiosity.

For better or worse.

At times she suspected she had experienced the worst and seen only occasional glimpses of the better. Perhaps now the state of affairs between them would change. He would treat her more as an equal, cease ordering her around, allow her more freedom.

Don't count on it!

The girl in the mirror looked so young and frightened. Her color was a trifle too pale, amber eyes a bit too wide, lips slightly parted and trembling.

She examined the ring on her finger. Topaz and emerald stars. For the first time since entering their suite at the inn, a smile eased the tight line of her mouth. 'Twas not some cheap bauble bought without a moment's thought. Notwithstanding his panicky state and hasty action, he'd not married her on the spur of the moment. The ring was fashioned especially for her.

She recalled that enchanted night in the desert when she snatched the stars from the velvety sky to the accompaniment of Christian's laughter. The first night they spent together. The first time they truly talked with civility. As she inspected the ring, she knew he remembered that night, too, and marked it as the beginning of a special bond between them.

Christian came through the doorway, crossed the room, and stopped behind her. She drank in his image in the mirror. He buried his hands in her hair and sifted his fingers through the tangle of curls. Lifting them to one side, he bent and pressed his lips to the nape of her neck, searing her skin like a brand of ownership. Samantha closed her eyes and leaned back into him.

"Nervous?" he asked quietly.

She nodded.

"Then I'm in good company."

Her eyes flew open, and she swiveled her head to gape at him. "You? Nervous?"

One corner of his mouth lifted in a half smile. "I've never married, and I've never made love to a virgin."

She returned to the mirror. "I find that difficult to swallow."

"What?"

"About . . . virgins."

"Why?"

"You are s-so knowledgeable," she stammered, her fingers fiddling with a silver-backed brush on the vanity. "You always seem to know what you're doing."

He removed the brush from her hand and swept it slowly through Samantha's tresses. Her eyelids drifted half closed at the rhythmic stroking. "I never had the desire to deflower a virgin," he replied. "That task I leave to Garrett. He has a penchant for tender, young things. In the past, I've preferred my women with more experience."

She opened her eyes and fixed them on his reflection. "And now, do you have regrets?" she asked in a small voice.

"For marrying you or for your virginal state?"

"Either. Both."

Would he repent this precipitous action? For thirty-eight years, Christian had avoided becoming too deeply involved with any one woman. Did being literally trapped aboard a ship for months on end force an intimacy he had neither sought nor required? Were he and Samantha to part at some point, would her memory fade as quickly and easily as the others? What did the little imp possess that enticed, no, compelled him into marriage, when with all the others, he'd not even come close? He could have had her anyway, without the benefit of vows.

Was he sorry? No. At this moment he could truthfully say he was not. However, he had no knowledge of the future and what it would bring. He could envision a lifetime with Samantha, a home and children. Would the newness of his current bliss last, or, like a silver tea set, would it tarnish with age?

At Christian's silence, Samantha examined his face, seeking his answer, the reassurance she required. He seemed to sense her insecurity and lowered his gaze to her. A warm smile spread across his sensual mouth.

"No, tigrina, I have no regrets."

He pulled the brush once more through her hair, from scalp to ends, and slid his hands beneath her arms to bring her to her feet and turn her toward him. His lips hovered over hers and skimmed them, tracing their outline with his tongue, dipping into the corners and parting their softness. The kiss was tender, breathtaking, and full of sweetness, flavored with champagne from the wedding dinner, sugar from their wedding cake, and his dark, underlying desire.

When his tongue moved into her mouth, she met it and followed when he retreated, probing, exploring. His arms tightened around her, molding her smaller, softer body against his larger, harder one, and he took control of the kiss. It deepened, his lips firmer and hungrier, his throbbing erection burning into her belly.

Her heartbeat escalated out of control. At that point she became aware, truly aware, of what would happen between them this night. It seemed she had sought it for an age. The notion accelerated her pulse, spread delicious sparks across her skin, and knotted her stomach.

She eased away from him and searched the expression in his eyes, encountering his dark, turbulent gaze. "Will it hurt?" she asked, her voice trembling.

"Only the first time."

She took her lower lip between her teeth, then released it and asked, "How much?"

He shook his head, smiling apologetically. "That I cannot tell you. For every woman the experience is different, or so I've heard. It depends on how thick and firmly lodged is your maidenhead."

"Will it hurt you, too?"

His brows raised a notch. "I have no reason to believe I should feel any pain."

A familiar mutiny reared its head, and she frowned. "That does not seem fair."

He grinned, clearly amused by her reasoning. "Would it salve your demand for equality were I to suffer the agonies of the damned?" When she declined to answer, he went on. "Please believe me, Sam. I've experienced my fair share of pain these past months. Wanting you and not being able to have you has caused me more misery than you can imagine. I retired to bed in wretchedness more nights than not." He twisted her around and started undoing the buttons down the back of her gown. "Now I want to look at you," he said, his voice rough-edged and husky. "I've dreamt of the day when I could feast my eyes on you with no barriers between us."

When he unbuttoned her sleeves and slipped the bodice off her shoulders, a blush flushed her skin. Unlatching her skirt, he pushed the gown to the floor. After he untied her petticoat ribbons, the garments joined her skirts. "Step out of them," he said, his words a plea more than an order, and she moved away from the pile of frothy lace and lawn, spinning around to face him.

After unlacing her chemise, he pulled it off over her head and knelt on one knee to untie her drawers and glide them slowly down her hips, leaving her clad only in white stockings, lacy garters, and white leather shoes. Sitting back on his heels, he inhaled a slow breath and made a leisurely, thorough inspection of her body. Samantha's blush turned fiery. She lifted her hands to shield her private parts from his smoldering eyes.

He brushed her hands aside. "Please, Sam, we're married. You have no need for modesty." Reaching up, he smoothed his palms down her arms and across her breasts to span her waist. He slid them over her hips and belly and the curves of her thighs and calves.

"Turn around," he said with a catch in his voice. She slowly pivoted. His fingers explored her sloping shoulders and the arch of her back. They cupped and kneaded the cheeks of her buttocks and roamed down her legs again. "Exquisite," he whispered. "You are perfection."

After bringing her around to face him, he removed her shoes, garters, and stockings. Once he came to his feet, he handed her a silk dressing gown. "Slip into this," he said, his hands shaking, "though it pales in comparison to the silkiness of your skin." While he crossed the floor to a table in a corner of the room, she draped the robe over her nudity.

He returned, holding two snifters of brandy, placed one in her trembling hand, and winked. "I know you enjoy brandy. This might calm your nerves. Both our nerves."

Samantha recalled the brandy she drank in Boston before their first meeting and smiled. Did he never forget anything? She sipped from the glass and gazed into his eyes. The green pools softened, darkened. This was the Christian she loved, the one she had seldom encountered. At last he had lowered his barriers and allowed her to see him as he truly was, as he could be. This was the man who loved her. Her nerves fluttered with expectation of what was to come. Her heart beat faster, not in fear but in anticipation.

Still holding her gaze, Christian began to remove his clothes. She followed the motion of his fingers, noting that his hands trembled as much as hers. More than anything, that tremble gave her confidence. However, when he moved to the fastenings of his breeches, she averted her face.

"No, you don't. Do not fail me now." He took her chin in gentle fingers, tugged on it until he could meet her eyes, and pointed to the bed. "I would ask that you sit there. It would please me for you to watch. It's only fair I stand for your inspection as I asked you to stand for mine."

She perched on the edge of the bed but closed her eyes. His fingers cupped her chin once again, and she lifted her lids.

"Keep your eyes open, Sam. No mysteries will lie between us. The time has come for you to learn what a man looks like. Though my shape is not as pleasing as yours, it all belongs to you."

He stepped back and pushed down his breeches and drawers in one smooth motion, as though he expected her to bolt. While he balanced on one leg, then the other, he stripped. At last he stood before her in all his nude, highly aroused glory.

Samantha's eyes stretched wider. She forgot how

to breathe. His broad chest and shoulders, covered in dark hair, were familiar. The dense mat on his chest narrowed as it moved toward his trim waist, running in a dark line down his flat abdomen and thickening again around his groin. His erect penis jutted from the curly nest, and she sucked in a choking breath at her first sight of a man's aroused phallus. 'Twas so much more than she ever imagined. A thick, long shaft bulging with veins, a rounded, purplish red tip with a cleft in the center, and . . . big, surely much too big.

"How can this possibly work?" she sputtered. "'Tis too large. I have changed my mind. I have no wish to continue with this." She gave him a pleading look and attempted a smile, but she expected it looked sickly. "You don't wish to injure me, do you?"

Christian laughed softly, though his compassionate expression revealed his empathy with her virgin fears. He stepped forward, crouched down, and took her cheeks between his hands, looking deeply into her eyes. "I would imagine it's a frightening surprise, but I give you my vow, it *will* work. Right now you find that impossible to believe. Nonetheless, our bodies are designed to fit together. I'll not hurt you any more than is necessary." He straightened his legs, moved to the bed beside her, disposed of her robe, and eased her onto her back. "Now it's time to rid you of that pesky virginity before you have more time to agonize over it."

CHAPTER TWENTY

Christian began with kisses, deep, hot, slow kisses that flowed through Samantha like liquid sunshine, his mouth sweeping over her skin. Tonguing her breasts and nipples and grazing them lightly with his teeth, he suckled rhythmically. The tugging produced that familiar pulling sensation, and moisture dampened her inner thighs.

He bent her legs at the knees, braced her feet on the bed, and spread her legs. Kneeling between them, he caressed the petals of her sex, dipped a finger inside her while his thumb strummed her spot of exquisite pleasure. Adding another finger, he stretched her, and she grunted. The fit was so tight, her passage so small, his fingers so large. Perhaps Christian was mistaken. He might *not* fit! A fishhook of tension pulled at her abdomen, and her thighs trembled, her nether mouth squeezing his fingers.

"Relax, Sam," he said. "Breathe deeply and loosen your muscles. We're doing little more than we did before. Trust me, and you'll make this easier."

She admonished her body to relax, because she did trust Christian, despite his blustering nature. Her scolding came to naught, and her muscles stiffened even more. She anticipated what would come next, and her belly quivered with strain.

He parted her folds and slipped the head of his penis inside her. She grew more rigid. Her body clenched, trying to expel his shaft. He grunted and set his jaw, positioned his fingers over her woman's center, and stroked. Gradually her muscles softened, and he eased farther inside.

"So hot," he murmured. "Like a silken oven. So hot and wet and tight." He inched inside her clinging passage, and the tendons on his neck stood out. Her delicate folds gave way, shifting to conform to his size and shape.

Stopping abruptly, he drew back. His fingers on her mound drove her higher and higher, made her hotter and hotter. The stretching fullness of his penis now added to her pleasure, and she spiraled upward. Her orgasm burst in an explosion of stars behind her eyelids. Her hips bucked, her channel gripping his shaft in convulsive waves. At the peak, she cried out his name.

With her release distracting her, Christian slipped his hands beneath her buttocks and lifted her, driving forward and breaking through her maidenhead, immersing the length of his phallus in her to the hilt.

"Ow!" she blurted, the sharpness of the sudden pain interrupting her pleasure. Needles of burning spread out through her arms and legs. She struggled to squirm out from under him. He pressed on her shoulders and held her still.

"Don't move, Sam." A strained laugh escaped him. "I beg you. Don't move. Try to remain very still. The pain will pass momentarily. I promise." He kissed her ears and eyelids and licked the tears from her cheeks. "Forgive me for hurting you. But it's the only way. I'll never have to hurt you again. Lie still and tell me when you no longer feel pain."

While he placed soft kisses across her face and breasts, tears leaked from the corners of her eyes. Their joining fell far short of the ecstasy she had dreamt about. 'Twas an invasion. Smarting pain had eclipsed the glorious delight of her climax, taking away her memory of it. Could she truly tolerate this agony time after time? Then, as he promised, the sharpness of the pain faded, leaving her with only a lingering burning and the sensation of being stretched and filled with his hardness.

She wriggled about a bit, testing the feeling. Though not unduly distressing, neither was it enjoyable. When Christian grunted, she peered up at him. His jaw clenched so tightly she feared he would break it. Veins and muscles stood out alarmingly in his face and neck. Though a smug smile threatened, she suppressed it. The poor man seemed to be in greater pain than she, but she realized the wisdom of refraining from pointing out the inaccuracy of his earlier statement.

"Sam," he said in a strangled voice when she wiggled once more, "are you still hurting?"

"Only some burning and fullness." She sent him a look of concern. "Has your pain passed?"

He seemed to choke on a laugh. "No, it hasn't. I'm going to move now. I fear I'll give you little pleasure this time. I've waited too long to be inside you and will be unable to hold back. I'll try not to hurt you again."

Her mouth drew into a frown. "Should you feel certain you are well enough to continue."

He grimaced and drew back slowly. "If I don't, I'm liable to expire." He flexed his hips and drove forward. She lay still and silent beneath him. After two more rapid thrusts, he released his semen in convulsive shudders. His hot seed gushed into her and bathed her abused tissue. With a guttural groan, he collapsed. Sweat covered him. His penis, still inside her, twitched with small aftershocks.

She had felt only mild agreeable friction when he moved, but it ended too soon to arouse her to passion after the hurt inflicted on her poor flesh. She felt cheated of something wonderful. Her only consolation was that he appeared to have recovered from his discomfort and derived no more pleasure from the act than she.

As wrung out as Monday morning laundry, Christian shifted his weight to his elbows, looked down at her, and lifted his brows.

Samantha's eyes seethed with rebellion. "I had no liking for it, and from what I could determine, neither did you. Must we do it again? I would wish to spare you any more pain."

Christian laughed, shifted onto his back beside her, and rested his hand on her damp nether curls. "You're not much of a salve to this old man's ego, my love, though I appreciate your concern for me." He turned back to her, leaned up on an elbow, and toyed with her hair spread out on the pillow. "Naught is ever easy with you, Sam," he said in a more serious tone, "and predictably, your maidenhead was as sturdy and as hard to breach as Hadrian's Wall. I'm well aware you didn't care for it. Women rarely feel pleasure the first time. I promise you, it will become better, much better, for us both. Before you know it, you'll be pleading with me to make love to you."

"If I were you, I would not place a wager on that occurring," she said with a frown.

He grinned. "Nonetheless, in answer to your question, yes, we must do it again and again and again. I don't know if I'll ever have my fill of you."

She stiffened and tried to roll away. He stretched out an arm, drew her close, and held her fast to his side, sprinkling kisses on her eyelids and the tip of her nose.

"We have no need to do it now. You're sore and require time to recover." He covered her lips in a soul-searing kiss. "Now you'll soak in a tub," he said when he raised his head, "and we shall see if we can work some of that soreness out of you."

"A hot bath?" she asked with such delight it brought laughter to his lips again.

Samantha lounged in the copper tub in bubbles up to her shoulders. Fragrant steam caressed her, and the soreness between her legs ebbed. She closed her eyes with a sigh and rested her head against the rolled edge of the tub.

All these mysterious inner workings of her body, this biology of which she had so little knowledge. It seemed that biology consisted of more than snakes, turtles, and lizards.

Why did no one explain before now what happened between men and women? When she had a daughter, she would know what to expect long before she experienced it. As usual, Christian was right; knowledge vanquished fear.

Movement drew her gaze to the far side of the room where Christian, still breathtakingly nude, lolled in a chair. His need, judging by his penis, had arisen again. Heat surged into her face, and her stomach tightened.

She licked her lips. His gaze caressed her from beneath half-closed lids. The blaze in their depths threatened to boil her bathwater.

"So soon?" she asked.

A crooked smile tugged at his mouth. "I've been ready since the moment I left you."

She ducked farther under the bubbles.

He chuckled and left the chair, his bare feet whispering on the floorboards. Picking up the soap and washcloth, he knelt behind the tub. "Move forward," he said. "I'll wash your back." The cloth painted circles across her skin. He rinsed her, then stood, lifting her by the waist to her feet and onto the hearth rug.

While water ran in silky rivulets down her body, he stripped the coverlet off the bed and laid it before the fire. He came down on his knees in front of her, held her still, and licked the water from her skin. She closed her eyes and eased back her head at the exquisite caress. "I much prefer this to what you did before," she murmured.

"Lie down," he said softly, pointing to the pallet. "On your stomach."

Once he straddled her hips and poured lotion into his hands, his fingers traveled over every inch of her skin in a gentle, soothing seduction.

"It smells heavenly," she said, her voice heavy with languor. "What is it?"

"Garrett's wedding present."

His magical fingers continued, and he slid backward, kneading her buttocks. She sighed, her knotted muscles unraveling into ropes of warm taffy.

"Part your legs," he said.

When she complied, he moved between her legs, massaged the lotion deep into her thigh and calf muscles, bent each leg at the knee, one by one, and rubbed her feet. Her nerves shimmered. She felt as if she might sink straight through the floor. When he rolled her onto her back and concentrated on her upper chest and breasts, her nipples grew stiff and distended. A shiver danced across her skin.

"I feel like a bag of bones," she said, sighing.

Christian smiled and reached for another bottle. He sat back on his heels and stroked the ointment into the folds of her womanhood. "This is different, Sam. It's made from aloe."

When his fingers stroked her and worked their way inside, she sucked in a deep breath. His touch and the soothing balm produced heat and slippery moisture. Before she could protest, he placed his mouth where his fingers had been. Flushing caused the tips of her ears to burn. She knew she would die from embarrassment, though rapture ran a close second. His tongue stroked her slickness, flickering over the pearl of flesh and delving inside her furrow. She tangled her fingers in his hair. Heat pulsed through her body, a searing volcanic heat.

She arched her hips toward him, clutching his hair tighter, and strained to catch her breath.

His mouth left her, and he shifted forward. When his shaft glided into her with little effort, she twitched a bit, but then an incredible fullness stretched her, and she melted around his length. He pulled out slowly, paused, and slid the tip of his cock, glistening with her juices, over her pleasure bud and drove back inside, filling her completely. When he did it again, she rose up to meet his downward thrust, her hips soon catching the rhythm.

"Still sore?" he asked while pulling ever so slowly to the edge.

Unable to wrap her mouth around the words, she shook her head, dug her fingers into his shoulders, and pulled him back into her cleft. She dissolved, the gliding on her flesh growing maddening, the pause before his thrust torturous. Tension coiled in her legs and belly, and she rose higher and higher on a wave of euphoria. He resisted her efforts at controlling the pace, continuing to pull out slowly, stroke the exquisite flesh of her sex, and drive back in hard. Farther and farther. She wanted him deep inside her, stretching her, touching her, and she whimpered when he slipped out.

When her limbs shook and her head thrashed from side to side, he gripped her left knee and bent the leg against her chest. Shifting again, he plunged with directed thrusts. The friction assaulted her swollen bud. The change in position initiated strong waves that undulated down her passage, clasping and unclasping his thickness, and he filled her each time to unimaginable depths.

He drove even faster. The spasms grew stronger. Her body tightened, sparks moving outward through her blood, spreading like wildfire. A burst of intense release seized her muscles. She pressed her hips against him, taking him as deeply as she could. Receding into darkness, she was barely aware when Christian reached his own orgasm, releasing an explosive breath with the strength of it and flooding her with his searing essence. His cry came as though from a distance, or was it her own?

Christian picked up a sleeping Samantha and carried her to bed. He settled on his back with her nestled against his side under his right arm, her head resting on his shoulder, hand splayed across his chest and entangled in his hair. She mumbled, snuggled closer to him, and threw one thigh across his leg. Strands of butterscotch hair drifted over his chest.

Christian folded his left arm under his head and stared up at the ceiling. Sleep was far from his mind. He already ached for her again, but considerate of her recently deflowered state, he allowed her to sleep. They had years to explore the limits of his past months' erotic dreams. He wanted her not only mentally willing but physically capable to fulfill those fantasies. Eventually he joined her in sleep.

Liquid tranquility poured through her veins. She settled into the meadow, crushing the grass beneath her. The clean scent of hot sunshine and bursting life rose to inundate her senses. His green eyes caught her gaze, holding her in thrall, and the world fell still, all sound and motion ceasing beyond this one spot in this golden meadow. Beyond the sphere of sunlight, the sky turned as black as the ocean depths, drawing a curtain of life around them, as if nothing existed outside its enveloping folds. They were the only living creatures left on Earth.

The Smilodon moved up beside her, lay down, and stretched out his front legs. His thick mane, a fusion of dark and light strands, arched upward from the nape of his neck. His canines, long and curving, gleamed in the sun. His wide mouth lifted into a knowing grin. A grin he gave to no one but her. His paws flexed and pushed against a tuft of grass. Rumbling came from deep in his throat, and he washed his legs. His pink tongue and sharp teeth moved closer with every movement.

She eased back in the grass with a sigh, and the cat became Christian. He rose and lay between her legs. His

strong hands kneaded the flesh at the juncture of her thighs.
His tongue, soft and wet, licked her legs, moved higher and
higher, closer to her core, wet with need and pulsing for
his touch. Her eyes drifted shut, and she moaned, lost in
the pressure of his touch and the wet heat of his tongue.
She soared, and as Christian had merged with the cat, she
merged with him, absorbed his strength, his fire . . .

Hands ran over her skin, pulling her closer to the
warmth beside her. Her breasts swelled, nipples tightening, callused palms caressing them. She sighed, turned
onto her side, and burrowed backward. Her buttocks
met a hard body, and she slowly awakened to pale light
sifting through the curtains. He took hold of her hips
and drew her into the cradle of his groin. His leg parted her knees; his velvet-covered penis slipped between
her legs and into her sex. With a firm grip on her hips,
he thrust strongly. She angled her bottom to take him
deeper, producing a heavy ache. When she picked up
the pace he set, his arm came around her waist. He slid
a finger into her from the front, bending it to place pressure on her responsive nub.

Her heartbeat escalated into a mad cadence, and
she catapulted into orgasm, crying out, the walls of her
passage rippling, gripping, and pulling him even farther inside. She trembled, and he withdrew and flipped
her onto her back, propping her legs over his shoulders.
While on his knees, he lifted her bottom and plunged

into her, deep enough to touch her womb. She climaxed again, calling out his name. He drove into her with fast, hard strokes that made him shatter into pieces, spilling his release deep inside her.

Christian slipped out and fell back onto the bed, panting and slick with sweat. He turned to her and grinned. "I promised myself I wouldn't touch you again until daylight. Good morning, tigrina."

"Um," she murmured, her voice husky, her body still throbbing in the afterglow of his loving. "A *very* good morning."

He rose on an elbow and stared at her with a puzzled expression.

"What?" she asked.

"I was just thinking about what you said when you came."

"I said 'Chris,' did I not?"

He shook his head.

"Then what did I say?"

"I believe you said 'Smilodon.'"

A flush roared over her skin, and she hid her face in the pillow.

CHAPTER TWENTY-ONE

Four days of bliss followed the wedding night. A red-faced maid delivered meals to the suite, carting back empty trays, and countless tubs of water were filled and emptied. The newlyweds spun a cocoon of erotic pleasure around them. Samantha soon learned lovemaking involved positions and activities she'd not believed possible, and she basked in a glow of satiation.

Even as the most ideal times come to an end, theirs came in the form of Garrett, who haunted the inn's public room for two days, debating whether to disturb the newlyweds. Finally, he had to intrude. The information he uncovered could wait no longer.

As a maid with a breakfast tray proceeded to the stairway, Garrett stopped her. "Is that for Professor Badia's room?"

She bobbed her head, tossing her curls and smiling. "I swear, I don't know what they could be doin' up there! With all the food goin' their way an' the baths, ye'd think they was feedin' an' washin' a regiment. Me legs are that sore from trampin' up an' down. An' the sounds comin' from their chamber, 'tis enough ta make me blush."

Garrett doubted that but gave her a sympathetic look. He flashed his most bewitching smile, which had melted many a Boston lass. The maid trembled and looked as if she would swoon, though she recovered her aplomb quickly enough.

"May I trouble you for a favor, Miss?"

"Sarah," she said. "O' course. I'd be thrilled ta 'elp any way I can." She batted her lashes and smiled.

"Sarah." Garrett sighed. "A lovely name for a lovely lass." He handed her a folded paper. "It's imperative Professor Badia receive this message as soon as possible. You must give it only to him, not to Mistress Badia. May I count on you to carry out that task?"

"Certainly, sir." She tucked the note into her bosom and bobbed a curtsy, giving him an unrestricted view of her cleavage. "An' should ye like another favor later, say t'night, I'd be much obliged." She trailed her fingers across his chest.

Garrett grinned. "I'm not certain I'll be free tonight, Sarah, but the first night I find myself desirous of company, I can assure you I'll come knocking on your door."

Starlight & Promises

She blushed a rosy red, turned, and started up the stairs. Stopping halfway up, she twisted toward him, saying over her shoulder with a coquettish glance, "Just be sure ye knock on number eight."

Garrett watched her sway up the treads, her gait exaggerated a bit for his benefit, and expelled a sigh. In all likelihood, he wouldn't have a free night for quite some time.

Sarah knocked and cracked open the door to the Badias' suite. Laughter issued from the bedchamber, and a woman's voice became clearly audible. "Chris, surely that is impossible. It cannot work." A male voice, the words too low to decipher, rumbled in the background. The woman spoke again. "Very well, if you are certain—" She erupted into giggles.

Sarah shook her head. *Worse than rabbits in a wee hutch.* Knocking louder, she called out, "Would ye like ta break yer fast?"

Fumbling sounds issued from the bedchamber, and Professor Badia emerged, dressed in a silk dressing gown, his feet bare, hair tousled. Though the time was close to noon, a sleepy expression covered his face. 'Twas obvious he had tumbled the missus not long ago. Sarah tsked to herself and set the tray on a table in front of the fireplace. *Rabbits!*

"Morning, Sarah," he said and yawned, stretching his arms over his head.

Professor Badia was a striking man with his tall, brawny frame, and Sarah flushed at what must lie beneath his robe. "Mornin', sir." She beckoned with a furtive gesture. "I've a message fer ye," she whispered. "T'gen'leman told me to give it only ta ye, not ta t'missus." Reaching into her bodice, she withdrew the note, handing it to him.

When Mistress Badia, wearing a night rail covered by a lacy peignoir, strolled into the room, the professor slipped the note into his robe pocket and nodded at Sarah. "I thank you," he said, smiling. "Breakfast looks sumptuous as usual. We shall have a bath in an hour."

Sarah curtsied out after retrieving the empty tray and dishes from the previous night's supper.

Samantha jumped into a chair at the table and tore into the food. "I'm starving," she said through a mouthful of biscuit topped with melting butter. She waved one at Christian. "Want some? They are heavenly." She washed down the food with a cup of chocolate.

"In a few minutes. I would rather shave first. Then I'll join you." He winked and gave her a wolfish grin. "Keep my place warm for me."

She grinned back. "I shall do that, but should you dally, I give fair warning, you will get only crumbs. You've kept me so shockingly busy, I've not had nearly enough to eat. If it weren't for the bed play, I could believe myself back in the brig."

When he returned to the bedchamber, leaving Samantha cooing and aahing over the food, he removed and opened the note from Garrett. It began with an apology: *Much as I hesitate to interrupt your honeymoon, I've come across some information we must act on immediately. Meet me in the private parlor at one, if you can tear yourself away from your lovely bride. Don't mention this to Sam. Garrett.*

Christian frowned. Garrett must have discovered news of Richard Colchester. From the note's tone, unfavorable news. He whipped up lather and shaved, then dressed and joined Samantha.

She sent him an arched-brow look, gaze running over him. "Suddenly I feel underdressed. Either that or you are overdressed." She made an airy gesture with a hand holding a biscuit. "Take off some significant item of clothing this very instant," she ordered.

He leaned over to kiss her, long and lingering, and swiped the biscuit from her fingers, taking a bite. "I have to go out for a short while," he said while pouring a cup of coffee.

"Out?"

He offered a lopsided grin and sat down to pile his

plate high with sausages, biscuits, and sirloin. "I have a need to stretch my legs, and business in town calls."

Disbelief crept over her features. "Have you not obtained sufficient exercise for ten men the past few days?"

"Spot-on, my love, but I truly must go out." His mouth curved to a rakish angle. "I daresay I'll return before you finish your bath. I may come back even sooner and join you. I have a suspicion that tub is large enough for two."

He could still make her blush, and she did so charmingly. When she looked at him again, a glint appeared in her eyes. "I suspect you're endeavoring to flee from me, Chris. Is the honeymoon over so soon?"

"Never," he avowed, catching her hand and trailing his lips up her arm in small kisses and bites. He stood abruptly and pushed the partially empty dishes off the table.

"Sweet merciful heavens," she said, her jaw dropping. "You're making a fair muddle!"

"I quite agree." Grasping her by the waist, he plucked her out of her chair and sat her bottom on the table's edge. After sliding her skirts out from under her, he pushed her back to the tabletop.

She raised herself on her elbows. "Whatever is in your head?" she asked with a saucy grin.

"Finishing breakfast." He shoved up her skirts, pushed apart her legs, which dangled off the table edge, and moved between them. While she watched him through lowered lashes, he dipped his head to lick the folds of her inner flesh. "Delicious," he murmured when she moaned and threw back her head. He unbuttoned his breeches, releasing his swollen shaft. Holding it in his fist, he slid his hand up and down its length. Beneath her gaze and his ministrations, it grew longer and thicker. Positioning the tip at the entrance to her sex, he teased her with the blunt head. She inhaled sharply, falling back against the table. Clasping her buttocks, he slid into her, inch by slow inch. She was already slippery and wet. The storm overtook her, and she dropped all mention of what they were discussing.

When Sarah knocked on the door, Samantha found herself still sprawled spread-legged on the table, too enervated to move, and Christian had departed. She struggled up, collected the plates and spilled food from the floor, and piled them back on the table. After bathing, she curled upon the bed to catch up on some much-deserved sleep. She'd not dreamt marriage could be so exhausting.

When Christian entered the private parlor, Garrett eyed him. "Are you ready to come up for air?" Garrett asked, his words blatantly teasing with a tinge of envy.

"Not hardly," Christian replied. "Not for at least another month."

"I fear I cannot grant you a month, old man. Though no doubt you need more than a month's rest at your age, merely for recovery. I would imagine Sam has given you a run for your money."

Christian grinned and headed for the coffeepot, pouring a mug of the brew. "What was important enough for you to pull me from my nuptial bed?"

Garrett settled with his own coffee into an armchair in front of the fire. Christian dropped into a chair across from him.

"I ran into an interesting character a few nights ago at the Cock and Crow," Garrett said. "He told me he once sailed on the *Manta Ray*, a pirate ship masquerading as a merchant vessel and captained by a piece of filth named Miggs. The particular fellow whom I met has a problem holding his grog, a disability you know I've never suffered from. He talks, a great deal, when he's in his cups. Last year, the *Manta Ray* engaged in a sea battle with another pirate ship, Jack Fallon's *Rapier*. According to my informant, the *Manta Ray* emerged the victor and sank the *Rapier* but not before sustaining considerable damage to the hull. During the fight, they lost valuable cargo. Miggs was fit to commit murder. Insisted the cargo was worth a king's ransom."

"Richard Colchester and James Truett?"

Garrett inclined his head. "The same."

"Are they dead, then?"

Garrett shrugged. "No one seems to know. They vanished during the fight. Miggs believes they washed out through a hole in the hull. According to my drinking companion, who gets his jollies applying the cat, they were in less than sterling condition. In fact, he swears Truett had already succumbed to the cat's persuasion. It's assumed that if either were alive at the time, they soon drowned, but no bodies were recovered."

Christian came up from the chair and paced in front of the fireplace. "If Miggs was expecting payment, it would not have been ransom. Neither man was particularly wealthy or well-known, except in the scientific community. The two scientists possessed only one treasure worth their lives, the Smilodon, which would be of no interest to an unlearned man such as Miggs. So, the question then becomes: who hired Miggs?"

Garrett's gaze tracked Christian's movements. "My companion didn't know. He knew only that the employer was a local gentleman. However, I would suspect, in his estimation, anyone with a clean cravat is a gentleman. Apparently only Miggs knows the man's name."

Christian halted and stretched an arm across the mantel. "What else did he tell you?"

"The *Manta Ray* is currently docked in Macquarie Harbor up the western coast. The spot is a known enclave for pirates. Word in town is that the military garrison pays them no heed. It's a sure bet the swinish Sergeant

Dobbins holds some responsibility for turning a blind eye and has lined his pockets for extending that favor to the pirates. Escaped prisoners established the village years ago. It quickly became a center for their activity. It's easily defensible and has a protected, deepwater harbor. To all accounts, Miggs visited Hobart lately, though I've had no success in locating him."

Garrett returned to the coffeepot and came back around to Christian, who was staring into the flames in the fireplace. "I did manage to pry from him the coordinates of the *Manta Ray*'s battle with the *Rapier*, the spot where Colchester and Truett disappeared," Garrett said. "I fear it's far from any landfall. The chance they survived is less than slim, assuming they escaped at all and were alive at the time."

Christian turned around, his mouth set in a firm line. "Don't mention this to Sam if you should happen to see her, and ready the *Maiden Anne*. We leave tomorrow morning."

Garrett lifted a brow. "What do you plan to tell her?"

"I have no idea." Christian scowled. "But she'll not go with us. I'm leaving her here with her family."

Garrett released an audible sigh. "You're not telling her at all, are you?"

Christian gave Garrett a look that answered the question without words. He would tell her naught until it was too late for her to follow him. He refused to allow their connubial bliss to disintegrate into a battle of wills, was unwilling to spoil what might be their last night together for a long time.

That night Christian made long, tender love to Samantha, clasping her to him as she shook with orgasms, crying out his name repeatedly. He couldn't bear to let her go and finally drained her with his attentions. As dawn seeped through the window, she fell into an exhausted sleep. He edged away and dressed in silence. Before departing, he bent over and touched his lips one more time to her velvety mouth, still swollen from his kisses. She smelled of lavender soap and sex. A heady combination.

"I love you, Sam," he whispered into her butterscotch curls, then departed, locking the door behind him. On his way out of the inn, he left instructions with the innkeeper along with two missives, one for Lady Delia and one for Samantha. Delia's letter also contained his will, witnessed by Garrett and the innkeeper.

When Christian boarded the *Maiden Anne*, he first inspected the supplies and munitions. He was hunting pirates this time, not cats, and had every intention of returning to his wife in one piece.

The ship hoisted anchor and sailed out of the harbor on the dawn tide, headed for the coordinates supplied by Garrett. The sails filled with a fresh wind, and Christian stood at the stern, watching Hobart recede in the distance. He lost sight of the inn, but he visualized Samantha, warm and soft, curled up on her side like a sleeping nymph in the large bed. She would think badly of him for leaving her behind. Regardless, he could not expose her to the dangers he was apt to face. The Smilodon hunt was a jaunt along Brighton Beach compared to an almost certain confrontation with pirates. At best, he would return in a few weeks, or months, with or without her uncle. At worst, she would never see him again. Would she be too irate to mourn him? He knew now that he loved her beyond reason. She had spoken words of love in the night when he held her close. Did she truly love him, or was she merely infatuated and overwhelmed by her first experience with carnal bliss?

God, he wished he could be certain of her feelings. He could have used the knowledge to carry him through this journey. After exhaling on a sigh, he drew in a lungful of sea air. The ocean rolled out before him, calm, deep, and clear. Turquoise water merged with azure sky until the horizon disappeared. Blue spread out in every direction, as though the *Maiden Anne* sailed inside a sapphire crystal bowl.

As the ship's sails strained against the wind, he tied back the hair blowing across his face, turned away from Tasmania, and made his way to the helm.

CHAPTER TWENTY-TWO

Samantha dozed, halfway between sleep and wakefulness. In spite of her fatigue, a sense of comfort and serenity covered her with a blanket of happiness and love. Thus far, marriage was not the prison she had imagined, unless she wished to consider their suite a prison. Christian had yet to chain her to the bed, and the dominance he displayed at other times was in no danger of smothering her identity. However, time would tell. True, he proposed in an unorthodox manner and uttered no words of love. Nonetheless, he showed her every day and night in his lovemaking how much he cherished her.

She stretched with a wiggle and scooted backward toward the bed's center, expecting to encounter the warmth of Christian's back, or better yet, his front, seeking his morning erection. Her breasts tingled, and she contemplated waking him in a way he especially enjoyed. Her body was already damp and eager.

She reached across the space. At the touch of cool sheets, a frown slid over her mouth. If he had arisen, why did he not rouse her? Sitting up, she looked at the mantel clock above the fireplace. Good Lord, nearly eleven! He must have gone downstairs to the common room for breakfast, allowing her to laze about in light of their strenuous night. 'Twas a considerate gesture, worthy of a loving husband.

She smiled slowly. His lovemaking had contained a fierce, almost desperate quality. Perhaps he had left to plan an outing. After cloistering themselves in the suite for four days—not that she desired to complain—an outing would be a welcome change. What she had seen of Hobart to date could fit into a thimble. Filled with energy over the prospect of some wonderful surprise, she jumped out of bed to wash at the basin.

She searched the chests, looking for items discarded for days. Christian kept her unclothed and in bed most of the time. She blushed simply thinking about it. After drawing out a butter yellow cambric dress with a matching jacket trimmed in white velvet, she slipped into it and brushed out her hair, plaiting it and coiling it at her nape. She pulled out wisps of curls and allowed them to fall about her face.

While she was at her toilette, a knock came at the door.

She grinned. 'Twas Christian, impatient for her presence downstairs. When the knock came again, her grin slipped. Why would he knock? Did he forget the key? She hurried to the door and turned the handle. 'Twas locked. "A moment," she called out and hunted for the key, first checking the mantel where Christian always left it. The key was not there. She pursed her lips. What was happening? Who would take the key? Who would lock her in the room?

Christian?

A key scraped in the lock. When the door opened, Aunt Delia and Chloe stood on the threshold. Both displayed nervous expressions.

"Aunt Delia . . . Chloe," Samantha said carefully. "How pleasant of you to visit. I'm not certain where Chris has gone, but surely he will return soon." She motioned for them to enter, waved them to chairs before the fire, and rang for tea and scones.

Worry lined Aunt Delia's forehead; her smile seemed forced. "Samantha, darling. You look wonderful. Marriage must agree with you." She twisted a handkerchief as though she would tear it into pieces.

Samantha declined to answer. Instead, she gave Chloe a sharp look.

With a stricken expression, Chloe lowered her eyes.

Sickly cold seeped into Samantha's stomach. Her heart pounded in her ears. "Something has happened to Chris." She turned back to Delia. "Tell me. Where is he? Is he hurt? I must go to him."

Delia patted Samantha's arm with a gloved hand. "No, my dear. Christian is quite well."

Samantha panted, not quite able to catch her breath. "Then why are you here? And where is he?"

Delia drew back her shoulders, pushing out her bosom. At the familiar gesture, Samantha's heart dropped to her knees. "Now, Samantha, brace yourself. I have no wish for you to become hysterical. You are a married woman. I expect you to accept what I have to say in a mature manner. You will be moving in with us while Christian tends to important business."

He left? Without her? No wonder he lulled her so sweetly the previous night. He planned all along to leave her behind. "The hell I will!" Samantha sprang from her chair and clenched her hands until the remnants of ragged nails dug into her palms. "Where is the bastard? I shall kill him!"

"You have no need to use profanity." Deep grooves appeared beside Delia's mouth. "This is a serious matter. Christian received information regarding Richard and departed to investigate its accuracy. He felt it best you remain behind with us, because the situation is not without danger."

"Bollocks!" Samantha sputtered. "He crept out like a thief in the night, not even bidding me good-bye or giving me the opportunity to decide my own course of action. I shall never forgive him for this! I shall divorce him! I'll not have a lying sneak for a husband!" The bolt of pain that shot through her heart weakened her knees and brought tears to her eyes.

Delia rose gracefully and curved an arm around Samantha's shoulders. She squeezed gently and held out a handkerchief she drew from her sleeve. "Now, now. Remember that words said in anger can seldom be taken back. The situation is less dreadful than it appears on the surface. Christian left a letter for you, explaining his actions." She pulled a sheet of paper from her reticule and placed it in Samantha's hands.

Samantha didn't even glance at the missive. She crumpled it and tossed it to the floor. "I have no desire to read his *explanation*, which is naught more than an excuse. He took what he wanted and then scurried off, like a hound with its tail between its legs. I should have had more sense than to trust him."

From remaining silent with a hapless look on her face, Chloe now reached down and picked up the letter. After smoothing out the creases, she offered it to Samantha. "I beg you, read what he has to say. If you know only part of the story, how can you make an informed decision?"

Chloe acting calm and sensible? Struck mute, Samantha stared at her cousin as if she were a circus oddity. But then Chloe's husband did not just desert her. Samantha accepted the letter with reluctance as Sarah brought tea and scones into the room on a tray and set it on a table. Samantha sent the maid a glare, as though she were a coconspirator. Judging from the locked room, the inn's entire management had participated in the deed. Sarah averted her eyes. Her face reddened. She bobbed a clumsy curtsy and darted out the door.

Samantha pulled herself together, breathing deeply to calm her throbbing head and churning stomach. After pouring the tea, she settled stiffly into a chair and opened Christian's letter. Her eyes swimming with tears, she could scarcely read his sprawling script.

My dearest Sam,

I'm well aware of how you feel at this moment. For that I apologize. I cannot, however, apologize for what I've done, only for the way I left you with no proper good-bye. I would have explained everything to you last night, but I'm a selfish son of a bitch. I didn't want to spoil what might have been our last night together for some time. I know you may not forgive me for this, but in light of the information I seek, it's a chance I was compelled to take. I'll carry the memory of our last night together in my heart for however long it takes me to return.

Garrett uncovered news of Richard and James. I must tell you the news is not encouraging. But do not lose all hope. Miggs, a pirate captain, abducted them and carried them out to sea on his ship, the Manta Ray. An unknown gentleman paid for their abduction, presumably to learn the location of the Smilodon. A battle ensued at sea, and the captives disappeared during the conflict. It's unknown whether they escaped or died, though no bodies were found. Garrett was able to learn the location of the battle as well as the current position of the Manta Ray.

When you engaged my services, you charged me with two tasks: to find your uncle and to track down the Smilodon. I'm now undertaking the first duty. I intend either to find Richard or bring back certain proof of his death. I trust you understand why I couldn't allow you to accompany me on such a dangerous mission. Knowing you well, you're fuming by now, and this letter will end up in the fire. Before you destroy it, pay heed to the rest of my words.

You are to move in with Lady Delia and Chloe. Pettibone has agreed to remain behind to protect you, as have Cullen and Jasper. Above all else, remember that someone, possibly even now in Hobart, is willing to kill to find the Smilodon. He paid to have your uncle taken. He'll not hesitate to come after you next if he no longer has Richard.

You will go nowhere without Jasper as an escort. You'll not pursue this on your own and will not attempt to follow me. This is not a request, Sam. I am your husband, and as such, I'm instructing you to follow my orders. Should Lady Delia and the others deem the situation too serious, you will return to England with them. I shall join you there when I complete my mission.

You must remain safe. Trust no one with whom you are not already acquainted. This mystery man is treacherous in the extreme. Your life means nothing to him. If my words don't convince you, perhaps this will. You could already be carrying our child and have a responsibility beyond that of your own safety. Should I fail to return within six months, Lady Delia has instructions regarding my finances and your welfare. But I plan to return, and when I do, we'll seek the Smilodon together.

I'll miss you and think of you every day, tigrina. You've changed my life in ways I cannot describe. I can tell you that I love you madly, insanely and always will.

Chris

By the time Samantha finished the letter, tears poured down her face. True to Christian's prediction, she wadded it up and threw it into the fire, but first she tore off the last few lines, the part where he declared his love. Folding the strip of paper, she stuffed it into her bodice next to her heart.

Samantha moved into Talmadge House with Aunt Delia and Chloe that very day. She presented no arguments and declined to discuss her circumstances. In fact, her face and manner reflected a composed mien. Too composed to Delia's mind. Samantha was up to mischief. She understood her niece better than anyone. Since Samantha's last display of temper, when she burned Christian's letter, she had become a docile wife. However, Samantha had never been docile. Delia closeted herself with Pettibone, Cullen, and Jasper.

"I suspect Samantha is planning some foolishness," Delia told them. "You must give me your word that you will watch her at all times and guarantee she undertakes no rash actions."

Meanwhile, Samantha's mind raced. Beneath her calm exterior, she plotted. She recovered from her initial anger at Christian, the main part of it, though she would still make him pay when he returned. Once again, he had questioned her competence, treated her as if she were incapable of making her own decisions. Perhaps if he had explained the situation to her. But no, he had decided for her. It was not to be borne.

Christian had unwittingly provided her with clues, clues she could investigate. Were she to identify the mystery man who kidnapped Richard, perhaps she could find her uncle and save them all a great deal of time and misery. Sitting about idly and waiting for Christian to return with word of Richard was not an option.

She mulled over what she knew and took out a leaf of paper to make notes, listing what she recalled from Christian's letter while ruing her hasty act in destroying it.

First, the man sought the Smilodon. That, in itself, was a valuable hint. Only a scientist or an equally educated man would understand the significance of the discovery.

Second, he was privy to information only she, Richard, and James knew. She added Christian, Garrett, and the ship's crew to her inventory of knowledgeable people as well as the scientists she had originally contacted at the academy. However, Richard's abduction was a fait accompli by the time the others on her list learned of the Smilodon's existence. Therefore, either Richard or James told the man of their find, or he learned through some nefarious means before Richard contacted her.

Third, he was someone Richard knew, someone he trusted, or the man knew of her uncle's fame but was not of the earl's social circle.

Fourth, he was present in Hobart at the time of the discovery a year ago, and according to Christian, he might still be here.

Fifth, a pirate captain named Miggs had snatched Richard and James. The ship he commanded was the *Manta Ray*.

If she was able to track down Miggs or one of his fellow pirates, she might discover the name of their employer. That person would know where Richard and James were being held, for her heart told her that the two were still alive.

When she gleaned as much as she could from her memory, she planned her next move, taking into account her appointed watchdogs, Jasper, Pettibone, and Cullen, who dogged her heels. She could scarcely inhale a breath without brushing up against one of them or take a step without treading on their feet.

Once again, the Blue Boar Inn seemed the most promising place to begin her investigation. Dare she dress as a boy, assuming she could shake her shadows? She shuddered when she recalled her last excursion into that filthy den and the degrading experience in the garrison gaol.

Then again, Sergeant Dobbins might know of Miggs and his ship. Contemplating another encounter with the unsavory sergeant brought her dinner up into her throat. She *must* find another way. Sergeant Swine had to be her last resort.

"I have naught to wear," Samantha said. "All my frocks are too heavy for this climate. I'm a married woman now, and my gowns make me look like a school-room miss. Since Christian insisted I remain in Hobart, I may as well spend his money. 'Tis the least he deserves."

Delia looked up from her sewing, eyes narrowing at Samantha's sudden and uncharacteristic interest in clothes and fashion.

Samantha turned guileless eyes on her aunt. "Have you found a decent modiste in Hobart? I vow I feel as dowdy as a governess."

Delia's suspicions waned. Samantha had cooperated admirably the past few days. This was her first mention of Christian and his absence. The desire for a new wardrobe could be an encouraging sign that she had accepted her husband's decision and would follow his orders with good cheer.

"Certainly, dear." Delia smiled. "Madame Louella provides gowns for all the ladies in Hobart. With so few real ladies in residence, she has a smaller number of quality clients than she would like. I heard she is even contemplating returning to England for lack of business. I'm certain she would be thrilled to whip up a few frocks for you. Shall I make an appointment for her to come here?"

"Oh no. I would rather go to her shop. I could not expect her to fetch bolts of fabric and heavy pattern books all the way out here. And I would enjoy the outing."

"Be certain to take Jasper with you."

"As if I could shake him off my tail," Samantha mumbled.

"Did you say something, dear?"

Samantha smiled. "I shall visit Madame Louella tomorrow without fail."

That night as Samantha lay in her cold, lonely bed, she longed for the feel of Christian's arms around her, his warmth against her, his hard length inside her. She released a breath and twisted the bedsheets into a jumble as she had done every night since he had left. Heat surged beneath her skin, ignited in her veins, and Christian was not here to put out the fire.

She closed her eyes. As happened so often, her thoughts turned to the Smilodon, and the Smilodon morphed into Christian. His suntanned hands kneading her mound, his tongue slipping across her sex. With his forest green eyes holding hers captive, she arched off the bed and climaxed, bursting through the barrier in a cataclysm of ecstasy. She fell slowly to Earth and opened her eyes, her hand tangled in her pubic hair, her fingers sticky with her dew. She blushed and rolled onto her side. She had pleasured herself exactly as Christian had taught her one long-ago evening under the desert stars on a South Sea island. She sighed. To be perfectly truthful, self-gratification was better than naught, and she finally fell asleep.

The following morning, Samantha dressed for her visit to the modiste. Excitement and an element of danger tumbled through her in irrepressible waves, making it all but impossible to maintain her poise in front of the others. Nonetheless, she managed to rein in her emotions. If she should fail to escape Jasper, he would never give her another opportunity. She would become a prisoner in Talmadge House.

Madame Louella was a woman structured from iron, but perhaps 'twas the whalebone corset that made her frame so erect and unbending. Dark auburn hair pulled back into a bun at her nape allowed no hair to escape. From her impeccable dress, not a wrinkle or a line out of place, and long, thin face with a fashionably pale complexion, to the toes of her glossy shoes, she presented an inflexible picture.

Despite her outward appearance, she greeted Samantha with a welcoming smile, revealing a warm nature beneath the stern exterior. "I shall find it a delight to dress you, Mistress Badia," she said in dulcet tones as she examined Samantha's small figure with a critical eye. "You have an exquisite frame and such unusual coloring."

When Jasper strolled into the shop, Madame Louella looked askance.

"My bodyguard," Samantha explained with an apologetic smile.

Jasper grinned, teeth white in his ebony face.

Louella placed a shaky hand to her breast and drew a quavering breath. "Perhaps Mister—"

"Jasper," Samantha said.

"Perhaps Mister Jasper would be more comfortable waiting outside. This is bound to be a lengthy session. I'm certain he will become bored."

"Madame Louella is quite right, Jasper. You would be bored silly. You may take the carriage back and return for me in, say, three hours?" She looked at Louella for confirmation and received an affirmative nod.

"I shall wait outside in the carriage, Mistress Badia," he said. "I'm not supposed to leave you alone."

Samantha frowned. "I'll not be alone. Madame Louella is here, as are her seamstresses. I'm in capable hands. I feel assured Mister Badia would not insist you be present when I'm in a safe place."

"I'll wait outside," he said firmly.

Samantha wanted to tear out her hair. He was going to be harder to pacify than she had hoped. She stopped short of making a fuss that would rouse his suspicions. "Certainly, Jasper. Wait in the carriage if you wish." Her smile was thin. "Perhaps next time you should bring along a book to pass the time."

His grin penetrated her pique. "Perhaps I shall."

He whirled on his heel, left the shop, and climbed into the carriage Pettibone drove. *Two* watchdogs she was obliged to dodge.

With a conspiratorial look, Samantha turned to Louella, who had closely watched the exchange. "Servants," Samantha said. "'Tis so exceedingly difficult to engage good help."

Madame Louella quickly recovered from the encounter with Jasper and ushered Samantha into the salon for measuring. Once the modiste had completed her task, Samantha and Madame Louella discussed designs and viewed fabrics. Samantha lingered over the details, spending nearly four hours in the shop. When she finally emerged and Jasper helped her into the carriage, he wore a bored, impatient look. By the third visit, he would be asleep on his feet, as Pettibone was already on the driver's perch, and she could slip out. No one would miss her for hours.

Chapter Twenty-Three

Samantha entered the modiste's shop the following week for the first fittings. With tears conjured up with pepper grains, she related the tale she had fabricated for Madame Louella. "I married only recently against my family's wishes. My husband is an untitled American and"—sniff, sniff—"my father has threatened to disown me."

Madame Louella looked suitably sympathetic.

"My only contact with my family is my brother, Arnold," Samantha continued, "but my husband, outraged by my family's position, refused me permission to meet with him. My husband can be so stubborn, such a tyrant. He has me watched day and night to prevent my arranging a meeting."

"Mister Jasper," Louella said with an empathetic nod.

"Yes." Samantha's smile wobbled. "I must see my

brother again. It may be the only time we shall have this opportunity. Arnold followed me here, all the way from England, on the chance of just such a possibility. He loves me that much." She drew a trembling breath. "I need your help."

"I sympathize with you, Mistress Badia, but how can I possibly help? Were your husband to discover I aided you, he would ruin what little business I now have."

Samantha waved away the woman's objection. "You see, my husband is away for a few weeks. If he were in town, I should never attempt this. He will never know. I need merely a few hours without my bodyguard following me. During the final fittings next week, I could duck out the back door, meet my brother, and return before Jasper discovers I'm gone."

If Louella harbored suspicions, she hid them well. After being fed a story as thin as turtle soup, the woman probably believed Samantha had an assignation with a lover. Samantha shrugged. 'Twas none of Louella's business, unless Jasper uncovered her absence. But she had laid her plans carefully. So long as she kept her excursion within the allotted time, she could carry it off.

"In that event, I would be pleased to help you," Louella said. "I find it so disconcerting when families cannot get along. However, you must promise you will return before your Mister Jasper comes looking for you. I'm not averse to admitting he frightens me."

Samantha clasped Louella's hands in hers. "Oh, I shall. Thank you so awfully much. You have no idea what this means to me."

This time, Samantha kept Jasper waiting almost five hours.

When the day of the final fittings arrived, Samantha's nerves twitched as violently as a mouse deer's held in the stare of a hungry python. She bit her fingernails with abandon, drawing censorious looks from Delia and a spate of tsking from Chloe. Though the day was warm, indeed sultry, she swept up a hooded cloak and draped it over her arm while Pettibone pulled the carriage in front.

"Will you not be overwarm in that, dear?" Delia asked, pointing to the cloak.

Samantha managed a laugh. "Oh, I have no intention of wearing it. I'm taking it along to see how it fits over my new gowns. Should it not look quite right, I shall be obliged to have another made. When Christian sees the bills I run up, he will regret his decision to leave me moldering in Hobart."

By the time Jasper handed her into the carriage, Samantha's limbs trembled. Reservations wreaked havoc on her confidence. Did she truly believe she could succeed in this mad plan? Was Delia suspicious? Was Jasper onto her? Would Madame Louella remain silent and cover for her? So many factors to consider. Regardless, she had committed herself and refused to turn back.

She sat in the carriage across from Jasper and forced an air of gaiety, gripping the folds of her skirt so tightly her fingers cramped. A tension headache gathered at the back of her head, and her stomach roiled.

You'll escape easily. You'll escape easily, she chanted silently.

Madame Louella greeted Samantha with her customary warmth. When Jasper retired to the carriage with his well-thumbed copy of Omar Khayyám's *Rubái-yát*, Louella escorted Samantha toward the fitting room. They passed it and threaded their way through sewing rooms to a door leading into an alley. Samantha threw her cloak over her shoulders and pulled up the hood.

"I shall return in three hours," she said. "Should Jasper come looking for me before then, tell him I'm in dishabille and unable to see him until we have finished."

Louella's thin lips pinched together even tighter.

Samantha smiled and squeezed the woman's hand. "You have no cause for worry. He'll not come for me early. I informed him that today's session would be longer than usual. He will wait patiently until I finish. He has no reason to suspect anything untoward."

A snappy breeze laden with the strong aromas of seaweed, fish, and sewage blew in from the sea and made the temperature at the docks cooler than in town. Samantha thanked God for that small respite. After her frantic flight from the shop to the quay, perspiration dripped from her temples and slid down her cheeks. She flipped back the cloak's hood and let it fall to her shoulders. She had braided and coiled her hair to avoid looking like a tavern wench and attracting unwanted attention. Gulls wheeled overhead, their raucous cries competing with the shouts and curses from the dockworkers, whose bare backs gleamed with sweat as they hefted heavy loads on their shoulders and tramped up and down the narrow gangplanks.

Teeth worrying the inside of her cheek, Samantha searched for someone she could approach for information regarding Miggs and the *Manta Ray*. Someone other than the rough lot of half-naked laborers. When she contemplated striking up a conversation with one of them, her courage deserted her. From the glances they sent her way, she feared being dragged into an alley and ravished to within an inch of her life.

As she strolled along and inspected the men for a respectable person, a ship's officer perhaps, someone tapped her on the shoulder. Whipping around, she released a startled breath. 'Twas the man with sandy hair and beard and hazel eyes who had sheltered her during the fight at the Blue Boar Inn. He wore well-tailored clothes today, a gentleman's outfit, with dark brown trousers, a white linen shirt, a flawless cravat, and a bottle green coat.

Bemusement beetled his brows. "Sam?" he said.

"Sam Colchester?"

She smiled. "How did you know?"

He tilted back his head and laughed, a hearty, melodious sound. "Well, Sam, you make an unconvincing boy up close, and I would recognize your golden eyes anywhere."

His warm manner contained no hint of unseemliness. When he held out his elbow, she automatically hooked her hand in it. "Shall we take a cup of tea," he asked, "while you tell me what is certain to be an interesting story?" He glanced around, concern etching his face. "This area is unsafe for ladies, you know."

Before she could object, he led her away from the docks. "I know a respectable tea shop," he said, "where we can converse in private. However, first we should observe the amenities and properly introduce ourselves." Pausing his step, he bowed and doffed his beaver hat. "Steven Landry, merchant, exporter and importer."

"Mistress Samantha Badia," she replied in turn.

His eyelids lowered a bit, and he resumed walking. "I thought you said your name was Colchester."

"I married recently. Colchester is my maiden name."

"I see. You're a newlywed, then."

"Yes," she said softly. An *abandoned* newlywed. "I fear I told a small lie the night we met. Richard Colchester is my uncle, not my father."

"Ah, at last the truth comes out." He smiled. "But what are you doing at the docks? Where is the husband?"

She pursed her lips. "He shipped out for a few weeks on business."

Steven's uncanny ability to put her at ease allayed Samantha's nervousness. Soon they addressed each other by Christian names and took tea and biscuits like old friends. Samantha explained away her disguise the last time they met as resulting from a lovers' spat. She made no mention of what happened after she left the tavern.

"Samantha," Steven said, "I told you I once knew your uncle. As boys we were close friends. We even attended Oxford together. Of course, not being a peer, I was there on scholarship and pursued commerce while Richard studied his plants. Is that why Richard traveled to Tasmania? Was he on a plant expedition?"

Samantha nodded, not elaborating.

"I wish I'd been able to renew our acquaintance while he was in the vicinity, catch up on old times, you know. Unfortunately, I sailed to Australia on business at the time and learned of his visit only after I returned."

Could she take Steven into her confidence? He had established himself in Hobart as a respectable merchant and might be able to help her. She hesitated, recalling Christian's warning. Then she dismissed her concern. Steven had no resemblance to the kidnapper's profile she had so carefully developed. He was a merchant rather than a scientist. Though acquainted with Richard, they'd not seen each other for years. With the man's gentle manner, he deviated too greatly from her conception of an amoral character.

When a clock chimed at the back of the restaurant, her stomach flipped like a netted fish. Surging to her feet, she made her apologies and stammered out words about a previous appointment.

Steven rose from his chair, paid their bill, and led her to the door. "May I escort you somewhere?" he asked.

"That will not be necessary. I have only a short way to go, merely a few blocks. I thank you for the tea and conversation. I truly enjoyed speaking with one of Richard's friends."

He lifted her hand and patted it in a paternal manner. "Then may I call on you at your residence? Though Hobart has become crowded, there are few one can call friends. I would find it refreshing to have a friend in town who reminds me of home. And I suspect you would welcome an escort while your husband is away."

Samantha smiled warmly. "Certainly, I should be pleased to see you again. I'm certain Aunt Delia, Richard's sister, would embrace your company." After giving him her direction, she sped off with a little wave over her shoulder.

Clothing clammy with perspiration, hair tumbling around her shoulders, Samantha practically fell through the back door into the shop as her three hours expired. Madame Louella stood with her mouth agape, and Samantha rushed past her to peek out the window. Jasper paced in front of the carriage.

"Any problems?" Samantha asked, gasping to catch her breath.

The modiste shook her head. "You look a fright. I cannot send you out so disheveled. You will have to sponge off, fix your hair, and wear one of the new gowns."

Samantha hurried to the fitting room, stripped, and mopped away the perspiration. Foregoing a corset, she struggled into the new dress in record time. When she left the shop a few minutes later, she was smiling and chatting with Madame Louella. Every hair was in place. Except for the hectic flush on her face, she looked normal, even to Jasper's discerning eye.

"I shall have everything ready tomorrow and delivered by afternoon," Madame Louella said.

Behind Samantha, Jasper expelled a heavy breath.

"Wonderful, madame," Samantha said. "Your creations are just the thing. I'm certain I shall return for my winter wardrobe."

Samantha preceded Jasper into the carriage and smiled inwardly for outwitting him so easily. She took delight in boring him further by running on about lace ribbons and trim and the advantages of cotton and linen versus brocade and silk taffeta the entire way to Talmadge House. By the time they arrived, his eyes had nearly rolled back into his head.

When Steven called at Talmadge House two days later, Delia was expecting him. Earlier, Samantha explained that Mister Landry was a friend and schoolmate of Richard's whom she met at Madame Louella's. Appalled that her niece should speak to a strange man without an introduction, Delia read her a lecture on wifely duty and proper etiquette until Samantha convinced her naught was improper in Landry's interest.

Delia tapped a finger against the dimple in her plump chin. "Landry? I have no recollection of a Landry, but then Richard and I were not as close once he left for Oxford, so I knew few of his school friends. I must admit my memory is less sharp than it used to be. What is Mister Landry's Christian name?"

"Steven. He is a merchant."

"I recall just one Steven. Of course, I was younger and had my own circle of friends, so I saw him only once or twice. I cannot even bring to mind his appearance. I do recall he was a scientist, like Richard, and the eldest son of the Marquis of Lansdowne. His family estate adjoined ours when we were children. However, his family name was Burdett or Burnett, I believe. Certainly not Landry. Details become so foggy when you reach my age. I do remember some awful scandal ensuing when his father disinherited him and pensioned him off to America. My parents never discussed the details in my presence, of course, but servants gossip, and children listen. Shortly thereafter, some dastardly housebreaker murdered the marquis. The papers laid the motive to robbery. Can you imagine?" She paused and fanned herself with a handkerchief she drew from her sleeve. "What can the world be coming to when even peers are at risk in their own homes? I believe the younger son took up the title after his father died. No one ever heard from Steven again. I imagine he is still living in America."

"This man could not be the same Steven. Mister Landry attended Oxford on scholarship and owns an importing and exporting business. He told me he has never even visited America. You will take a liking to him. He is quite gentlemanly—harmless, quiet, and unassuming."

"I'm certain I shall, dear. Nevertheless, bear in mind what Christian told you. You are to go nowhere unescorted, even with a harmless man." Delia bustled off to her sewing.

Samantha glowered at Delia's back. Christian's orders still had her on a leash. However, if she and Steven were to ride in a closed carriage with Jasper outside on the driver's perch, they could talk privately. After much reflection, she decided to trust Steven. With his shipping connections, he could research information on the *Manta Ray*.

When Steven arrived, the butler answered the door, and he chafed at the servant's inspection as he took his hat and swept a disdainful gaze over his attire. Seemingly satisfied Steven was suitably dressed for calling and respectably sober, the staid man led him to the drawing room and announced him in a nasal voice.

"We shall take tea, Pettibone," Lady Delia said from her position on the couch. She stretched out her arm.

Steven bowed, pressing her hand.

Delia simpered. "Mister Landry, would you care for something stronger than tea? Brandy or sherry, perhaps?"

He allowed his mouth to form his most polite smile. "Tea will be fine, Lady Delia. I'm not a drinking man." He greeted Samantha, careful to address her as Mistress Badia in her aunt's presence, and bent over her extended hand in the same graceful gesture. He grew hard as a pike inside his trousers and went through hell to suppress his reaction. A shame she had married. His revenge would have been sweeter had she remained a virgin.

"I understand you export and import, Mister Landry," Delia said after Steven settled into a chair, crossing his legs and making himself comfortable. "What sorts of goods do you trade?"

"Many items, Lady Delia. You may not be aware that Tasmania is the center for trade with the Far East. Through my contacts in Asia, I import jade and other jewels, spices, and silk, then sell them to merchants in London, Paris, and Milan. I operate a fleet of ships for importation to Tasmania and export my acquisitions on vessels operated by other firms."

"My, my, should you not mind me being blunt, your business sounds highly lucrative and adventuresome." Delia poured the tea Pettibone provided and handed a cup to Steven. "It must occupy a great deal of your time. Do you often travel on your own ships to such exotic locales?"

Smiling, he shook his head. "I used to enjoy the adventure of voyaging. As I grow more mature, I find the comforts of home suit my bones better than a swaying deck in a high sea. My most recent trip was to Australia last year."

"I suppose your wife is content now that you are at home."

He grinned. "Lady Delia, I fear I'm unwed. My business, with its frequent absences, left little time for a wife and family."

Delia's eyes sparkled. "Oh, my," she said on a breath.

The visit ended after two hours, during which Samantha said little. Steven asked whether he could call again in a few days and take the two women for a carriage ride around Hobart. Delia accepted with enthusiasm, while Samantha gave Steven a strained smile. He responded with a conspiratorial look and took his leave, confident he had managed to charm both Samantha and her aunt, drawing himself closer to his goal.

Chapter Twenty-Four

Steven, Delia, and Samantha took carriage rides, picnicked along the Derwent, and attended socials at the settlers' homes. Samantha found no opportunity to question Steven alone, and as the days raced by, her desperation rose.

Chloe, who had fallen into a short-lived depression over Garrett's departure, soon had a veritable regiment of young military officers knocking on the door of Talmadge House. Few eligible young women of good family and reputation resided in Hobart, even fewer as well-favored as Chloe. She preened under the attention, flirting and toying unmercifully with the callers. Hardly a day passed when Samantha had no reason to push her way through the crush of Chloe's suitors in the drawing room.

When Gilly had other duties, the responsibility for

chaperoning Chloe fell to Aunt Delia. 'Twas not long before the afternoon arrived when Steven showed up for a carriage ride and Delia and Chloe found themselves swamped with eager swains.

Delia wrung her hands. "I dare not leave Chloe unchaperoned. Gilly has taken herself off to bed with the sniffles. Though I know 'tis not entirely proper, I must allow you to go along without me. After all, Samantha is married now and has no real need for a *dueña*."

Steven offered his condolences for Gilly's condition, features expressing his disappointment at missing Delia's scintillating company. "Perhaps we should reschedule," he suggested.

"No," Samantha blurted, drawing a puzzled look from Delia. "I-I mean, that is hardly necessary. Steven is already here, and you are overwhelmed with Chloe's beaus, Aunt Delia. I was looking forward to an invigorating ride."

Delia looked frazzled but smiled nonetheless. "Samantha is quite right, Steven. Why should we confine her to the house simply because I have other commitments? You two run along and enjoy yourselves."

Goose bumps rippled along Samantha's arms. At last she would have the opportunity to confer alone with Steven. Four weeks had passed since Christian's sailing with no word of his whereabouts or when he would return. Samantha burned to pursue Miggs and the *Manta Ray*. The colder the trail became, the more difficultly she would have in finding him.

When Steven handed Samantha into the carriage and followed her, sinking into the facing seat, Jasper loomed in the doorway, clearly intent on joining them. Samantha sent him a thunderous look. He scowled, closed the door, and climbed up on top with Pettibone.

Alone at last was the foremost thought on Samantha's mind; however, Steven had retreated to the past.

_* *Lansdowne, England*
1872

As was his habit, the marquis dismissed the servants for the night. He allowed no witnesses, no interference in the ritual chastisement of his son. 'Twas not the first time they had played out the dance this way.

The old man sat behind his desk, his white, winglike brows crouching over censorious hazel eyes, brittle with anger and disappointment. He showed no inclination to extend an invitation to sit, and Steven braced himself, legs apart and hands clasped behind his back. Though he was now nineteen, on uncounted occasions since the age of ten, he had stood exactly this way, in this same room, while facing his father's wrath.

Edward Burnett, 7th Marquis of Lansdowne, got

to his feet. "Steven, I am forced to a difficult decision. You've allowed your indiscretion to taint the family name. I find I cannot tolerate or forgive this outrage. We've held the Royal esteem for six hundred years, fought honorably in England's wars, and imparted favors to kings and queens. Before your precipitate action, no scandal dared touch our name, nor will it ever again."

Steven set his jaw and flattened his mouth. His fingers wove tighter together, every muscle growing tense. "What are your intentions?" he asked, vocal cords as taut as cello strings.

Lansdowne walked to the walnut sideboard, where he poured a glass of brandy and motioned with the decanter.

Steven stiffly declined with a shake of his head.

"I have decided," Lansdowne said with clear remorse, an emotion he seldom expressed, "that your brother, John, will succeed me."

Steven erupted, hands fisting at his sides. "You cannot mean that! The title rightfully belongs to me. Is it not entailed?"

A door of dispassion closed across his father's face. "Indeed, I can and already have. Her Majesty and the House of Lords agreed to approve the change, precipitated, I daresay, by your dishonest actions."

"And what in bloody hell do you expect of me?" Steven shouted.

"I *expect* you to leave England—forever. You inherited

funds from your mother. In addition, I'll add a yearly remittance that will ensure you live comfortably."

"You must be mad!"

His father sighed. "Steven, a young man such as you, intelligent and with a talent for scientific inquiry, should have no difficulties coping. I see no reason why you should not live a productive life in a place such as America. The Americans tend to be more forgiving of scandal than your peers. You will have the opportunity to make a fresh start."

"I'll not go."

Lansdowne picked up the brandy glass and gave his back to Steven. "Martin packed your baggage and booked your passage on a ship leaving England tomorrow morning for Boston. Be on it."

Tears stung Steven's eyes. He strode sharply from one side of the room to the other, halted, and turned to his father. "Can I say naught to change your mind?"

"You cannot."

"So be it," Steven said bitterly. His father's antique dueling pistol lay on a bookshelf at his right elbow. As though in a dream, he picked it up, pointed it, and fired.

Who knew the old fool had kept it loaded all these years?

Richard Colchester!

The name stabbed like a saber thrust. If not for Richard Colchester, Steven would have covered every contingency, destroyed the evidence, ensured his colleagues' silence, and weathered the storm with a dig-nified air and affronted attitude, as befitted a peer of the realm. It didn't have to come to this . . . this travesty.

Were it not for his father's cooling corpse, he would be tempted to believe it didn't truly happen.

With limited time in private, Samantha could hold her silence no longer. "Have you heard of a ship named the *Manta Ray*?" she asked.

Steven visibly started and averted his face, taking an audible breath. "Where did you hear that name?"

She looked down at her knotted hands. "I've heard gossip. The *Manta Ray* is a merchant ship. Since you have a shipping firm, I imagined you might have knowl-edge of it." She lifted her gaze to his face. "Have you?"

He returned her look with an unreadable expression. "Indeed, I know of the *Manta Ray*. However, I conduct no business with its captain. The information you have is incorrect. The *Manta Ray* is no merchant but a pirate ship."

He knew the ship! A shiver raced across her skin. "My word! I was unaware of the ship's connection with pirates. Are you then acquainted with its captain, a Mister Miggs?"

"Unfortunately," he said slowly. "We have crossed paths a few times, though I would hesitate to count him among my acquaintances. He has a reputation as a dangerous, vicious man." His eyes narrowed. "Why do you ask about Miggs and the *Manta Ray*?"

She expelled a mental breath. Now or never. She must either trust Steven or drop the subject entirely. "I understand Mister Miggs may have abducted my uncle and his friend James Truett."

Steven looked shocked. "My dear, you cannot be serious. Miggs is certainly capable of abduction, but he does naught without profit. Why would he take Richard?"

In for a penny, in for a pound. "Some despicable character paid him. I've no notion of whom. But I must discover the identity of Mister Miggs's partner and whether Richard is still alive."

Steven took her small, cold hands in his large, warm ones. "Samantha, Miggs is a monster. You dare not involve yourself in his business, even if it concerns Richard. Your husband may not be present to prevent you from taking foolish risks, but as your friend, I feel a responsibility to guard your safety. I could not possibly allow you to pursue this pirate."

"I have no other leads, Steven. Will you help me? You can ask questions where I cannot." Tears welled in her eyes. "I beg you, as Richard's friend and mine, help me. I need only to know whether Richard still lives and, if he does, where I might find Mister Miggs and the *Manta Ray*."

He released her hands and combed his fingers through his beard. "You ask the impossible. I applaud your motives. Nonetheless, you cannot embroil yourself in such a perilous undertaking."

Her tears spilled over. "I beg you, Steven. Please do this for me."

He sighed. "If I should aid you, will you vow to do nothing rash or foolish, such as trying to find Miggs on your own?"

A tremulous smile curved her lips. "I promise. I'll not make a move without consulting you. If we should uncover his location, we can notify the garrison."

"Very well." Steven took out his handkerchief, wiping away her tears. "I shall discover what I can, but I caution you, prepare for the worst. If this man has Richard in his clutches, your uncle's chances of surviving are quite slim. You must understand, my dear, that what I learn may not be what you wish to hear."

"I realize that. But I must know. If Richard is dead, I can face that fact. What I cannot abide is not knowing his fate."

Steven moved across the carriage aisle and sat on the bench next to her. He enfolded her in his arms and placed a chaste kiss on her forehead. "I vow I shall try. Then we can allow the military to handle the situation."

The day after his conversation with Samantha, Steven

met with Miggs in the back room of the Blue Boar Inn. After quaffing a swallow of ale, Steven asked Miggs, "Is the *Manta Ray* still anchored in Macquarie Harbor?"

Miggs nodded and scratched at a louse crawling through the hair covering his bare belly.

"I have Colchester's young niece," Steven said, looking at the pirate with disgust.

Miggs's hand jerked, and he spilled ale on the table. "Where?" he sputtered.

"Not here, you half-wit. But I have her trust. She will do whatever I say."

Miggs leered, his gap-toothed mouth a gruesome sight.

"You'll keep your hands off her or see not a penny of payment." With a smirk, Steven lifted his tankard. "I have plans for her. Perhaps when I have what I want," he added at the lustful look in Miggs's eyes. He pointed a stiff finger at the pirate. "But not before! I want this one alive. A dead girl cannot lead me to the cat."

When Steven showed up the following morning at Talmadge House, Pettibone stared down his nose at the early intruder. "Neither Lady Delia nor Mistress Badia accept social calls before ten," he stated.

Steven stood his ground. "'Tis imperative I speak with Mistress Badia."

When Pettibone shook his head, Steven handed the butler his card. "Please inform her I called on urgent business."

Starlight & Promises

Samantha had slept poorly and arose earlier than was her usual habit. Due to the promise of Steven's assistance, her mind had raced throughout the night. She could now set her plan in action.

While she was dressing, Steven's and Pettibone's voices drifted up from the downstairs foyer. She rushed her toilette, scraping a brush through her hair, and flew down the stairs as Pettibone was turning Steven away. Stopping on the bottom step, she pressed a hand against her stomach.

"Steven," she said breathlessly when Pettibone began to close the door, "Aunt Delia is indisposed, but will you stay for breakfast?"

Pettibone twisted around with a scowl.

Over breakfast in the morning room, Steven exuded an impatience that fueled Samantha's hopes. "You have information for me," she whispered when the maid left them alone.

Pettibone entered the room before Steven could answer. The butler took up a post by the door, standing stiffly like a rusty suit of armor. Though Samantha glowered at him, he remained on watch.

When Steven nodded fractionally, her heart leapt. They limited further conversation to inconsequential matters. At the conclusion of the meal, Steven asked whether she and Delia would care to join him for a carriage drive.

"Aunt Delia suffers from the same unfortunate ailment Gilly contracted and is taking her rest. Gilly is nursing her. But I would love a jaunt in the fresh air."

This time Jasper ignored Samantha's downturned mouth and sharp looks and hefted himself onto the carriage bench next to her. Again she was unable to converse freely. Steven slid her a wink and suggested they stop at Government House gardens to stretch their legs. She swiftly agreed.

With Jasper following from a ten-foot distance, they ambled through the flowers on crushed-shell paths. Samantha and Steven kept their faces turned forward or bent over the blossoms and carried on a whispered conversation.

"Richard is alive," Steven said first.

Samantha's breath jammed in her throat. Her pulse beat wildly. "Alive?" she said in a strangled whisper.

He nodded.

"Where?"

"In a hidden cove where the pirates anchor their ship."

"How did you discover this?"

"One of Miggs's men values coin more than loyalty."

"What action do we take now? Can the military aid us?"

He shook his head and glanced at Jasper, judging the distance between them. "Samantha, I have other news . . . news of a distressing nature."

She peered at him but could discern no inkling of what he was thinking.

"After checking about, I uncovered shocking allegations of corruption in the military leadership," he said. "They have known of the pirates' cove for some time. The pirates pay them tribute for protection. They'll not come to our aid. If we should attempt to involve them, word will most certainly get back to Miggs."

Heart sinking, Samantha plopped down on a stone bench among the blooming roses, while Jasper took up a position farther down the path. What could they do? Christian and Garrett were far away, obviously off on a false lead. Who knew when they would return? If she waited, Richard could die in the interim. Jasper would not help her. He would lock her in the house were he even to suspect she was considering rescuing her uncle from pirates. Steven was her only hope.

She lowered her head and whispered her question. "What shall we do? We cannot confront pirates alone, but every day that passes further endangers Richard's life."

He smiled and turned his head toward her. "We are not alone. I have loyal men, men I trust. I shall go after Richard."

Her fisted fingers mangled her skirt. "I must go, too. You'll not leave me behind."

"No, 'tis too dangerous. The pirates Miggs deals

with are killers. I'll not place you in jeopardy. We have another problem," he said before she could object. "I failed to learn the cove's exact location. When I know more, I'll get back to you."

Jasper shuffled his feet in the shells, and Samantha darted a glance at him, then came to her feet. With Steven beside her, they wended their way through the garden to the carriage.

Steven handed her into the conveyance and whispered, "I shall be in touch soon."

As if she didn't have enough worries, another complication reared its thorny head. Samantha had missed her monthly course. She recalled Christian's letter and sought out her maid. "Gilly, how does a woman know she is breeding?"

"Ooh, that's marvelous, ma'am."

Samantha waved off the maid's speculation. "Refrain from jumping to conclusions. I ask only so I shall know if and when I'm with child."

Gilly's face fell. "Well, usually the first sign is missin' the monthly courses. Then the mornin' sickness comes on, though some women never have the sickness."

Samantha did not feel ill. Surely an encouraging sign. Someday, should her detestable husband ever return, she would quite like a child or two, though she had no desire to rear a child alone.

"By about three months, the breasts become tender and swell," Gilly said, "and by the fourth month, ye develop a little belly. But all women are different. Me mum had four babes without even knowin' she was breedin' 'til they popped out of her."

"Popped out of her?" Samantha twisted her mouth into a frown. What a disconcerting vision!

"Are ye breedin', ma'am?"

"I-I'm not certain. I mean, do a husband and wife not have to have . . . relations for a long time before they make a baby?"

Gilly chuckled. "Nay. Just one time. That's all it takes. But most women don't catch so quickly."

Samantha sighed. So much for that theory. "Say nothing, Gilly. I missed only one of my courses. That could be a result of my upset over Christian's leaving so abruptly."

"Mum's the word, ma'am. It'll be our secret 'til ye're certain." Gilly grinned. "I hope 'tis a little lass, so we can dress her in frilly frocks."

Samantha gave Gilly a warning look. "Nothing. Say nothing to anyone."

Gilly made a gesture of buttoning up her lips and grinned again.

Samantha pushed the worry from her mind.

A week went by without word from Steven, and Samantha's fretting wore her nerves to a nub. She began to believe he had deliberately lied to prevent her from taking off on her own. She moped about the house in a dyspeptic disposition, causing her family to remark upon her behavior.

While tossing about in her lonely bed a few nights later, a rustling came from outside her window. She rose up on her elbows and turned toward the sound. When a black shape blocked the moonlight, she opened her mouth to scream.

Boot steps thudded forward, and a hand clamped down on her lips. "'Tis me, Samantha. Steven," a voice whispered. He slowly removed his hand.

She blinked and strained to make out his features in the pale light. "What are you doing here?" she hissed. "If Jasper were to catch you, he would tear you limb from limb."

He dismissed her words with a gesture and eased down on the edge of the bed. "I acquired a paid informant in Miggs's crew. He agreed to lead me to the cove for a price and on one condition. He knows of your presence in Hobart and insists you accompany me. He will accept his reward only from your hands."

"Reward?"

"I shall, of course, provide the coin."

She shook her head. "That will be unnecessary. I have my jewels and will gladly give them up for Richard's safety."

"Can you dress and quickly pack a bag?"

She hesitated. "Can you not simply tell me the location?"

"He refused to disclose it, offering only to guide us there. I would never take the chance of harm coming to you if there were any other way. My informant guarantees your safety. To be certain he tells the truth, my men will guard us. If we are to rescue Richard, we must leave tonight. The trip will take some time over rough territory, and the *Manta Ray* returns to sea in a couple of weeks. Should Richard still be alive, I give you my word he will not be by the time they sail."

She posed one more question. "Were you able to discover who hired Miggs to kidnap Richard?"

He shook his head. "I dare not push my informant further and risk losing his cooperation. Perhaps we shall learn all there is to learn when we find Richard. Making certain he escapes safely is my greatest concern. I have no doubt the man you seek will eventually reveal himself. Will you come with me? I have men and horses waiting below."

Samantha bounded out of bed, flew into her dressing room, and pulled on a riding habit. She stuffed a small bag with essentials, including her jewels, and joined Steven in the bedchamber. "I'm ready. We should go before someone discovers us." Steven headed toward the open window, and Samantha stopped beside the desk to take up a pen. "I must first leave a note for Aunt Delia. She will be frantic if I should suddenly disappear."

Steven crossed the room and laid a hand on her wrist. "That would be unwise. If your family discovers our plans and applies to the military garrison for help, Miggs will learn about it. It may endanger our lives and Richard's." He held her gaze in a sorrowful look. "'Tis best for now they know nothing. When we return with Richard, you can explain everything."

"I-I suppose you have a point, but I cannot simply leave them to worry about me."

"Samantha," he said firmly, "if you truly wish to save Richard, you have no choice."

She squared her shoulders and dropped the pen on the desk. "We should leave now."

He helped her climb down the trellis supporting a thick growth of trumpet vines on the side of the house. At the back entrance to the garden, six men sat on horses and held two other mounts by the reins. "Can you ride astride?" Steven asked.

Samantha answered by swinging into the saddle with no assistance, gathering up the reins, and applying her heels to the horse's flanks.

They left in a clatter of hooves and a cloud of dust. Samantha looked back over her shoulder only once and wondered what her family would think of her sudden disappearance. Her thoughts turned to Christian, and her heart ached.

Chapter Twenty-Five

In the Tasman Sea

Christian leaned back in the captain's chair and crossed his ankles on top of the desk corner. He held a glass of whiskey in his right hand and a cigar clamped between his teeth. Garrett occupied a similar chair, feet also on the desk. He preferred brandy to whiskey and puffed on a slim cheroot. A pile of charts depicting the islands and waterways of the surrounding sea lay between their feet. A collection of navigational instruments sat atop the papers.

The *Maiden Anne* was anchored dead center over the spot where the *Manta Ray* engaged and sank the *Rapier* over a year ago. For hours, Christian and Garrett had pored over the charts, but the results remained unchanged. The nearest landfall lay hundreds of miles from their present location.

"Assuming they escaped the ship," Christian said, "did they survive? If so, how?"

Garrett picked up Christian's train of thought. "Miggs's man said he applied the cat to both. Truett was either dead or nearly so. We can assume the beatings, along with the little food and water they'd have been allowed, would weaken them. They couldn't go far under their own power, even if they managed to escape the ship during the battle."

"So they didn't swim away." Christian sent Garrett a pointed look. "If you were starved and beaten and too weak to swim, what would you do?"

Garrett lifted a brow. "Float?"

"Float," Christian agreed. "In the wake of a battle, debris litters the ocean. A determined man could latch onto a floating keg or spar and, perhaps with a large dose of luck, hang on to it long enough to make land, if the sun and sharks didn't get him first."

He swung his feet off the desk and snapped at Garrett, "Find a chart showing the currents at the time the *Rapier* sank. Assuming Richard and James floated away from the ship, we should be able to determine in which direction they headed."

Garrett dragged out the chart and spread it on the desk. Swirls on its surface indicated the ocean currents. Garrett drew a line from Hobart, Tasmania, to Wellington, New Zealand, the *Rapier*'s home port. The line crossed their present location, which lay in the center of the East Australian Current of the Tasman Sea. The current swept down from the Coral Sea along Australia's eastern coast, then curved westward at the northwestern tip of Tasmania, creating a circle that passed by the western edge of New Zealand and moved northward.

From there it fanned out in two directions: back into the circle of the East Australian Current or southwest along the northern tip of Australia to pick up the South Equatorial Current, which eventually led up the western coast of South America.

Christian traced a finger along the second route. "If they passed New Zealand and floated eastward, we have no hope of finding them alive. The passage is too distant and leads back into cold water. If we're to assume they reached land at some point, they must have caught the same current in which they began their journey. What lies in that path?"

Garrett read the names off the map. "Lord Howe Island, Norfolk Island, the Loyalty Islands, the Hebrides, and New Caledonia. The closest, Lord Howe Island, is over eight hundred miles from here." He looked up. "It's impossible, Chris. They couldn't have made it that far."

Christian frowned. "We either believe they're alive or give up all hope and return to Hobart empty-handed. As we're committed to the former, we must assume another island exists between here and Lord Howe Island, uncharted but there nonetheless."

"And we find it how?" Garrett asked. "By floating on the current?"

Christian rubbed a hand across his chin. "You may have an idea there."

Garrett emitted a short laugh. He took a turn around the room, puffing hard on his cheroot. "I was being facetious. Have you any idea how long that would take a ship this size?"

Christian lifted one shoulder in a shrug. "Longer than I would wish. However, after a year, we're no longer searching for survivors at sea. They had to make landfall to endure this long. Hopefully, their situation will be no more dire than it already is no matter how long it takes for us to find them."

The next day the sailors lashed together a line of empty water kegs. A lead line attached them to the ship's bow and allowed the crew to haul in the buoys at night or during rough seas. The line remained slack while the ship, under boiler power at low speed, followed the kegs, which floated freely in the current far ahead but still within sight of a spyglass wielded by a lookout in the crow's nest.

The plan proceeded well. The *Maiden Anne* trailed the barrels for eight days, bobbing northeastward in the East Australian Current. Then Neptune intervened, taking them by surprise.

The *Maiden Anne* received warning of only a few

minutes. When the lookout spied the seawall, Christian was at the helm with Captain Lindstrom and Garrett. The three men tied themselves to the wheel, and the captain bellowed out for the crew to turn the ship's stern into the wave and lash themselves to the masts. The *Maiden Anne* would surely go beneath the tremendous wave, but it might not sink. A man secured to the ship had a greater chance of surviving than one swept out to sea.

The ship turned. Close to half the crew managed to comply with Lindstrom's order before the wave smashed into them. It lifted the ship a hundred feet in the air. The *Maiden Anne* surfed along the crest for endless minutes, then dropped like a stone into a trough, pushed along from behind, while Lindstrom, Garrett, and Christian fought the wheel to keep the ship's stern turned into the waves following the initial seawall.

When the hull suddenly crashed into a coral reef, it broke into pieces and took on water. Those still conscious after the impact untied their ropes and rushed to help the others before the ship slipped beneath the waves. Christian, Garrett, and the captain, still lashed to the wheel, were knocked senseless by a falling timber.

When Christian cracked open his eyes, he lay on his back. A bright red and black honeyeater, with a long curved beak, cocked its head at him from a branch over-head. He tried to sit up. Blood dripped into his left eye, his head spun, and he sank back to the ground.

He rolled his head to the right to view a wall of luxuriant vegetation. Exotic birdcalls rang through air redolent with tropical flowers. He saw no sign of humans, the ground beneath him was hard, and he ached like hell.

With a groan, he turned his head to the left and came face-to-face with a pair of dusty brown feet and the pointed end of a spear. He panned his gaze up the long, sturdy body, naked except for a loincloth, and covered from waist to knees in fantastic designs, swirls, circles, lines, and dots, tattooed into the skin with blackish blue ink. He reached the man's face, a harsh countenance, bare of whiskers. His dark, golden brown complexion appeared even in color. Blue black hair hung straight to his shoulders. A pair of arrogant obsidian eyes glittered under heavy, prominent brow ridges.

He recognized the tattoos as Samoan, but surely the wave couldn't have pushed them all the way to Samoa.

The spear prodded Christian in the side. He grunted and struggled to sit up again. When he failed, falling back once more, the man motioned to two others standing behind him. One was a veritable giant. He pulled Christian up by his arms and slung him over one massive shoulder, carrying him like a sack of grain. Christian passed out from the pain.

Christian awakened for the second time in a dusky space. Moaning came from the surrounding dimness. He stretched out a weak arm, and his hand brushed up against a body that stirred when he touched it. When his eyes adjusted to the low light, he made out shadowy figures next to him. Instead of bare ground this time, he lay on a reed pallet. Gradually, walls with tiny, silvery lines of light leaking through cracks, indicating a reed construction, became visible.

Gazing up, he gained an impression of clouds that parted at times and allowed starlight to filter down. When he flexed his limbs, pain filled every inch. It was an aching pain rather than a sharp one that would indicate broken limbs or internal damage. Lifting his hand to his forehead, which seemed particularly sore, he found a wound, smeared with a poultice, above his eye. He brought his fingers to his nose and sniffed. Vile-smelling stuff, but that someone was tending to his injury indicated his captors, should they fall into that category, had some humanitarian values.

He would have to wait until morning to determine his circumstances. Then he could count the survivors. He closed his eyes, and his thoughts turned to Samantha, as they had every night since his departure. Despite his pain and fatigue, his groin tightened. He managed a weak smile. At least *that* part of him still worked properly!

Starlight & Promises

Early morning sun threw stripes of light through the slats in the reed walls. When the sunlight hit his eyes, needles jabbed Christian's brain. He lowered his eyelids and moaned. A hand slipped beneath his nape, cradling his head and raising it a few inches off the mat. A bowl of sweet liquid touched his lips. He sipped the moisture into his dry throat. When he inched open his eyes, a woman was leaning over him with the bowl balanced in her hand. Sun seared his retinas. He glimpsed only a blurry impression of long, dark hair and a rounded brown face.

She laid his head back on the mat, and he tested his voice. "Who are you? Where am I? How many survived?" The words emerged in a mere whisper from his scratchy, dry throat.

The woman remained silent and moved away from him.

He turned his head, searching for familiar faces among the men on the pallets scattered across the floor. His heartbeat accelerated when he recognized Garrett lying against a wall on the other side of the room. There were others, all seamen from the *Maiden Anne*. Captain Lindstrom was not among them. He counted seven men, plus Garrett and himself. Unless another room similar to this existed, only nine from a complement of twenty-seven survived the wave. His breath shortened, and he strained for air, inhaling slowly, deeply.

By the look of the natives, they hadn't landed on the coast of New Zealand or Australia, so he assumed the ship had fetched up on an island. They were fortunate to be alive. Even nine of twenty-seven was a miracle. Nonetheless, he would hold off celebrating until he learned where they were and who held them. They could have fallen, quite literally, from the sea into a cooking pot, if their hosts turned out to be cannibals.

He took another look around the corral. No other word accurately described it. Closely woven reed walls rose about eight feet high. No windows and only one door. A bumpy reed floor beneath him. The structure appeared flimsy, although he suspected it was sturdier than it looked. Small brownish geckos no larger than his finger scurried about, on and between the reeds.

Christian gazed up through the open ceiling. Their room, or prison, hovered above the ground. Treetops soared not far above him. Colorful emerald doves, parakeets, and lorikeets, with shining feathers of green, blue, orange, and yellow, fluttered back and forth, chattering in competing voices. Large bats, their leathery wings folded about them like capes—flying foxes, his scientific mind told him—clung upside down to the uppermost branches of the trees in massive brown colonies.

The woman returned and knelt beside him. The sun had risen higher and shined through the enclosure's open top. Her features were clearer. Fortyish with a plump figure encased like a sausage in a leaf-printed sarong that wrapped around her ample waist and fell to her calves. A string of shells draped around her neck, hanging to her bare breasts. Heavy black hair rippled to below her bottom, and a pink flower with multiple tubelike florets, a species of *psychotria*, peeked out from behind her right ear. The flower, birds, and bats gave Christian additional clues to his location—somewhere near New Caledonia. Though the people appeared to have a Samoan source, they could easily have come from Polynesia at some point in their history. The woman's black eyes were kind in her unlined, expressionless face as she fed him a tasteless paste with her fingers.

CHAPTER TWENTY-SIX

Christian recovered rapidly on a diet of fruit, bland paste, stringy meat that tasted like pork, fish, and a fortifying drink with an alcoholic content and a beneficial effect on his constitution. Garrett recouped his strength more quickly, having received only cuts and bruises from the ropes binding him to the wheel and a glancing blow from the spar.

While Christian lay on his pallet, Garrett related what he recalled. "I came to my senses soon after the ship hit the reef. After cutting your bonds, I managed to pull you from the wreckage before waves swept the carcass beneath the sea. I then dragged your limp body across the reef and through the lagoon. I apologize for the cuts from the coral. Our nurse been tutting over them."

Christian knew of the dangers from coral, a living

animal, though it appeared to be inert rock. Coral embedded in flesh could grow and cause a fatal infection. The daily poultices of a smelly concoction that burned like carbolic acid seemed to be keeping serious damage at bay.

"Captain Lindstrom died," Garrett went on, "I suspect from the impact of the falling timber. The other survivors have cuts, bruises, broken limbs, and internal injuries, but all seem to be on the mend."

Garrett also relayed his impressions of their captors. For indeed they were captors. "Our hut sits in a tree about twenty feet off the ground. It's the dry season. I suppose that explains the lack of a roof. I would hope they apply thatching when the winter rains come, not that I believe we'll be here that long. I've found only one way down. By ladder. They remove it when they have no need for it."

"What are their intentions?" Christian asked.

Garrett shrugged. "The only native I've seen close-up is the woman who tends us. I don't believe she understands English, that or she's mute. She hasn't uttered a word. From what I can see through the cracks in the walls, we're in a large camp situated on a mountainside. I counted over a hundred men and more arriving every day. Less than twenty huts at ground level, proper roofed ones but with open sides. They look hastily thrown together, and many of the new arrivals appear displaced. I assume the tsunami flooded their homes. The village looks to be a temporary gathering place. I still cannot get a sense of whether we're on an island or on the coast of a larger landmass."

With much groaning and hissing through his teeth, Christian pushed himself to his feet.

"Hey! You shouldn't be standing yet."

Christian held up a staying hand and limped around the small corral. "If I remain idle much longer, I'll be crippled for life." He stopped and panted, bracing himself against the wall, and talked softly with another invalid. Then he turned back to Garrett. "I gather this is the only prison, and we're the only survivors."

"As far as I can determine. Some may have been taken to another location. However, I believe what you see here are all who remain of the crew."

Christian grunted and eased back down the wall until his bottom rested on the reeds. "The one warrior I recall seeing appeared less than friendly. Any sign they're cannibals or headhunters?"

"From up here," Garrett said, "I can see little of significance. They haven't removed anyone yet, are feeding us, and have seen to our injuries. Surely that's an encouraging sign."

Christian gave him a crooked smile. "Perhaps their purpose is to fatten us for a feast in which we're the featured guests."

Garrett returned the smile. "I must admit that's a possibility I hadn't wished to consider. Now that you mention it . . ."

"Assuming we come up with a plan, how many men are well enough to attempt an escape?"

"If I'm to count you, whom I'm sure you mean to include, five, maybe six. We have no weapons. They stripped us of our knives and guns before they carted us up here. We even eat with our fingers. If we're to have any hope of arming ourselves, we'll have to take weapons from the men below."

"Who's our best climber?"

"Cullen." Garrett grinned. "Unfortunately, you failed to foretell our predicament and left him in Hobart."

Christian scowled at Garrett's attempt at humor.

"Among the ambulatory men, I suppose I am," Garrett said with a sigh. "I have the least severe injuries, and I'm pretty agile."

Christian arched a brow. "I would imagine from climbing out windows when husbands return unexpectedly."

"Actually, I was thinking about my second-story work with the gang in Frisco. Though I haven't had the occasion to use my skills for some time, I still remember the fundamentals."

"Neither are you twelve years old any longer."

"But I'm younger than you, old man."

Christian threw a glance at the tree branches overhanging the open hut. "Think you can climb up there and swing over to another tree? I've watched the parakeets climbing about. Surely you're as nimble as they are."

Garrett directed his gaze upward. "Perhaps. I'd have to attempt it in the dark, find the ladder, steal weapons, and break down the door. And, of course, I'd have to complete these tasks in utter silence amongst a hundred natives, thirsting for my blood and breathing down my neck."

"You have a problem with that?"

"God, you're a hard man to please, aren't you?"

"The dark of the moon comes in two weeks," Christian said with a sharp nod. "If we should manage to hold on to our heads that long, up and out you go."

"By all means," Garrett replied with a sickly smile. "Up and out and into the stewpot."

The night was moonless. Once the sun's light vanished and the sky was at its darkest, Christian hoisted Garrett onto his shoulders and boosted him high enough to grab a branch above the hut. Garrett swung his legs until he gathered momentum. Releasing the branch, he flew across the dark space to a lower branch on a neighboring tree.

His position allowed Garrett to view the entire encampment. Though the night lay as black as the lava sands, cook fires burned below. Men reclined on pallets around the fires. Silence, broken only by the rusty screeches of nightjars, reigned over the village. A suggestion of movement in the forest ringing the open space caught his attention. As he scrutinized the area, shadows crept out of the trees toward the sleeping men.

"Chris, something's happening," Garrett whispered from his perch among the foliage.

"What?" Christian called out in a low voice.

"Shhh, I believe we're in for some excitement. Men have surrounded the village. It doesn't look as if it's a friendly visit."

When the village erupted in war cries and weapons clashing, Christian shouted up to Garrett, "Come down!"

"No," Garrett said, his gaze fixed on the melee below. "This may be my only chance. While they're busy slaughtering each other, I can slip through unnoticed and find the ladder."

Christian yelled, "Garrett!"

But Garrett was already making his way down the tree toward the ground.

Garrett dropped from the last branch and looked about. He was too exposed, too far out in the open. Warriors careened past him or wrestled in combat. Clubs split skulls and broke legs and arms. Darts whistled past his head. After dodging a warrior intent on stabbing him with a wooden dagger, he sped to the forest verge. He paused to hug the trunk of a sandalwood tree and sidled around the bole, casting his gaze about the clearing for the ladder.

With his attention riveted on the mayhem beyond the trees, Garrett tripped over an obstacle. Looking up from his sprawled position, he stared directly into a pair of blue eyes. He blinked in slack-jawed amazement when the man sitting on the ground extended his hand.

"Hello," the man said as calmly as if they were meeting at White's on St. James Street in London. He grasped and shook Garrett's hand. "James Truett. Pleased to make your acquaintance. Who are you, and what in the name of Zeus are you doing here?"

Chapter Twenty-Seven

Though speechless, Garrett could not seem to close his mouth. He examined the man with auburn hair, blue eyes, and Caucasian skin spotted with brown dye like a leopard's.

James made a waving gesture. "Do you mind? Were you simply to move to one side, I would be ever so grateful."

Garrett clambered to his feet, crab-walked to one side, and peered over the man's shoulder. What was this man, a white man, doing sitting cross-legged on the jungle floor and sketching a tribal massacre with sharpened charcoal sticks? Garrett felt as if he had climbed down from the tree straight through Lewis Carroll's looking glass.

Once Garrett moved out of his view of the action, James resumed his drawing. "You had best sit behind me," James said. "You stand out like a ghost with your white skin."

As though to punctuate his point, a javelin whizzed past them, close enough to stir the air above Garrett's ear. He threw himself to the ground and inched behind James. His mind barely registered the words the man was saying. A moment later, it did. "James Truett?"

James nodded and pursed his lips while the charcoal flew across the sketchbook page made from pressed tree bark. "And you are?" he muttered.

"Garrett Jakes. We've been searching for you."

James turned his head, cocking a brow at Garrett. "Have you now?" His eyes lit with sudden revelation. "By 'we' you mean Samantha, do you not?"

"Well, yes, but we left her in Hobart."

"Good for you." James returned to his illustration. "This is hardly a proper place for a lady. Imagine she gave you a bit of trouble over it, I mean, leaving her behind. She can be a bit willful."

"I know," Garrett said. He remembered what he'd meant to ask. "Is Lord Stanbury with you?"

James pointed with his charcoal stick to a man in the thick of the fighting. "Right there. He's been posing beautifully for me. Has a great economy of movement, don't you think?"

Garrett followed James's gesture. Richard, dressed only in a loincloth, his body painted with tigerlike stripes, wielded a knife in one hand. In the other he held a short javelin. "Damnation!" Garrett swore when Richard took a jab to the ribs with a spear and warriors swarmed over him. He appeared to be losing ground and fighting for his life.

Garrett took off at a run. He plucked up an abandoned spear as he swept by it, ducked a war club, and skewered the warrior swinging it. Grabbing the war club, he threw himself into the fight beside Richard, disabling two of Richard's assailants. When he lunged at another native, Richard stayed his hand. "No," he shouted above the din. "They're on our side."

The battle lasted less than an hour. Warriors lay bleeding on the ground, dead or dying. Women and children remained to one side, calmly awaiting the outcome, while the captured chiefs, guarded by a contingent of armed men, stood in stoic silence, their chins held high, shoulders thrown back in defiant postures.

Garrett finally caught his wind, turned to Richard, and grasped his hand. "Garrett Jakes," he said, panting. "We've come to rescue you."

"Capital," Richard replied. "James and I have a wager. Is Samantha among your number?"

Garrett shook his head. "Not at this time. We left her in Hobart, but her husband accompanied me."

Richard's brows shot up. "Husband? Samantha married? Where is he?"

Garrett pointed to the hut of reeds high over their

heads. "In there, along with our surviving crew."

The hut door burst open, and Christian's tall frame filled the doorway. He glared down on the carnage and cupped his hands around his mouth. "Find the damn ladder, Garrett. Now!" he bellowed.

Garrett raced to follow Christian's order, and Richard chuckled. "By Jove, Samantha's husband. This is one man whose acquaintance I *must* make."

Garrett located the ladder under a tree, and Christian climbed down, followed by those men well enough to negotiate the rungs. Then he strode directly to Richard and put out his hand. "Stanbury?" he said.

Richard grinned and clasped Christian's hand. "I understand you wed my niece, Samantha. My condolences."

Christian smiled dryly. "I would have observed the formalities and sought your permission. Unfortunately, you had gone missing and were presumed dead."

Richard studied Christian, a glimmer of recognition kindling on his face. "You are an American. I know you. Wait a minute; it's on the tip of my tongue. A zoologist, ah, Professor Badia, Christian Badia. We met briefly during a conference at Oxford some years ago."

"The same."

"How did you become involved in a search for me?"

Christian gave him a pained look. "It's a long story. Suffice it to say, Samantha can be rather persuasive."

"You mean stubborn, I daresay."

"Of course."

A glint sparked in Richard's gold-colored eyes. "I begin to understand. Samantha must have contacted you about the Smilodon. How did you come to wed?"

"It's quite complicated. As I said, Samantha is a persuasive woman." Christian cleared his throat. "But we suit well. I should probably qualify that statement by saying we shall once she resigns herself to a wifely role. She'll eventually learn to find contentment as a wife and mother."

James walked up beside Richard, and they exchanged a glance. Both doubled over in laughter.

Christian eyed them as though they had gone daft.

Richard wiped a tear from his eye. "I beg your pardon, Badia. I fear you are in for a bumpy ride with Samantha. Have you heard her 'modern woman' theory?"

"She has yet to explain it to me. Nevertheless, I'm well aware of her . . . peculiarities and shortcomings. I daresay I can handle her."

"I wish you luck." Richard patted Christian on the back. "I don't envy you the task ahead. How did you manage to sail out of Hobart without her?"

Garrett jumped in. "He locked her in their honeymoon suite until the ship sailed."

Richard and James laughed again. "Perhaps you know her better than I supposed," Richard said. "You will have hell to pay when you return."

"No doubt," Christian said with a frown. He gestured

to the warriors surrounding them. "Who are these natives, and where are we?"

"The *o tagata o fanua o la'ua*," Richard replied, "which loosely translates as 'People of the Tree Land.' The other chaps are their traditional enemies, the *o tagata o fanua i afi*, 'People of the Fire Land.' Kiha, the son of the high chief, Kamaiole, pressed for a preemptory attack while the *afi* were recovering from the effects of the tsunami, the goal being the capture of women and livestock. 'Tis a familiar occupation. The tribes battle on a frequent basis. The majority of the women have moved back and forth between them numerous times. As to our location, I'm not truly certain, but I suspect somewhere near New Caledonia, judging by the flora."

"And the people?" Christian asked. "Surely they are Samoan."

"Yes, or at least of Samoan origin. The culture resembles that of Samoa, and the language is a Samoan dialect."

While they conversed, the priests decapitated the dead *la'ua* warriors, buried the bodies with ritual, and deposited the heads in decorated animal-skin sacks. They dispatched the injured *afi* warriors on the spot, taking the heads, which they collected in large nets, and leaving the bodies on the battlefield for the scavengers. They loaded the bodies of their own chiefs onto litters for ceremonial burial in their village.

When Kiha and the other chiefs approached, Richard

turned and introduced Christian and Garrett. They retrieved the remainder of the *Maiden Anne*'s crew from the hut. Preceded by the captured chiefs, the women and children, and the *la'ua* warriors, they took off through the jungle toward the southern coast. Additional litters, constructed for the injured crewmen and warriors, transported those unable to walk.

With the burden of carrying the injured and the presence of several dozen women and children, the return trip took six days. The well-traveled path linking the two villages curved like the spine of a serpent through a dense forest of Araucaria pines and sandalwood trees. Torches carried by warriors flickered through the leaves, painting checkerboard patterns of light and shadow on the leaf-carpeted ground. The four white men exchanged stories during the journey.

"After being attacked on the streets of Hobart and rendered unconscious, we came to in the hold of a ship, which we soon discovered to be manned by pirates," Richard said, his eyes turning hard. "They flogged us without mercy. I was certain the beastly creature wielding the whip had killed James. When the crew of another ship boarded ours, I managed to slip overboard with James and tie us to barrels, where we floated for an endless time, eventually fetching up on this island. The *la'ua* rescued us. Tapia, the *taulaitus*, their spiritual leader, nursed us back to health."

A silent flight of flying foxes glided overhead, torch-light reflecting off their furry bellies, making them golden beneath, black above. The close encounter of their large bodies stirred the air like a gentle wind, though none, other than Christian and James, paused to observe them.

Turning his gaze from the bats, Christian explained how they had also utilized barrels to follow the ocean currents.

Glancing up and back down to his sketchbook, trying to render an image of the foxes as he walked, James replied, "Ingenious. Never would have thought of it myself."

Garrett took up the story. "We didn't count on the tsunami and were right in its path. It pushed us back-ward onto the reef, and the ship broke apart. The natives captured us and locked us up in that aerie. We still have no notion of what they intended to do with us."

"Probably eat you," Richard said with a straight face, ducking and sweeping a leafy frond the size of a dinghy out of his way.

Garrett grinned at Christian. "Seems you were right, old man."

Christian shrugged.

"The tribes on this island are cannibals," Richard said, "but they differ in their habits. The *la'ua* are ritual-istic cannibals and consume only the flesh, which they call *io*, of enemies defeated in battle. But some other tribes eat human flesh as a regular part of their diet. They believe it gives them strength. The *afi* are among those."

"What is our fate now?" Christian asked with a frown, raising his voice to be heard over the whistling duets of an abundance of indigenous nightjars and the crashing of the flying foxes into the foliage, where they attempted to catch hold of branches, then swing upside down. Once attached and hanging, a fox would draw food to its mouth with one of its hind feet or with the clawed thumbs at the top of its wings.

Richard laughed and said loudly, "Have no worry. You now fall into the category of friends, *uo,* and are in no danger."

"You said we were on an island. How did you discover that?" Christian asked. The nocturnal birds' calls faded, and Christian resumed in a normal tone of voice. "Have you explored it?"

"Not completely. The *la'ua* have no word for 'island.' They call this land *lau'ele'ele i sami,* which translates as 'land in the sea.' From the descriptive name, I always assumed it was a volcanic island. You'll soon see two peaks, *fanua o la'ua*, the forested caldera of an extinct volcano, and *fanua i afi*, an active volcano. As the other natives are less accommodating to strangers than the *la'ua*, we've remained close to the village. This excursion was our first extended trip."

"Is *fanua i afi* the highest point?" Garrett asked. He bent and picked up a slender black branch that resembled ironwood, tapping it against his leg as he walked.

Richard looked pointedly at the stick. "You might want to watch where you put your hands and what you retrieve from the brush. This area has an interesting gecko species with sharp teeth, and a giant gecko. If you hear some animal growling in the trees, it's probably a giant gecko. The natives call it the 'devil in the trees.'"

Garrett peered at the stick as though he expected it to come to life in his hand. When it remained naught more than a stick, he shrugged and employed it to poke about in the leaf litter beneath the trees.

"As to the volcano," Richard continued, "I would assume it to be the highest point, since it's still active."

Christian rubbed his whiskered jaw. "If we climb to the top, perhaps we could gain a sense of what we're facing." He looked at Richard. "I gather you wish to leave?"

"Certainly. I've enjoyed my little holiday, but the time has come for us to depart and commence searching for the Smilodon."

"Whoa!" Garrett yelled and jumped back when his stick-probing elicited a crackling and slithering beneath a pile of leaves.

After sending Garrett a black look, Christian turned back to Richard with a cynical smile. "You're *certain* it was a Smilodon? I would hate to have come all this way because of a dream you had one night when foxed on brandy."

Richard's brows lowered. "Most certain, but even

are we not fortunate enough to find the Smilodon again, you'll not return empty-handed. You found Samantha."

"That I did." He sighed. "I'll be paying the price for that lapse in sanity for the remainder of my life." He pushed aside thoughts of his wife and struggled to refocus on their predicament and the one mystery that still bothered him. "Other than Samantha, to whom did you disclose your discovery?"

Richard frowned. "I've asked myself that same question. The answer is always the same. No one. James and I discussed that sticking point and concluded that someone must have overheard us making plans to contact Samantha. The pirates kidnapped us shortly after I sent the missive off to her, requesting her aid in putting together a proper expedition."

"You came across no old acquaintances in Hobart? A scientist, perhaps, who would understand the significance of your find?"

"No. In fact, James and I spent little time in Hobart."

"I suppose we'll have to wait until we return to uncover the name of your abductor," Christian said. "When we arrive at the village, we can devise a workable plan to remove ourselves from this island and return to Hobart."

The nightjars began their serenade again, the eerie music a perfect complement to the deep, evergreen forest, black night, sputtering torches, and softly padding bare feet.

A smile played across Richard's mouth. "Anxious to return to the little woman?"

"Partly," Christian said, his look more grim than amused. "Mostly I fear for her safety. The last I heard, the mystery man who paid for your abduction may still be hanging about Tasmania. More likely than not, Samantha has been stirring up mischief during my absence. I expect that locked door slowed her no more than an hour or two."

Chapter Twenty-Eight

Hobart

Cullen slept in a room over the stables at Talmadge House and had taken up the task of caring for the horses and helping Jasper and Pettibone guard Samantha. Cullen carried out the latter duty in his own way. With ships arriving and departing Hobart's harbor daily, the streets in town saw much activity. Young boys—ships' cabin boys and settlers' offspring—swarmed the byways as thickly as flies in a slaughterhouse. Cullen moved among them like a will-o'-the-wisp. He possessed a knack for moving quickly, blending in, and remaining unobtrusive, managing even to avoid the notice of Samantha's other two bodyguards.

On the day Samantha slipped away from Madame Louella's, meeting Steven Landry on the docks, Cullen had, as was his usual habit, stationed himself outside the back entrance to the shop. Samantha's recent passive attitude and willingness to follow Christian's orders had struck him as suspicious. Less trusting than Jasper and Samantha's family and being a schemer himself, he sensed she was up to tomfoolery. Therefore, he often tagged along at a discreet distance whenever she went into town.

He was unable to figure out the significance of her assignation with Landry and kept the meeting to himself. After that incident, he subjected Samantha to even closer scrutiny.

Landry made his skin crawl. Even though the merchant was a welcome visitor at Talmadge House, Cullen watched him like the last piece of salt pork on a becalmed ship. The man made numerous visits to the Blue Boar Inn, a tavern no respectable gentleman would frequent. His business there remained a mystery, though Cullen suspected it was dirty business. He debated confiding in Jasper or Pettibone. However, he had no evidence against the man, only suspicions, and after that first meeting with Samantha, she and Landry never met in secret again.

One moonlit night several weeks after Steven Landry became a fixture at Talmadge House, Cullen lay awake on his pallet, the skin of his nape prickling. Something was brewing. Something bad. He wished, as he did each day, that Christian and Garrett would return. They would know what to do. He couldn't verbalize his unease, though he felt it deep in his gut, like pressure dropping from a storm on the horizon before a typhoon.

When voices in the alley drifted in the window above his pallet, he sat up and strained to distinguish the words. At first only murmuring. Then hooves stamping, horses snorting, clinking bridles, and creaking saddles. He jumped up, pulled on his clothes in the dark, and covered his shirt and trousers with the black cloak he used as a blanket. At the last minute, he shoved a revolver he'd borrowed from the ship into his belt.

Cullen slithered out of the barn with the caution of a hayloft cat. He slipped into the gardens, where he crouched among the rhododendrons, positioning himself within view of the back of the house and the gate leading from the yard. The moon's light revealed the silhouettes of riders in the alley.

At a motion from the house, he turned his head. A man climbed out of Samantha's window and made his way down the trellis between the trumpet vines. Another figure, shrouded in a cloak, followed the first. The moon came out from behind a cloud, and Cullen recognized the two—Steven Landry and Samantha. His chest tightened. Samantha was following Landry, not being dragged away or carried off. She was leaving with him willingly, running away from Christian.

His hands fisted. How could she do this to Christian? Bitter disappointment and shattered illusions fell about his feet, bringing the sting of tears to his eyes.

Cullen dashed to the stables, saddled his favorite horse, a fleet-footed black gelding, and took off after the group. From his location behind the riders and off the road inside the tree line, he counted six men in addition to Landry and Samantha. Their racket and the dust they stirred up masked his pursuit.

He followed throughout the night and all the next day. Nonetheless, he fell behind. His twelve short years of life included survival on the London docks and duties aboard a seagoing vessel but lacked the services of a riding master. He slid around on the gelding's back like a lopsided bag of potatoes. The clatter the horses made kept him on track at first. When they crossed the Derwent and traveled farther from town, however, heading southwest along a roughly hewn road leading to the primitive settlement of Huonville, he lost sight of his quarry. Hours sped by, and his dubious skills as a horseman caused him to lose more ground every mile he traveled.

When night lifted and Samantha's escort emerged, fully visible in the weak morning light, her earlier reservations resurfaced. She shivered and shot an appalled look at the men accompanying her and Steven. A repulsive lot, ugly, dirty, and scarred, they wore a mélange of cast-off finery and sailors' breeches swathing their muscled bodies in tatters. Weapons bristled. Daggers in their boots, pistols, and the occasional cutlass shoved through their belts. She transferred her gaze to rest on Steven. Though his features were devoid of emotion, when he glanced her way, he sent her a reassuring smile.

She tried to return the gesture, but her lips had frozen into a clenched-teeth grimace.

They pounded the road as though all the demons of Hades rode on their heels. With the exception of Steven, the men were poor riders. The horses labored under the strain of keeping their bouncing loads mounted. Steven's trusted friends? They more resembled pirates or footpads than merchants. Her hasty decision to leave Hobart with no word to her family now seemed ill-conceived. No one spoke to her. Only the occasional encouraging smile from Steven kept her moving forward.

They reached Huonville, located on the banks of the Huon River twenty miles from Hobart, and prepared to board a raft. The men cursed fluently, struggling with the horses, whipping them, and having to drag them aboard the tipping craft. Samantha watched in horror the display of inept handling and cruel behavior. When she voiced a suggestion to blindfold the animals, the men snarled and brushed her off as though she were a blood-sucking fly.

She made her way to Steven's side. "Where are we

heading? Who are these men? They look dangerous, and they are incompetent. They know naught about horses."

He laid a hand on her shoulder and pressed lightly. "From this point, our journey turns westward into wild territory," he replied, voice calm though his features strained, as though he wrestled with some inner demon. "We require adequate protection." When he looked at her, his eyes were unfocused. "My men may be rough around the edges. Nevertheless, in a pinch, they are good companions. In the event we meet with hostiles, you'll be thankful for their presence."

Though she bit her lower lip and said nothing more, serious doubts bedeviled her. When Steven motioned to her, she boarded the raft, and they pushed away from the shore to catch the river's westward current.

Dusk settled over the land, and Huonville came into sight. Tracks on the road indicated that the riders had turned and headed for the river. When his horse stumbled and came up lame, Cullen swore. Every nerve and muscle screaming, he slipped off the gelding's back and checked its hoof. A thrown shoe. The reins in one hand, he hobbled toward the riverbank as Samantha and Steven pulled out of sight down the Huon around a bend in the river.

Cullen approached the rough raftsmen along the shore. "Ye know where that raft's 'eadin'?" he asked one man with a peeling bald head and a face like a bowl of bread pudding.

The man glowered as if Cullen were a louse that needed squashing. "What's it ta ye, nit?"

Cullen cinched up his breeches. "They be friends o' mine. I was supposed ta meet 'em 'ere, but me 'orse threw a shoe."

The man studied Cullen with an air of suspicion. "Well, be they friends o' yourn, I reckon ye know where they be 'eaded."

Cullen let out his breath in a noisy exhalation. "'Ave ye another raft fer 'ire?"

The man shook his head. "Nay. They's all promised."

"'Ow about a smithy?"

"Nay. Ye'll 'ave ta take yer nag ta 'obart."

From the look on the man's sullen features, Cullen had reached a dead end. Perhaps if he had a hefty purse with him, but he didn't. His shoulders dropped. Gathering up the gelding's reins, he trudged back down the road toward Hobart.

Three days later, an exhausted, hungry, and very dusty Cullen led his lame horse into the stable at Talmadge House.

Samantha, Steven, and their contingent of body-guards floated down the river for four days, past tremendous Huon pines, some more than eight hundred years old, carpeting the rolling hills on both banks, creating dense forests that often crept up to the river's edge. Myrtle beech and swamp gum vied with the pines for space and light, along with the occasional leatherwood, swathed in white and pale pink blooms. Samantha drew in the heavy fragrance they threw across the water.

In infrequent grassy meadows, wallabies grazed, hopping on powerful back legs. Shorter rufus wallabies and shy pademelons flitted through the forest underbrush. Samantha watched with wonder as an im-possible-looking creature foraged on the river bottom. It had a sleek, furred body, a beaverlike tail, a duck's bill, and webbed feet. Parrot, cockatoo, honeyeater, and scrubtit cries swirled about them, and the sporadic eagle or falcon wheeled overhead.

At night they pulled the raft to shore and tied it to the trees before bedding down on the pine needle-cov-ered ground. Samantha huddled in her bedroll close to Steven at the feet of the pines and tried to ignore the lecherous looks cast her way by the others in the party. The farther they traveled from Hobart and civilization, the greater her apprehension.

Steven's friends remained taciturn, rarely uttering

more than a few words and never to her. Steven stayed close, presenting a buffer between her and the rough men. She welcomed his protection, for though the men kept their distance, their hungry eyes caused her heart to pound painfully. She failed to shake the worry that some malady might overtake Steven before they reached their destination. What would she do then, unarmed and alone with these men?

Even Steven's company failed to completely erase her anxiety. Though gentlemanly, displaying an outward solicitude toward her and concern for Richard's fate, he grew more remote each day. At first she believed he fretted over the coming negotiations. However, she soon suspected he hid some dread secret. Something she should know. Why did she leave Hobart in such haste? What if they should reach the ship and Richard was already dead, no longer there, or had never been there? If that were the case, what could be the pirate's reason for insisting she appear in person?

In spite of her welling reservations, she never once considered departing the company and making her way back to Hobart alone. Even asking Steven to return to Talmadge House was unthinkable. Such a move would be a step backward to exactly where she was before, if, taking into account Steven's determination to push forward, he even respected her request. If nothing more should come of it, she would learn more about Richard's fate than she had known before.

One night after many days of travel, they roasted a wombat over the fire. Samantha had suffered from nausea from the journey's onset and had eaten little. This night her appetite returned, and she consumed the marsupial meat with relish. When Steven offered her a cup of warm ale from a canteen, she drank deeply despite its sour taste.

With a full meal in her stomach and the ale's warming effect, she moved to her bedroll and stretched out. She fell asleep a short time later and descended into a benumbed state of oblivion.

CHAPTER TWENTY-NINE

Lau'ele'ele i sami

The day dawned bright and hot, the sky painfully blue. A young girl with a shy smile emerged from the shadows of Tapia's hut. Garrett eyed her with a rake's appreciation. She appeared no older than sixteen, slim and tiny and as graceful as a swan. Sooty lashes rimmed liquid black eyes. Her golden skin and black tresses glowed with health, and her firm breasts thrust up proudly from her chest.

"My word," Garrett said, bestowing his most devastating smile on her and turning to James. "Who is this exquisite creature?"

The girl ducked her head and pressed herself to James's side. "Masina," James replied with a note of reservation. "Tapia's daughter. Her name means 'moon.'"

Garrett caught the possessive undercurrent. "I see,"

he said, his smile fading. "Not to worry, old chap. I don't require a weather vane to determine which way the wind is blowing."

James nodded, and his adoring gaze settled on the girl.

When Richard and Christian joined them at the cook fire, James turned to Masina. "Will you show us the path to the top of *fanua i afi*?"

Masina touched each man with a wide-eyed gaze, and her eyes came back to James. "It is *tapu* to climb *fanua i afi*. This you cannot do. *Tagaloa* will be angry. He will punish you and the *o tagata o fanua o la'ua*."

James grasped her hands and looked into her fright-filled eyes. "We must, Masina. My friends wish to leave *lau'ele'ele i sami*. You must help them. *Tagaloa* does not exist. You know this. You studied with the missionaries who taught you of the One God."

"Your god will not help us." Tears sprang to her eyes. "Will you leave with Richard and your friends? Will you leave Masina?"

His throat bobbed, and he swallowed. "Will you come with me?"

She bowed her head, face stricken with sadness. "I cannot. I am *o tagata o fanua o la'ua*. I cannot live in *lalo'lagi*." When they turned to depart, she pushed past them, looked back over her shoulder, and dashed the tears from her cheeks. "But I will lead you because James wants it so."

She started up a narrow trail leading into the jungle. The route appeared little used, no more than a track for the wild pigs brought to the island by the missionaries, overgrown with ferns and lianas. Richard and Christian slashed a path with daggers through the foliage where no passage seemed to exist.

The forest air was heavy and moisture laden, the way ill defined and shadow filled. At the passage of a goshawk, great conclaves of horned parakeets, red-fronted parakeets, and rainbow lorikeets screamed like demented lunatics from the uppermost canopy, resulting in jumpy muscles and unsettled nerves among the company. Several of the giant geckos scurried beneath ferns and drew Christian's gaze downward. Overhead under the broad leaves, like ripe, russet coconuts, hung fruit bats the size of a man's hand, wings secured about their bodies, awaiting dusk. Large and small rats, feeding on insects and succulent vegetation, scampered along branches beneath the bats, creating a noise like wind rustling the foliage. As most oceanic islands had no indigenous mammals other than bats, the rats were clearly another fauna introduced by white men.

The group emerged from the jungle onto a black, glassy plain, broken by fissures through which lava had flowed, rising in a nearly seamless, obsidian wall. The cauldron churned far above them. Masina circled the lava field and took up another faint track. After traversing the mountain's eastern base, they came across a field of basalt, dark gray and crumbly, with bubbles on its surface formed by steam from the expanding lava. Halfway into the field, she turned into a cleft bisecting the basaltic flow. There within its gloomy interior, rough steps carved out of the rock led upward.

Masina came to a halt at the crater's top, her body shaking like a palm in a gale. Sulfurous fumes arose in a turbid atmosphere below them. Magma seethed under its surface with flames erupting and burning in the molten soup. Looking into the volcano's heart was like glimpsing the gates of Dante's *Inferno*. Heat baked their skin. The arid air scalded their throats. When they took a breath, it seared their lungs, and they inhaled in shallow pants.

Christian and Garrett turned their backs on the cauldron to gaze out over the entire island and beyond. Puffy clouds drifted across the azure sky, against which red-tailed tropic birds dipped and soared. Beyond the rise of the volcano, riotous jungle clothed the land and the nearby green-carpeted peak of *fanua o la'ua*. The coral reef enclosed a turquoise lagoon with transparent water revealing the shadows of large fish swimming beneath the surface. The ocean beyond the reef became emerald with rolling swells breaking in white foam on the coral. Between the trees and the water lay a narrow belt of black volcanic sand. To the northwest, the tsunami's destruction revealed itself in a swath of broken coconut and breadfruit trees and another lagoon filled with floating debris.

Christian pivoted slowly, shading his eyes with his hands. He wished for a spyglass. Nonetheless, a faint hump of land rose from the sea to the east and another, larger outline far beyond that. He pointed, and Garrett peered in that direction, shading both eyes with cupped hands. "Unless my eyes deceive me," Christian said, "we're on a chain of islands. If we travel east, we may eventually make the mainland. What do you think?"

"That we have no other choice," Garrett replied grimly, lowering his hands.

Christian nodded.

When the earth beneath their feet trembled, the cloud of gases over the volcano widened and streamed upward. A warm, noxious rain enveloped them. A gust of wind tore it apart, and Masina uttered a strangled scream. Christian whirled around. Her arm unsteady, she pointed down the path they had taken. Far below, Kiha led a heavily armed group of warriors up the side of the volcano.

"The *tapu*," she whispered. "Now Kiha will sacrifice us to the gods."

The volcano boiled behind them. The ground shook beneath them. Cinders and ash erupted from the cavity and dropped about them. As the activity increased, James grabbed the terrified Masina, and they sprinted toward the other side of the crater. Flaming lava bombs shot from the magma to fall into the jungle. The warriors making their way upward paused, turned about, and scurried back the way they had come. Lava seeped from fissures and streamed downward, cooling and depositing another layer of volcanic rock. Christian paced along the edge to look out into the jungle. The eruption appeared to be confined to one slope. With lava flowing across the eastern face of the volcano, the four men and Masina dashed toward a less-used path winding down the southern side. Following Masina's lead, they descended.

The trail was rougher than the one they originally climbed, and they backtracked often around precipitous rock sheets allowing no footholds. Evening fell by the time they stood on the shore beside the lagoon. When the sun dropped abruptly from the sky, darkness pressed in. Only a distant glow from the flowing lava relieved the night.

"Where do the *la'ua* keep their canoes?" Christian asked Richard. "I've seen them used for fishing. Now that we've violated the *tapu*, we have no alternative but to leave tonight."

"I will show you," Masina answered in a melancholy voice.

She took them to a cove hidden by overhanging palm trees. Within its shelter lay several small canoes and two larger catamaran-like vessels rigged with *tapa* cloth sails. James and Masina returned under cover of darkness to the village to retrieve the *Maiden Anne*'s crew while Richard, Garrett, and Christian gathered coconuts. They hollowed out the hairy nuts, filled them with freshwater from a stream trickling into the cove, and plugged the holes with coarse grass. After stripping the trees of fruit, they tossed it into the catamarans. When James and the men returned, they were ready to leave.

"Kiha and his warriors have yet to return to the village," James said. "The lava must have cut in front of them. The high chief, the *ali'i*, has called his council to debate our whereabouts. Conversation isn't likely to turn to action until Kiha returns. Tapia apparently suspects, because he's doing his best to extend the debate. That should give us a head start, though I have little expectation they will follow us. I have yet to see the *la'ua* venture beyond the lagoon."

Masina's small body pressed and shivered against James's. "Will you leave me now?" she asked, tears glazing her eyes.

James looked over her head to the men who waited by the catamarans. The battle waging in his heart between his past life and possible future shone clearly in his face. He released a sigh and tightened his arms around Masina. "I shall stay," he said.

Richard looked up from where he was tying coconuts

to the bulwark of a catamaran with a rope made from twisted vines. "What of Kiha and the *tapu*? If you and Masina remain behind, Kiha is likely to kill you."

Masina smiled and shook her head. "We will live with my mother's people and be safe there."

"Have you set your mind to this?" Christian asked.

James gazed down into Masina's eyes. "Indeed, I have."

Richard walked over to him and extended his hand. When James took it, Richard said, "Luck go with you, James. Perhaps we shall cross paths again someday."

"Should God will it," James said softly and pulled Richard to him for an embrace.

Christian witnessed the emotional moment between two men who had worked and traveled together for many years; still, the possibility of being caught before they crossed the reef made his gut twist. Having no desire for his limbs to end up in an oven, he loudly cleared his throat.

Richard patted James on the back once more, bent down and kissed Masina's cheek, and turned away, striding back to the boats.

James stood on the sand, his arm around Masina's waist, while the men pushed the two catamarans into the lagoon, climbed aboard, and picked up the paddles. Once the boats cleared the reef, James raised his arm in farewell. When Richard waved back, James and Masina turned and disappeared into the jungle.

Starlight & Promises

Two weeks of sailing eastward from island to island and paddling when the wind died, and they ran out of islands with no larger landmass in sight.

"Continue on eastward and pray we find New Zealand, or go back?" Christian asked Richard. "If we continue, we'll be heading into open sea."

"I'm for going on," Richard said. He polled the other men, and they seemed of one mind—go on.

They filled their stores of coconuts and breadfruit, though the island had no freshwater. Coconut milk would have to do. Then they set out again, sailing ever eastward. One week passed, another, and no land, only endless open sea lapping against the sides of their boats. On dawn at the beginning of the third week, one man sighted the sails of a ship to port. They adjusted their sails to intersect with its course.

"What if it's a pirate ship?" Garrett asked, a gloomy look on his face.

"Shut up, Garrett," Christian replied, "or I'll throw you overboard. A ship is a ship and better than a watery grave."

Garrett gulped and closed his mouth.

As they drew nearer, the Union Jack flying from the ship's topmast brought a rousing cheer from the men on the catamarans. The ship heaved to and brought them on board, and two weeks later, they made landfall on the coast of New Zealand. Though sunburned and dehydrated when they sighted Auckland, the men voiced their elation with prayers and hoorahs. They had made the arduous trip with few mishaps and no loss of life. After a few days' recovery, they caught a British military troop ship headed for Hobart.

With Samantha on his mind, Christian stood at the rail as Hobart came into view. He imagined the delight in her eyes when he reunited her with her uncle Richard. A smile stretched his mouth, his heart warmed, and his cock hardened. He'd been so long without a woman, he would likely come at the sight of her. He had eschewed the attentions of the native maidens on the island, his thoughts only on Samantha. Now that he had returned alive, he resolved never to leave her behind again. A gust of wind ruffled his hair, and he breathed in the heady harbor scents. Civilization at last. Hobart was far removed from Boston, but it was better than a reed pallet in a hut and eating breadfruit paste with his fingers. Never had he been so anxious to return from the wilds. But then he'd never had a woman like Samantha waiting for him.

The ship set anchor in the harbor. After the troops and the *Maiden Anne*'s crew disembarked, Christian, Richard, and Garrett climbed into a dinghy and were rowed to the docks. They rented hacks from the nearby stable and galloped through the streets toward Talmadge

House, their haste underscoring their impatience to end their journey.

Pounding hoofbeats brought Cullen from the barn at a run. His mouth dropped open, and he darted toward the riders pulling to a halt in a scattering of crushed shell. "Chris!" he shouted while grabbing the horse's bridle in one hand. He turned his head toward the house, cupping a hand at his mouth. "Christian's back! And Garrett, too!"

Pettibone opened the door at the commotion and lost his composure. He ran down the steps and left the door swinging on its hinges. Jasper, Delia, Chloe, and Gilly appeared a few seconds later. They milled around the men, hugging bodies and bussing cheeks. Delia held Richard in her pudgy arms as if she would never let him go.

Christian embraced them all, swept up in the hub-bub. After a few moments, he realized he'd not yet seen Samantha, whom he had expected to be the first to greet him. He stepped away and searched the courtyard in vain, the lightness in his heart dying. His smile slowly turned into a frown, and his stomach tilted with a sickening wobble.

Clasping Delia's shoulder, he turned her away from Richard. "Where is Sam?" he asked, barely able to curb his urge to shout.

Her gaze fell, and she linked her arm in his. "You had better come inside."

At her paleness, his heart moved into his throat.

"The yard is no proper place for a discussion," Delia said. "Come into the house where we shall be more comfortable." She turned at the waist to include everyone in her invitation. "I shall ring for tea."

Christian twisted his mouth bitterly. Typical aristocratic reaction to any unpleasantness. As though tea would drown his worry. He laid his hand on the arm curled within his. His fingers tightened unconsciously. He remained very still, though panic crackling in his brain crawled through his limbs and weakened his knees. "Will someone please tell me what is going on and where my wife is?"

Delia patted his arm. "Not here, Christian."

He wanted to shake her, but he could see he would get nothing more from her in the yard. Delia, in her own way, could be as stubborn as Samantha. An argument would only delay the information he demanded. "Shall we go in?" he said, capitulating and tucking her arm more tightly in the crook of his elbow.

The others took seats in the parlor. Christian remained on his feet, leaning one shoulder against the fireplace mantel and crossing his trembling arms over his chest. He drew on all his reserves to remain calm and civil. "Now that we've seated ourselves and tea is on its way, would you kindly tell me where my wife has gotten herself to?"

When all the Talmadge House inhabitants began to talk at once, Delia made a shushing gesture. "Leave this task to me. Samantha is my niece."

Christian remained cool and unemotional outwardly, but his fear for Samantha's safety strained at the leash of his composure.

"Samantha met a man," Delia began.

Christian's body turned to stone. He barely exerted command over his temper.

"His name is Steven Landry," she said. "He told us he knew Richard from school."

Richard frowned. "I have no recollection of a Landry, but he could have been in a different year from me."

She turned to Richard with a plea in her expression, as though she wished to be spared this conversation. "He is a mature man. I would imagine about your age. A quiet gentleman. When Christian sailed without her, Samantha took his absence badly. She soon reconciled herself to remaining in Hobart, or so we believed. I approved when she began seeing Steven. He treated her like a daughter and occupied her time, chaperoned at all times, of course, by Jasper and Pettibone. Her disposition brightened. She began to take an interest in her appearance and in enjoying herself and exploring Hobart." Her gaze swiveled to Christian. "I vow I never saw any improper behavior between the two of them."

"She ran away with 'im," Cullen interjected.

Christian straightened with a jerk. An indrawn breath hissed between his teeth. "She did what?" Reality spun away; numbness settled over him. He cast a baffled gaze at the room's inhabitants. Their faces reflected pity. His mouth hardened. He had no use for pity; he wanted answers.

"That appears to be the case," Delia said with a sigh. "We have no notion what truly happened. She departed six days ago and left no word behind. As we feared foul play, we contacted the authorities. When they heard Cullen's story, they informed us they could do little other than issue an order for the constables to send word should they happen to come across her. She *is* of age, and from what we can determine, Steven did not coerce her."

Christian narrowed his eyes on Cullen. "Tell me," he said.

Cullen moved to the center of the room, settled on the carpet as if he were on the deck of a ship, and took a deep breath. He proceeded to relate what he'd observed and his impressions of what happened.

Christian stopped him only once, managing to ask, though the words nigh stuck in his throat, "Why would you assume she wasn't coerced?"

"She weren't tied nor nuthin'," Cullen said. "An' Landry wasn't pointin' no pistol at 'er back."

"Go on," Christian said, dimly aware that a vein in his temple throbbed in concert with his pounding heartbeat.

By the time Cullen finished, Christian's muscles were coiled as tightly as a leopard's haunches tensed to leap. He turned to Jasper. "I presume you inquired into Landry's character and business. What did you find?"

Jasper released a breath, as though relieved Christian had finally allowed him to join the discussion. "The man is a legitimate merchant. He owns a fleet of ships and imports luxury items from Asia. Neither the garrison nor the other merchants had word of any unpleasant gossip. He arrived from England about fifteen years ago and, to all accounts, has been a model citizen ever since. He is unwed, forty-five years of age, and of outstanding moral character, according to his acquaintances."

Christian locked his hands behind his back and strode back and forth in front of the fireplace. His shoulders and back ached under the strain of maintaining a civilized demeanor. He felt as if he stood outside his body, observing the group from a distance. When he glanced in the mirror above the mantel, he was amazed at how unruffled he appeared, considering he felt like howling loudly enough to raze the house. He struggled to consolidate his thoughts and rejoin his body.

Once his initial gut reaction drained from his brain, the cloud over his reasoning cleared. Would Samantha abscond with a man she barely knew, a man who approached her on the streets of Hobart, so soon after their marriage, with no word to her family, no consideration for him? She was devious; she was manipulative, but she was not intentionally cruel or dim-witted, except when it came to defending her family. She would not distress them like this. Neither would she torment *him* like this. He was fairly certain she loved him.

Unless . . .

He halted and swung around. "I believe you, Cullen, when you say Landry didn't coerce her, but I expect he enticed her. Only possible news of Richard would convince her to leave so abruptly." He directed his next statement at Richard. "She was obsessed with finding you. If someone were to convince her they had word of your location, she would follow them to perdition itself." Shoving a hand through his hair, he pulled it loose from its queue, and it fell down around his shoulders. "Landry may be only a minor character, perhaps even duped into doing Sam's bidding. What worries me more than Landry is the other men accompanying them. They could be part of Miggs's crew. Damn it!" He slammed his fist into the mantel. "I warned her to be wary of anyone unduly interested in Richard. It's my own fault. She never listened to me before. I don't know why I expected her to do so this time."

"Find us food," he said to Delia. He swept a hand toward Cullen. "Saddle and pack the horses for a trip into the interior." He turned to Garrett. "Recruit four or five hale men from the *Maiden Anne*'s crew who are handy with weapons and have no compunction about using them. We're going after her."

"How will you find them?" Pettibone asked as the others ran to carry out Christian's orders.

"Track them," Christian answered with a humorless smile. "That's the reason Samantha commissioned me. I track animals."

CHAPTER THIRTY

Eight men pounded out of Talmadge House courtyard, the horses' hooves kicking up shell fragments and a white haze. Waving from the top of the steps, Delia, Chloe, Pettibone, and Gilly prayed for their success. Cullen, a sullen frown on his face at their insistence he stay with the women, stood alone in the stable doorway.

With the seamen less adept on horseback than the three gentlemen, Christian, Garrett, and Richard left the others behind, forging ahead to Huonville to seek transport and information.

Christian learned from the raftsmen that only a few small settlements existed between Huonville and the western coast. However, the inland towns held no interest for him. He sought the pirate's enclave, Miggs's rat hole.

Only three inlets west of Hobart appeared suitable for hiding a deepwater ship. Bathurst Harbour lay south of the river and across the Arthur Range, rugged mountain terrain covered in Huon pine, scrub brush, and nearly impenetrable forest. Mostly uninhabited, the area enjoyed a reputation for its inhospitality. Payne Bay, the outlet for the Davey River, also lay across the Arthur Range. Only one tiny outpost existed along this route, a tin mine at Melaleuca. A track of sorts led from the end of the Huon River to Gordon Bend, but to reach Payne Bay, they would be obliged to sweep around the northern edge of the mountains and turn south to Port Davey. The third possible inlet was Macquarie Harbour situated northwest of the Huon River at the end of the Gordon River. It ran westward out of Lake Gordon and through a long track of wilderness to the sea. The last Christian heard, Miggs had anchored his ship at Macquarie Harbour, but that information was months old.

By early evening, the company wended its way westward along the river on two sturdy rafts. They rode the river by day, pulled to the banks at night to camp, and reached the end of their journey on the Huon River after four days. Bathurst Harbour and Payne Bay lay to the south, Macquarie Harbour to the north.

Christian took over. Knowing they were at least six days behind Samantha and Landry, he studied the ground, using his tracking skills to search for signs of

recent passing. Most traffic had taken the path leading to Gordon Bend. Only one group of hoofprints,
less than a fortnight old, led northward. It bypassed the
track to take the shorter route to the lake region. So it
was Macquarie Harbour. If he was wrong and Samantha
suffered as a result, he would have to live with his mistake for the rest of his life.

They headed north toward the lake through heavily
forested land and tracked northwest when they reached
the southern edge of Lake Gordon. When they came
across the Gordon River, they followed it westward to
Macquarie Harbour.

Almost two weeks passed before they reached their
destination. A rocky, narrow entrance, dubbed Hell's
Gates, protected the harbor, and an island lay in the
middle of the inlet. At one time, the island had housed
Tasmania's most brutal penal colony. The government
abandoned the site over sixty years ago after establishing
an escape-proof colony at Port Arthur.

A rude town sat at the far end of the mainland close
to Hell's Gates. Tall cliffs ringed the southern edge of the
encampment, and forest swept down on the north and
east. While the men set up a temporary camp beyond
the cliffs, Richard and Christian took out their spyglasses
and moved to the cliff edge. There they stretched out
on the ground and surveyed the town. Offshore lay the
hulk of Miggs's ship, the *Manta Ray*.

"Over there," Christian whispered, not knowing how far his voice would travel.

Richard swung his glass to the location Christian indicated, to a man walking across the compound toward a cabin larger than the others and set back a short distance from the town.

"Recognize him?" Christian asked.

"I would recognize his stink with my eyes gouged out," Richard said harshly. "'Tis Miggs. I would wager a hundred guineas that if he has Samantha he keeps her in his hut."

"That's a bet I'll not take," Christian said softly, then asked, "How many men do you count?"

Richard scanned the ship and the town area. "A dozen, mayhap a few more inside or at the harbor entrance on watch."

"I make it fourteen with the three who just went below deck."

Miggs entered the cabin, drawing their gazes, and another man left, closing the door behind him.

"Fifteen," amended Christian. "What do you make of that small hut on the forest edge?" He pointed to it.

Richard focused in on the tiny, windowless hut. He turned to Christian with a grin. "Munitions?"

Christian smiled grimly. "Our ticket in."

They scrabbled backward on their bellies away from the cliff and stood when no longer within sight of the village. After brushing themselves off, they made their way back to the camp Garrett and the others had established inside the encroaching forest. They made no fire when night fell but sat in a circle and discussed their plans for penetrating the pirates' midst and retreating in one piece. A tawny frogmouth called in the tall pines, and the cries of hapless creatures, prey to prowling predators, pierced the darkness at intervals, shredding the men's nerves.

"I would prefer to watch the town for another day to determine for certain where the prisoners, if any, are being held," Christian said. "Most likely it's in Miggs's own cabin, the large one at the eastern edge of the village. Nonetheless, we can't afford to be wrong. Once we enter the area, I have no wish to waste time in trying to find them."

"As much as I deplore leaving Samantha in the hands of those villains another day," Richard said, "I agree with Christian. Miggs must believe Samantha is the only person with the information he so desperately wants. He would assume James and I are dead. Surely he'll not take the risk of her dying, too, and taking the secret with her."

"Wouldn't she have told him by now?" one of the seamen asked. "Then he would have no reason to keep her alive."

Richard and Christian exchanged a knowing glance. "Samantha would tell him naught, even were he to keelhaul her," Christian said in a dry voice. "I imagine she and her gentleman friend found their way here expecting to find Lord Stanbury. When she learned otherwise, she got her back up. When Samantha becomes stubborn, Beelzebub himself couldn't compel her to cooperate."

When the men looked skeptical, Jasper nodded and said, "He is right, you know. Lady Samantha is as tough as a moray eel."

"Besides, she has been here but a short while," Richard said. "With a lady among their company, I seriously doubt they traveled as quickly as we did. I would imagine Miggs would give her and Landry some time to mull over their fate before moving on to the heavy persuasion. Miggs would have no reason to expect pursuit and therefore might believe he has all the time he needs."

"There is another factor," Christian added. "The man who paid Miggs for Richard's abduction, a gentleman from Hobart. I have yet to see anyone who fits that description. Miggs will wait until this mystery man arrives. I would expect his employer plans to interrogate Samantha personally before he pays, so he may be certain the information comes from a reliable source. More than likely, he'll arrive by ship through Hell's Gates. I can't see a gentleman tackling the overland route. Only one ship sits at anchor. Unless he has already come and gone, we've arrived before him."

They turned in for the night and curled up in blankets beneath the trees in beds of thick pine needles.

Richard shook Christian before he fell asleep. "In

the event I fail to make it out of here, I want you to find the Smilodon."

"In order to do that, I would first have to know its location," Christian replied.

A smile pulled crookedly at Richard's mouth. "You mean Samantha didn't tell you yet?"

Christian shot him a speaking glance.

"That little minx." Richard shook his head. "Well, as you are officially family now, the secret is yours as well as ours." He proceeded to relate the island's coordinates to Christian.

When morning came, they monitored the village from the cliffs. Men came and went from the area of Hell's Gates, and only two pirates kept watch on the sea passage. None appeared to guard the forest near the munitions hut nor any other location. Two sailors from the *Maiden Anne* scoured the village perimeter to confirm their observations.

The pirates clearly felt secure from attack by land. One man always remained in the cabin they had designated as belonging to Miggs. Food was taken in, empty plates carried out, and visitors knocked before the door opened. If the pirates held Samantha and her gentleman friend, they were in that cabin, and the door remained locked from the inside.

As the sun westered, the men gathered again. "We require two diversions," Christian said. "The first will distract the pirates after Garrett, Richard, Jasper, and I make our way to the hut. When we set off the fireworks, we trust the man guarding Sam and Landry will unlock the door and come outside. We can get to them in the confusion."

The men collected their weapons and divided into two groups. "Give us one hour to reach the forest nearest the ammunition hut," Christian said, handing the spyglass to one of the seamen. "Once you see my signal, come down the cliff. Fire your guns and make as much commotion as possible. About a third of the way down, you'll find a ledge fronted by boulders, where you can hold off the pirates until we return."

The two groups split up. One moved toward the cliff, with ropes to rappel down the slick face. The other slipped through the forest to circle around to the ammunition hut. The four men ran silently and swiftly through the trees, barely disturbing the wildlife in their passing. In less than an hour, they positioned themselves on the edge of the forest directly behind the hut.

Sunset came in a blaze of glory, the sun sinking in an inferno of crimson and pink into the sea off Hell's Gates. Christian pulled out a small mirror and held it up to the last rays of the sun. The light's reflection bounced off the top of the cliff where his men waited. A few minutes later, all hell broke loose.

The men atop the cliff threw ropes over the side. They slid downward and fired their repeating rifles into the village. Pirates burst from the cabins and left cook fires, hiding from the snipers behind makeshift barriers of barrels and wooden crates. With the pirates' eyes riveted on the cliff, the four men in the forest crept into the open and approached the hut.

Jasper smashed the lock with his pistol butt and stood guard while Garrett, Richard, and Christian moved inside the murky interior. Christian was the last to enter. He paused at the doorway, waiting for Richard to go ahead, and thought he heard Samantha calling out to him. Glancing around, however, he failed to see her. Ducking inside, he blamed his confused senses on the uproar in the camp and wishful thinking.

Gunpowder barrels and cannonballs littered the rotting wood floor. Rifle and pistol bullets filled wooden boxes along one wall, and cutlasses and sabers hung from the rafters. Cannon grease sat in tubs near the door.

Christian pulled out a length of rope and coated it with grease. He broke open a barrel of gunpowder, buried one end of the rope in the black powder, and motioned to Garrett to leave. When Jasper and Garrett sped toward the woods, Christian knelt and lit a match, touching it to the end of the rope.

"Come on," he yelled to Richard, taking him by the arm and pulling. "I don't know how long that fuse will burn."

As they spun toward the door, Richard following on

Christian's heels, a bullet came through the side of the hut. A tremendous force slammed into Christian's back at the same instant the world ripped apart.

CHAPTER THIRTY-ONE

Macquarie Harbour

Samantha slept for what seemed like time without end. Whenever she climbed upward through the gloom, wetness poured down her throat. She swallowed convulsively and sank deeper into a dreamless sleep. When she finally awoke, she blinked stupidly, her body sluggish, mind disoriented. Rough-hewn logs chinked with mudlike mortar enclosed her in a dirt-floored space no more than six by eight feet. One window, shuttered with wooden planks, cut into the wall opposite her. A door lay to her right. The room held naught for furnishings save for the straw mattress she occupied on the floor. By the pallid quality of the light sifting through spaces between the shutter boards, either dawn or dusk approached.

When she sat up, her head spun with the sudden movement. A batten of cotton wool wrapped around her mind, and her eyes felt heavy and gritty. A foul taste lingered in her mouth, her throat as dry as ashes. Her last memory was of falling asleep beside the fire in the forest on the banks of the Huon.

She cleared her throat and tested her voice. "Steven?" From the pounding headache coming on through her mental confusion and the enervation of her limbs and body, she suspected she'd been drugged. "Steven, can you hear me? Where are you?"

A faint rapping came from behind her.

She crawled off the mattress and dragged herself to the wall. "Steven? Are you there?"

The rapping came again and a whispered voice. "Samantha?"

"Oh, Steven. What happened to us?"

"Quiet," he said. "Keep your voice low, or they will hear us."

She shoved her tangled hair back from her face. "Who?"

"Miggs," he responded. "The pirate betrayed us. Miggs caught us at the camp after you fell asleep. He killed my men, knocked me out, and took us captive. We are being held in the pirates' village at Macquarie Harbour."

"I was drugged, Steven. I remember naught. Who drugged me?"

"One of my men. I believed him loyal to me, but he also worked for Miggs. I found out only too late. Miggs interrogated me earlier, said you are privy to some information he desires. He wanted to know about a cat and your uncle."

Samantha inhaled a breathy gasp.

"They've been waiting for you to revive. Then they plan to question you," he continued. "What do they want? What cat are they talking about?"

"I-I have no notion," she said, her voice breaking.

"Samantha, listen to me. These men are killers. They took your uncle, and I must tell you, though I know how much you hoped to hear otherwise, but they killed him, murdered him.because he refused to talk. They have convinced themselves you have the information they seek. What do you know? What could be so valuable they would kill Richard to obtain it? Pray believe me, they will not bat an eye at torturing us both to extract what they desire.

"What do you know?" he asked again when she remained silent. "Is it worth dying for? Allow me to help us. Would Richard have wanted you to keep his secret at the cost of your life?"

"Oh, Steven, I don't know. I'm so confused. Had I imagined it would come to this, I would have told the world. No secret is worth Richard's life." Her throat constricted and ached with the strain of holding back tears.

"Hear me well, Samantha. I know Richard's demise has devastated you, but you must share your secret with me. If I was to know what the pirates seek, I might be able to stall or misdirect them while I devise a plan that will allow us to leave here alive. I can withstand more torture than you. They will beat you, mayhap even rape you."

"No, I cannot allow you to sacrifice yourself for me. I shall tell them what little I know."

"Did Richard die in vain? Will you now make a mockery of his life and kill us, too? Mark my words. If you tell them everything; that is exactly what will happen. Once they get what they want, they will murder us and dump our bodies at sea. Tell me, Samantha. Allow me to help us. I can bargain with them, while you cannot."

She expelled a weary breath. "They want to know where to find the Smilodon."

"Smilodon? A saber-toothed tiger? Are they not extinct?"

"Indeed, they are or were. Richard found one, a living one. And some person, another scientist, wishes the cat to be his discovery. He hired Miggs to kidnap Richard and James and coerce the locality of the find from them."

"If what you say is true, Richard has made the greatest discovery of the century, or so I assume, not being a scientist myself. I now understand why his life was in danger and why the pirates want you. Did Richard inform you of where he found this cat?"

She held her tongue, considering Steven's question. 'Twas overmuch to process, what with her headache and their desperate situation. Circumstances were unraveling too quickly. Not really understanding why, she equivocated. "He did, but the coordinates are in Richard's last letter back at Talmadge House. So you see, I cannot reveal what I do not know. I fear 'tis hopeless. They will not believe me and will kill us anyway."

"Do you recall anything from the letter, anything I can give them to stay their hand at least for a time until we concoct an escape plan?"

He sounded so terribly desperate. Was she not obligated to provide him with something? 'Twas she who had put his life in danger. "Only that the cat is on an island in the Furneaux Group."

"That area contains over fifty small islands and hundreds of atolls," he said with a note of exasperation. "Can you not be more specific?"

An unexplainable instinct warned her to guard her tongue. "No, I truly cannot remember. I require Richard's letter."

"Very well, save your strength. Try to rest. When they come for you, pretend you still suffer from the influence of the drug. I shall think of something."

Steven rose and walked out of the room into the cabin's main living area.

Miggs sat at a battered table where he wielded a

knife to carve into its wooden top by the light of a whale-oil lantern. He raised his head at Steven's entrance. "De she 'ave what ye want? I know she 'as what I want." A smarmy grin covered his mouth.

Steven caught up a chair and swung it around, straddling it backward. "She has it but says it's in Hobart, meaning this trip was a useless waste of time."

"De ye believe 'er?"

He rubbed his chin with a hand. "I don't know." He met Miggs's one rheumy eye with a silent challenge. "You'll not touch her. That was part of our agreement."

Miggs laughed. "An agreement atween gen'lemen, eh?"

"Correct, and I shall gut you should you revoke it. I require her alive, at least until I obtain the information from her."

"An' 'ow will ye de that? De ye really think she'll give ye what ye want once she's back wi' 'er lovin' family an' them bodyguards?"

"I shall get it. How I accomplish that is none of your concern. You've received your pay. Now we must come up with a plausible escape scenario that will make her forever obligated to me for saving her life."

"I don't know," Miggs mused. "I think this job's worth more'n ye paid. If this cat's so bloody valuable, I may jest want it fer meself, an' the girl, too."

Steven exploded from the chair. He caught Miggs's wrist in an iron grip and squeezed. The unholy look he gave Miggs was enough to make the pirate shiver.

"'Ey now. She's yers if'n ye want 'er that bad," Miggs said in a pained voice.

"You're bloody right she's mine," Steven spat and dropped the pirate's wrist.

A knock came at the door. Rubbing his wrist, Miggs shoved back from the table and lumbered to his feet. He made his way across the room and cracked open the door. "What de ye want? I'm busy 'ere," he said to the pirate in torn breeches with two cutlasses hanging from leather bands crossing his chest.

"We 'ave trouble." The man swallowed visibly. "There's men comin' down t'cliffs. Not garrison, no uniforms, but not ourn."

"'Ow many?"

"Four o' five so far."

Gunfire erupted from the direction of the cliffs. The man swung his head to look over his shoulder.

"Then take care o' 'em!"

While Miggs berated the man, Steven slipped a stiletto out of his boot and silently got up from the chair. He came up behind Miggs. When the door slammed closed, he clamped an arm around Miggs's neck and thrust the knife deep into his kidneys. The pirate struggled briefly before sinking to the floor. Blood poured from the wound.

Samantha leaned against the rough wall, tears streaming from her eyes. Finding Richard alive after all this time had been unlikely. Nevertheless, she had still held out hope. She cursed the Smilodon and the expedition that brought her uncle to Tasmania. Her stomach cramped, and she vomited on the floor. Though Steven vowed he would find a way for them to leave this place, she no longer had the will to believe him. He was as much a prisoner as she.

She tapped on the wall. "Steven?"

He failed to answer; only muttered voices came from the room beyond her prison. The guards. How many? How in God's name did Steven expect them to stroll past an entire pirate crew?

Diminishing light bled in from the window, indicating coming night instead of day. Samantha pushed herself up from the floor and stumbled over to the boards. Her legs, still weak from the drugging, scarcely held her upright. She peered out. A bar braced along the outside width secured the shutters. Men in dirty clothing, some with bare chests, their bodies swarming with knives, pistols, and cutlasses, ran past the window. Other cabins sat in the forefront in a space denuded of vegetation. A log corral to the right held horses, and straight ahead on the edge of the settlement, the waters of Macquarie Harbor made a blacker shadow against the darkening sky. A battered ship, its near side stove in, bobbed in the water beside a hand-hewn wooden dock. Sheer cliffs rose in the distance above the enclave.

A sudden volley of gunfire shattered the silence, and a suggestion of movement on the face of the cliff attracted her attention. However, the light had become too faint to make out details.

When her door flew open, Samantha swallowed a scream. Her heart pounded, and she whipped around. Steven stood in the opening, holding a cutlass.

"Come," he said and motioned sharply. "I disabled the guard. We must leave while the pirates are distracted."

"How?" she asked, moving toward him. "How did you escape?"

The door to the outer room banged open, and Steven spun away, the cutlass raised. At the clash of metal on metal, Samantha ran to the door, and her hand flew to her open mouth.

Steven was engaged in a battle with a pirate twice his size. The pirate slashed down, his cutlass a lethal arc of steel. Steven stepped aside, blocked the blade, and the men circled the room in a furious flurry of thrusts and stabs.

The pirate's blade nicked Steven's arm, and blood flowed. Steven seemed to gain strength from his wound and pressed the larger man toward the door and the body of another pirate lying on the floor. The man fell back with the onslaught and in his haste slipped in a pool of blood and went down on one knee. Steven plunged his blade through the man's stomach, pushing him onto his back and pinning him to the floor. As he fell, the pirate smashed into the table and toppled the lighted lantern. Blazing oil spread outward, igniting the table and racing across the floor toward the wall at terrifying speed.

Steven turned to Samantha, breath ragged, and gestured violently. "Come! Now, while we have a chance."

She hurried to his side. He bent over and snatched up the dead pirate's cutlass. Pulling a pistol from the man's belt, he shoved it beneath his own. With the cutlass in one hand and Samantha's palm in the other, he left the burning cabin.

With the sun slipping far down the horizon, shadows spread over the encampment. Glowing light from smoky fires illuminated pirates firing rifles and moving purposefully toward the cliffs to the south. Steven pulled Samantha up against the cabin wall into a pool of darkness. Once the men fled past their location, they sprinted toward the horse corral. Steven cut down the guard coming at them out of the gloom and retrieved his pistol, passing it to Samantha. She tucked it into her waistband.

They caught up two horses and stole along the verge of the town, moving toward the trees at the eastern edge of the cliffs. With deafening rifle and pistol fire and the pirates' concentration on the intruders, Steven and Samantha slipped by unnoticed.

Their path took them close to an outlying shack. A flicker of movement near its door made Samantha pause. She grabbed Steven's arm and pulled him to a halt.

Four men crept toward the building in the gathering darkness. Samantha became paralyzed, her breath suspended. Hairs along the back of her neck rose as though touched by a chill wind. The man in the lead resembled Richard. She released a choked sound. When the last man approached the door, a flare from the fire outlined his features. The air gushed from her lungs.

"Chris!" she screamed. She dropped the horse's reins and stumbled forward, her heart knocking so hard against her ribs she feared it would burst outward.

The man at the door paused, turned his head in her direction, then entered the shack. A second later, two men ran out and into the woods. Neither was Christian.

Steven clutched an arm around her waist and pulled. She fell back, limp against him. A bullet whistled past her head and into the wall of the hut. When the night exploded in a blast of heat and fire, Steven pushed her to the ground. The shock wave rolled over them, and hot wind peppered their bodies with wood splinters.

Samantha lay stunned beneath Steven, searing agony tearing at her heart and stomach. She dared to look up, eyes awash with tears, heart rent with pain. The conflagration choked her, robbed her brain of air. The blast had demolished the shack. 'Twas utterly gone, the two men still inside. Her husband, the partner of her heart, was dead. She receded into a numbness welling up from the deepest recesses of her soul.

CHAPTER THIRTY-TWO

By the time Steven and Samantha approached Talmadge House three weeks later, Samantha's bleak depression showed no signs of lifting. Even the certain fact that she carried Christian's child could not pull her from her grief-stricken state. Breeding sickness had finally claimed her body, further slowing their journey, and withdrawing into a frightening silence, she refused all food, other than what Steven forced on her.

Whenever Steven attempted to draw Samantha out during their trek, he came up against a blank stare. Distant and silent, withdrawn and wan, she shed no more tears and followed his lead like an inanimate puppet. She never asked how he overcame and killed Miggs, and his questions to her remained unanswered. Steven was soon at an impasse as to how to reach her. If she were to linger indefinitely in this state, he would never convince her to give him the Smilodon's location. Anger and frustration beat like bat wings inside his breast and grew more frantic with every mile they traveled.

When the riders entered the courtyard, Pettibone shouted for Delia and hurried out to meet them. Delia, Gilly, and Chloe spilled from the house, brimming with questions and flooded with tears of joy. Cullen, drawn by the commotion, edged out of the stable door and leaned back against the sun-bleached wood.

"Samantha!" Delia cried, running forward. When Steven dismounted and lifted Samantha to the ground, Delia bustled up to her and swept her into her arms.

Gilly and Chloe hung back, hugging their arms to themselves and eyeing Steven with pained confusion on their faces.

"I do declare, my dear, you are naught but skin and bones," Delia exclaimed. Her concern ran deeper than she dared express. Samantha was gaunt and pallid, her riding habit torn and splattered with mud. Scratches and bruises marred her sunburned skin. Her eyes, however, caused Delia the greatest alarm. Cold and distant, their normal bright gold had dimmed to a pale, sickly yellow.

Delia cradled the stiff girl in her arms, gaze skittering to Steven, who waited silently beside the horses. "What happened to her?" she asked with uncharacteristic sharpness. "And where is her husband?"

Steven lowered his eyes. "I believe you should allow Samantha to retire. She has had a rough time of it. Then we can speak more freely."

Delia nodded. She turned Samantha toward the house and led her inside. A bath was drawn and, under Delia's watchful eyes, Gilly bathed the silent girl. When Chloe brought up a tray of food, Samantha averted her head. They tucked her into bed, and she closed her eyes, drifting off almost immediately. She still had spoken not a word. Gilly watched over her while Delia returned to the parlor to confront Steven.

When Delia entered the room, Steven stood beside the bank of front windows, a brandy in his hand. He looked as beaten and road weary as Samantha. A bloody rag circled his right upper arm. Exhaustion and a despondent air clothed him.

"I'm not sure you are welcome here," Delia said, her words chilly as she settled on the edge of an armchair near the fireplace.

When he raised his eyes, bewilderment wreathed his features. "Whyever not?"

"Cullen told us of your departure with Samantha. He followed you to Huonville."

Steven expelled a loud sigh, walked to the settee, and sank down on it. Leaning forward, he rested his elbows on his knees and bowed his head into his cupped hands. "This incident was entirely my fault, all of it," he said when he finally straightened.

"Explain," Delia demanded.

"Samantha asked me to assist in finding her uncle. I knew him at school. Though we never enjoyed a close friendship, we were jolly acquaintances. She swore me to secrecy for fear you would worry. I agreed because I had every intention of returning Richard to your arms by myself, if I were to find him. When I uncovered a clue to his location, Samantha insisted on accompanying me. I told her I would not allow it."

Chloe and Pettibone eased into the parlor and stood along the wall beside the door. Cullen also came in from stabling the horses and found a spot on the floor against the wall. His eyes on Steven, his brows hunkered together in a scowl.

"Was your information correct?" Delia prodded.

"I certainly believed it was." He smiled with a touch of irony. "One of the pirate crew told an associate of mine that Richard was still alive and being held at a pirate cove. I met with the man the next night to demand his terms. He wanted ransom money. When I offered to pay whatever he asked, he insisted Samantha pay him in person and accompany us in the event we were planning to notify the garrison. She and I were to be his insurance against arrest."

Delia drew a careful breath. "Knowing Samantha, this condition thrilled her."

Steven fixed his gaze on a distant point outside the parlor window. "Indeed, it did. I should never have told her."

"I quite agree. You should not have."

He released a shaky laugh. "Truer words were never spoken. We soon discovered Richard was already dead and had been for a long time."

"But Richard is alive," Delia said, her gaze sharpening, voice rising. "Christian found him and James on an island off the coast of New Zealand."

Steven regarded her in dumbfounded silence. "Alive?" he choked out.

"Indeed," Delia said with a nod. "He accompanied Professor Badia in a quest to rescue you and Samantha. What puzzles me is why they failed to return with you. Did you escape on your own before they arrived?"

Steven relaxed. His features assumed a look of sympathy, and he let out his breath slowly. He extended his arms to lightly clasp Delia's hands. "My dear, I fear I have further bad news. I beg you, allow me to continue."

Delia slipped her hands out of his, drew herself up, and motioned for him to go on.

"Unbeknownst to us, the pirate we trusted made a secret pact with Miggs and one of my men. From what I understand, Richard was searching for something of inestimable value. Miggs became convinced Samantha knew where to find it. He took Richard to discover his secret and truly believed Richard had died in a sea battle before the extortion succeeded. Now, with Richard gone, Miggs wanted Samantha, but she was too well guarded in Hobart.

"He duped us, using me and her obsession with finding her uncle to lure her to him." He shook his head. "I simply wished to aid her. Six of my sailors accompanied us. A traitor within my group drugged us two days out from the pirate town and killed his compatriots. When we awakened, we were in the pirates' camp and held under guard in separate locked rooms."

Delia came off the chair and moved to the window, anger in her breast and tears in her eyes.

"An' 'ow did ye escape all by yerself surrounded by bloodthirsty pirates?" Cullen asked.

Steven snapped his head toward Cullen. A hard spark appeared to flicker in his eyes. It disappeared so quickly, Delia must have only imagined she saw it. Steven addressed his answer to Delia. "Miggs interrogated me first. He was saving Samantha for more . . . more refined questioning."

Delia made a soft, strangled noise and clasped a shaky hand to her throat.

"You need not worry, Delia. The situation never became that dire."

The anguish in her face slowly faded.

"I soon learned that Samantha occupied the room next to me," Steven went on. "We managed to communicate briefly through the wall. Her time was running out. I had no knowledge of the information Miggs desired nor any way to stay his hand. He was growing impatient. Thus far the pirates had harmed neither of us. I knew I would be obliged to act soon and was prepared to sacrifice myself to save her. I seized my chance when Miggs brought me out for another interrogation session and a commotion arose in the camp at the same time. When Miggs was called to the door by one of his men, I came up behind him with a bottle. As he closed the door, I smashed it over his head."

"Did you kill him?" Pettibone asked.

"Good heavens, no." Steven looked aghast. "I could never take a life, even to save my own."

Cullen sneered from his position on the floor. "So ye just left 'im there ta come after Sam again?"

Steven shot him a disdainful look. "I'm fairly certain he'll not do so."

"What makes ye so sure?"

"Because by the time I released Samantha and we found horses, a battle raged in the town. I believed at the time the attacking party to be rival pirates and blessed their timely interference. I had no notion they were otherwise until we passed the munitions hut. Samantha saw a man and two others entering and called out her husband's name. I've never met Mister Badia and cannot confirm his identity, but she seemed convinced it was he.

Before we could make our way over, a bullet must have pierced the hut, and it exploded."

"My God!" Delia gasped.

"Fortunately, we were far enough away to sustain only minor injuries, such as this cut on my arm." He gestured to the bandage. "However, I fear the explosion obliterated the building and killed the men inside. Since you say Richard accompanied Mister Badia, I presume two of those who died to be Samantha's husband and uncle."

"Did ye check ta see if'n they was dead?" Cullen asked.

Steven shot him a sharp glare before returning his gaze to Delia. "No one could have survived that catastrophe. Pandemonium was breaking out around us. I was obliged to see Samantha to safety. As we departed, the battle was ending, with the pirates holding the advantage. Flames engulfed the cabin where I left Miggs unconscious." He sent a pointed look toward Cullen. "'Tis for that reason I know he'll not bother us again."

Steven left the chair, walked to Delia, and wrapped an arm around her shoulders. She was crying and stiffened at first. Gradually, she leaned into him and wept on his dusty coat.

"I am desolate, Delia," he said. "I accept full responsibility for this horrific tragedy, that you should lose your brother so soon after finding him, and Samantha, still a newlywed, should lose her husband. Understandably, she has taken her husband's death hard and shown no spark of life or interest since that day. If I were able, I would give my life for her husband's to alleviate her grief."

"No," Delia sobbed. "You did what you could. You are so little acquainted with Samantha. Even had you insisted she stay behind, she would have found a way to follow you if she believed you would lead her to Richard."

"I truly regret his death. Please forgive me. This disclosure must pain you dreadfully."

She looked up with a tremulous smile. "Unlike Samantha, I held out little hope for Richard's safe return after so much time. I made my peace with his death long ago. That it came now rather than a year ago matters little. God did allow me to hold Richard in my arms once more. I'm grateful to Him for that small mercy."

Chloe and Pettibone exited the parlor, motioning to Cullen to come with them, and left the two alone. Delia remained in Steven's arms, crying quietly. He leaned back and lifted her chin with two fingers. "I must tell you something more, Delia, and I do beg pardon if I speak too plainly."

Delia's pulse pounded at the prospect of additional dire news. "Speak as plainly as you must."

He inhaled a deep breath. "Samantha is with child. She suffered from breeding sickness the entire trip back. When I told you and Samantha that I was unwed, I fear I was less than forthcoming. I married once as a young man before I took to sea. My dear wife died birthing a stillborn child. Her death pains me too much to speak about it. So you understand I recognize the signs of breeding. If we are unable to pull Samantha from her depression, she is likely to lose the babe."

Delia's eyes widened. "I-I had no notion—"

"Though I know I have no right to ask," he continued, "and why you should grant me the privilege, I cannot fathom, but I should like to see Samantha and help her recover. I blame myself for her current distress and wish to atone for my faulty judgment. She requires love and support now. Though I realize we've been acquainted for only a short time, I have grown to care for her. I have become fond of her. No, I must be truthful, Delia. I have fallen in love with Samantha."

CHAPTER THIRTY-THREE

She stood in a meadow carpeted in tall grass as golden as ripened wheat. Where was he? Squinting into the sun, she shaded her eyes with a hand. Then off to the edge, where the light met a world as black as the ocean depths, the grasses parted. He grew closer, panting through parted teeth and sniffing the ground, following her spoor. A tawny head with a thick mane, a fusion of dark and light strands, arched upward from the nape of his neck.

He raised his head, and green eyes caught her in their gaze, holding her in thrall. The world fell still, all sound and motion ceasing beyond this one spot in this golden meadow. A curtain of life drew around them, as if nothing else existed outside the enveloping folds of light. They were the only living creatures left on Earth.

A quiver ran through her. Her heart soared. She

eagerly awaited his touch. His canines, long and curving, gleamed in the sun, and the wide mouth spread into a knowing grin, a grin that filled her breast with love.

When a lyrebird cried in the distance, its voice like liquid sunshine, the cat's ears pricked toward the sound. He gazed once more into her eyes and turned away. His footfalls grew more distant, and she wept. Somehow she knew: she would never see Christian, never feel his touch again.

Over the next month, Samantha slowly emerged from the depression leeching her soul of all feeling. Every night she dreamt of the Smilodon. Every time, he left her.

Steven called on her and Delia daily. He expressed his remorse and cast at her feet promises, like withered bouquets, to care for her and her babe. Gilly wept over her, and Delia derided her selfishness, telling her she owed it to Christian's child to pull herself together. Pettibone watched over her at night, and Cullen avoided her. Only Chloe truly understood. Chloe, a romantic at heart, believed in fated lovers and everlasting love.

As Samantha grew stronger, she contemplated her future with Christian and Richard gone. She healed on the outside, yet ice still sheathed her heart. She felt insubstantial most days, as though she were only spirit, not flesh and blood. All joy fled from her life. Even the prospect of bearing and holding Christian's child could not warm her.

On the day she rose from her bed, she searched through her belongings for Richard's letter. She found it among her petticoats, crushed it in her fist, and tossed it into the fireplace. Flames licked up, consuming it as voraciously as the cat had consumed her life. The Smilodon quest had brought her the greatest love she could ever imagine. It also culminated in her greatest sorrow. Watching the letter curl and brown in the fire's heat eased her sorrow somewhat and brought her a degree of peace. From that day, she began to recover. Soon she was riding in the carriage with Steven, taking walks in the gardens at Government House, and accompanying Chloe on shopping trips into town. She still was not herself, prone to prolonged silences, and seldom smiled, yet her family took heart.

One day a few weeks later, when the babe inside her fluttered against her rounded belly, she took stock of her life and what lay before her. She placed her hand against the stirring child, and contentment washed over her. Steven asked for her hand in marriage that same day.

He came upon her in the garden, went down on one knee, and took her hands in his. "Samantha," he said, "I know you still grieve for your husband. However, I pray you can find some room in your heart for me. I cherish you and wish to provide a home and security for you and your child. I shall forever regret the role I played in Christian's death and can only hope that someday you will see fit to forgive me. I beg you. Allow me to be your protector, your husband. Allow me to comfort you."

She smiled inwardly at Steven's extravagant proposal, remembering the less than romantic way Christian hauled her from her cabin aboard the *Maiden Anne* and dragged her to the Hobart chapel. That memory made her realize she could never love Steven the way she loved Christian.

"I cannot forget him, Steven, nor do I wish to," she replied with a sad smile. "His image dwells in my heart. Though I'm flattered by your proposal, I cannot accept, knowing I would be unable to share your sentiments. I place no blame on you for Christian's death. You merely tried to help me and Richard. You will always remain a friend, but I can promise you no more than friendship."

Despite her resistance, Steven crumbled her defenses, his suit aided by Aunt Delia and Chloe, who expressed their belief that she required someone to look after her and the baby needed a father. Steven seemed the perfect choice to Samantha's family. Wearied by their persistence and battered by her emotions, she finally agreed to marry him. She would never love again but admitted the logic of their arguments. She could not allow her baby to suffer without the love of a father because of her selfishness.

In the Tasmanian wilderness

Christian lived in a world of pain with no memory of the final moments before the ammunition exploded. When he swam up through the darkness, Garrett's voice echoed from the ether, vague, far away, and muffled by a ringing inside his skull. He tried to open his eyes, but a soft object pressed against them. He raised a hand to his face to touch the bandage wrapped around his head, and agony shot through his arm.

"Hey, none of that," Garrett said, his words as faint as a breeze. Christian's hand was clasped gently and his arm moved back to his side. The slight effort exhausted him. He fell back into the dark void.

Though the bandage still covered his eyes when he awoke again, his hearing had improved. The words spoken by Jasper and Garrett, who talked nearby, now clearly penetrated his senses.

"It's been three weeks," Garrett said. "He needs a doctor. It's a miracle he's lived this long."

"We cannot move him yet," came Jasper's voice. "The breaks were clean, and I see no sign of fever or infection. Internal damage would be evident by now. But if we were to move him, he may suffer more injury."

"M-may I vote?" Christian asked, his voice as corroded as an anchor chain.

"Chris!" Two voices resounded as one. Rapid footsteps clattered on a wooden floor.

"You're awake," Garrett said.

"A-astute of you." He wet his lips to aid his speech. "Don't dare m-mince words. What happened?"

"Do you remember the explosion?" Garrett answered.

"Ap-apparently not. Refresh m-my memory."

"In the munitions hut at the pirates' camp in Macquarie Harbour."

Images swamped him like a tidal wave. Samantha and Landry. Miggs and the pirates. Creeping into a hut stinking with cannon grease and black powder. Then nothing.

"A bullet must have set off the charge early," Garrett said. "Jasper and I made it to the tree line, but the blast caught you and Richard."

"R-Richard?" Christian questioned with hesitance, though he suspected he knew the answer.

Garrett cleared his throat. "He . . . he didn't make it. We found him lying on top of you. You fell through rotten floorboards and into an earthen cellar beneath the hut. The blast hit Richard in the back. He died instantly and shielded you from the worst of it."

Now Christian remembered. "Powder ex-exploded. Something slammed against me. Richard. S-saved my life." Sorrow ran through his pain. He didn't want to ask. He had to. "S-Samantha?"

"We saw no sign of her. Miggs's cabin was in flames. If she was locked inside . . . I'm sorry, Chris. Our first concern was to get you away from the town. The *Maiden*

Anne's men were barely holding off the pirates. As we dragged you from the splintered hut, they were climbing back up the cliff. I assume they made it."

"Yes," Christian said, unable to vent his grief at Samantha's probable death. He recalled a moment outside the hut when he thought he heard her call his name. He buried the memory with his pain but made a silent vow. If she was dead and Miggs the agent of her demise, he would return to the pirate town and burn it to the ground. "Where?"

"We are in Queenstown," Jasper said, "a silver mining settlement north of Macquarie Harbour. We could hardly fetch your large carcass all the way back to Hobart, so we made for the closest settlement. It consists of no more than a few shanties, a saloon, and a mining office, but we have walls, a bed, and freshwater."

Christian tried to nod and groaned instead. He sucked in a tortured breath. "When?" He avoided asking about his injuries, wanting to delay for as long as possible what they would undoubtedly tell him.

"Three, four weeks, perhaps," was Garrett's reply. "You broke both legs and your left arm in the fall. All were clean. Jasper straightened and splinted them. Fortunately you were unconscious at the time. You probably cracked a few ribs, suffered a concussion, and the remainder is merely scrapes, cuts, bruises, and burns. No internal injuries, we trust."

Christian attempted a laugh. It came out as a rusty chuckle and ended on a deep cough that brought sharp pain to his chest. Leave it to Garrett to blurt out the gory details with no finesse. "As good a-as new," he managed to say. He struggled to lift his arm again. A hand caught it. "My eyes?"

"Powder burns," Jasper said. "You caught a powder flash. You must have looked back as the ammunition exploded."

"Must confess . . . don't remember that." He hesitated before asking, "Am I b-blind?"

Jasper sighed. "I cannot tell you, Christian. I have seen this kind of injury aboard ship. Some recover their sight. Some do not."

"I see." His lips twitched at his pun, and he bobbed his head. "Wait and see."

"Indeed. Once your bones knit and you can sit a horse, we shall return you to Hobart. If you should fail to regain your sight by then and not find a doctor there, surely someone in Boston can help you."

"Brilliant," Christian uttered bitterly. No denying the fact that science had little use for a tracker who could not even see the ground beneath his feet.

"Concentrate on getting well," Garrett said, his voice breaking. "Mind Nurse Jasper, and you'll soon be up and about."

Christian turned his head on the pillow and fell asleep,

moisture oozing from his eyes beneath the bandage.

In another four weeks, Christian could stand and hobble for short distances with the aid of two wooden canes, though his legs remained in splints. Jasper removed the splint from his left arm and the bandages from his eyes. When he opened his eyes for the first time, he encountered no more than what he expected—darkness. His bruises and other injuries healed and became but part of a painful past. At last he could draw breath without feeling like a boulder was crushing his chest. Two more weeks, Jasper told him, and the splints would come off his legs. He could then learn to walk and ride again. When, or if, he would recover his sight was a subject they shunned in mutual, silent consent.

The weeks soared by in anticipation of Samantha's wedding. Steven hungered to question her regarding the Smilodon, but the bitch fell mute whenever he brought up the subject. When she was absent, he took to scouring her bedchamber.

Though he riffled through every piece of clothing and read every scrap of paper, he failed to find the letter from Richard. Impatience twisted in his gut like a knife, and he dared not push Samantha too vigorously for fear she would cry off from the wedding and her family would exclude him from her life entirely. Therefore, he bided his time. Once they married, she would give him the letter one way or another.

The cat's discovery became only a small part of his revenge on the Colchester family. By marrying Samantha, he would control her fortune and Richard's, since she and Chloe were her uncle's only heirs. He would also control Samantha herself. With that thought, he barely kept a tether on his lust. Since the night in that dingy tavern when he had looked into her golden eyes and recognized her as a Colchester, he had wanted her. Since Richard could no longer pay for his sins, Samantha would. She would pay dearly with her body and her soul.

Over Samantha's objections, Delia dragged her to the modiste, to fittings for a wedding gown. Since the first wedding had been such a hurried affair, Delia demanded that this time Samantha would wed in a manner befitting an earl's niece.

Samantha stood on the platform at Madame Louella's while the modiste draped material across her for Delia's approval. Her eyes remote, features indifferent, Samantha nodded to any and all of Delia's suggestions concerning cut and fabric.

Delia pursed her mouth, and her brows came together

in a frown. "Samantha, do you have no preference at all for your wedding gown?"

Samantha looked up, and Delia's chest tightened at the emptiness reflected in her niece's eyes. In the girl's deep state of mourning, she had accepted Steven's proposal only with great reluctance. Delia convinced herself that love would develop over time, or in any event, contentment. She had reservations about love, as written about in novels, even existing. Should it prove to be more than myth, the emotion was more likely to be detrimental rather than beneficial to one's peace of mind. She had felt no burning love for her own husband. Nevertheless, they had suited, become friends and congenial companions. What Samantha needed, for her sake and the baby's, was a comfortable friend who would take care of her.

Samantha stepped down and began to don her walking outfit.

With a sigh, Delia pointed to a bolt of cream silk brocade. "That one will do, Madame Louella, with the gold lace trim."

The arrangements were finalized, the church reserved, the flowers chosen, and the invitations sent. Samantha played no part in the preparations. Most days, when she could elude Steven, she spent in quiet contemplation in the gardens. She thought about her baby, Christian's baby. Would she deliver a green-eyed boy or a golden-eyed girl? At those times, she drew out her wedding ring that she wore on a ribbon around her neck. The sparkle of the topaz and emerald stars caused her such pain that she soon tucked the cherished ring back into her bodice against her heart.

Oh, Christian, she asked time and time again, *am I doing the right thing or making a terrible mistake? What would you have me do?* Christian never answered her plea, and events swept her along as though she were naught but flotsam caught in a strong sea current. Her wedding day advanced with alarming speed. The closer it drew, the more helpless she felt.

When Jasper removed the splints from Christian's legs, Christian took his first blind, tentative steps with only a pronounced limp as testimony to his injuries.

"Your right leg did not heal as straight as I had hoped," Jasper said. "Perhaps it will improve with exercise."

Once again ambulatory, Christian fought to recover his former strength. At long last, the day arrived when Jasper pronounced him well enough to weather the journey to Hobart. Jasper packed supplies while Garrett saddled the horses. They left Queenstown behind on the long overland journey around Lake George and on to Hobart.

Christian rode like a novice rider on a lead rein behind Garrett. His temper suffered, but he bore the indignity in silence. His two friends were doing the best they could. He stubbornly clung to the hope that soon he would regain his sight. Though with Samantha gone, naught remained that he wished to see.

They caught the ferry at the western end of the Huon River, and the three men grew eager for the journey to end. They spoke of beds instead of bedrolls, beef in place of bush-tail possum, and water that tasted clean, unlike that from canteens, which left a metallic aftertaste. For as much good as it did, Jasper bathed Christian's eyes every night with an acidic solution he had purchased from an Aborigine medicine man.

"Damn, that stings," Christian complained, as he did each time Jasper soaked the cloths and laid them across his eyes. "And it has no effect."

"Patience, Professor, you must have patience and faith," Jasper said. "You sustained much damage. You cannot expect miracles overnight."

Christian grumbled, but two days out of Hobart when he opened his eyes at dawn, the darkness he had lived with for weeks lightened. By the time they reached Hobart's outskirts, his vision had improved. Objects in the distance appeared fuzzy. A headache arose when he strained to focus, but he could see well enough to reclaim his reins from Garrett.

The day of the wedding at hand, Samantha rode in a carriage beside Delia, Chloe, and Gilly to the church where Steven awaited her. Pettibone drove. Cullen, despite their urging, refused to accompany them. He made his feelings clear: he wanted no part of Steven Landry or Samantha.

While Cullen mucked the stalls, a clatter arose in the courtyard. He laid aside the pitchfork and strolled to the door, wondering if the visitors were looking to lease Talmadge House. They had received several inquiries in past days. Steven planned to move Samantha into his town house directly after the wedding. Her clothes had already been sent ahead. After a weeklong honeymoon, the remainder of the family would join them and stay until Samantha gave birth. As soon as the baby was old enough to travel, they would return to England to settle the details of Richard's estate. They had invited Cullen to accompany them, but he couldn't stomach Samantha's betrayal of Christian's memory. If Jasper and Garrett didn't return before the family departed, Cullen planned to sign on to a ship headed for America.

He wandered outside to greet the visitors and failed at first to recognize them. Jasper's great bulk and dark skin finally registered. He drew closer to the other two bearded, dusty men, and his eyes stretched wide. His heart gave a hitch. "Chris!" he shouted and accelerated into a run. He reached them, stopped short, and knuckled at his eyes. "Ye can't be 'ere. Ye're dead!"

"Much as I hesitate to disappoint you, I'm not dead yet. However, I've certainly been in better health," Christian said, stiffly swinging his leg over the horse and dismounting. He caught Cullen up in a hug that nearly cracked his ribs.

Cullen struggled out of his arms. "Ye don't understand. If'n ye're not dead, ye can't let 'er de it!"

Christian's brows drew together. "What are you prattling about? Not let who do what?"

"Sam," Cullen panted. "Sam's gettin' married!"

"Married?" the three men echoed.

"Aye, married ta Steven Landry, may God rot 'is soul. Ye've got ta stop 'er!"

Grimness tightened the line of Christian's mouth. "When?"

Cullen pointed down the road. "Now! At t'church!"

Stiffness suddenly loose fluidity, Christian grabbed the reins and swung up onto the horse. He pivoted the mount on its hindquarters and dug in his heels. The horse shot forward with a leap. Jasper and Garrett chased after his heels.

Starlight & Promises

Samantha clutched the cushions until the springs pressed painfully into her palms. She desired naught more than to remain in the carriage and instruct Pettibone to drive on. 'Twas a vain wish. Everyone awaited her at the church door, with strained smiles on their faces. She inhaled a breath, released her grip on the cushions, took Pettibone's hand, and stepped down onto the roadway. Every instinct screamed for her to end this debacle before it went too far. Nevertheless, her feet moved her forward. She managed that first step, and inexplicably a sense of calm slipped over her. 'Twas as though Christian was by her side or nearby, watching with approval as she took this action for their child. She forced a smile and entered the church on Pettibone's arm.

Flowers of all varieties and hues of the rainbow crowded the church this time. Ribbons decorated the pews and altar, and a massive candelabra burned with dozens of sweet-smelling candles. Steven stood at the altar with the pastor. He turned and looked at her, hazel eyes blazing in the candlelight. With Pettibone holding her up, she lowered her veil and proceeded down the aisle. Her dress of cream silk brocade whispered. When they reached Steven, the butler handed her off to her future husband and took his seat.

Samantha met Steven's gaze and saw not tenderness,

as she had seen so often, or pity, as she had come to expect, but raw lust, and her knees threatened to give way. Goose bumps broke out across her skin. She'd not considered the physical aspect of this marriage. Her only concern was her child's welfare. The remainder she had blocked from her mind. Could she bear it? Could she allow Steven to bed her and touch her as Christian had done? When she placed her hand over her stomach, the baby kicked, as though in response to her thoughts.

A small smile touched her lips. She had no desire for Steven's attentions but surely could endure whatever was necessary to ensure her child's future. Were she obliged to close her eyes and pretend Steven was Christian, she would do so.

The pastor intoned the words that would make them man and wife, and her thoughts returned to the ceremony.

"If any man present can give reason why this man and woman should not be joined in holy matrimony, let him speak now or forever hold his peace," the pastor said, looking out over the assemblage.

Silence reigned, and everyone craned their necks to examine their neighbors, as though expecting some objection. None came.

The pastor smiled and looked down on the couple. "Then, with the blessing of the Church of England, I now pronounce—"

"I have reason," a strong voice echoed from the back

of the church, clearly heard by all assembled.

Heads turned around, and eyes focused on the large, bearded man poised in the open doorway with his legs apart and hands on his hips.

The pastor blinked. Bewilderment crossed his face. He cleared his throat, directing a stern look at the man. "And what would be your reason, sir?"

"She is already married," Christian said and strode up the aisle.

The pastor's mouth dropped open. His gaze returned to the bride when she slumped to the floor in a froth of cream silk brocade.

Chapter Thirty-Four

Steven dropped to one knee and patted Samantha's pallid cheek.

Christian stopped beside him. "Remove your hands from her before I break them."

Steven's eyes sparked with fury. "Who are you, sir, to issue orders to me?"

Christian squatted on his heels, scooped Samantha into his arms, and straightened his legs. "Christian Badia, Samantha's legal husband. Who the hell are you to wed another man's wife?" His gaze barely touching on the burden in his arms, he looked with contempt over the slender, middle-aged man. Samantha planned to marry this aging roué? The least she could have done was select a man her equal. He shifted his gaze to the pastor. "Should you require confirmation, ask them."

He nodded toward the pew where Samantha's family sat.

Aunt Delia and Chloe had fainted. Gilly hovered over them, fanning the air and darting incredulous glances at Christian. Pettibone appeared frozen to the pew.

"I protest this!" Steven whipped his head toward the pastor.

"And I don't give a damn," Christian said. He turned and left with Samantha cradled against his chest.

The pastor swayed on his feet with his mouth catching flies.

As Christian headed down the aisle, he examined Samantha. Cheeks and lips as white as sea foam, her breathing shallow. While he reacquainted himself with her lovely face and form, his gaze lit on her rounded belly, and he drew in a tight breath. Exactly how well did she know Steven Landry? He harked back to what Cullen and the others had said about Landry at the time of her disappearance. She and Landry were close . . . close friends. And more? Pain hit him as surely as if someone had socked him in the gut. Were they "close" from the time he had shipped out on the *Maiden Anne* to search for Richard, she could be carrying the man's child. In a moment of clarity, the reason why she decided to marry Landry abruptly made sense. And why did Cullen so fervently pronounce his demise? Once Samantha recovered from her swoon, he would demand some answers.

His mother's face flashed before his eyes, her features

superimposed on those of Samantha's. The woman's perfidy had destroyed his father, transformed a strong, rational man into a rambling child. Never would Christian forgive his mother for the misery she had caused. Now it seemed he was doomed to walk the same path as his father. How had he allowed himself to fall into Samantha's trap? He would be damned if he did! Though his wife had managed to worm her way into his heart, he could just as easily expel her. Her actions this day confirmed the opinion he'd held for so long of women as untrustworthy creatures. He'd thought Samantha was different. He'd been wrong.

When Christian exited the church, Jasper and Garrett were waiting by the horses. He handed Samantha off to Jasper and mounted, then reached out for her.

Jasper looked down into her colorless face. "You didn't have to kill her," he said with a dry smile. "A good scolding would have done." At Christian's black look, Jasper passed her up without another word.

Samantha came to in her bed and raised her head from the pillow. Gilly knitted in an armchair by the fireplace. The curtains were drawn. For a moment, Samantha believed it to be the morning of her wedding to Steven. Then a vision of a bearded face, an angry, bearded face, flooded her mind. Christian! She bolted upright in the bed. Had she only dreamt him, like she dreamt about the Smilodon? Or had Christian showed up in time to prevent her marriage to Steven?

Gilly dropped her knitting and made haste to Samantha's side. "Oh, Miss Sam, we've been ever so worried about ye," she said, wringing her hands. "Ye've been out fer so long, we was afraid ye'd never wake up."

"Is Chris here, or did I merely swoon and dream about him?" she asked, her voice small and tight.

Gilly nodded. "Aye, he's here al'right. An' in sech a tempest. T'house is in an uproar o'er him an' Master Garrett an' Jasper, o' course."

Samantha's heart swelled. "He is alive," she whispered. "He is truly alive." She swung her legs out of bed, noticing only then that she wore her night rail. "Find a gown, Gilly, any gown." She ran to the vanity and began to brush out her sleep-snarled hair.

She tripped down the staircase ten minutes later, heart beating a rapid tattoo and her head spinning like a carousel. She felt like laughing out loud. Christian was back! He didn't know yet that she was carrying his child. He would be so extremely happy! Of course she would first have to explain why he found her willing to wed another man. However, he would understand when he learned the entire story and she told him about the baby.

She darted into the parlor, looking for Christian. Frowning, she came to a stop in the empty room. The mantel clock struck one. Luncheon. They were surely in the dining room. She smoothed back her hair with one shaky hand, having been unable to wait for Gilly to put it up, and sped into the dining room. When she burst through the doorway, everyone looked up, and she halted to drink in the sight of the man she loved.

He sat at the head of the table. He had shaved and trimmed his hair to its normal length and tied it back with a leather thong. The same recalcitrant strands escaped the queue and brushed against his face. A few additional silver hairs threaded through the sides. His face looked bronzed and a bit gaunt, as if he had undergone hardship and barely managed to pull through. Of course he had; he must have faced near death in the explosion.

When her eyes encountered his, she nearly took a backward step. His fierce expression, his cold, hard stare, set off an alarm in the pit of her stomach. Why? Taken off guard, she could scarcely maintain her smile, and her hand came up to circle her neck. Though she had tried hard to rid herself of the annoying habit of biting her nails, the urge to indulge nearly overwhelmed her. Then . . . *Oh, but of course.* Naturally he was angry with her for going after Richard and for almost marrying Steven. When he granted her the opportunity, she could easily explain both incidents.

She brushed aside her hesitance and crossed the room, throwing her arms around his neck and placing butterfly kisses on his face despite the audience. "Oh, Chris," she said with tears running down her face, "I believed you were dead. I have missed you terribly."

Stiffening, he shoved back from the table and stood, breaking her hold. His napkin slid off his lap onto the floor. His hand clamped her wrist, and he nodded to the company. "If you will excuse us, my wife and I desire some privacy." His voice dripped pure ice, his words curt and sharp. He looked down at her, gaze running straight through her. "Madam." He uttered the one word and stepped away from the table, taking off for the garden, pulling her behind.

When they reached a bench, safely hidden from view of the house, Christian released her and motioned for her to sit.

Samantha knew his moods as well as she knew her own. He was in a quiet fury and would brook no disobedience, so she sat. Very well, she had flaunted his orders again. But was that tiny detail any reason for him to be less than pleased to see her, when her own heart, in spite of his reception, burst at the seams? After all, her waywardness was a common enough occurrence and no occasion for the world to end. Setting her mouth firmly, she studied the forbidding line of his body, the taut skin over his cheekbones, and her spirit wilted.

He laced his hands behind his back, his accusatory gaze raking her and lingering on the belly her dress could no longer hide. "Do you have something you wish to tell me, madam?"

She wished he would cease calling her madam, as though she were a stranger. Regardless, she resolved to speak her piece. Once he learned her secret, his mood would change. The corners of her mouth tilted a bit. "Indeed, I do. We are having a baby."

Christian reacted not as she anticipated, with a grin and the elation swelling inside her breast. Instead, his eyes narrowed further. "I see," he merely said. "And whose baby are we having?"

Cold, like an Antarctic wind, swept into her veins. "Whatever do you mean?"

He glanced away, as though her question, her mere presence, irritated him. "I mean, whose baby are you carrying?"

Each word dropped like a stone.

For a moment, she forgot how to breathe. Coherent thought burned to ashes. She leapt up from the bench, all but knocking him over and causing him to take a step back. Her hands curled into fists, fingernails, short as they were, digging into her palms. "*Your* baby, Chris. I'm carrying *your* baby!"

He remained stony and inaccessible, unmoved by her declaration.

She raised her fists, more in protest than to strike him. Catching her wrists, he pulled her arms down between them. "'Tis your babe, Chris," she sobbed, feeling as though he had ripped out her heart. "I swear to God it is. Why would you even imply otherwise? Ask Gilly. She will tell you I suspected I was breeding soon after you left. Go! Ask her!"

"I already spoke with Gilly and Chloe and Delia," he said, voice rising in volume, a flicker of outrage breaking through his indifference. "Gilly informed me that you missed one of your monthly courses before you left with Landry. That was *after* you began seeing him. How do you know the babe is mine? It could just as well be Landry's. One does tend to wonder. Correct me if I'm mistaken, but you were fond enough of him to marry. Had I not interrupted the wedding, you would be ensconced in his bed at this moment."

"The babe is not his. I thought you were dead. We never . . ." The strength flowed from her body like water through a broken dike. She sagged against the bench, weeping, torn inside, baffled and devastated by his accusation.

He pulled her upright by her shoulders. "So you say. I suppose only time will tell."

She froze at his touch and, twisting around, broke his hold. Stepping back, she strove to gain her composure. "What are you saying?"

"To pack your bags. We leave tomorrow for Boston. Delia, Chloe, Pettibone, and Gilly will return to England."

"I'll not go." She wiped at her flowing eyes with the backs of her wrists.

He fisted his hands on his hips. "Despite your attempt to change your status, you're still my wife. You'll go wherever I tell you to go."

Tears coursed down her face, yet she met his eyes without flinching. "I refuse to go anywhere without my family," she said through a jaw so tight she barely formed the words.

"We shall see." He swung around and walked away from her. "Go inside and pack."

"I shall do that," she screamed at his back. "And I shall pack the largest gun I can find so I can blow a hole in your black heart, if you still have one."

Samantha prevailed on one account: her family accompanied her on the return to Boston, along with Jasper and Cullen, who voiced their preferences for a life ashore rather than a career at sea. Christian hired Jasper as cook and majordomo of his Massachusetts farm. Cullen, who discovered he liked horses better than spars and lines, accepted a position as a groom in the extensive stables. To avoid another unpleasant scene, Samantha grudgingly agreed to stay at Christian's farm. Aunt Delia, Chloe, and Pettibone declined, saying they would lodge with the Colchester relations in town. In deference to her pregnancy, Christian allowed Gilly to continue as

Samantha's maid.

With the *Maiden Anne* a shattered hulk in the Tasman Sea and Samantha's condition delicate, they booked a safer, longer route, taking a steamship to San Francisco and then crossing the country by rail to Boston. The trip would take three months. Along the way, Christian showed his solicitude for Samantha's health and was polite to a fault, yet he never once touched her in love or affection. Her despondency grew in concert with the child.

After the information Garrett had imparted in Hobart, Samantha suspected Christian's distrust came from his childhood experience, his mother's betrayal, his father's madness. She remained at a loss how to address the issue. She had tried tact to no avail. At any rate, tact was not her most endearing trait. One evening when Christian acted particularly cold and distant, she finally lost her temper. "I am *not* your mother," she shouted. "I am *not* Lady Jane!"

His head whipped around at her words. "Don't dare speak her name in my presence," he replied, face turning a puce color.

"I shall say what I wish as long as you continue to treat me as if I were some highborn whore!" She rushed at him with fists flailing.

Garrett and Delia broke up the confrontation before Samantha did an injury to herself.

In an icy fury, Christian smoothed his trembling

hands over his dinner jacket and stalked away. They avoided each other for days.

Samantha felt as though she had lost her husband a second time; only she was obliged to suffer his company daily. Her pain at his desertion and mistrust hardened the knot in her heart whenever she encountered him.

"He will come around," Delia said one glorious, delicate dawn as they steamed into San Francisco Bay. "When he sees the babe, he will come to terms with his feelings and forgive all."

"There is naught to forgive," Samantha replied, waves of despair beating against her chest, "and by that time, I may not want him any longer."

"You must view the circumstances from his point of view," Delia reminded her. "I realize you are overset. Your pregnancy has made you emotional. Christian can see only that you broke your trust with him once again in pursuing Richard, and you kept company with another man. Garrett told me of Christian's estrangement with his mother. I would think it particularly difficult for him to trust a woman after what happened in his family. I'm sure he knows deep inside you have nothing in common with his mother. Nonetheless, the hurt he feels brings back painful memories. You must allow him to deal with that pain. When he does, he will realize how much he loves you." She dabbed at her eyes with a lace handkerchief. "I take the blame on myself. I encouraged your friendship with Steven. Had I known of Christian's past, I never would have interfered."

Steven. A man she had not thought about for so long. The mention of his name brought back a memory and a mystery. Where was he? After learning what happened on her wedding day, pangs of guilt at having left Steven at the altar propelled Samantha to seek him out, to explain, apologize. He must have suffered great embarrassment and disappointment. However, she found his house closed up and no word of where he had gone. To England, she supposed, back to the life he had there before coming to Tasmania. Someday she must try to contact him again. But not now, not until she straightened out her own life. For now, she relegated him to the past. One bewildering man was more than enough to deal with.

"The fault is not yours, Auntie," Samantha said on a sigh. "I realize Chris has issues with trust. But if he truly loved me, he would know I could never betray him with another man."

"Allow him some time to come to grips with the situation. He nearly died searching for you, and then to return and find you wedding another man . . ." Delia paused for a breath as though at a loss for words. Her sorrow for her niece's predicament showed plainly on her face and in her eyes. "He does love you, Samantha. Keep your chin up and give him time."

Through the tears blurring her vision, Samantha

looked out over the approaching arms of the bay and seagulls drifting above in graceful flight. "I have given him naught but time," she said in a soft voice. "How much does he need? I find myself running out of time. When all is said and done, love may not be enough to repair the breach between us."

CHAPTER THIRTY-FIVE

Though she loved the farm outside Boston and kept busy with tending house and working in the gardens, as the babe grew larger and more active, time weighed heavily on Samantha. Meanwhile, Christian continued to keep his distance, spending his days at the university or on business in Boston. He treated her like a houseguest, providing her with luxurious separate accommodations, anticipating her every need, and calling her madam. They tiptoed around each other like polite strangers, cordial yet isolated, going their own ways in a deafening silence. The rift was slowly strangling Samantha. If she could not find a way to span the gulf between them before the babe's birth, she feared they would never resolve their differences.

As more time passed, she began to understand and

accept her heart's message. In spite of what she had said to Delia, the love she bore Christian grew only deeper and more urgent. She wanted him—in her life, in her bed, in her future—though she was mystified about how to achieve that result. She inspected her swollen body in the mirror, and her lips canted into a lopsided smile. She was as puffed up as a bullfrog. How could Christian ever want her again? Now was obviously not the time to try seduction as a solution to their problems.

The burden of the babe now awkward and fatiguing, Samantha grunted when she tried to fasten her bodice over her grossly expanded breasts. All her gowns fit tightly and uncomfortably, as though she were trying to squeeze a tomato through the eye of a needle.

"Let me do that," Gilly said, entering the room with Samantha's shoes and hat. She moved behind Samantha, pulled the bodice edges together, and fastened them with effort.

"I shall never again fit into my clothing," Samantha lamented. "I require an entirely new wardrobe."

"Nay, m'lady, I can still let out these gowns a bit more. An' after ye give birth, ye'll be back to yer slim self in no time."

"You have more faith than I. I have no doubt I shall forever be a mouse in an elephant's body."

Gilly knelt and slipped stockings up Samantha's legs, followed by lacy garters that tied at the thigh. She eased on the half boots, with which she struggled a bit, Samantha's feet having swollen with fluid. Stepping back, the maid tugged Samantha to her feet. Samantha winced at the tight leather shoes. Slowly, she made her way to the window and gazed out. Christian came into view for a moment as he entered the barn. She released a melancholy sigh.

"What should I do, Gilly? He acts as though I'm a boarder and not a very welcome one."

Gilly's lips tightened, and she shook out her skirts. "He does love ye. He's just full o' male pride. As soon as he sees his babe, he'll come round an' feel guilty fer distrustin' ye. Just ye wait an' see."

Tears slipped from the corners of Samantha's eyes. "By then he will have allowed his chance to slip away. If he cannot trust my word, our love, what hope is there for us?"

"Now, now," Gilly soothed.

Samantha interrupted the maid before she could mouth more platitudes. "See if the carriage is ready. I have no desire to keep Dr. Finney waiting."

Gilly bobbed her head, her own anger and frustration at Christian's cruel behavior toward his wife simmering on her features, and left.

After agonizing for months over the impasse between her and Christian, Samantha saw only one clear course. Her husband may have loved her once. 'Twas now obvious he no longer felt that way.

She returned to her dressing table and withdrew

money from a drawer, funds she had hoarded for passage to England should she ever need them. Now it seemed she did. Stuffing the American dollars into her reticule, she told herself she had come to her senses at last. She had lost patience with Christian and had no inclination to endure his conduct any longer. What was the point? After seeing her doctor and visiting with Aunt Delia, she would purchase the tickets. She and her babe would leave. Christian assumed she had no choice but to remain with him. He was mistaken. She would do what was best for her and her child. Languishing in Massachusetts, unloved and unwanted, was best for no one.

Moisture coursed down her cheek. She brushed it away. A one-sided love was a poor reason to cling to Christian. If he no longer wanted her, no longer loved her, had indeed he ever truly loved her, she could not suffer his apathy. Her conscience tugged a bit at the thought of taking his son or daughter from him. But then, he had declined even to acknowledge it. So what would he be losing? Slipping away quietly would be best. In truth, Christian would likely rejoice at her departure.

Gilly stomped down the stairs and threw open the front door. She remained on the porch with her hands on her hips and hailed Cullen. "'Tis about time," she huffed when Cullen pulled the pair of chestnuts up in front of the steps. "The missus is ready ta leave."

Christian emerged from the stables and propped a

shoulder against the wood frame, arms crossed over his chest. Gilly blew out a breath and turned to call Samantha. Her mistress stood behind her, gaze fastened on her husband, who stared back. Though his hat shadowed his face, his posture spoke volumes. Gilly took Samantha's arm, guided her down the steps, and helped her climb into the carriage.

Christian returned to the dimness of the barn and inhaled the dusty scents of hay and oats. His chest ached, as always seemed to be the case when he caught a glimpse of Samantha. She looked so ethereal in her pregnancy. He struggled to draw breath and longed to hold her against him, to absorb a little of the glow emanating from her. So why didn't he?

He entered the stall with Triton, picked up a brush, and curried the horse in short, savage strokes. His anger had long since abated. Now bewilderment swirled inside him like a whirlwind. Overwhelming love for Samantha squeezed his heart as though it were caught in a bear trap. But with his hasty jumping to conclusions, his unwarranted suspicion, he had badly muddled the state of affairs.

Triton shifted and crowded him against the stall boards. Christian pushed against the horse's flank.

A thousand times he had cursed himself. Never

having experienced jealousy, he had fallen hard to the emotion, allowed it to rip him apart. He had also permitted his mother's betrayal to dictate his life and destroy his marriage. Was this, then, to be the rest of his life? Was he resigned to going through it alone? Was permanent estrangement from Samantha to be his fate?

Setting aside the brush, he measured out grain, pouring it into a wooden bucket and placing it in the manger.

A thousand times he had burned with the urge to fall on his knees before Samantha and beg her forgiveness. Her words aboard ship the night of their last argument rang true. Samantha was not his mother; she bore no resemblance to Lady Jane. And he was not his father. For all his father's humanitarian qualities, he had been a weak man. Lady Jane didn't destroy his father; the man granted Lady Jane license to destroy him. So why did *he* allow the image of Samantha standing beside Steven at the altar to intrude, like a demon sitting on his shoulder, and goad him? Christian now recognized the demon's true face—pride—and racked his brain over how he could repair their relationship.

This was madness. Samantha's baby was his, not Steven's. He knew it, had accepted it long ago. He suspected he had known it all along. He had feared that if he gave himself permission to love, he would lose his mind and soul, as his father had. In truth, all he had lost was his heart.

Starlight & Promises

Dumping an armful of hay into the rope sling above the manger, he scooped up the water bucket, carrying it to the pump to fill it, and returned it to the stall.

Now he had dug himself in so deeply he no longer knew how to claw his way out. He was terrified he had killed the love Samantha once had for him. He twisted his lips into a poor facsimile of a smile. Undoubtedly he had, and he could place no blame on her for withdrawing her affections.

He had to confront her, apologize, admit he was wrong, and let her know he loved her. What if she spurned him, as she had every right to do? Tore his heart from his chest and shredded his declaration of love? What would he do then? He'd never considered himself a coward; nonetheless, his hesitation to face her rejection had kept him from taking that first step. His tangled thoughts seemed to tell him that if he refused to deal with the situation, it didn't exist or, at any rate, could not get any worse.

"Fuck!"

The horse turned his head and stamped a foot.

"Sorry, old boy." He patted the animal's hide and set the bucket on the stall floor. "I suppose I'm not fit company."

Triton snorted.

Christian left the stable and walked over to the barn housing his basketball court. Kicking off his boots, he closed and locked the door, picked up a ball, and savagely dribbled his way across the floor. He always concentrated better with a basketball in his hands, as though the world became clearer when reduced to no more than a ball, a basket, and a polished wooden floor. He charged across the court, dribbled, and shot, struggling to devise a solution to the impasse he had created.

When he had first met Samantha, wide-eyed and innocent, scratching up his court with her boots, his gut cautioned him to send her away before she hooked his heart with those golden eyes. Considering himself impervious to her charms, he scoffed at the warning and fell in love, ass over teakettle, with a bloody English *lady*. Visions of a frozen angel saving Cullen's life, an enchanting pixie snatching stars from a desert night sky, and a sultry siren writhing on his bed in a cloud of silken butterscotch hair compressed his chest so tightly he could scarcely breathe.

An hour later, blowing and dripping with sweat, his defenses collapsed about his feet. He had allowed the acrimony to fester for too long. Pride be damned; his fears had ruled him long enough. He would tell Samantha he believed her, tell her he loved her more than life itself. If she tossed his love back into his face, he would let her go, if that was what she desired. Slamming the basketball against the wall, he made a dash for the house and pulled off his damp clothes. After washing and dressing, he saddled Triton and spurted off in pursuit of Samantha's carriage.

Starlight & Promises

Cullen dozed on the driver's seat while he waited for Samantha in front of Dr. Finney's office on a Boston side street. She had visited the doctor weekly for the past month, and Jasper generally drove her into town. Today, with Jasper feeling poorly, Cullen took over the duty, which he enjoyed. Spending more time with Samantha, he had developed sympathy for her situation and estrangement from Christian. In regard to Steven Landry and the baby, well, the more he came to know Samantha, the more difficulty he had accepting she would betray Christian in that way. Gradually he had come around to her side.

When Samantha appeared in the doorway, Cullen jumped down to help her negotiate the steps. With her huge belly, she found walking a chore. It being his first experience with a breeding woman, he handled her as carefully as a china vase. She waddled toward the carriage door, looking like a goose fattened for Christmas dinner, and he fought back a smile.

"All's well?" He clasped her elbow and hoisted her into the carriage.

She caught her breath and smiled. "Indeed, Cullen. We should welcome an addition to the family soon. And about time. I feel as clumsy as a tortoise with three legs." She dropped onto the padded seat with a heavily expelled breath.

Chuckling, he climbed onto the driver's seat, took up the reins, and released the brake. He clucked to the horses and snapped the lines on their backs. The pair took off in a sedate trot as though they understood the precious burden entrusted to them.

A half-mile drive lay between the house where Delia resided and the doctor's office. The road wended through residential streets and a warehouse district along the docks. As Cullen drove through the narrow passageways between the towering buildings, he kept up his guard. Itinerant sailors and other unsavory characters hung out around the alehouses squatting amongst the respectable businesses like pickpockets in a crowd of gentry. With the radiant sun imparting a sparkling quality to the air, Cullen relaxed his vigilance.

A produce wagon appeared, overturned ahead, its owner ambling about and retrieving cabbages and squash from the cobbled street. Cullen slowed and halted the horses. He resigned himself to waiting until the wagon moved, but at the corpulent grocer's unhurried pace, Cullen vented a soft curse.

"I'll be right back," he called down to Samantha. "If'n I don't 'elp this bloke, we'll be 'ere fer 'ours." After setting the brake, he tied off the reins and climbed down from his perch.

Samantha leaned her head out the window and released a sigh at the mess in the roadway. Easing back against the seat, she closed her eyes. When the carriage door opened after only a handful of minutes, she smiled. Cullen seemed to have quickly sorted out the grocer's dilemma.

Rough fingers clamped over her lips. Her eyes flew open, and her heart ceased to beat. A hand seized her wrist and hauled her upward with force. She fell out of the carriage door into strong arms.

Though his breath gushed out in a hiss against her cheek when her bulk toppled into him, he quickly recuperated. With an arm wrapped beneath her breasts and his hand pressed against her mouth, he dragged her away from the carriage and into an alley between two warehouses.

Samantha struggled to free herself, but her abductor seemed possessed of an unholy strength. After shoving her through an opened doorway, he kicked the door shut, engaged the lock, and released her.

She stumbled to her knees, bruising them on the dusty wooden floor, and her size prevented her from climbing immediately to her feet. Samantha panted with the exertion. A sudden, sharp pain, stabbing low in her belly, followed. She grunted and looked up. "Steven!" she sputtered. "What are you doing here?"

"Shut up, bitch!" He extracted a length of rope from his jacket pocket and bent over her.

She twisted away, ending up on her back, straining to roll over and get to her feet but managed only to writhe about like a turtle stranded on its back.

Steven grabbed her arms and jerked her up onto her knees. Pulling her hands behind her back, he looped the rope around her wrists.

A pounding came on the door behind them. Cullen shouted her name from the other side. Samantha jerked her head toward the sound. "Cullen! Get h—"

Steven whipped out a handkerchief and tied it over her mouth. She sank down on her side, gasping from her struggles and the lack of air. When Steven moved out of view into the shadows along the wall, a chill swept over her skin.

Cullen kicked at the door, rattling it on its hinges. Finally the lock gave way, and the boy stormed into the gloomy space. He sprinted to her side and knelt.

Steven came up behind him.

Samantha screamed behind the gag, tried to signal Cullen with her eyes, but her bound hands held his attention.

Steven drew a gun and brought the butt down on the back of Cullen's skull.

When Cullen collapsed, a deadening fog swept through Samantha's brain. Her belly convulsed and squeezed her womb in a long, throbbing contraction that made her fight for breath. Her chest compressed at a sudden realization. The pain came, not from her fright but from the babe. She battled an agonizing wave, and tears sprang from her eyes. She strived to relax her muscles until the contraction passed.

Steven loomed over her, legs braced apart, eyes as

hard as diamond chips while he regarded her with a pitiless expression. Snagging Cullen's collar, he dragged
the boy away to a far corner. When Steven returned, he
squatted on his heels and removed her gag. Cupping his
hands beneath her arms, he slid her along the floor and
propped her into a sitting position against a wall. Resting a shoulder against the boards, he smiled coldly.

"Well, now, Samantha, here we are, my runaway
bride and I. Did you truly believe you could leave me at
the altar without even a backward glance?"

"Why, Steven? Why are you here?" Through the
dull roaring of blood in her ears, she swallowed thickly
and tensed at another contraction gathering. Breathing
through her mouth, she rode out the long, dark, rolling
waves. When they ebbed, leaving her breathless, she
looked up at him. "What do you want from me?"

"What do I want?" He laughed harshly. "I daresay
I want my wife."

Every instinct cautioned her to keep her wits about
her, to remain calm and still, though the thought of her
baby coming now in this dirty warehouse was a river of
icy water washing over her. Nevertheless, she was unable to still her mouth. "You know full well I'm not
your wife. Christian is my husband. We wed in Hobart.
Why are you doing this?"

He spun away from the wall and paced in front of
her in short, heavy strides that thudded on the wood

louder than the beating of her frantic heart. When he brought himself up short, he jabbed a finger at her. "You owe me! Your family owes me! I intend to collect the debt."

She shook her head, making every effort to follow the thread of his words. An insane light glittered in his eyes, warning her to hold her tongue.

"The Colchesters owe me!" he continued, spittle flying from his lips. "Your dear uncle Richard ruined my life, my career. He made me a laughingstock in society and caused my father to disown me."

"How, Steven?" she asked as softly as her nerves and the coming baby would allow. She sensed his preoccupation with the past and encouraged his tortured mind to release the memories it seemed he longed to air, though how it would help her, she did not know. Nonetheless, every moment she could gain was precious. "How did Uncle Richard ruin your life?"

Swinging his head in her direction, he cut the air with the blade of his hand. "You care nothing for me or the pain your family visited upon me."

A film of sweat broke out on her forehead with the crouching pain. She had to force her tone to remain even. "I do care for you. I would have wed you had my husband not come back from the dead. I was legally obligated to go with him. It had naught to do with how I felt about you." Soon Delia would miss her, and surely someone would come looking for her. She had to keep him talking. "I beg you, tell me why you hate my uncle so dreadfully. Perhaps I can help."

He tilted his head and looked at her. The madness faded from his eyes, but now they looked far away, as though he were peering into the past. Lifting his chin, he gazed up at the dust motes dancing in thin streamers of light, released a breath through his teeth, and leaned back against the wall beside her.

"Richard and I were the best of friends," he said, his recitation strangely wooden, as if repeated by rote. "Our love of nature compelled us to spend countless hours combing the meadows and woods on our fathers' adjoining estates." He lowered his gaze to rest on her. "You never knew I was Steven Burnett, Richard's neighbor, did you?"

She shook her head, though she recalled Aunt Delia mentioning the Marquis of Lansdowne and some scandal broth. "Please go on."

He inhaled a breath, and his eyes glazed over again. "Our devotion to science grew with time, and a mentorship beneath the aegis of Charles Darwin spurred us on to Oxford and serious scientific research."

"Then you didn't attend Oxford on scholarship, nor did you study commerce," she interjected, unsurprised by his lies.

A chuckle rumbled from his chest. His mouth lifted in a cynical smile. "Hardly. After all, my father was a marquis. I held title as a viscount. As our careers began,

Richard catalogued flora and studied its fossil remains, reconstructing climate change progression and plant evolution. I gained a reputation for my discoveries along the pathways of human evolution." His voice grew softer, a wistful expression coming over his face. "We were a jolly good team. Together we painted a picture of time in flux. In those golden days, Richard and I were like brothers. We stuck so closely to each other's sides, one could not have separated us with a shoehorn."

Samantha stiffened, occupied in riding out a contraction squeezing her belly like an anaconda's coils. "When did it change?" she asked with only a modicum of strain in her voice. "What happened to that friendship?"

The flesh across the bones of his face stretched as tightly as the skin of a drum. "We had been accepted into the membership of the elite Royal Academy of Science, rivals yet colleagues. But while Richard's fame grew, important discoveries and their elusive meanings falling from his pen like autumn leaves, I encountered naught but roadblocks to my continued professional success.

"You must understand," he said, "human fossils are a great deal rarer and more difficult to uncover than plant fragments. My work suffered, and my reputation waned. I required some major discovery, something . . . spectacular." His gaze caught and held hers. He gave her an earnest look, as though he wished to sway her to his point of view. She returned what she hoped resembled a sincere smile. "You see, the academy was close to ejecting me. My father would never have allowed me peace should I have permitted that to occur."

She nodded, praying the gesture conveyed sympathy.

Steven's gaze drifted away. "I was reaching the end of my tether when I encountered a man who offered me a chance for redemption. A partially intact skull, meticulously constructed, a chimera of ape and human parts." He grinned. "It was quite nearly perfect. I presented it to the academy as the first solid evidence of the missing link between apes and humans. At first, accolades propelled me to the scientific forefront. Scientists bandied my name about the London salons in the same breath as Darwin's. Then Richard Colchester emerged, like the Grim Reaper from the London fog." He raised fists, and his voice turned bitter. "His righteous scythe cut me to the knees, exposing the fossil as a fraud. Richard vowed he did so, not out of jealousy but through scientific outrage that one of his own should go to such lengths to gain notoriety." He paused, his chest heaving as he gulped in air.

"What happened then?" Samantha asked cautiously.

He laughed and waved an arm in an airy gesture. "Oh, quite a bit, indeed. A storm of censure descended. The ensuing gale blew through London, wiping out my reputation and erasing all my previous, legitimate scientific contributions. My friends shunned me. I became a social pariah virtually overnight." The maniacal light that so concerned her before surfaced again in his eyes. "The academy expelled me, and my father summoned me." He chuckled. "But I took care of him as I believed I had taken care of Richard."

With an intake of breath that had naught to do with her worsening physical condition, Samantha recalled Delia's words: intruders had murdered Steven Burnett's father shortly after the marquis petitioned the House of Lords to elevate his younger son. Surely Steven could not have killed his own father? Another thought struck terror in her soul. Richard's abduction by pirates. Steven orchestrated that situation, too? *He* was the gentleman who paid Miggs? She could not quell a loud gasp.

Steven pushed away from the wall and looked down with a chilling smile. "Quite right, my dear. Miggs was to dispose of Richard after he learned where to find the Smilodon." He stretched out his arms with a plea on his face. "Can you not see that Richard owed me the Smilodon? Its discovery would restore my standing. However, circumstances intervened, and your damned uncle has more lives than a cat. Like all the others in my past, Miggs turned out to be a disappointment." Lowering his arms, he pulled back and smiled reflectively. "Yet, now Richard is dead, as fairness dictates he be, and I have you."

After his confession, if that was what it truly was and not merely a boast, she discarded any sympathy, false or otherwise, she might have had for the man. "Christian will come for me. When he finds us, he will punish you for your transgressions, both past and present."

His laugh echoed off the rafters, setting into flight a roost of bats in the far reaches. Dust and wood fragments sifted downward, and he brushed off his shoulders, glanced up at the bats. His gaze came back to her. "Your beloved Christian despises you. He believes that brat you carry to be mine."

When she flinched, he said, "Oh yes, I know. I followed your affairs with a vested interest. Even should he search for you out of some misplaced sense of responsibility, he will soon join Richard and my father in hell." He brandished the gun. "After all, we cannot properly wed until you become a widow."

Samantha tried to discard Steven's assessment of her marriage as the ravings of a madman, though it held more than a grain of truth. Christian had no earthly reason to rescue her. He *did* believe she carried another man's child. Even so, she refused to abandon all hope. "What do you truly want, Steven? You obviously have no love for me." The abdominal pain, which had briefly quieted, gripped her womb once again. She fought to bear it and hold back the scream swelling in her throat. When the curtain of agony lifted, Steven was speaking.

"—my dear. I've not an iota of love for you. Quite the contrary. As the spawn of a Colchester, I loathe you.

Yet I desire what you possess. Your fortune, respectability, and social consequence." He leaned down into her face. "Most of all, I desire the Smilodon, *my* discovery. It will propel me back into the ranks of eminent scientists. With your money, my scientific achievement, and you as my respectable wife, doors will again open for me."

She battled the pains coming closer together. She must keep him talking. "What about the scandal? Marriage to me will hardly undo the past."

"*You* will. Your words will redeem me. You will let it be known that Richard confessed to constructing the fake fossil and made me his pawn out of jealousy. Before he died, he regretted the injustice he perpetrated on me and my family."

"Wh-whyever would I utter such an untruth and smear Richard's name?" she asked, incredulity infusing her words.

He hunkered down and pressed a hand cruelly hard on her rippling belly.

She grunted with pain.

"Because of this, Samantha. Because of your child. The child whose future depends upon my charity."

Despite the heat inside the warehouse, she shivered. He meant what he said. He had already proved he was not above murder, and he would harm her child were she to defy him. A red wave of agony sunk its teeth into her guts, causing a moan to slide past her lips. The baby was coming quickly. If help did not arrive soon, they could die here.

Steven rose and turned away.

"Steven," she gasped, "the baby is coming. You must fetch me to the doctor, or we shall die, and you will have no one to restore your reputation."

He pivoted around, his brows gathered in censure. "You cannot give birth now. I forbid it. You will have to wait until we board the ship. My driver will arrive presently."

Samantha blinked open eyes she hadn't realized were closed while wrestling with the contraction. Her jaw sagged. *Wait?* He was more insane than she supposed if he believed she could wait! "I cannot wait. This child demands to be born now. I have no capability of stopping it. You must find help for me."

His face thunderous, he strode away, muttering to himself like a bedlamite. Coming to a halt, he glared back. "You will wait, I say. I shan't countenance any disobedience. As you are my wife, you will obey me!"

She collapsed against the wall. Each time a contraction seized her belly, she drew up her knees and bent over them, muffling her cries in her skirts. She could not allow Steven to become aware of the true state of her distress. No telling what he would do. When he asked questions, she waited as though in thought until the pain eased, then answered in a low, controlled voice. Steven had lost all grasp on reality, retreating into a delusion of his own invention. With the impending birth continuing to wreak havoc on her body at regular intervals, she fought to keep from instinctively pushing her child into the world.

CHAPTER THIRTY-SIX

Christian exited the doctor's office and jogged down the steps to the post where he had tied Triton. When departing over an hour ago, Samantha had mentioned to Dr. Finney that she planned to visit her aunt Delia before returning home. The doctor told Christian that Samantha was healthy and her pregnancy progressing satisfactorily. He expected her to deliver in no more than a few days. He assured Christian he would remain on call, although he didn't anticipate any difficulties.

Familiar with the route to Delia's Boston accommodations, Christian made good time through the residential neighborhoods and soon came upon the dockside warehouses. After passing four lofty wooden structures, he turned left around the far corner of the fifth onto the narrow road leading out of the commercial district. His carriage was three-fourths of the way down the street beside a weather-worn warehouse with the sign "McCreedy Brothers, Steamship Equipment Fitters" painted on the front. He frowned and halted Triton.

The carriage driver's seat was unoccupied. Moving closer, he leaned down and peered into the carriage. His jaw muscles firmed. Where was Cullen? More importantly, where was his wife? Swinging down from Triton, he hitched him to the side of the carriage and tried the front doors of the warehouse. Finding them locked, he walked into the alley.

Cullen opened his eyes to filtered light floating with dust. At first he had little remembrance of where he was or what had happened to him. Then voices came across the cavernous space, one of them belonging to that scoundrel Steven Landry, and his memory came back. Revulsion moved into his throat. Easing up on his hands and knees, Cullen crawled closer.

Landry loomed over Samantha and berated her. The gleam of a pistol picked up a stray beam of light from the windows far overhead. Samantha sat with her back against the wall and her hands behind her. Though her voice sounded calm, beneath the words, Cullen detected pain and fear. Chill bumps rose on his arms and legs. He stole a look about for a weapon. Nothing presented itself, and Landry began to stride back and forth across the floor between Cullen and the door.

Cullen scooted backward until his heels bumped up against a wall, and he inched along it. Surely a building this size had more than one door. Every nerve stretched tight, the need to escape and find help drove him. He'd always held the opinion that Landry was a bad egg. He'd told everyone the man was a snake, but no one had listened to him. Now, with the man threatening to harm Samantha, Cullen drew no comfort from his keen assessment of character. He would trade all his insight for a weapon and another fifty pounds of muscle. That being unlikely, he would settle for a constable.

A faint light outlined the seam of a second door. Cullen found the latch and snuck another glance at Landry. The man had turned his back, waving his arms and stalking about in front of Samantha. Cullen cracked open the door and rolled out into the dirt alley. He prayed Landry did not notice the slight creak of the door and the light streaming in. Climbing to his feet, he quietly closed the door and took off running, pelting down the alley toward the street where he had left the carriage.

He rounded the corner of the warehouse, and the silhouette of a man appeared in the shadows. One of Landry's men! Cullen stifled a groan, skidded to a halt, and spun about. A familiar voice called his name, and he looked back at Christian trotting toward him.

When Cullen emerged from around the far corner, Christian was planning to try the doors on the side of the warehouse. "Cullen!" he shouted, and the boy stopped. When Christian reached him, Cullen was shaking as though with the ague, and blood dripped from a cut on the side of his head. "Where is Sam?" Christian asked, clamping a hand on Cullen's shoulder. His heart beat at thrice its normal rate.

"Inside," Cullen panted. Christian turned toward the door, but Cullen stopped him. "Steven Landry's in there, an' 'e 'as a gun. Looks like 'e's tied up Sam."

Christian compressed his lips and nodded. "Listen carefully to me. Triton is tied out front. You are to take him, hie to the nearest police station, and send them back here. Then ride on to Dr. Finney's office and inform him that we may require his services."

Cullen's head moved from side to side, hair flying into his eyes. "Ye can't go in there by yerself. Landry's armed. Ye need me ta back ye up."

Christian shook him. "Do as I say, boy! Sam may be hurt. I have no time to argue with you!" He shoved the boy toward the alley entrance.

Cullen hesitated, rocking from foot to foot before sprinting off.

At the sound of Christian's voice, Samantha turned

her head toward the alley. She sucked in a breath, praying she had sufficient strength left to scream, but her attempt came out as a tortured squeak.

Steven threw himself beside her and slapped his hand over her mouth. He drew forth the handkerchief, gagged her, and dragged her to the middle of the space, where a trickle of sunlight spilled down on her. "One false move and he dies," he whispered, face only inches from hers.

Her heart flipping in her chest, she watched him disappear once again into the darkness along the far wall, the gun gripped in one hand.

Christian inched open the door, slipped through the opening, and eased the portal shut behind him. Stale, heavy air filled his lungs. Dust particles swam in dirty ripples of light and distorted his vision. His breath coming quick and shallow, he stood motionless and blinked in the semidarkness. Deep shadow hugged the walls, and mountainous wooden crates were arrayed on the gritty floor at irregular intervals. Wan light bled through two high, grime-encrusted windows to limn the rafters far above.

He focused in on Samantha, who sat on the floor, hands behind her and a gag covering her mouth. When she shook her head, his knees wobbled. She looked unharmed and as furious as a caged leopard.

Where was Steven? Nearby. Christian all but smelled the gun pointed at him. Since arriving in Boston, Christian had commissioned an investigation of Steven and his business dealings. Then Landry disappeared, two steps ahead of the British authorities. Though Christian tried every avenue to track him down, the man had left Tasmania on a ship bound for Malaysia and then vanished with no trace. Never had Christian considered that Boston might be Landry's ultimate destination, not with a Royal warrant for his arrest on charges of murder.

To think that Samantha had come so dreadfully close to wedding the man froze his blood. He had believed Steven was out of their lives forever, and thus, not mentioned his findings to Samantha. Not surprising, considering he had granted her no more than a few words of conversation in the past months. Now, knowing the man's true nature, Christian felt certain Steven would decline to emerge from his hiding place and face him like a man. A coward who hired others to carry out his dirty deeds would more likely shoot from ambush.

Christian leapt forward and dove into a forward roll, aiming for the darkness behind a large crate. A bullet whined, slicing the air above his tumbling body, and he snapped a glance toward the sound. A curl of smoke wafted from a black area along one wall. The air stank of cordite. He rose behind the crate, and a grim smile spread across his lips. Listening intently, he waited for the man to move again. A slight shuffling came from the wall to his right.

Christian pulled off his boots and climbed the side of the wooden crate. Once on top, he fished a pen-knife from his pocket and tossed it to the floor. The gun roared again, the flame from the barrel lighting up the man in the shadows, and Christian launched himself into the air. He plowed into Steven as the man spun toward him. The gun went off again, the bullet passing by harmlessly.

Christian's weight and impetus knocked the man off his feet. They lay in a heap on the floor for a heartbeat. When Steven swung the gun, Christian took a glancing blow to the side of the head. It stunned him long enough for Steven to scramble to his feet.

Christian flung out an arm, caught the man's ankle, and Steven stumbled into the wall, giving Christian time to get his feet beneath him. Then Steven pushed away from the splintered boards and raised the gun.

Christian seized the outstretched wrist. He squeezed and twisted until bone snapped. Steven gave a sharp cry, and the gun dropped from his hand and fell to the floor. Christian bent and picked it up.

A red haze filled his vision, and he gazed down at the man who had destroyed his marriage and threatened the lives of his wife and child. He rested the metal barrel against Steven's temple. Steven clutched his broken wrist in his other hand, and with eyes as cold as a New England blizzard, glared up at Christian.

"I should kill you," Christian said, his voice shaking but the gun steady, his finger on the trigger. "You deserve to die." He pulled back the hammer. Temptation to fire blew through him like a typhoon. This man was responsible for all their troubles: Richard's death, his estrangement from Samantha, not to mention the death of Steven's father, a respected peer and an honorable man. He would find it easy to end everything here in this dusty warehouse.

"Why?" Steven laughed. "Because I fucked your wife and she now bears my child? Because you were not man enough to keep her faithful? Though you can kill me, you will see me every time you look at my son or daughter." His words were pitched to goad, as though he truly wished to die. Tears of laughter ran down his face.

Christian flexed his finger, more than willing to grant Steven his wish. Landry's words lashed like a whip at the jealousy Christian had nursed for so long, and though he accepted the words as falsehood, they still stung. But the main brunt of his anger came from Steven's placing Samantha and her unborn child in mortal danger.

"Chris!" Samantha screamed.

He turned his head quickly toward her. She had worked the gag down onto her chin. At the sight of

Samantha, heavily pregnant with their child, his desire to end Landry's existence wavered. Could he allow her to watch him murder a man in cold blood, even a man like Steven, who deserved death? Would this act of retribution forever color their lives? Would she remember this moment every time he held her in his arms? He examined his heart and knew her good opinion weighed more heavily than Steven's miserable life and the momentary satisfaction he would gain by taking it. He had many bridges to repair between his wife and himself. He didn't need to add to that burden.

Christian turned back to Steven and slowly released his breath. He eased the hammer forward and tilted up the revolver. "You're as mad as a rabid fox, Burnett, and not worth the effort I would have to expend to kill you," he said with disgust. "Samantha carries *my* child. She loves me. I'm the only man she's ever had and the only one who'll ever have her. As much as I would love to put a bullet in your skull, I love her more. I'll not upset her. The law can mete out your punishment. I daresay they'll arrange your return trip to London and an appointment with Tyburn Tree for murdering your father. In the end, you'll have your wish for death granted." He leaned over and, without another thought for the man, backhanded Steven with the gun.

When Steven slumped to the floor, Christian turned to his wife. He had badly misjudged the focus of

Samantha's attention. Rolling onto her side, she writhed in pain. He ran to her, ripped off her gag, and loosened her bonds.

She squeezed her eyes closed and bit down on her lower lip. Veins stood out on her forehead.

"Sam," he said, his hands shaking, "did he harm you? What did he do? Are you hurting? Where do you hurt?"

Her rigid body at last relaxed. "Of course I hurt, you witless ass," she gasped. "I'm having a baby."

His arm behind her back, he eased her up to sit and lean against him. The coil of tension twisting his innards slowly eased. A grin wobbled on his mouth. "I know you're having a baby, sweetheart. You're having our baby. And I agree with your evaluation. I'm an ass. I love you so profoundly. I'll never be able to tell you how much I regret my insensitive behavior. Can you ever forgive me?"

She sucked in a pain-whistled breath between her teeth. "Not now, you lackwit. You fail to understand. This is hardly the time or place for an involved discussion. I'm having a baby *right now!*"

He jerked back as though she'd slapped a red-hot iron on his hide. "Now?" he repeated.

She threw him an exasperated look. "*Now!*"

He started to rise. "I'll fetch you to the carriage. Within thirty minutes, we'll be at Dr. Finney's home."

Her head whipped back and forth. "I suspect this

babe will not grant me thirty minutes. 'Tis coming right now!" With those words, her water broke, and clear birth fluid gushed out from under her skirts.

"My Lord," he whispered. "You're having a baby."

"God save me from bird-witted men," she groaned.

He ceased breathing and glanced at the door, praying Cullen and help would miraculously appear. Despite his wishes, they remained alone in the warehouse except for the unconscious Steven and the bats stirring in the rafters. A glacial shroud settled over him. "I can do this," Christian mumbled. "I'm familiar with all the parts and how they work, theoretically. I think I read a paper about it somewhere . . . sometime. I've brought foals into the world. How much difference can there be?"

Samantha writhed beneath a massive contraction catching her in its clutches.

He first helped her into the illumination coming from a hole in the roof. He would need light for what he was about to do. Tearing off his coat, he rolled it and slipped it under her head, laying her back on the floor. After loosening her bodice, he unhooked her skirt at the waist, then reached beneath the skirt and stripped off her soaked petticoats and drawers.

"I trust you know what you are about," Samantha said when the contraction subsided.

He hoped his smile looked more confident than macabre. "Don't worry, tigrina. I'm a scientist. Catching babies cannot be any more complicated than catching wild cats."

Her chuckle unraveled into a scream when she bore down on the next pain. He pushed her knees up and her legs apart and knelt between them. Shoving her dress to her thighs, he made a bundle of the driest petticoats and padded the floor beneath her heaving body. She arched her back, contractions tearing through her, fingers scrabbling at the boards. Her screams shredded his nerves and composure like confetti, though he suspected she might be having a worse time of it than he. She proved him right. In between contractions, she cursed him to the devil while he wiped her brow with the handkerchief Steven had used for a gag. Though he was the singular object of her vitriolic words, he could not help but marvel at the creativity of her invective. When her body stiffened again, he gripped her hand and helped her through the pain.

After a lengthy time, minutes crawling by like snails, she panted weakly, "I'm sorry, Chris, but I cannot do this anymore."

"Yes, you can," he said, voice trembling, smile smoothing the worried furrows from his brow. The head of the infant was crowning between her thighs. "You're the strongest woman I know. It's nearly over. When the next pain comes, I want you to push as fiercely as you can."

"I cannot," she whispered.

"You can and will. That is an order. If you'll recall,

we have a contract."

"I do not believe I read that clause," she grated out, her back bowing with another contraction.

"Now push!" he yelled.

She panted through her open mouth, features screwing up as she pushed. The baby's head cleared the birth canal. With her next hard push and an earsplitting scream, the shoulders popped free, and Christian's child slid into his waiting hands.

Pulse throbbing in his throat, he gazed down on the miracle he held. A daughter. Fuzzy, wet, butterscotch hair curled around the top of her head. Her eyes scrunched shut, and her rosy mouth puckered into a wail that pierced his eardrums. His heart melted like a candle, his grin spreading from ear to ear.

He laid the squalling infant on her mother's belly. "We have a daughter, Sam. She seems to have your disposition."

Samantha lifted her eyes to his, her face wet with tears and a tremulous smile on her lips.

His grin widened. "Thank God she has my good looks," he added.

The door behind him opened, and he pulled down Samantha's skirt to preserve her modesty, then glanced over his shoulder at two policemen, Cullen, and Dr. Finney entering the warehouse. The policemen took care of Steven, who was coming around, while Dr. Finney and Cullen crowded near Samantha and Christian.

The doctor sent Christian a chagrined smile. "It appears you two performed my job for me." He canted his head toward Cullen. "Why don't you take the lad outside while I finish up here?"

Christian and Cullen followed the police and Steven to the street. Soon Dr. Finney called Christian back in. Christian lifted Samantha and his new daughter into his arms and carried them to the carriage, the beaming doctor filing behind.

CHAPTER THIRTY-SEVEN

An uncharted island in the Furneaux Group
off the coast of Tasmania

Wind from the Tasman Sea sifted through her long tresses and tossed them about. Samantha raised a hand to brush the hair back from her face and tuck it behind her ears. The island spread out before her from the promontory on which she stood. For want of a better name, they called it Cat Island. Sandy hills undulated to a sparsely populated scrubland below her. Small orange and blue lizards scurried across the sand. An albatross with a six-foot wingspan circled on the air currents high above. Closer to the water, blue-footed boobies attempted a landing on the beach. Graceful in the air, they were ungainly on land. They touched ground, tumbling head over heels, spewing up sand and drawing a delighted giggle from the small person beside her.

A tiny but insistent hand tugged on her skirt.

Samantha looked down.

"Look, Mummy," a young voice piped up in a high, clear tone. Five-year-old Adrianna clung to her mother's skirt and pointed to the left side of a nearby hill. "Look. Papa has put the kitty to sleep." Her young face, suffused with excitement, turned up to meet her mother's gaze. Adrianna's eyes were like her father's, a deep emerald green, though she had inherited her mother's butterscotch hair. The child danced in place, unable to keep her short legs still. Narcissus, the iguana, in a harness and leash attached to the girl's wrist, danced, too. "Please may we go see? Maybe it's a girl kitty."

The tugging on her skirt became more urgent. Samantha shaded her eyes with a hand and concentrated on the activity below her. Christian got to his feet and waved, signaling that he had sedated the cat and it was safe to join them. Samantha looked down on her daughter with a fond smile. "Very well, poppin, you may go down." She got out only the first few words before the child and attached iguana shot forth as though propelled from a cannon. "Remember to speak quietly," she called out. "When the cat is sleeping, loud noises disturb him."

Adrianna ran down the hill and threw an impatient look, one reserved only for silly parents, over her shoulder. "I know, Mummy. Papa already told me. He said I'm nearly as good a scientist as he."

Samantha couldn't hold back a grin. Adrianna's

enthusiasm for science seemed boundless. At five, she already knew her letters and numbers and could read and write. However, much to her father's dismay, she had the same unfortunate propensity as her mother to challenge authority and sidestep orders.

Samantha adjusted the carrier on her back, which held the newest member of the Badia family, nine-month-old Richard, and strolled down the hill toward the group. Adrianna and Narcissus had already joined them. A mountain of golden fur lay on the ground, surrounded by the team. Due to the delicate nature of the expedition, they had restricted the company to friends and family.

Garrett, now twenty-six and very much a man, stood beside Christian. This would be Garrett's last expedition. He was talking about getting out on his own. The war of freedom in Cuba called to him, and he had a burning desire for new adventures.

At eighteen, Cullen had grown into a tall, lanky young man who caught the eye of many a young maid around Boston. His wild black hair was now dressed into a queue like Christian's, and his dark blue eyes had a brooding quality that made the girls sigh. He still worshipped Christian, but independence, youthful rebellion, and a passion to race horses had begun to surface.

Jasper's bare black torso gleamed with sweat in the sunlight after the exertion of raising the cat from the pit. The shark-tooth earring still swung from his ear. His white teeth flashed when he grinned down at Adrianna, and his large, dark hand reached out to smooth her wind-blown hair.

Pettibone had also stripped off his shirt, and ropy muscles defined his arms and chest. He wore a straw hat to protect his bald dome from the harsh sun.

Chloe, dressed in breeches and a shirt with her hair pulled up under a battered hat, had surprisingly turned into a fine field scientist. She knelt on the sandy ground beside the cat and called out measurements that Adrianna dutifully entered into a dog-eared notebook.

Only Aunt Delia was absent from the company. She had passed away the previous year when an influenza epidemic swept through Boston.

Samantha joined the others, and Christian looked up from where he knelt beside the cat's head. The smile spreading across his face warmed her to her bones. "Is it a female?" she asked hopefully.

He shook his head. "Another male." His gaze returned to the cat, a frown crimping his mouth.

Samantha's thoughts mirrored his. This animal was the seventh cat they had caught in a pit trap. Dug eight feet into the soft earth, baited with meat, and covered with tree limbs, the pits had proved successful in trapping the animals. As the uninhabited island's largest preda-tors, indeed one of its only predators, the Smilodons had no fear of humans or their scent, and the bait drew them like blossoms to sunshine. After catching a cat, Christian sedated it with a weak solution of a substance he had obtained from natives in the South American rain forest on one of his expeditions. It came from the skin glands of small frogs. Once the team examined, measured, and marked the cat by notching one ear, Christian then released it back into the island's interior.

Unfortunately, they had trapped only males to this point.

After inspecting the cat's teeth for age and wear, Christian straightened and hooked an arm around Samantha's waist.

"Where are the females?" she asked more to herself than to Christian.

"I wish I knew." A deep crease marred his forehead. "It makes no sense. Four of the males were young adults, and the island's size limits the number of predators it can support. I wouldn't expect us to find more than two or three more cats. They must be the females."

Other wildlife on the island was scarce. From observation, they learned that the cats preyed almost exclusively on seabirds that nested along cliffs on the eastern coast and seals that bred among rocky pinnacles amidst the beaches.

"Perhaps they died," Samantha said.

"Perhaps. They could have contracted a disease fatal only to females. However, I doubt that. In general, diseases pass only from animal to animal and are species specific. With no influx of new animals, where did the disease originate?' Then again, the female, being the warier of the species, could simply be more difficult to trap." His arm tightened on her waist, and he looked down at her. Her nerves sang. After six years of marriage and two children, he could still thrill her with a look promising later delights.

Two weeks and three additional male cats later, they discussed their findings around the campfire. Samantha listened for a while and finally said, "Christian, if no females remain to breed, when these males die, the species will truly become extinct, will it not?"

"I fear so," he said glumly. "In the last few days, we've trapped only marked animals caught at least once before. I daresay we've examined the majority, if not all, of the population."

Much later, when Adrianna and baby Richard had fallen asleep, Christian and Samantha curled up together on their pallet on the other side of the tent. She crawled on top of him and worked on the buttons of his shirt.

"Quietly now," he whispered. "You cannot scream when you come, or you'll wake the children."

She smiled wickedly, a slow curving of her lips, and kissed her way down the strip of skin and wiry hair marching down his chest muscles.

He groaned, rolled her over, and quickly stripped

her clothes from her.

"No fair," she protested. "You are still dressed."

He grinned and silently stood, tugging off his clothes in record time. "Satisfied?" he murmured, lying back down.

"Not yet," she purred, "though I shall be soon."

She pushed him onto his back and straddled him, her core already wet and throbbing. She slowly lowered herself onto his penis, and he growled deep in his throat. Grasping her waist, he pulled her down until he filled her to the maximum. When she swayed forward to sweep her hair across his chest, he lifted his head to fasten onto a pebbled nipple. He suckled, and she moved back and forth and circled her hips in a figure eight. Her spine straightened, and she braced her hands behind her on his thighs while he thrust from beneath.

"No screaming now," he gasped, settling his thumb between her thighs where they joined to rub against her swollen clit.

She drew in a sharp breath. Coiling tension gathered in her groin and spread like liquid fire down her legs. When the contractions began, he pulled her forward onto his chest and took her cries into his mouth. His hands pressed her downward, and he thrust up into her sheath for a final lunge that exploded through her like a blazing sun. Drained, she collapsed onto his chest and panted like a winded racehorse. He stroked her hair, his heart dancing against her ribs. Kissing the top of her head, he lifted her off him and fitted her under his arm against his side.

She recovered her breath. "See, I performed admirably. I did not even wake the children."

He chuckled. "Nonetheless, it was a close call."

She snuggled next to his moist, heated body, throwing an arm over his chest, a leg over his thighs, and fell into a contented sleep.

The Smilodon stalked her through a meadow carpeted in tall grass as golden as ripened wheat. She parted the stalks, and bright sun penetrated to her bones. Stopping, she slowly turned. How close was the cat? He panted as he followed her spoor, snapped grass stalks when he drew closer. He raised his head, and clear green eyes caught her gaze, holding her in thrall. She stood motionless, unable to move. The world fell still. All sound and movement ceased beyond this one perfect spot in this perfect golden meadow on this one perfect day. Yellow sunlight poured down on them. The rest of the world turned as black as the ocean depths, and a curtain of life drew around them, as if nothing else existed outside its enveloping folds. They were the only living creatures left on Earth.

A quiver shook her limbs, an exhilaration that stole her breath and made her heart flutter. His long, curving canines gleamed. His wide mouth spread into a knowing grin. A grin meant just for her.

Liquid tranquility poured through her, as bright as the

sunshine, as golden as his coat and her eyes. She lowered herself to the ground. Moving up and laying down beside her, the Smilodon crushed the grass beneath him. The meadow's sweet scent rose in waves. He stretched out his front legs, his paws flexing, pushing against the grass. Rumbling came from deep in his throat, and he washed his legs, his sharp teeth moving closer with every swipe of his tongue.

When she lay back, the cat failed to move. She opened her eyes and sat up. His paws still gently kneaded the grass, mashing it down. He lifted his head, and his gaze meshed with hers. She drowned in his eyes, merged with the cat, and with the connection, a sudden, oppressive sense of loneliness, of hopelessness, washed over her. Tears seeped from the corners of her eyes.

The Smilodon was fading, turning to mist, the sun growing wan, cool, and pallid. A stiff wind rustled the grass, carrying the acrid scent of ashes. Dark clouds gathered, throwing shadows and further dimming the light.

She scarcely saw him now, his image growing fainter and fainter until nothing was left other than two glowing green eyes touched by a melancholy that tore open her heart. Then they, too, faded away. The meadow grass, once so golden and bursting with life, grew withered and seared, leaving behind a dead, barren land.

She cried out, but her voice made no sound, except inside her head in the bleak landscape of a dying Earth.

Her cries woke Christian, and he tugged her close.

"What's wrong, tigrina?" he whispered. "A bad dream?"

Tears burned her eyes, the dream still very much with her. The words welled inside her, but she could not voice them. "Indeed," she replied, snuffling against his chest, "merely a bad dream. Return to sleep. I shall be fine." Wiping her face on his mat of chest hair, she laid her head on his comforting strength. Though he fell back asleep almost immediately, she lay awake for the remainder of the long night.

Morning came in the strident calls of circling gulls and terns and delicate pink light in a pastel wash in the eastern sky. Christian found Samantha on a hill above camp where she sat on a hummock of sea grass with her legs pulled up to her chest. Her arms wrapped around her legs, her chin resting on her knees, she stared out at the beach below, where a Smilodon in the distance stalked a young seal.

When he eased down beside her, she turned and gave him a watery smile. Moisture pearled on her lashes.

"Why the tears, tigrina?" he asked, moving behind her to pull her into the cradle of his knees. Her back met his chest, and he bent forward, dropping a kiss on the side of her neck and pressing his cheek against her hair.

"They are truly extinct, are they not?" Samantha asked while she watched the powerful cat stalk its prey.

"That appears to be the case unless we find a female or two."

"You have no real expectation that we shall, do you?" She turned and looked into his eyes. Christian once said her eyes resembled the golden light of the sun. His reminded her of the mossy green Earth. Gold to green . . . sun to Earth . . . both were necessary for life. Unfortunately, so were male and female.

His breath echoed harshly. "No, I don't. As I said, it makes no sense. Nevertheless, I have this gut feeling that all the females are gone. If they are, it's merely a matter of time. These males are probably the final remnants of a dead species."

"Let them go," she said softly.

He scooted back, got to his feet, and pulled her up to face him. "You mean keep the secret? Not inform the scientific community?"

She grasped his hands and threaded her fingers through his. "That is precisely what I mean. Allow them to live out the remainder of their lives in peace. I have no wish to see them captured and put on display. They deserve a more dignified end. They are so very beautiful and have managed to exist for such a long time. Allow them to remain free now that their time is nearly over."

He took on a serious expression. "Have you any notion what you're asking? This could be the greatest discovery of the century. You're suggesting I throw it all away."

She returned his look. "Yes, I am."

He smiled slowly, released a laugh. "Very well. I

was having reservations, in any event. I agree with you, my feisty wife, the mother of my children, the love of my heart. They deserve to live in peace. I have no use for additional accolades or species bearing my name. The greatest thrill is in finding and studying them, not writing the damned papers. We shall keep the discovery strictly among our company."

"Would that be a promise?"

Christian caught her face between his hands and brushed a kiss across her mouth. "Absolutely, Sam, and you know I always keep my promises."

She threw her arms around his neck and tugged his head down for a real kiss. He cupped her bottom, lifting her. His cock grew hard as it always did when she wrapped her legs around his waist and pressed her heated center to him. With her head spinning, she pulled back. "Thank you, Chris. I truly believe you are the best of husbands, the best of fathers, and the best of scientists. I promise I shall love you forever with all my heart. And that promise is one I shall have no difficulty keeping."

When they left Cat Island behind, Samantha also left behind her dreams of the Smilodon and its ultimate fate. Now she dreamt only of Christian.

Epilogue

Faint mewling came from the side of the cliff on Cat Island, causing the seabirds to take to wing in sudden flight. Deep inside the cave carved into the volcanic rock along a seemingly impassible ledge, a Smilodon curled up around her litter of kittens. They were an orange hue with white spots splattered across silky fur, and they had wide, padded feet with pointed little kitten claws that kneaded their mother's side as they fastened onto her teats and sucked greedily.

The mother Smilodon sighed and lay back on her side, giving the kittens greater access to the rich nourishment. A deep purr rumbled from her throat, her brood pushing and pulling and suckling. Rounded bellies soon stretched tight with milk.

Cat Lindler

The litter was large for a Smilodon, six healthy kittens.
And, as Mother Nature somehow managed to find a solution in times of adversity, all six were female.

BIBLIOGRAPHY

Barker, Francis, Peter Hulme & Margaret Iversen. 1988.
    Cannibalism and the Colonial World. University
    Press: Cambridge.

Bier, James A. 2003. *Reference Map of Oceania.* University
    of Hawaii Press: Hawaii.

Bjerre, Jens. 1974. *The Last Cannibals.* Drake Pub.:
    New York.

Goldman, Irving. 1970. *Ancient Polynesian Society.*
    University of Chicago Press: Chicago.

Kirch, Patrick Vinton & Roger C. Green. 2001.
    Hawaiki, Ancestral Polynesia. Cambridge
    University Press: Cambridge.

Krieger, Michael. 1994. *Conversations with the Cannibals.*
    Ecco Press: New Jersey.

Markham, Clements R. 1878. *William Hawkins, Voyage
    into the South Seas.* Hakluyt Society: London.

McGaurr, Lyn. 1999. *Tasmania.* Lonely Planet: Melbourne.

Mead, Margaret. 1970. *People and Places*. Bantam: New York

Mytinger, Caroline. 1942. *Head Hunting in the Solomon Islands*. The Macmillan Company: New York.

Oliver, Douglas. 2002. *Polynesia in Early Historic Times*. Bess Press: Honolulu.

Pizzey, Graham. 1980. *A Field Guide to the Birds of Australia*. Princeton University Press: New Jersey.

Walker, James Blackhouse. 1914. *Early Tasmania*. John Vail, Government Printer: Hobart.

Watts, Dave. 2000. *Field Guide to Tasmanian Birds*. New Holland Pub.: London.

Author's Note

Dear Reader,

In my books, I pull from many inspirations. The idea of a living Smilodon is one that particularly appealed to me because of my zoological background and my research with wild cats. When I first conceived of *Starlight & Promises*, my animal of choice was the Tasmanian tiger, a marsupial from Australia and Tasmania, thought to be extinct, that filled the same niche as the lion in Africa and the tiger in Asia. However, as I began the book, a small group of living Tasmanian tigers was found in Australia. As a scientist I was thrilled by the discovery, but it ruined my story. Therefore, I shifted gears to the Smilodon, a less likely candidate for sudden rediscovery.

Steven's scientific hoax was based on a true incident. In 1912, workmen discovered skull fragments in a gravel pit in Piltdown, England, during a time when

English anthropology had suffered a decline in popularity and success. The workmen first unearthed a large skull, and soon after, uncovered an apelike jaw. Scientists, ecstatic with the discovery and its anthropological implications, named the fossil "Piltdown Man" and touted it as the "missing link" between apes and men they had sought for so long. Scientists even assigned the fossil to a genus, *Eoanthropus* (dawn man), and a species, *dawsoni*, after Charles Darwin. Forty years later, in 1953, Piltdown Man was exposed as an ingenious hoax, the juxtaposition of a modern human skull with the jaw of an orangutan.

My hero, Christian Badia, is a lover of basketball (as am I), and it gave me great pleasure to introduce this sport in its infancy. James Naismith, a Canadian instructor at the Young Men's Christian Association Training School (now Springfield College) in Springfield, Massachusetts, invented the game of basketball in 1891. His superior, Dr. Luther H. Gulick, had challenged him to develop a vigorous athletic sport suitable for indoor winter play. Using a soccer ball (known then as a football) as his inspiration, Naismith incorporated elements from football, soccer, and hockey. The original teams had nine players, and peach baskets were nailed to the walls as goals.

The Bornean Bay Cat (*Catopuma badia*), formerly *Felis badia*, was not (unfortunately) named after my hero, Christian Badia. It was first described by Gray in 1874, but no photograph was taken of the species until 1988, and no live specimen captured for examination until 1992. Until then, only a few skulls and skins, which were collected in the late 1880s, existed in museums. To date, it is one of the rarest and least known of the wild cats.

I hope you enjoyed reading about Sam's and Chris's adventures as much as I enjoyed writing about them.

May you always have romance. I love to hear from readers. You can reach me at my Web site, http://catlindler.com.

Cat Lindler

Kiss of a Traitor

CAT LINDLER

Wilhelmina Bellingham is an ardent Tory and has two goals in her young life: catching the rebel traitor, General Francis Marion, and avoiding marriage to the fool to whom her father betrothed her when she was only a babe, a man neither she nor her father has ever met. Her first goal is within reach. Willa knows South Carolina's swamps and byways as well as any rebel. With judicious searching and a large dose of luck, she will eventually catch the partisan general. Shedding her betrothed is another matter.

Captain Brendan Ford, a spy with Marion's patriots, stumbles across the perfect way to infiltrate the Loyalist high command when his half brother is killed shortly after arriving in Carolina. Ford assumes his brother's identity as Lord Montford, fiancé to Wilhelmina Bellingham. But his masquerade requires he actually court her, and the untidy little wren of a girl is not a female to inspire courtship. He is thankful his ruse will end as soon as the patriots drive the British from South Carolina.

Neither Willa nor Brendan are prepared for the consequences of war or the betrayals of the heart—but will their allegiance to outside forces keep them from the love they just might find within each other's arms?

ISBN# 978-193383651-5

Mass Market Paperback / Historical Romance

US $6.95 / CDN $7.95

AVAILABLE NOW

www.catlindler.com

EMERALD EMBRACE

SHANNON DRAKE

Devastated over the premature death of her dearest friend, Mary, Lady Martise St. James ventures to foreboding Castle Creeghan in the Scottish Highlands to dispel rumors surrounding the young woman's demise and retrieve a lost emerald. Beneath the stones of this aging mansion lurks a family crypt filled with sinister secrets. Locked within this threatening vault is the answer to the most dangerous question, and the promise of the most horrifying death.

Amid jaded suspicion, underlying threats, and the dreaded approach of All Hallow's Eve in 1865, Martise encounters a witch's coven and meets Lord Bruce Creeghan, the love of her friend's life. Mysterious, yet passionate, Mary's husband elicits a deep desire and a profound fear in the core of her soul. He knows . . . something. And it's up to Martise to reveal what he hides from her prying intrusion.

Lord Creeghan wards off the invasion of his private fortress, yet he cannot resist his magnetic attraction to the beautiful sleuth. As strong as the inevitable pull toward the catacomb beneath their bed, an overwhelming obsession propels them into disheveled sheets of unquenchable hunger and lust. While savoring an affair that cannot be denied, Martise must discover whether her lover is a ruthless murderer or a guardian angel.

ISBN# 978-160542082-0

Mass Market Paperback / Historical Romance

US $7.95 / CDN $8.95

AVAILABLE NOW

www.theoriginalheathergraham.com

Plum Blossoms in Paris

Sarah Hina

Daisy Lockhart is a searcher. She just doesn't know it yet.

Burdened with an unlikely name by her father, a preeminent Henry James scholar, Daisy is a tightly wound grad student on her way to fulfilling the American dream. When her boyfriend breaks up with her, though, Daisy succumbs to the vertigo of uncertainty for the first time in a scripted life.

Embracing the plunge, Daisy flees. Her namesake chose Rome; Daisy Lockhart settles on the celestial city: Paris.

There, Daisy finds a soft landing in the arms of Mathieu. An impassioned writer, Mathieu has been rocked by the recent death of his mother, who left him for her American dream when he was a boy. Reeling from the loss, he latches onto Daisy with a fierce commitment that exhilarates, and suffocates, her.

Over a golden autumn day, Daisy and Mathieu clash over religion, art, Iraq, food, the metaphysical possibilities of a good shoe, and the murky memories tunneling up from their pasts. Dancing along a razor's edge of desire and discretion, the lovers lie to one another in minor and meaningful ways, until finally the deceptions and passion explode.

Torn between her blossoming love for Mathieu and the family and dreams she's left behind, Daisy must discover if the flickering flame of her self can survive the vacuum of this brilliant, difficult man, who will always take her breath away.

ISBN# 978-160542126-1

Trade Paperback / Contemporary Romance

US $15.95 / CDN $17.95

AUGUST 2010

www.sarahhina.blogspot.com

Passion's Blood

Cherif Fortin & Lynn Sanders

Lady Leanna is a flame-haired beauty loved by her betrothed, Prince Emric, desired by his loathsome brother, Prince Bran. Although in love with Emric, Leanna has still not made her peace with the knowledge that this arrangement was forced upon her.

Prince Emric, noble and courageous, rides to war, ignorant of his brother's dark treachery.

In a net of betrayal and violence, the young lovers must preserve their faith, and Leanna must keep Emric alive with her love and the magical powers she herself does not fully understand . . .

ISBN# 978-160542062-2
Hardcover Adult / Illustrated Romantic Masterpiece
US $25.95 / CDN $28.95
AVAILABLE NOW

There Be Dragons
Heather Graham

Nico d'Or was a kind and gentle man who lived in the age of dragons. Through a simple twist of fate, Nico married the lovely Princess Elisia, and the couple were blessed with a beautiful daughter, Marina. Would they live happily ever after?

Well, not quite. The neighbor's wife, Geovana, was neither sweet nor lovely, but a devious sorceress who spent her time casting dreadful spells, devising vile tricks, and mixing powerful potions with eye of newt and the horn of a toad.

Geovana used one of her favorite spells—strategically hurling rocks through windows to smash into the heads of her victims—tragically killing both Nico and Elisia, and leaving the beautiful Marina all alone. To make matters worse, Geovana became Marina's guardian and, greedy for power, arranged a marriage between Marina and her own evil son, Carlo Baristo.

But Marina was in love with someone else. And as Christmas Day approached, Marina was faced with a terrible choice: save her land and her people, or follow her heart and believe in the magic of Christmas and true love.

ISBN# 978-160542071-4

Hardcover Adult / Illustrated Romantic Masterpiece

US $25.95 / CDN $28.95

AVAILABLE NOW

www.theoriginalheathergraham.com

MEDALLION

P R E S S

Want to know what's going on with
your favorite author or what new releases
are coming from Medallion Press?

Now you can receive breaking news,
updates, and more from Medallion Press
straight to your cell phone, e-mail, instant
messenger, or Facebook!

twitter

Sign up now at <u>www.twitter.com/MedallionPres</u>
to stay on top of all the happenings in and
around Medallion Press.

For more information
about other great titles from
Medallion Press, visit
m e d a l l i o n p r e s s . c o m

Insanity is doing the same thing over and over and expecting different results. If you're not getting the results you want out of life, than it's time to do something different! *MOTIV8N' U* will focus on taking a look at where you are now and how you want to spend the rest of your life—and will teach you how to restructure the beliefs and behaviors that are keeping you running in circles.

If you're not where you want to be, this book will show you how to unleash the spirit of strength and the power of fitness in every area of your life. I will walk you through twelve fundamental keys that will enable you to unlock the life-transforming fitness you've been dreaming of!

There is nothing more empowering than self-discovery, nothing more inspiring than self-direction, and nothing more rewarding than self-discipline—I will equip you to transform your life by motivat8n you in the spirit of strength! The spirit that already resides within you!

MOTIV8N' U is the only book you'll ever need to become the fittest you possible!

ISBN# 978-160542092-9
Trade Paperback / Motivational
US $15.95 / CDN $17.95
DECEMBER 2010
www.staciboyer.com

DARK SECRETS

⇐ OF THE ⇒

OLD OAK TREE

DOLORES J. WILSON

Following the end of her fifteen-year marriage to a high-powered attorney, Evie Carson returns to her small, Georgia hometown to open a fashion boutique. From the protective covering of her father to the tarnished shield of her husband, Evie has always lived behind the armor of a man. But she sees this move as her first step toward the peaceful, happy life she wants.

Trying to recapture a few moments of her youth, Evie climbs to the ruins of her childhood tree house. While hidden by the massive branches of the old oak tree, Evie is stunned into deadly silence as she watches Jake—a mentally challenged community member—enter the clearing below her with a nude, lifeless body over his shoulder. Hovering above the macabre scene, Evie is forced to look on as a grave is dug. When the body is rolled into the hole, Evie realizes the dead woman is her childhood friend whom she hasn't seen in years.

The authorities are sure once Jake is arrested, the town's nightmare will be over. But when he turns up dead and Evie's home becomes the center of bizarre events, Evie and an investigating state trooper fear she may be the next victim. Wondering if she can trust him, or anyone, Evie alone must face the *Dark Secrets of the Old Oak Tree*.

ISBN# 978-160542106-3
Hardcover / Suspense
US $24.95 / CDN $27.95
AVAILABLE NOW
www.doloresjwilson.com

Diary of a Confessions Queen

Kathy Carmichael

Seven years ago Amy Crosby's husband, Dan, disappeared under baffling circumstances in the little town of Independence, Kansas. No marital dispute. No warning. No suicide note. As bizarre as taking out the garbage and never coming back.

She has no hope of seeing him again and presumes he's dead. So Amy begins legal proceedings to have the inventor of unusual devices declared deceased. Simple . . . that is, it would be simple without his valuable patents and insurance money.

What starts as a normal procedure turns into a fiasco. With her take-it-in-stride, confessions queen sense of humor, she endures black-mail, threats on her life, and repeated burglaries. Then someone close to her is murdered, and she realizes that an enemy wants to do more than frighten her. Whoever has an interest in her husband, everyone from his business partners to his family members, isn't playing games.

Sexy police detective Brad Tyler is assigned to the case . . . in more ways than one. Amy teeters on a precarious line between convincing him of her innocence and seeking his protection. An overpowering attraction makes their relationship a high-stakes race against the clock to find the killer. Coffee, tea, or murder anyone?

ISBN# 978-160542095-0

Trade Paperback / Mystery

US $12.95 / CDN $14.95

AVAILABLE NOW

www.kathycarmichael.com

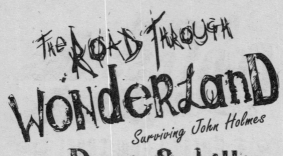

Dawn Schiller

The Road Through Wonderland is Dawn Schiller's chilling account of the childhood that molded her so perfectly to fall for the seduction of "the king of porn," John Holmes, and the bizarre twist of fate that brought them together. With painstaking honesty, Dawn uncovers the truth of her relationship with John, her father figure-turned-forbidden lover who hid her away from his porn movie world and welcomed her into his family along with his wife.

Within these pages, Dawn reveals the perilous road John led her down—from drugs and addiction to beatings, arrests, forced prostitution, and being sold to the drug underworld. Surviving the horrific Wonderland murders, this young innocent entered protective custody, ran from the FBI, endured a heart-wrenching escape from John, and ultimately turned him in to the police.

This is the true story of one of the most infamous of public figures and a young girl's struggle to survive unthinkable abuse. Readers will be left shaken but clutching to real hope at the end of this dark journey on *The Road Through Wonderland*.

Also check out the movie *Wonderland* (Lions Gate Entertainment, 2003) for a look into the past of Dawn Schiller and the Wonderland Murders.

ISBN# 978-160542083-7

Trade Paperback / Autobiography

US $15.95 / CDN $17.95

AUGUST 2010

www.dawn-schiller.com